The Ruins of Daemor

C. K. DRADER

Copyright © 2023 by C. K. Drader

All rights reserved.

No part of this book may be reproduced in any form or by any electronic or mechanical means, including information storage and retrieval systems, without written permission from the author, except for the use of brief quotations in a book review.

 Created with Vellum

Dedication

This is a threefold dedication to my sons, Hunter Sage Wolokoff-Drader & Reed Apollo Wolokoff-Drader. You two are the reasons I worked so hard to finish this book. I wanted you to see proof that you can make your dreams a reality no matter how long it takes. Lastly, to Heather Halls. The first person to encourage me to keep writing this book. The character Milthra is after Heather's D&D character. Rest in peace.

Acknowledgement

My thanks to Sarrah Kam @ Paper Polish, Sara Williams, and Davida De La Harpe for their exceptional work in editing and proofreading this novel. This book would not have been possible without you.

Contents

Chapter 1	1
Chapter 2	6
Chapter 3	21
Chapter 4	29
Chapter 5	36
Chapter 6	47
Chapter 7	62
Chapter 8	69
Chapter 9	73
Chapter 10	80
Chapter 11	90
Chapter 12	101
Chapter 13	107
Chapter 14	116
Chapter 15	126
Chapter 16	135
Chapter 17	143
Chapter 18	151
Chapter 19	158
Chapter 20	163
Chapter 21	173
Chapter 22	181
Chapter 23	185
Chapter 24	193
Chapter 25	201
Chapter 26	211
Chapter 27	220
Chapter 28	227
Chapter 29	237

Chapter 30	247
Chapter 31	254
Chapter 32	260
Chapter 33	265
Chapter 34	270
Chapter 35	277
Chapter 36	284
Chapter 37	292
Chapter 38	300
Chapter 39	305
Chapter 40	313
Chapter 41	321
Chapter 42	326
Chapter 43	335
Chapter 44	347
Chapter 45	350
Chapter 46	358
Chapter 47	369
Chapter 48	379
Chapter 49	387
Chapter 50	394
Chapter 51	401
Chapter 52	403
Chapter 53	411
Chapter 54	413
Chapter 55	420
Chapter 56	426
Chapter 57	439
Chapter 58	447
Chapter 59	455
Chapter 60	461
Epilogue	470

Chapter One

EARTH

DENVER, COLORADO

The dawn's morning light was a welcoming sight to Taylor; it had been dark still when he had risen to prepare for his hiking trip. Every piece of his gear had been inspected, then thoughtfully organized in the backpack that now leaned against the door. It would all be needed for the two-week trip through the remote mountain trail.

The backpack had been there for over an hour while Taylor sat on the couch, all the while pondering the trail he had picked.

Is this the right choice? Am I doing the right thing going on this trip?

As the thought passed through his mind, a glint of light off the frame on Lilly's desk caught his attention. It was like a sign from her, expressing her agreement with his decision to make the trip. His heart sank a little as he stood and walked over to the desk, picking up the picture. It was the last photo they had taken of themselves. He smiled; she had joked that his long blond hair and bright-blue eyes made him look like an eighties rockstar. She had died two days later.

"One last journey together, Lilly," he said as he looked at the box containing her urn. The image of Lilly's kayak overturning in the rapids of the mountain river they were traveling on that day flashed through his mind. A tear leaked out of his eye as he put the picture down.

While he tucked the urn into his backpack, his phone dinged. But before he could answer, there was a knock at the door.

"Taylor?" He heard his friend Brian's voice. "Sorry I'm late, man! Cassie needed a ride to work."

"Be right there," Taylor called back as he wiped his wet cheek. "I'm in the bathroom," he lied.

Taking a minute to compose himself, Taylor unlocked the door and opened it. "Hey, little guy!" Taylor jested. Taylor, standing at six-foot-one, often bugged Brian about his five-foot-nothing height. "Thanks for giving me a ride to the trailhead. I hope Cassie didn't give you too hard of a time for volunteering to drop me off out there." Taylor feigned a smile. "I'm almost ready. Can we grab breakfast on the way?"

Brian frowned when he looked at Taylor's damp face. They had been friends since childhood. He knew Taylor was hiding his hurt about Lilly behind the joke. Brian's eyes slid past him to the couch, where the crumpled blanket and the pillow were. "Nah, she's glad you're taking some time to yourself. She misses Lilly too." Brian looked back at Taylor. "If you need a moment, I can meet you in the car."

Taylor did not look back. Brian knew that he had trouble sleeping in his bed; most of Taylor's close friends knew. It was a harrowing reminder of Lilly and their unborn child.

"Yeah, I'll meet you down there," Taylor replied, closing the door as Brian walked away. His heart ached as he looked around the apartment. The next two weeks would be a good break from his everyday routine. There would be no distractions on this trip; not even his cell phone would work where he was going.

He gathered his backpack and headed down the apartment steps to the car.

WORLD OF DAEMOR

THE REFUGE

The steam rising off the grass in the meadow was a reminder to Rayla of how early it was. The sun had been up for only a short time, but she would need every bit of light; the walk to Glydane, the Capital city, and back was a journey of many days. She breathed in the morning air just outside the entrance of the Refuge and smiled a knowing smile.

"Good morning. Rayla." Kalamar's old voice creaked. "Off for a bit of thievery so early this morning?"

Rayla laughed. "I would hardly call liberating the property of our people thievery." She turned to her old friend and one-time mentor. A tall and frail-looking man of immense age, his long white hair and beard framed his old, dark, withered face. He stood basking in the morning sun only a few steps from the cave entrance of the Refuge.

"I've been seeing him again, in the visions," she said, a note of concern in her voice. "I have to return to the Great Library to retrieve the book of Prophecy you spoke of. I had only a moment to glance through it the last time. The information inside that book may lead me to him. The true man of Prophecy we have been waiting for."

Kalamar's ancient looking face revealed he knew there was more to her angst. "I know you worry for our people as much as I. But don't let that be a reason for being impulsive—as you can be. Take care that you're prepared for the consequences that may follow should you initiate the coming of the Savior. His coming will affect us all, as will the war he brings to our world."

Rayla turned, looking back through the meadow and across, to the path leading to Glydane. "We can wait no longer. Our people have suffered dearly during Tarak's reign. I need to stop it."

Kalamar said not another word, slipping back through the ward that hid the entrance to the caves. He had seen the world before the fall and had lived with the occupation. Three hundred years was a tragically long lifetime of suffering and loss. Not even Rayla, despite the unnaturally long life bestowed upon her by the Power, could understand what he felt. Her life stretched a hundred and fifty-some years back—she understood her people's losses. However, not as Kalamar did.

Rayla's hand went to the sword at her side for a moment, then to the Orb at her chest. She had dressed in as plain a cloak as she could find, hiding most of her appearance. It hid her jerkin and the rest of her light leather armor perfectly. Only her dark hair and olive-skinned face stood exposed.

Behind her youthful twenty-something appearance,

none would suspect she was a wise and powerful woman. A woman that had led the militia into battle many times, a woman that could be dangerous if pressed.

Rayla set a quick pace on the path to Glydane. With luck, she could be there in only three or four days. She smiled to herself this time; sneaking into Tarak's domain to liberate the book that would help bring an end to him was a sweet thought indeed.

Chapter Two

DAEMOR

GLYDANE, THE CAPITAL

The echoes of heavy footfall filled the torch-lit hall outside Tarak's rooms. Someone was coming, coming toward his room in the early hours of the morning. He could feel it even as he slept. His heart sped up, his breath heavy as his chest rose and fell, his mind still deep in sleep.

His dreams were always of the tormented sort. The trauma of his childhood laid their foundation. The faces of those he had killed were imposed by magic onto the nightmare, a constant reminder of the terrible things he had done.

Tarak had been innocent once, long ago. Scavenging on his desolate home world of Kardan while his mother had cared for and protected him. Even now, so many years later, he sobbed in his sleep.

"People in pain cause pain in others, Tar," his mother had said as his boyhood-self looked into her eyes. The dream unfolded—the two of them, hiding once again in a deserted building in the desolate, rundown city he grew up in.

"Why are others so cruel to us, Mum?" he had asked. Fright arose in him, for himself, but even more for her. The raiders were coming, and they were so close. Tears fell down his cheeks as he shook with fear.

A loud crash from the outside world ripped him from his nightmare. His mother's face, which he only remembered in the dreams, vanished.

A tall man with pale skin stretched over his bones had burst into the bedchamber, waking him. The door had swung open, crashing into the wall and startling him back into reality.

"Tarak! Tarak!" Godry yelled in his shrill voice. His dark, unwashed hair flew about as spittle sprayed from his mouth.

Tarak, a muscled mountain of a man, sat up, filling himself with the Power. Using the magic of the Orb that hung from the chain around his neck, he picked up Godry and slammed him against the wall. The red pulse of the Orb illuminated Godry's face. It took Tarak a moment to comprehend where he was and who this person was that had disturbed him. As his mind cleared, he began to recognize his oldest servant.

His four-poster bed made of fine oak came into vision, and he felt the sweaty sheets against his skin. The torches burned low, making the chamber's stone walls blurry to his eyes. *I'm in the legislative building, the glorious castle of the Capital. I remember now, yes, in the first minister's residence.*

With fury in his voice, he scolded Godry. "I told you not to disturb me!" Tarak, at the edge of his temper, had almost killed him. He hated being woken but he would not slay him, not Godry. No, Godry had been one of the first men he had tainted and twisted with the Power so long ago.

"Has it really been so long?" he said aloud.

"Yes, my king. You welcomed me into your service three hundred years ago," Godry sputtered, compelled by the web of magic that Tarak had, at some point, put in his mind. Godry squirmed against the pressure keeping him against the wall. "So that I might help you take over this world. And we succeeded." The man squirmed; other things were compelling him to speak. "Mina has detected her in the city. The Orb Bearer... Rayla is here in the city."

"At last!" Tarak shouted. He grabbed his house-robe and put it on, covering his sweat-stained nightclothes and keeping out the chill. *Rayla thinks she's so intelligent. That I don't know she has an Orb. One of your spies told me before he met his end, Rayla.* A sense of jubilation swept over Tarak. For so long, the other Bearers had been at large. His frustration that his sleep had been disturbed faded away at the news that Rayla was here. He had been waiting for this moment for over a year. He had managed to capture several of the Vidre shards, pieces of broken Orbs, that these people had fashioned into jewelry during his reign. That they held less magic was not of consequence; the Power in them was priceless all the same. No one here realized what the magnitude of the magic they held meant in other worlds. They could never comprehend the vast value of the one Orb he possessed, let alone the Power three Orbs held. This world was rich in refined Vidre, the crystal giver of magic and the source of all magic in the universe.

That Tarak held only one Orb was of no consequence, as he ruled here unchallenged. The people in this world hadn't warred in generations until he had arrived. *But still, to have them all.*

"Where is she?" Tarak's voice boomed in the large chamber. His temper rushed back in, he was still on edge after the dream of his mother, and he was having trouble controlling it. "Tell me! Has she made it to the library?"

Godry's voice shook as he spoke. "Mina is still new as a carrier. Finding someone who could use the shard to sense others was a challenge. She can only detect people as far as the city's outer walls. And it's foggy for her. Mina will see Rayla better as she closes on the city center."

Disappointment flooded Tarak; the people of this world were below him in every way. While he could have only performed small bits of magic without the Orb, he was still better than those without magic, the ones his people called the Navaden. The people here would not be able to perform magic if it were not for the unique type of Vidre here. Vidre that could lend a Navaden magic was something he had never heard of until coming to this world. The constant failure of these people was an annoyance. Tarak released Godry, and he fell to the floor in a heap.

"Bring Mina to me!" Tarak said. When Godry did not move fast enough, Tarak righted him using magic; an invisible hand picked him up by the scruff and tossed him out the door. "NOW!" he shouted as Godry skidded to a halt, sprawling on the floor, his dark robes jumbled about him. The man picked himself up and ran down the hall. He was spry for his age. Keeping Godry alive was only one of the many things the Power of the Orb could do.

Tarak lost himself in watching the man run down the hall, forgetting for an instant why he was so excited. Something caught his attention, and he glanced in the mirror that hung to his side on the wall. Inside the mirror, a specter, deformed and mangled, crawled on the floor toward him. The specters only appeared on reflective surfaces, haunting him. This was one of many that he had killed—the ones the Orb would not let him forget.

"Get out!" Tarak shouted. The thread of magic was instantaneous—he hardly even thought of it. The weave lashed out and created an invisible void of pressure on the mirror's surface, shattering the glass so his image was broken and distorted. The two ever-present room servants sprawled on the floor caught his eye as they stood and bolted for the door. This time the thought was conscious, and the weave formed, slamming the door closed. "Not you!" The two men scurried back and pressed themselves to the floor once more.

Tarak paused, gathering himself. "I'll need my armor and my sword!" he demanded in a dignified voice. The men sprang to their feet, rushing to the chest that held Tarak's armor. The breastplate stood prominently displayed on a stand beside the chest; his well-crafted longsword leaned up against it.

Tarak stood with his arms outstretched. His men moved about, fitting his armor upon him. Stroking the breastplate with his large bare hand, he tired of the distorted image and wove a bit of magic repairing the mirror. "I rather like looking at it," he said. "This one is something to wonder at. Don't you think?" The men did not answer as they continued attending to him. He watched intently as they attached each piece of armor to his body. "I only recently had this one made. The artistry is amazing. I rather like how the gold inlay accents the black. Don't you agree, Godry?" Tarak looked around. "Where has that man gone now? You there, where is Godry?" Tarak addressed one of the servants collecting a piece of armor from the open chest.

The man shook with fear but did not answer. "Well, speak up, or I will have your tongue."

"Beg your pardon, my king," the other man said as he approached with a gauntlet. "You already took his tongue for speaking too much." The man's voice quivered as he spoke, and he looked back down to the floor as he came to a halt.

"Do you know where Godry is then?" Tarak inquired.

"You sent him away to fetch Mina, my king," he replied, looking about for a possible escape if need be. "He should be back any moment."

"So, I did! There is so much to remember. Well, carry on then. I need my armor on, move faster!"

The men moved about, fastening the last of his armor. Had the mirror not stood before Tarak for him to admire himself in, he might have lost his temper with how long it was taking. It eased his lack of patience. "My cropped blond-gray hair and striking blue eyes make me look fierce," he said aloud to himself. He had ignored the first specter that appeared in the newly-repaired mirror. However, now there were several creeping about in the reflection. With the last piece of armor in place, he was glad of the footfall that brought his attention to the chamber door. Godry stood there with a young woman in a well-made dress of dark-green satin with jewels about her neck. Both had sweat at their brows and were a little winded.

"Mina," Tarak said in a smooth voice. "I'm glad you could join me. Godry has said you have detected Rayla in the city with the fragment in the pendant you were given. Have you found out exactly where she is yet?"

Mina bowed low to Tarak; her dark hair was up in a bun, contrasting with her pale skin. She bent a knee in respect, as sprawling on the floor would have been beneath her station; she was part of the minister's court. Mina briefly touched the pendant she wore containing the fragment of the same material of which the Orbs were made. "I have been working to see clearer, my king. She has definitely closed on the library." Cautiously she waited for a response.

Tarak frowned; it had taken a long time to find this woman, and he could not afford to kill her out of hand. "How long have you been a carrier again?" he asked in a strained voice.

"Almost a month now, and I have refined my ability much since receiving your gift. I work continuously to become better with the shard." She spoke with difficulty as if her chest were constricted, and she seemed uncomfortable.

She should be uncomfortable standing in front of her king. Perhaps she had worn one of those binding garments under her dress to make her look thinner. He watched as she held her breath; he was growing impatient with her.

"Be sure you improve with using the shard before the next circle of the moon," he demanded. It was then that Tarak realized he was clenching his fist. He understood then that she was not holding her breath. He had lost control of the Orb's power again and had begun to squeeze her chest. She could not breathe. A tear leaked out of her eye before it occurred to him to release her. She dropped to her knees like a sack of stones, gasping for breath.

"Where is my sword?" Tarak hollered. *I must pay more attention to my magic. It slips away so easily these days. Why?*

The servant that had dared to speak to Tarak earlier stepped in front of him with the sword held out. *Who did this man think he was, interrupting his thoughts and disrupting his meeting?* "Have you sharpened it?" he snapped. It did not need to be sharpened. He could keep the blade sharp with the Power of the Orb, but he liked to have it worked with a stone. Something about the sound soothed him, a sound from his past he could no longer recall. Reaching over, he drew the sword from its scabbard. The steel of the blade rang as he did so, sending shivers down his spine. "How I love this sword." Tarak drove the sword toward the man's chest in one fluid movement, stopping short, the tip piercing the man's chest. A weave of magic flowed through him as he pulled the Power out of the Orb. Seen only by him, the weave twisted along the blade in his hand, then slipped into the cut at the end of the blade. The man stood frozen as Tarak used the weave to drain the life out of the man, adding it to his own. Tarak stared into the servant's eyes, watching the life slip out of him.

With his anger at Mina relieved, he took the scabbard and sheathed the sword.

"Let us get moving," Tarak commanded. "And stay back and out of sight. I don't want Rayla to suspect we have seen her. I want her Orb and the location of her followers. If we aren't quick enough, she will disappear, and my chance will be lost. Her ability to mask herself on her previous trips will make her sloppy in covering her presence." Mina stood shakily and joined Godry, and they trailed behind.

On her fourth day of travel, Rayla was nearly at the gates of Glydane. There was a small stream of people flowing through the gates. This was now one of the last trade ports left, and carts of all shapes and sizes were making their way amongst the crowd in the morning sun. Soon Glydane would be full of people, buying, selling, and in some cases, thieving—much like her.

She would be little noticed amongst all these people, blending in with her worn and tattered cloak. Where she was going and the task at hand needed her to be invisible. She reached into the Orb with her mind and formed a web of power that would shroud her. If the others here could see magic, they would have seen something like a spiderweb settle upon her cloak. A nifty bit of trickery that she had learned from Kerisa. She frowned. *That friendship needs some tending to. Not today, though; I have some fun to partake in.*

With the web about the cloak, people would see her but not take any particular notice. The magic was a bit fragile; if she moved too quickly or made any sudden movements, the magic fell apart. Rayla made her way through the gate and in no time was before the Great Library, a glory in its time. Her eyes fell upon the angular exterior of white limestone, in contrast to the rest of the building. The columns at the door and the corners of the building were smooth, a one-piece, rounded stone of white-veined dark marble.

The massive oak double doors stood open, allowing the visitors ample room to enter and exit. She was confident that no one knew who she was. Rayla touched the Orb that lay muted in her brigandine, its blue glow hidden from notice. She made sure her cloak hid her armor and sword from prying eyes. Her long dark hair hung down her neck and chest, further obscuring the glow. She needed to get to the library and back out as fast as possible. Stealing the book she needed out of the library would be challenging, but it had to be done. It would tell her where to find him. The man that would help her save the world.

Rayla frowned. She would have been one of the leaders

of her world as a Bearer before Tarak came. The true Bearers now only oversaw the Refuge and the small resistance that had formed. She had learned of the Prophecy from Kalamar only days after she revealed the Orb in her possession to him. That was over a hundred years ago, yet she still looked in her early twenties. She had spent those years learning to lead, becoming skilled with using the Orb's power, one of the fastest Kalamar said in history to gain control, and had developed impressive battle skills with a sword.

That all changed twenty years ago, to this day, when she felt a ripple in the fabric of Prophecy. A ripple that gave her one of the most potent visions of the man who would help save her world. She had been driven by the death of her family to rid her world of Tarak—the vision had made her almost zealous about it.

Rayla had spent her years at the Refuge helping raise countless orphans, helping the sick and injured, and spending time with the elders she had once raised. She had repeatedly seen the damage Tarak did, through the refuges. It drove her, made her into the leader she was. She had taken lovers over the years, but it was hard to be with someone you would likely outlive. With that thought, she broached the distance toward her destination.

After mounting the stone steps of the library, Rayla could see that there were more soldiers about than usual. These were the men who patrolled the streets, the everyday sort of soldier meant to keep the peace. That was the premise anyway. She need not be concerned about them, that she knew. They were a show of force that was obsolete and would not notice her if she did not draw attention to herself. The web of power she had put around herself was slight and easily broken by unexpected movement. She could not risk using more power. Tarak had some of the shard jewelry; one of the Carriers might detect anything more powerful. She could not abandon her goal now. If she turned around on the stairs now, that would break the web of power. She would surely arouse suspicion, especially since she was almost at the doors. Most of these soldiers collected bribes, created more crime than prevented it, and often looked for an opportunity to squeeze coins from unsuspecting citizens. The soldiers were likely bold enough to harass her for a fee here in broad daylight. Her ruse would be over then, once they searched her.

Rayla slid into the library before wandering into the busy foyer. The tall shelves filled with books were roped off on the first floor. The second floor was open to the foray—its wooden banisters and rails polished to a gleam, as were the ornate wall panels of the library itself. She could see the rows of books above that stretched back into the unseen. The upper level was restricted; only Librarians were allowed up there. Before slipping unnoticed up the barricaded stairs that led to the Prophecies section, she lingered a while. The upper floor was filled with several hundred scrolls and books about Prophecy. Most notable were the great prophet Egeldor's, many of which she had read. Being shrouded from notice gave her liberties like sneaking into the city and here as often as she liked. She had spent hours here, never once being disturbed. No one knew that the third, long-hidden Orb she wore had been found.

Walking amongst the shadows, taking care to go slow, Rayla looked below at the people who stared at the books they could not read. Tarak had opened up the Great Library a generation ago to the very people he had taken the written word from. None of them could read the books, and most of the library was cordoned off to "protect the books."

These people were from small villages and farms; most had likely never seen a book. She knew how to slip through, though. No one challenged the Librarians here—men easily picked out by their dark red formal dress robes. Being unchallenged for generations had made them lazy, giving her the advantage.

As the small crowd milled about, Rayla watched the Librarians take people through the library's finely built architecture and into the lesser restricted parts of the library. Disgust filled her at the mockery Tarak had made of the Librarians—well-muscled security guards were what they were in reality. Where once the Librarians had been peaceful men and women of great stature in society, they were now trained to fight and subdue anyone that tried to get to the restricted sections of books. Tarak rightly saw knowledge as power, and he had done a good job of taking it from them.

To view the books was a kindness given to them by Tarak, and they were allowed only to gaze from a distance. It infuriated her. She turned and made her approach to the very back of the Prophecies section, to the hidden alcove where books and scrolls of first-hand Prophecy sat laden with dust. Amid the shelves, lying open-faced on a roped-off stand, stood the book she had stumbled upon two months ago.

Taking it required her to take a chance, one she needed to plan for. Over the years, she had removed many small books and the odd scroll. This one, however, was large and prominently displayed. The Librarians patrolled this area often, and an empty stand would be noticed right away. She had watched the guards for half a moon cycle, and there was a small window of opportunity today. Removing the book from the stand, she placed it in her satchel. A sudden footfall at the other side of the shelves quickened her heart, and she froze.

"Is someone there?" A voice called out.

Rayla crouched and scurried back toward the hallway leading to the stairs. *The Librarian must have come in from the other hallway. What is he doing up here? He always disappears with one of the service girls on this day. Did he see me?* Her heart was pounding as she sidestepped down the hall with her back to the wall. She had planned the heist for this time of day, for when the light outside would be waning, creating long, dark shadows for her to hide in.

Rayla watched the tour below as she crept down the darkened stairs. She waited for her opportunity, stepping back in with one of the groups as they passed. Above, she saw a Librarian at the railing looking over the main floor, scanning the crowd. He met her eye for a second and lingered there. *Could they know? Albax, I need to get out of here.* The group she had merged with exited, and she moved down the steps. Was it her imagination, or were there more soldiers about? She moved as swiftly as possible to a side street and made for the nearest gate exiting the city.

Tarak could not have been happier when he saw her exiting the Great Library. The magic allowed him to see her even though she was masking herself. A smile spread across his face. "I going to enjoy this!" Tarak declared from the tower above the courtyard. "I have not had a good hunt in years. You see, Godry, my patience has proven to be fruitful." His heart pumped with excitement but also with anxiety. He had waited too long, and he could not lose his opportunity now.

Godry smacked his lips, "Yes, my king, it has indeed. Shall I wave the guard to follow?"

"No! She is mine to deal with." Tarak took off with a spring in his step, running down the stairs two at a time. "She will never see me coming," he said to himself. "In fact, I think I'll play with her a bit. See how fast she can run."

Tarak sprinted through the crowd, parting them with the Power—in some cases physically shoving them—shocked looks on their faces when they saw him. "I see that you all still know your places!" he shouted. "That you all still fear me, and justly so. If I had time, I would dispatch a few of you to make sure no one forgets." It had been a long time indeed since he had walked the streets. He had done so a great deal early on after taking over—striking fear into the people's hearts. He picked up his pace, fearing he might lose Rayla, "I must get to her."

Tarak caught a glimpse of Rayla as she closed on the door of latticed, wrought-iron bars of the side gate. The crowd here was thinner, but there were still enough people to provide cover. He slowed to a walk as she moved out of the small exit, so she did not see him. The people there scurried to the side as he approached, and the guards stood at attention. He peered around the corner of the gate to see Rayla just a little way up the path. As he turned to the guard and the people staring at him, he said, "What is the matter? Do you not recognize your King?"

"We do, my king," a guard said back meekly. "It's just, we don't see you in your armor much these days."

Tarak looked at his gauntleted hand, at his armor, then the guard. "She will see me. Give me your cloak!" The man quickly removed it, and Tarak snatched it away.

"Forgive me, my king, but the hood won't cover your helm."

Lifting his hand to his head, the clang of metal on metal sounded in his ears. He frowned, "Perhaps my full armor wasn't the right decision." He called upon the magic once more, and the armor he wore shifted and twisted. As it did, a cuirass formed at his chest, vambraces appeared on his forearms, and greaves at his shins. The helm and the rest simply disappeared. "Now I look like an everyday soldier, hey." He clapped the guard on his shoulder. The man winced, looking like he might meet his end.

Tarak stepped forward to move through the gate, then thought better of it. "Send some of these plebs up the north road and a few down the south road. I don't want her to realize I'm following. NOW!"

The guard shook with fear, stepping forward; he called out, "You heard the King. Start moving, and most of you head north. Get moving!"

The crowd began moving forward, and once a good part of them had moved out of the gate, Tarak moved with them. His cloak hid his armor well enough, and the people would do the rest. "You're mine now!" He muttered to himself.

Chapter Three

As Rayla walked along the road, she saw the footpath she needed to get back to the Refuge. While leaving Glydane, she saw a man who stood a head taller than the rest of the crowd. His cloak was a little too new and clean for her liking. *Has one of the Librarians sent a guard to follow me out for the book? If so, why wait?* The guard should have apprehended her and taken her back to make an example of her. To their surprise, they would have found an Orb Bearer. Then the real trouble would have started for her. She looked back several times over her shoulder. The soldier had remained where he was, amongst the people making their way along the road. He had made no effort to make any gain on her.

Glancing back once more, Rayla saw he was still there, several minutes back. *Maybe he's a new soldier sent out on an errand. He can't be following me; I'm masking myself with the Power. His gaze should slide off me as long as I don't draw attention to myself.* She placed her hand on the pommel of her sword.

"I hope I don't have to kill him," she spoke to herself.

It pained Rayla to have to kill her own people. She had only ever done it a few times in her hundred and fifty years. But it still weighed on her. She exited the road onto the small path, the first of many back to the Refuge. A few paces in, she stepped into the trees hidden from view. Few took this way; it led to farmland where not many people lived. As she watched, the tall man moved past the entrance to the footpath. After a few moments, she crept forward and saw that he had continued over the hill and out of sight. *Odd indeed! I better move quickly for a bit, just in case.*

She breathed a sigh of relief and turned back up the path. She could have run so fast no one could see her, if she needed to, but if anyone saw her disappear, that would cause trouble. Any indicators of where the Refuge was could give Tarak an advantage in finding them. She quickened her pace to that of a normal quick stride. She had never had anything like this happen to her in the hundred-plus years she had been sneaking into the city.

When dusk arrived, Rayla thought it time to take last meal. Using the Orb as she was made her hungry, the cost of the Power. Luckily; the amount of the Orb's power she was using to avoid detection was small. She was also eager to see what the book said about the man who would come here to help save her people. She even hoped for some clues about how to find him. Kalamar, the man that carried the other of the three Orbs, had told her of the book. He had tried to use it to warn that Tarak was not their coming savior. The fear of the Prophecy predicting the end of their world had made most people unreasonable back then. Hardly any had listened to the council. She had seen Godry, who had been the head minister when Tarak had arrived, during a trip to Glydane once. He looked like a wraith. That he was still alive meant that Tarak had used the Orb to sustain the man. It sickened her how he soiled the Power.

As the sun sunk low in the sky, she felt confident that she was alone on the path and broke her walk to eat. As she ate, she pulled out the book and opened it to the placemark she had put there on her last visit, realizing what this book was. She had not had any real time to look at the passage she had found that day. Her heart leaped that day when she saw the heading.

She sent a small weave of power, like that of a spider web, to keep the frail page from falling to pieces. With the utmost care, she flipped to the next page. A copy of the original Prophecy of Egeldor's, telling of the savior, was there on the page. Skimming through pages of the book Kalamar had told her of, she read about how "Taylor" would be brought here after being convinced he was needed. It also revealed that a Bearer would travel to his world and bring him back here. Her own visions of the man that would help save her world flashed through her mind.

Unexpectedly as she read, a second vision appeared, a frightening one. Death and sorrow filled her mind's eye; she pushed them away, unable to accept the image. "He will be mighty and will kill Tarak!" Flipping the next page, she noticed something odd; this page seemed thicker. She gently rubbed her fingers on either side of the page, but it seemed like a solid piece of thick paper. The Orb suddenly pulsed, and for an instant, a second web appeared on the paper. Rayla ran a counter web, and a second page appeared between her fingers. Her heart pumped a little faster; what were these hidden pages in Egeldor's Prophecy? With the pages splayed, the words at the top were as surprising as the web that had been there.

I, Egeldor, in the last days of being known to this world, have added these two pages to this book of Prophecy. When the man who unlocks Prophecy is to be found. Only she who bears my Orb will be able to unravel the web of secrecy I have placed here.

Below, filling both pages, was an illustration of eight spheres moving around a large yellow sun. The blue one, third from the sun, had an inscription, *"Earth."*

"Anything I might be interested in?" A man's voice broke in.

Rayla's heart jumped as she looked up at the tall cloaked man she thought had followed her earlier. *I'm so stupid!*

The man raised his hands to his hood, pulling it back and letting it fall. For a minute, she could not believe her eyes. Tarak stood before her. With lightning speed, he threw a dagger at her. She was instantly up and out of the way, with the book tucked in her satchel. *He cannot get this book!*

"Shall we play a game? Shall we see if you can outrun me?" The ring of Tarak's sword filled the air, and he stepped forward.

Tarak smiled as he lunged forward with his sword. Knowing that she was too fast for it did not make a difference. He wanted her to run. It would make killing her, in the end, more fun. She rolled and came to stand just a few feet away. "That is the spirit! I'm feeling generous today. How about I give you a lead. Say to the count of ten?" he jeered playfully.

Rayla darted away with a look of fear on her face. She was small and fast, but he had the advantage of longer legs. He would catch her in no time. "One, two, three, four..." he shouted. *Long enough!* Tarak tore off after her, his sword at the ready. The wind whipped through his hair as the Power of the Orb helped his legs pump at an unnatural speed. He caught sight of Rayla far sooner than he expected. *She must be more tired from using the Orb than I expected*. But then, in a few strides, Tarak felt his chest hit an unseeable obstacle. The breath rushed out of him as his legs whipped out in front of him. His momentum pulled him down and under an invisible barrier, and he hit the ground hard. His body tumbled and bounced over a hundred steps; he even collided with a tree at one point.

When he finally came to rest, he stared up at the trees, "An invisible weave!" he shouted. "Very clever, but you still won't get away." The Orb began pulling the broken bones together and mending them like new, the torn tissue stitched back together, and his cuts vanished. In only minutes, he could stand and was ready to be on his way. He took a deep breath and began running to the side of the path. This meant running slower, but he would catch her safely.

Only moments later, he could see that the trees came to an end ahead. It was then that he sensed something that troubled him. Something that he should have thought of but had not, considering it was the dry season. He did not know this area, and as he broke from the trees he was faced with a troubling sight.

A small lake lay ahead, and Rayla was kneeling at its edge. A flash of bright light in the water confirmed Tarak's fears. Rayla was opening a portal. He doubled his speed, and with the sword raised, he rushed her. Terror flashed in her eyes as she glanced back at him, causing him to smile to himself.

As Rayla broke through the treeline to the lake she was looking for, she heard Tarak shouting at her from a short distance back. He had found her little surprise on the path. The invisible weave of the chest-high barrier would give her the much-needed time she required to escape. At the water's edge, she halted and lowered herself beside it.

Rayla did not have plenty of time to open a portal back to the Refuge. She could hear Tarak coming, but when she set about to open the doorway, all she could see was the drawing in the book she possessed and the man named Taylor—who would help her save her people. The location of the man she had sought for years was finally revealed. All she needed was the proper web for the doorway to him, and she could in an instant be in his world and, with hope, close to him. She could retrieve the key person in the Prophecy to save her world. She pushed the thought aside, though; she did not have time for working out the web. Her life was in danger. She needed a quick exit, so instead she focused on the image of home, but again she could not hold it.

The image of Taylor slid back into Rayla's mind. *Albax, I don't have the time to figure out a weave for that kind of doorway.* The Orb was pushing into her mind what Prophecy required to happen instead of doing her bidding. An infuriating instance that occurred rarely. The Orbs sometimes formed a will of their own, but this was the worst time for it to happen. Or was it? There could be an end to the tyranny here! She was putting her life in danger; not one book in the library had mentioned a Bearer ever allowing such a thing.

I don't have much choice; Tarak will be here any moment. I need to take the chance that the Orb will open at the other end of the doorway where he is. She took a breath, understanding that Prophecy sometimes had its own way of fulfilling itself. She cleared her mind and took a leap of faith, allowing the Orb to form the necessary weave to open a doorway to Earth and to Taylor.

Focusing on the image of him from her visions and the illustration in the book, Rayla closed her eyes and opened her mind to the Power of the Orb. The Orb flared to life, turning a deep purple, and its power flooded into her, bringing with it a glorious rush of the Power's beauty. The world around her sharpened, the air crackled, and her awareness of her surroundings heightened. With her senses keen and the Orb's enormous power at her disposal, she reached her outstretched hand toward the surface of the water and willed the Orb to find the place and man she sought. The Power pulsated as she gazed into the water, and a weave she had never seen before formed by the Orb's own will. The small spot of light indicated the door opening she knew would come. The portal started to appear, swirled, then spiraled out. The doorway was solidifying, and to her surprise, Taylor was gazing back at her. What luck could this be? She stared at him in amazement. She was sure this was the man she had seen in her visions. He looked younger somehow. Innocent.

A crash of breaking branches from the woods behind Rayla brought her attention back to the reality of her situation. She swiveled her head back. She felt Tarak before seeing him rush out of the trees; he would be there in seconds. The doorway was not formed yet. She had never attempted such a great distance, and it was draining her of her own energy. She needed to go now, or she would likely find her death. Using the Orb, sending a weave of control over Taylor's will, she began to direct him to touch the water. If he would do that, she could circumvent the need for the door to be fixed. She would not be able to maintain the doorway much longer. He reluctantly reached out to the water toward her outstretched hand. There was a searing pain in her back as he touched the water, and her hand shot through, grabbing his. He was pulling her through, and she reached out with her other hand, latching on to him. Then everything went white.

Chapter Four

EARTH

ROCKY MOUNTAINS, COLORADO

As Taylor walked along the mountain path in the sweltering heat of the day, he was looking forward to a much-needed rest at the lake ahead. He rounded a corner on the trail and found himself immersed in a scene that took his breath away. The sun was high in the sky, and it cast a sheer gloss over the large lake that stood before him. Trees surrounded the lake almost to the very edge. In front of him, the trail opened to a glade where the ground gently sloped into the water.

Taylor sighed, "At last, we have arrived!"

Taylor looked for an appropriate spot to do what he had come here to do. There was a nook to the side where he stood at the edge of the clearing. Trees surrounded the nook halfway into the clearing, leaving a crescent-shaped shoreline. It was the perfect place for what he intended. He walked to the water's edge and lowered his backpack to the ground. Opening it, he removed an ornate wooden box, two hand-width's tall and a hand's-width wide. The weight of it was more than he remembered. Was the heaviness more than Lilly's ashes that lay inside?

"Here we are, Lilly. It's time." He slid the box open and looked at the dark urn inside. "It's time to let you go." The surface was not what one would expect of an urn; it was rough and clay-like. Taylor had made a special effort for the remains of his deceased wife. This urn was a 3D-printed composite of earth, meant to degrade. It could be placed under a tree to become part of it over time. That was not the purpose Taylor had in mind, though. Exposed to water, the urn would take less than a day to dissolve completely.

"You picked this spot for our fifth anniversary. A fitting resting place for you." Taylor had come to terms with Lilly's death almost two months ago. While going through her things on her desk in the living room, he had come across Lilly's trail book. Hiking had been one of their favorite outdoor activities. The book was well-worn, with folded corners inside and little sticky tabs poking out at points of interest. He had leafed through her book with the desire to see how she liked to plan their adventures, one last time. Inside, he found this location circled in her trail map book. An inscription of "5th anniversary" was written beside it. After that, he had committed to taking the journey here.

Taylor submersed the air-tight, weighted urn in the water. He dried his hands on his pants as he watched the urn begin to flake through the crystal-clear water. While he sat there, he thought of his memories of their time together. "Goodbye, Lilly!" A tear fell from Taylor's cheek, and he got up and walked with his pack to the other side of the glade at the water's edge. He pitched camp, taking his time with arranging the hiking tent and gear, and then set a ring for a fire.

Taylor wiped the sweat off his brow with a tanned forearm and pulled at his shirt, where it stuck to his chest. The thought of a refreshing swim to escape the heat brought a gratified smile to his face. He squatted down at the water and looked at his reflection on the mirror-like surface. His shoulder-length blonde hair hung down around his face, and he looked into his own deep brown eyes.

Reaching down, Taylor picked a small pebble out of the dirt and rolled it in his fingers. The stone's long years at the water's edge had left its surface smooth and round. Almost without thought, Taylor extended his arm and released the pebble out over the water. He watched the ripples dance across the water until they began to dissipate. As they disappeared, it allowed the water to show his reflection once again.

Taylor took in a breath and exhaled, attempting to relax. Then picked up another small pebble, tossing it into the water. The ripples distorted his face once more, but as they dissipated again, something seemed odd. As his reflection became clearer, it grew less like him. His mind worked to understand what was happening, but he could not grasp what he saw. The image that looked back at him was not him but that of an unknown, stunningly beautiful woman.

Taylor felt his heart starting to beat faster with confusion and then fear. His mind began to race to explain what he saw. Was this real? If it was, there was a dead body in the lake. He was thrown off further when the woman made eye contact with him, and he saw her smile.

It must have been a trick of the sun on the water—but then he saw a hand moving towards his. Drawn to touch the water, he moved his hand towards it, mesmerized by the woman's reflection. As if time had stood still, he tried to get his head around how on earth she could still be alive. Doubt sprung into his mind about what he was seeing; it must be the undercurrent. Had he just found a dead woman in the lake? He began to shake all over; visions of Lilly in the water rushed through his mind. At that moment, the woman in the water broke eye contact and looked back over her shoulder. When she turned around to face him, there was a look of panic now. She locked eyes with him again before closing them as if falling asleep.

She can't be alive!

As Taylor fought to keep himself in reality, he felt himself freezing up. He could not bear to witness another woman's death right before him. Taylor had just laid Lilly to rest; watching her death in the river came fresh into his mind. The woman-in-the-water's eyes popped open, and her gaze intensified. Taylor almost felt pulled into a trance as a compulsion took over his actions. He needed to place his hand in the water! She reached out to him when he did, and he touched her fingers, warm despite the cool water. Taylor could feel the warmth and solidity of her skin against his. At that moment, a strange tingling sensation swept through his body.

As Taylor came to the full realization she was alive, the woman's hand shot through the water and grabbed his wrist. It was so sudden, Taylor jerked backward and struggled to get his hand free from hers, but she held fast onto him. With his heels dug into the ground, Taylor pulled back as hard as he could to try to stand up, pulling her with him. As the woman's other hand emerged from the water, she grasped the strap on his backpack, securing her hold on him. He fell backward, the weight of her body crashing against his, as he landed flat on his back.

Taylor's heart raced, and terror and shock set in. The woman lay on top of him with her head resting on his chest. Her wet hair had begun soaking his T-shirt. She still held on to him, one hand gripped around the strap of his backpack, the other still holding on to his wrist. A strange sensation flowed through him, and with it brought a need to help her.

Taylor lay there for a moment, his heart pounding with fright. He pried the woman's hands from his wrist and backpack, then rolled her off to his side. The woman was petite, but weighed a ton and was unconscious. He slowly rose to one knee and looked at her as she lay there. As his mind cleared from the shock of this woman's appearance, his first aid training kicked in. He leaned over her, quickly felt her neck for a pulse, and found it weak and slow. "She's still alive! Thank goodness," he muttered.

The woman's beauty struck awe into him. Unable to resist, he reached down and brushed her raven black hair off her cheek, exposing her face. His eyes lingered there for a few seconds before his eyes were drawn down to her neck to the perfectly round Orb. It glowed a faint dark purple and hung from an ornate silver chain. He found it was hypnotizing, and a calming feeling moved through his hand where it rested on her cheek. She opened her dark, hazel-colored eyes to look up at him, drawing him in.

With great difficulty, she spoke in a soft and quiet voice. "I found you, Taylor," before her eyes slid closed, and she fell unconscious once again. The words bounced around in his head as his mind worked to comprehend what had happened. How was this possible? And how could this woman know him? Out of the corner of his eye, he noticed the pool of blood at her side.

That is a lot of blood! Taylor felt a moment of panic as a rush of painful memories flooded into his mind. The smell of cold, wet hair mixed with blood, the memory of cradling Lilly's pale, lifeless body in his arms as her blue eyes stared up at nothing. Then her upturned kayak floating away beside his, and the pain of building her temporary grave so he could hike back two days to town for help. The old emotions of that day were almost too much to bear; tears began to form in his eyes.

He shuddered, looking down at this strange woman as she took in a deep breath and moaned in pain. This woman was alive! Unlike Lilly, he had a chance to save this woman. Taylor's wilderness first aid skills kicked back in, and he began to look around, working out what he needed to do to save this woman. *I'll need to stop the bleeding....*

He needed to look at the wound on her back through her clothing. "Why are you wearing a cloak and a full-sleeved leather jerkin?" he said aloud. There was chainmail between it and her linen undershirt, to his further surprise. The jerkin fit tightly around her chest and abdomen, complicating things. At least she had linen pants with leather greaves over her shins, which meant less moving her around. "What on earth are you doing up here in this outfit? Is this some cosplay gone wrong?"

Even more astonishing was that she had the most spectacular sword Taylor had ever seen, running from her hip to three-quarters down her leg. It rattled and got in the way as he rolled her over. Cradling her with one arm across her shoulders, he looked over the wound.

The cut in the cloak and jerkin's leather started at her right shoulder and went down to her left hip. It was deep, going down through the skin and tissue beneath. "Damn, someone had to have wanted to kill you to do this much damage!" The armor had both lacing and straps along the sides of her body. These would have enabled her to tighten, loosen, and remove the armor. Taylor undid the straps and removed the lacing on the right side of her armor. He peeled the layers off her back and exposed the wound, which was more profound than he had hoped. The gash was all the way down to the bone.

He ignored the small bandages in his emergency kit; even all of them together would not have been enough. Instead, he used a clean T-shirt and the adhesive tape from his kit to cover the wound. Once it was secured, he folded the armor back into place and refastened it, hoping the pressure would keep the wound closed.

He pulled out his map, found their position, then the location of the watchtower he had passed on the trail earlier. There would be someone there during this time in the season, and they would have a direct line to help. He quickly traced the path from their position to the tower. The hike on his own would be almost two hours; carrying the woman would extend that time.

Now that her wound was taken care of, he rushed to look in the nearby trees and found two thick branches as tall as he. He unraveled his sleeping bag, then used his climbing rope to secure it to the branches, creating a stretcher. When he was finished, he rolled her upon it. Taylor grabbed the water from his pack and slung it over his shoulder. Leaving the backpack behind, pulling her all that way, would put enough strain on him. He knelt, grabbed the head of the stretcher, and began the journey toward the tower.

Chapter Five

The walk to the tower was arduous and left Taylor's body heavy, sore, and stiff. His arms trembled as he reached the watchtower, barely keeping hold of the stretcher. He laid the woman in the grass at the base of the tower, and his arms eased in relief. But they ached at every rung of the watchtower ladder as he climbed. To his relief, as he reached the top, the trap door swung open and revealed a middle-aged woman standing there.

"I caught a glimpse of you as you approached the tower. I have managed to reach the military base nearby. The helicopter should be here in a few minutes," the ranger said as Taylor reached the top. "Is she hurt badly?"

"Yes," is all Taylor could muster as he lifted himself through the opening in the floor and dropped in exhaustion. He heard the ranger descend the stairs, and some few minutes later, the chopping sound of the helicopter blades as he lay there. When it sounded like it had landed, he picked himself up with great effort and made his way down to the woman.

By the time Taylor reached her, the medics had transferred the woman onto a medical stretcher in the helicopter. It was strange, but he felt protective of her.

A man in a suit Taylor hadn't noticed broke his concentration. "Hop in; it looks like you could use a once over." He pointed to Taylor's blood-soaked clothes. "It's a good thing we were out looking for the source of an enormous anomaly we detected when the ranger called about your friend." The man looked down at the woman and then eyed Taylor with suspicion. "I'd like to chat with you when we get to the Denver hospital. Once we finish with our questions, we will get you to your home."

"That works for me. I'd like to know that the woman is okay. Does the army always dispatch medical helicopters to check out anomalies?" Taylor eyed him back.

"A precaution in case there were injured at the location or nearby the event. You never know what you might find." The agent smiled at him.

"I live in Denver. So that works for me." Taylor said dismissively. He hopped in the helicopter, taking the only available seat left.

One of the medics looked at him and motioned for him to put a headset on so he could talk to him. Taylor slipped it on, and the medic began to talk at once. "You did a good job packing the wound; what kind of training do you have?"

Taylor understood the urgency; "I have my wilderness and remote first aid. She had lost a lot of blood; checking the wound will only release the pressure," he had told them.

The medic nodded, "Good thing to have all the way out here. You could do surgery with that training." The medic went back to what he was doing and said nothing further.

Taylor slipped the headset off and sat back. The man in the suit, who Taylor had come to recognize as an FBI agent, could not ask him questions but stared at him for a time. The ride took less than half an hour, and before he knew it, he had been checked out by a doctor.

Agent Sadue made his formal introduction to Taylor before escorting him into a small hospital room. Sadue had the sword the woman wore in his hand, having confiscated it. "Please have a seat," the agent gestured to one of the chairs in the room.

Taylor sat down, somewhat uncomfortable with his situation. *I haven't been able to comprehend what had happened myself. How do I explain anything to this guy?*

Agent Sadue stood menacingly in front of him. "The military traced a high energy reading to the area you were in. Which piqued my agency's interest in the area. Could you tell me a little about what you were doing up there and how you came to be with the woman in the other room?"

Taylor had decided when he boarded the chopper; it was best not to reveal the actual events he experienced. Even if they did believe him. He had developed a strange protectiveness for the woman, something he could not explain. "I was hiking on my own; you can check the registry at the trailhead. I had hoped to take a swim but found her on the side of the lake instead."

"Just like that?" the agent grilled. "What do you suppose she was doing up there?"

Taylor shifted, "LARPing?" he shrugged.

The agent slid the sword free of its scabbard and held it up to gleam in the light. Before putting it on the table before him. "Do you see the edge on this thing? It could cut someone's head clean off with one stroke. What would she be doing up there with something like this?"

Taylor hunched his shoulders, "Extreme LARPing?

Maybe there are more of them up there; you could ask. Maybe there was an accident."

Sadue sighed, "I don't buy it. You aren't telling me everything. Something odd went on up there. I don't know that you're part of it, but you are a witness of sorts. And I can't hold you for finding her." Sadue pulled out a notepad and pen, dropped them on the table, picked up the sword, and sheathed it. "Write your information down, and you're free to go. I'll be contacting you in a day or two." He left Taylor there without another word.

Taylor left the hospital with a head full of questions and headed for home in a taxi, courtesy of Sadue. What had happened at the lake repeatedly played in his mind on his way home. He had to be sure he had heard her correctly. "I found you, Taylor." The vision of her opening her eyes and speaking those words still shocked him. How could she know his name? What had she meant? The whole experience seemed so fantastical.

Taylor looked at his watch after he got home. "7:00 PM," it read. "What a day. I'm exhausted." He plopped down on the couch. The small apartment Taylor lived in was still the same as it was before Lilly had died. He had been unable to put away her little touches everywhere in the small apartment. He had wanted to keep the last of what was left of her visible. What she had done to their tiny apartment had turned it into a home and a place of comfort. His gaze fell on the chair in the corner with her violin sitting on it. Memories seeped in of how Lilly had spent many evenings sitting there playing while he listened. Sheet music lay on the floor still from the last time she had practiced. It was long past due that he finished putting her life away. It was with thoughts of Lilly that he drifted into sleep on the couch.

Taylor lay awake on the couch most of the night and watched reruns of That 70s show in a marathon-style broadcast, letting the antics of Eric and friends help him forget his worries. Finally, he fell into a deep sleep in the early morning hours.

Taylor found himself on a tropical island, walking alongside a small stream. The beauty here was unbelievable; the rainforest, the vibrant beauty of the flowers, and their fragrance. Ahead, a small waterfall that came down off the ridge above into the gorge he was in drew his attention. He walked toward the bottom of the waterfall, where a clear deep pool had formed over the years. *How nice it would be to find such a place.* Peace and contentment flowed into him.

As Taylor walked along the stream and took in the beauty, he felt like he was not alone. Unrest came over him as he walked, and he began to look into the forest to the left and right of him. When he could see no one, he looked further upstream.

Taylor saw a small figure standing beside the waterfall struggling to pull something free from the water. He quickened his pace toward them, feeling the need to help. The person's appearance did not become any more evident as he approached; it remained blurry until he was about five feet from them. The figure turned toward him then, coming into perfect focus. He started in surprise; the person was the woman he had saved.

Taylor looked down at Rayla's hand to see what she struggled with. Around her wrist was a black iron shackle, attached to a thick black chain that led down into the water. As Taylor followed the chain with his eyes, he could see that a chain ran from Rayla's wrist to a large rock at the bottom of the pool. Taylor's heart pounded, and fear spread throughout him for her. Rayla turned her attention back to the chain and pulled, frantic to free herself once more.

Rayla paused after struggling for a minute with the shackle around her wrist. Rayla tried, again and again, to free her hand before she looked at him. "Help me, Taylor!" she pleaded. Blood now dripped from her wrist down onto her hand, and as the first drop fell into the pool, its bright red color flowed outward to turn the entirety of the pool blood-red. Rayla screamed out in fear and frustration, and tears ran down her cheek. She reached for him, and Taylor found himself beside her. She grabbed hold of his arm and held fast. "I need to get out of here. I haven't recovered my strength yet, Taylor—help me." Her eyes were fierce and determined as she looked into him. The moment she had touched him, he had begun to feel her fear and panic. It hit him at his core; his heart ached in his chest.

At that moment, Taylor started awake, dropped his feet to the floor, and clutched the couch's arm with his hand. His heart pounded in his chest. "What the hell!" he said aloud. He gulped for air and worked to calm himself. His mind raced as he tried to comprehend what had happened. *That's not possible! The dream felt so real; she felt real!*

Could she somehow have the ability to enter into my dreams? If so, how could she also affect my body? Whatever the case was, the dream he had left him with an overpowering sense, a sense that he should help Rayla. Standing up, Taylor walked toward the bathroom; as he passed the kitchen, he saw the clock read, "5:59 AM". *I cannot believe I slept that long.* He washed his face with cold water and looked into the mirror; he tried to reason things out. *If I go back to the hospital, it will look suspicious. Mostly for myself. But I need to help her!*

A sense of urgency pulled at Taylor. He could not seem

to shake the feeling. When he was unsuccessful in getting back to sleep, he headed to the kitchen to prepare a meal.

As Taylor ate his breakfast, the urgency pulled at him, wore at him, and told him he should be doing something. After eating, he cleaned up the dishes and decided to go for a run to clear his mind. After forty-five minutes of running, the urgency still remained. Taylor gave up and turned back home. He showered and dressed and, to his surprise, found himself at the door, unsure of how he got there.

With his keys in hand and his boots and jacket on, Taylor was ready to go to the hospital. He realized the persistent need that had nagged him since returning home would not go away. He could not understand his need to see the woman again, yet still, it was there.

Rayla had passed out after finding Taylor, the man from Prophecy. She did so in relief that she had escaped her pursuers and found him simultaneously. However, as she had slept, she had felt a danger of a sort. Several times, different people had tried to remove her Orb. As they had done so, the Orb had sensed their presence and protected her. In doing so, though, it had also transferred several tidbits of information about them into her mind. She had become aware of the information when she woke.

After what seemed like several hours between semi-lucid moments, Rayla felt herself waking, and as she did, she sensed trouble. With her eyes closed, she felt about with the Orb's power. She lay in a bed in a sizable, odd-smelling room. She heard the sound of a door open and the soft footfall of someone of small stature. The Orb had read the language centers of those trying to remove it. *So many languages and different peoples. This world is very different, indeed.*

Rayla reached out with the Power and brushed across the mind of the person who walked toward her. She could feel the woman's concern before her thoughts rushed in to her mind—*Such an odd way for a patient to come in, dressed like that. I've seen a lot in my time here, but nothing like her. I do hope she will be alright. There the screen goes again.* Rayla understood the woman was talking about the machine that listened to her body. It seemed that the Orbs' power was disruptive to the technology here. Each time Rayla used it, the machine stopped working. *Poor dear,* the woman thought.

Rayla listened for free thoughts from the woman that might lie on the surface of her mind. Looking further would have been an intrusion. She was forestalled when the door opened again, and a second person, a man, walked in. The room flooded with angst, then anger. Rayla's mind was assaulted with images of death as she brushed against his thoughts. War, machines that destroyed, this man firing his weapon at defenseless people, killing them. Then the thoughts of how his FBI badge protected him. Rayla retreated in horror. *He's a law man!* The others who had touched the Orb had dark thoughts, but this man and those like him were hateful beyond her imagining.

As Rayla withdrew from his thoughts, she saw Taylor's face. This man wanted to get answers from him. And this man, this agent, would hurt Taylor if need be to get them. *Oh gods, where are you, Taylor?*

"When might she awake?" the agent asked coldly.

"I'm not sure," she said. "You will have to ask the doctor."

A tidbit of the information the Orb had given her

rushed forward. The doctor was an FBI Agent like Sadue, but more important. There were several staff members here from the FBI, all there for her. Rayla's fatigue from traveling began retaking her. *I need to find you, Taylor, and get you out of here. I need to take you back to my world.* This place was filled with more danger and war than her world had seen in its remembering—something she could not fathom.

When Rayla awoke again, it was quiet in her room, and she felt a moment of ease. Her room seemed to have someone in it at all times. The wound at her back had healed, and the tissue inside had been repaired. The big breath she could take meant that she was almost ready to leave this place. A tray beside her bedside had the smell of food and, feeling famished, she made to sit up. The odd thing was there was a funny feeling in her groin. She reached down to find that there was a tube there; repulsed, she pulled it out. "What is wrong with these people?"

Taking the tray, Rayla put it on her lap and removed the cover to reveal small-looking eggs, a sort of white chopped-up root, and strips of meat. She devoured everything. Her body drew the nutrients out quickly; she was sad there was not more. Outside she heard the sound of people talking.

"She was still sleeping the last I checked on her, Cara. Let me know if you need a hand moving her to the gurney," a voice said.

"I will!" came a reply from the woman there. "Would you open the door for me, Officer?"

Rayla had sensed the man outside. A guard was placed there due to her unusual attire, sword, and the Orb at her chest which the staff could not remove. She would need to be quick to subdue him as she escaped. The sound of someone approaching the door and then telling the guard outside she needed in, alerted her. She quickly put the tray back and lay back down to not call attention to herself right away.

The door swung open to the sound of tiny wheels and the humming of a young woman. The wheels rolled up beside her, part of what Rayla assumed was a cart of some sort. She heard the woman move closer, and there were a series of clunking noises as she pushed the cart beside her.

"Alright, let us have a—Oh, your catheter has come out." The woman sighed, "A bit of a mess on the floor, but it will make moving you a little easier." Rayla felt a touch on her arm, "Miss? Miss? Wake up!"

To the woman's surprise, Rayla moved fluidly, and the Orb's power flared to life, flowing into her. She sat up and grabbed hold of the woman using one hand to clasp over her mouth and the other to hold her tight. "Sleep." The woman went limp, but Rayla had no trouble holding her upright. Rayla stood while holding the woman and noticed she had been pushing a second bed, not a cart. Rayla realized that the woman intended to take her somewhere on the gurney. Rayla hoisted her into the bed as a plan of escape formed in her mind.

Rayla looked down at the woman, her face calmly asleep. "You have made this a good deal easier." Rayla was still shaken from traveling through the doorway, but she could manage small bits of the Power. Closing her eyes, she spun a web of illusion upon herself. As it settled on her, she looked in the mirror, and Cara's face now looked back at her. To hide her escape further, Rayla spun a second web to make Cara appear in her likeness. It would fade in a short time after she escaped. She would not want that FBI agent to hurt this young woman. She quickly undressed the woman and put on her clothes. As she removed the woman's shirt, she noticed the tag on her shirt with the bold letters "C A R A" on it. The Orb had not yet given her the ability to read the language here. She would have to work on that.

Rayla covered the woman in the blankets, strode to the door, and left the room. The officer looked up at her and smiled. She closed the door, brushed her hand on the officer's shoulder, and nudged him toward sleep. If she had been rested, she could have done so from a distance. "I'll be back in a few minutes. I just need to use the washroom."

"Alright," the man there said, without looking up.

Rayla moved swiftly down the hall toward an office she needed to visit first. She had been able to plant a suggestion that Agent Sadue put her sword in the office of the doctor that investigated her. They were not working together, though; both had their own agendas. Sadue's fearful thoughts had been easy to read, as thoughts of that nature were; people tended to broadcast them.

When Rayla reached the office, she used the Power to sense inside to make sure it was empty. She opened the door and waltzed in. At the back of the room, behind a desk, was a long filing cabinet. She retrieved the sword and, almost without thought, spun a second web of the Power upon the sword that made it appear as a cane. "Time to go."

Chapter Six

Taylor started back to reality as his truck jerked to a stop when it hit the hospital's parking stall median. He looked around and realized that the last thing he remembered was closing his apartment door. *What is wrong with me? What is it about this woman that I can't seem to shake?*

Taylor sat with that thought a moment but was jarred out of it by a loud knock at the passenger window. A woman in a hospital uniform stood there waving to him. He rolled the window down to see what she wanted.

"Thank the gods you came!" The woman said as she looked at the outside of the door in confusion. "How do I get in? We need to hurry."

"Do I know you?" Taylor asked. She tugged at the handle, the door swung open, and she hopped in. "Seriously, can I help you?"

"This might freak you out a little. But don't go crazy on me." The woman closed her eyes, and her whole body wavered. Astonishingly the woman he had saved now sat before him, holding her magnificent sword.

Taylor slid himself up against the door. *I think I might be having a breakdown. Maybe the trip to the mountains was too soon.* His heart began to pound, "I, I, I ...."

The woman reached across the truck. Taylor retracted back but had nowhere to go, and she touched his arm. A warm tingle flowed through his arm and then into his body. With it, a sense of calm washed away some of his fear. "My name is Rayla, and I'll explain everything, but we need to go from here. Before they notice I'm gone."

"I don't understand what happened—"

"We need to go," Rayla said with firmness in her voice.

Rayla sat back, taking her hand away. Taylor could not explain it, but he complied, turning forward. "You need to do up the seat belt." She gave him a puzzled look, and he demonstrated with his own, then started the truck; the radio was on, and Billie Eilish began to play.

Rayla covered her ears, "It's so loud! Can you make it stop?"

Taylor felt puzzled; the music was not loud at all. He switched it off and backed the truck out, and she uncovered her ears but seemed surprised by the motion. This woman was strange indeed. With the truck in drive, he left the parking lot. Rayla seemed to look everywhere, awed by what she saw.

"Taylor, I need some food. Is there a tavern we can go to?" Rayla asked. "I'm exhausted."

Taylor heard her stomach growl loudly, "We can stop at a drive-through and grab a couple of burgers."

"What is a drive-through?"

Taylor thought, "It's a window at a ... tavern ... that you get food at."

"That sounds fantastic," was all Rayla could manage, still staring about.

Taylor pulled up to the window of his favorite burger joint, "What would you like?" he pointed to the pictures of the hamburgers on the menu.

Rayla looked at the board, "I've never seen such a wonder. I can pick any of them?"

Taylor nodded, "I like the double with cheese and bacon."

"I'll take four and some of those circle things," Rayla replied with eagerness.

"That is a lot. They're massive," Taylor said in disbelief.

"I'll take four!"

To Taylor's astonishment, he watched Rayla devour them while they drove. She had even eaten one of his. After she ate, the Orb began to glow a slight blue color, and after she finished, she fell asleep.

Taylor awoke on his couch to the sun shining on his face through the curtains. His short nap had refreshed but disoriented him. What had happened since finding Rayla filtered back in. *How can any of this be real?* Taylor stared up at the ceiling, allowing himself time to catch up with what had happened.

Rayla had still been exhausted when they had reached the apartment. So much so that she had asked Taylor to carry her. She had woken for a brief time, but not enough for her to walk. She had fallen fast asleep in his bed almost before he had laid her down. The Orb was still aglow at her chest.

"I can't explain things to you right now. I still need to rest from traveling." That was all Rayla had said on the way to Taylor's apartment. With her settled, he had plopped down on the couch, on which he had logged many hours since Lilly's death, and fell asleep.

The odd sense of need to help Rayla had all but gone after she had fallen asleep. *It has to be her that makes me feel and act this way. What else could it be?* Taylor felt curiosity build in him about Rayla, and he found himself in the hallway in front of his room.

The door stood open, as he had left it only two hours before. He tiptoed in with some apprehension. *Had that been real, the way her face had shifted in the truck earlier? She had looked like someone else, right?* As far as he could tell, Rayla had not moved from where he had laid her down. He went to the side of the bed and looked down at her. He could see her chest rise and fall, and when he looked at her face, he was still stunned by how beautiful she was. He reached down and gently touched her cheek with his fingertips without a thought. Her eyes snapped open, and he jumped back.

Rayla blinked away the sleep in her eyes before she sat up, "I'm starving! Can we eat again?"

Stunned, Taylor stood for a moment, "Ah, yeah, sure we can. I'll be in the kitchen," he said. Then, as he left the room, he turned. "It's right down the hall, and there is a bathroom through the door there." He pointed to the en-suite and then went to the kitchen.

What is happening? Why am I helping this woman? Taylor knew the answer in the back of his head, but he pushed it away. He had not been able to save Lilly; maybe he could save Rayla. Taylor warmed up the frying pan and rummaged around in the refrigerator. Retrieving butter and a carton of eggs, he closed the door and swung around to find Rayla there. With a start, the eggs and butter flew out of his hands and crashed to the floor. Eggs shattered and oozed everywhere.

"Did I startle you?" Rayla asked.

"Well, I guess you could say that," Taylor replied.

"Sorry, do you have some clothes that I could change into? These smell like the hospital."

Glancing at the mess on the floor, Taylor felt obligated. "Yeah sure," as he brushed past her. He went to his room into the closet and pulled a box from one of the shelves. His ears went hot, and his chest was tight with anger. Taylor sifted through the box of Lilly's summer things. Now he was giving this woman Lilly's clothes! What was wrong with him? He finally found a pair of shorts and a shirt that looked like they would fit her. He put the lid back onto the box and slid it into its place.

When Taylor returned to the kitchen, he found Rayla had cleaned up the eggs on the floor. "You didn't have to do that. I managed to find a pair of shorts and a shirt," he said, handing them over to her. "If you want, you can go through the boxes of clothes in the closet and see if anything else fits."

"I'd appreciate that ... why do you have clothes this small here?" Rayla threw the dishcloth in the sink as she stood and took the shorts from him.

"They were my wife's before she died."

Rayla stopped midway through holding up the shorts to see if they would fit. "Oh, I'm sorry. How long ago did she pass?"

"Just over a year ago," Taylor feigned a smile.

With a saddened look, Rayla walked toward the bedroom to change. "They look a perfect fit," she called out as she slipped them on. "You're a good judge of size."

"Ummm ... Thanks," Taylor said with discomfort. He

returned to the fridge and looked for something else to make for breakfast.

Rayla appeared moments later in Lilly's clothes and sat at the kitchen table. "The clothing your people wear is very strange. But comfortable."

"Okay...." He paused unsure of how to reply. "Now that you're safe for the moment, would you like to explain what is going on?" Taylor asked with curiosity while he stared into the fridge, avoiding her eye contact.

"I do have a little explaining to do," Rayla replied. "You had better sit down." She motioned to the chair across from her. Taylor reluctantly complied, closed the refrigerator, and sat across from her.

"I'll be blunt," Rayla began. "I'm unsure how long we are safe here. I came here to find the man that would help save my people. I traveled here using this," she held the Orb up for him to see. "I created a doorway—you would call it a portal I believe—to your world through the water in a lake on Daemor, my world." She paused, waiting to see that Taylor understood. "My world is in peril, and if I had the time to ease you into this, I would, Taylor, but I do not. You're the reason I came here. You're the person I must bring back to my world."

Taylor's eyes widened, and he laughed a nervous laugh. "That proposition is ludicrous; besides the fact that what you're saying is not possible, you have the wrong guy." He got up and paced in front of her. "I just finished my college degree to become an archaeologist, now I'm caught in a deranged person's crazy making." *Her world? What?* "My plans for adventure consist of me going to long-abandoned cities and digging up pottery. Now I'm in trouble with the law."

"Taylor, I don't have time for this. Prophecy has already

begun fulfilling itself on my world. My world has been conquered by a man named Tarak, enslaving my people and destroying everything we built. You are key in freeing my world. You must come with me."

Taylor sat dumbfounded, "Have you lost your mind?"

The Orb underneath her shirt began to glow, and she stood suddenly. "Albax, he's coming! The agent must have realized it was you that helped me escape," she said, concerned. "The FBI agent is on his way here. And there are others! We have to get out of here. I haven't recovered enough to open another portal to my world."

"There is no way I'm going with you anywhere," Taylor countered. "And how could you know that they're coming?"

Rayla reached across the table with a look of determination and touched Taylor's hand. "The agent is coming. You need to help me avoid him. So that I can remain safe here in your world while we work things out."

As Rayla touched Taylor, a tingling sensation swept through him. His desire to help this woman began to sway him. It wasn't enough to make him go anywhere with her, but he did still feel the need to help her. There was also the fact that he had a woman that escaped from the hospital and wanted by the FBI in his apartment. That would take some explaining.

"Please, Taylor, they will be here soon."

Taylor sighed, "I know a place they can't find us, but you need to figure out how to get yourself out of this mess without me. I am not *going* anywhere with you once we get there." Taylor said. He took a few steps from the table before he even realized it. He stopped and turned to her. "We will need to pack a few things. Follow me." Taylor continued to the closet in his bedroom. Frantically Taylor pulled out the boxes of Lilly's clothing and put them on the bed. Taylor grabbed two backpacks from the closet floor and gave Rayla one. "Fill this!" He busied himself, packing what he needed as fast as he could.

I can hardly believe I am helping this woman. Even if it's because I couldn't help Lilly. Everything is so mind-bending, how she changed how she looked, and her coming out of the water like that ... How could I disagree with her? Could it be true? And how did she know about the agent coming! Taylor would have thought her delusional if not for what she could do. But another world?

Taylor collected the bags and carried them to the front door when they had both packed. Rayla followed him after she finished dressing. As he wandered around the apartment, he thought of the supplies they would need. He had a cooler full of food, bags of dried goods, and snacks for creature comfort when he finished.

Rayla had had better hopes for the man who was to help free her world. But, as far as she could see, there was not anything she could say or do to make Taylor understand his importance. The one sure thing was that Taylor was not as she had expected. She would have to convince him. Time was running out for them both here and on her world.

Momentarily, the two stood at the door before Rayla reached out for the handle. *I need him to comply a little longer.* She knew Taylor felt less compelled to aid her, but he still did not have the will to resist his nature to help. She opened the door, and they began carrying things to the truck as fast as possible. Two trips to his truck later, the supplies were in the truck's box, and all they needed was their packs. The agent was close, but they would have time to get away.

Inside the apartment, Taylor whisked around, making sure they did not need anything else. When he was satisfied, they grabbed the packs. Taylor was about to open the door when Rayla reached out and locked the deadbolt. Taylor looked at her in surprise as she raised her finger to her mouth to silence him. The Orb had warned her of the men outside the door. She took his hand and began moving to the bedroom. She closed the door and turned to him, and spoke softly. "The FBI agent sent men in before he got here. He must have wanted to make sure we didn't leave." She paused in thought, "I believe I have enough in me to move a short distance. I can put us beside the truck."

"Ah, what are you talking about?"

"To move vast distances, I need to make a doorway. Moving a short distance is a little different; I call it shifting because I don't need water. The energy cost is smaller in comparison, however." Rayla pulled the Power of the Orb into her and fixed the truck in her mind. She took hold of his hand before calling the Power into herself. It swept through her, her whole body tingled, and she shifted them, draining every bit of energy she had gained in the last days.

Rayla knew she would only be able to compel Taylor to help her for a short while longer. Would he realize what she had been doing? If he did, he would be put out for being taken advantage of.

Taylor felt a cold prickling sweep over him, and everything went white. When he could refocus his eyes again, he stood beside the truck. "Whoa. What was that?" Rayla had fallen to her knees as they appeared at the truck.

"I need your help to get in," she was saying. Taylor could see police of some kind, in tactical gear waiting outside his door. He felt weak, and he had trouble understanding what had just happened. "Help me, Taylor!" Taking her hand, he guided Rayla to the passenger side and then tossed their backpacks in the back seat. He felt fuzzy and was having trouble thinking. "Taylor!" He heard Rayla shout. She put her hand on his chest, and he felt himself snap back to reality. Rayla looked like she might pass out. Everything became clear. He started the truck, dropped the gear shift into reverse, turned, looked out of the rear window, and backed up. As he put it into gear to head out, his heart jumped as a black SUV sped into the parking lot. Red and blue lights flashed in the grill, and the siren blared.

"Crap!" Taylor cursed.

Rayla closed her eyes, and the Orb flared to life, "Don't see us!" Rayla said aloud, with strain in her voice.

"I think it's a little late for that," Taylor said, exasperated as he drove forward right past them. But the agents did not pay any heed to them. Then, out of the corner of his eye, he saw the Orb's light wink out. Rayla let out an exhausted breath and flopped heavily against the door. When he looked into the rearview mirror, the agents were turning around, and he could hear the tires screeching. Whatever Rayla was doing had stopped when the Orb's light went out. "Well, here we go," Taylor stepped on the gas and sped off with the agents pursuing them.

Rayla managed a glance back and saw them following. She faced forward. "If I push much further, I'll slip into unconsciousness. Please get us somewhere safe." A pained look of urgency spread across her face; she straightened and closed her eyes. A calmness spread over her face, and her body relaxed.

"What are you doing?" Taylor asked as he looked back and forth between her and the rearview mirror at the black SUV that followed them.

Rayla did not answer; instead, she took a deep breath and exhaled. A violet purple glow radiated from the Orb that hung around her neck. A loud explosion drew Taylor's attention away from her to his rearview mirror. Behind them, the front of the SUV was engulfed in flames and had screeched to a halt.

Taylor looked at her in amazement, "You did that?" She managed a nod, closed her eyes once more, and focused again. Taylor felt a moment of disbelief and curiosity sweep over him. "How?" was all Taylor was able to say.

"I have many things to tell and show you," Rayla mumbled while concentrating, her eyes still closed. A second black SUV rushed toward them, lights flashing, then went right past. "Others are coming, but they're still a ways away." Her words were strained, but the Orb still shone brightly.

"We are going to have to find another way to get around. Any chance you could start a car without the keys?" Taylor asked. Rayla was one step ahead of him. The hood of the truck changed color from black to red, and the red continued to flow to the rest of the truck. Taylor let out a deep breath in wonder. "There is a numbered license plate on the front and back of the truck. Can you change that as well?" he asked hopefully.

"License?" Rayla panted, then peered at the oncoming traffic. "Ah, yes, I see. I can change that too," Rayla said with a smile. She nodded to him, "All done." The light of the Orb winked out, and Rayla slumped against the door unconscious.

Taylor's hands shook as he drove, intent on leaving the city. His whole world had been undone. *I think she apparated us! Is that what you'd call it? I think she called it Shifting.* He took a deep breath. *What have I gotten myself into?* Taylor navigated to the highway, but it was an hour before they reached the outskirts. The whole time, he tried to convince himself it was a trick of the mind. But he could not bring himself to believe it.

As they were almost about to leave the city, he remembered Rayla had taken Cara's clothes at the hospital, including the crocs that were too small for Rayla's feet, but she had crammed them in. They had looked through Lilly's shoes, but Rayla's huge feet were too big for Lilly's shoes too. He looked over at the stretchy climbing shoes she wore —the one thing that Taylor had owned that fit her; they were comfortable but not very practical. *Darn it, I forgot about that.* His brain felt a bit fuzzy today; all that had seemed paramount was to get out of the city. And what about women's products? He glanced at her sideways. That is not something I can ask her. Since Lilly had died, Taylor had had no need to think of such things.

"Relax, Taylor." Rayla stirred, "I don't require anything for my blood time in many years. Though that was thoughtful. I would, however, like a pair of shoes."

Taylor looked at her in surprise, "How....?"

Rayla smiled at him and said, "Your thoughts are quite easy to read when you leave your mind open. You're going to have to work on clouding your thoughts."

Taylor thought for a moment and realized what this ability to read his mind might have also revealed. "So you read my thoughts. Is there a limit to your abilities?" Taylor asked.

"There are some, but I can enter another's mind in almost every way. Though doing so is frowned upon in my world. Influencing another mind is hard, but compelling them to follow something in their true nature is easy enough," Rayla replied. "Dreams are a step easier; the mind is more open to ideas. It has been quite common for Orb Bearers to meet in the dream to talk in my world." Taylor thought back to how he had felt after finding Rayla, then again after the dream he had of her. Finally, he thought, "The dream! That was all created by you!"

"It was the only way to contact you, and I hoped you'd help me," Rayla replied. "When we touched hands at the lake through the door, I think the Orb left a small bit of power in you. That is why you're so drawn to save me."

Taylor was stunned, "How is it that the Orb can do such things?"

Rayla touched the Orb hidden under her shirt. "There isn't time to explain everything, but a simple explanation is that the Orb magnifies mental ability. That is how I could come here, read your thoughts, and contact you in your dream. It's how I know the things about your planet from the doctors, nurses, and staff at the hospital. I can explain more when we get to this place you're taking us. As for the Power the Orb left in you; they sometimes behave oddly. For now, that will have to suffice. We should get our items and go before your authorities find us."

There was a lot about what Rayla had done that Taylor couldn't explain. *Could this Orb be the reason she could do those things? Did I black out in the apartment and she dragged me out? Is this woman drugging me? I don't feel like*

I'm drugged, I feel too clear headed. I mean I believe psychics are real.

Taylor turned off the highway into a familiar mall parking lot. One of the signs read, "Jack's Outdoor Gear" on the mall signpost, a frequent stop for Taylor while heading this way. He was not sure how to feel about how Rayla had influenced him. But if Taylor understood her correctly, the magic of the Orb had connected the two of them and was doing something to him, but it was not directly controlling his actions. It made him second guess his motives at the moment, but he still felt he needed to help her. It was all very confusing. "One final stop before heading into the mountains then," he said.

Taylor headed to the outdoor store to find supplies for Rayla. Unfortunately, not all of Lilly's clothes had ended up fitting her. Rayla's legs were much longer than Lilly's, leaving her with only shorts that would work. After purchasing pants, socks, underwear, and a pair of hiking boots, they carried their items to the truck and returned to the highway toward the mountains.

"Tell me about this place we are going to," Rayla asked. She yawned and she looked as though she was having a hard time staying awake.

"And I thought you said you could read my mind," Taylor replied.

"That does tend to make things rather one-sided. But if you like?" Rayla waited for a response; when there was none, she carried on. "It's frowned upon on my world to peer into another mind unnecessarily. It's an invasion of privacy. But in cases where thoughts are left open or are directed toward me, they aren't private, and it's often hard to not hear them."

"I guess that makes sense. If someone is talking very

loud in a conversation near you, it's hard not to overhear it." Taylor looked over at her, "To answer your question, my friend Brian has a cabin in the mountains near the small town he grew up in. He has a few friends that know it's there, but other than them, the cabin is non-existent to the world. I've been up a few times to get away, and I have a standing invitation to use it anytime.

"There isn't much else to tell. If you want to be invisible, it's a great place to go. There is a generator for power, and water and a wood stove for heat. It's the perfect place for us." Taylor paused, "It's quite a long drive from here. Do you care to keep explaining why you've pulled me into this mess?" When he glanced over he saw that Rayla had fallen asleep. He sighed, *I guess that conversation is going to have to wait.*

Chapter Seven

Three hours after leaving the mall, Taylor spotted the side road that would lead them to their destination. He slowed down, turned, and followed the winding path up the mountain. *I must have lost my mind, doing this,* he considered as he watched for the driveway to the cabin. In the last few hours, civilization had become scarce; the last small town was an hour and a half back. The small farms in the foothills had dwindled before the final turn, and there had been only two driveways in the last half hour.

Taylor rounded a familiar corner in the road to see the two worn ruts marking the driveway he had been waiting for. He turned up the long dirt driveway to the cabin hidden within the trees. As the end of the driveway approached, the trees on each side opened up, and Taylor slowed to stop in a clearing. There, at its center, a cabin sat in a picturesque scene of beauty. Just short of the cabin, the trail turned into a gravel driveway. Brian had gotten tired of getting stuck in the mud in the spring, and had begun to fill it in. Taylor brought the truck to a halt and parked beside the cabin.

The small summer cabin had a homey look and was perfect for their purpose. Rayla still leaned against the door, curled up into a ball, asleep. Taylor reached over and shook her, "Rayla. Rayla. Rayla! We are here."

She stirred and wiped the sleep from her eyes. She seemed a little confused as she woke, and stared blankly for a moment before she smiled at Taylor in recognition.

"We're here," Taylor said to her in a gentle voice.

They stepped out of the truck, stretching their muscles from the long drive, before they collected their gear and brought it to the cabin. After retrieving the key, Taylor swung the door open and stood in the entryway. Memories of Brian and his friends playing poker during their getaways popped into his mind. The sparse furniture inside was covered with dust sheets.

Taylor led Rayla upstairs to one of the rooms, and after he was satisfied that she was settled, he left her to rest. He tossed his pack inside the door of his own room, then went downstairs. He started the generator and a fire, and began to cook dinner.

Taylor busied himself at the kitchen island and chopped vegetables as he watched *Battlestar Galactica* re-runs. After a time, the floorboards creaked upstairs, and Rayla came groggily down to sit on the couch and observe the show. She said nothing to him as she watched the episode intently, aside from when she asked who the "final five" were.

As Taylor finished cooking their dinner, he thought that at least they had the appearance of safety in his friend's cabin. "There, all finished," Taylor said to himself, and looked up to find Rayla there. With hunger in her eyes, she took in the sight of the food from the other side of the island. He handed her a plate of food, grabbed his, then followed her back to the couch. "I hope you like it. I'm not well known for my cuisine," he smiled.

"I'm quite sure it will do," she said and placed her plate on the coffee table. She dug in, and went back for seconds and thirds. Taylor could not believe it was possible to eat so much for her size. After she finished, he took their plates to the kitchen to wash them.

"Taylor, I'm still quite tired. I think I'll go back to bed," Rayla said. She heard Taylor say goodnight as she walked up the stairs.

While Taylor cleaned up the kitchen, he heard the floorboards creak in the room above and the old mattress springs groan. The silence that followed meant Rayla had fallen asleep. He took a deep breath of relief that he had some downtime; the stress of the last few days wore on him. With the dishes done, he grabbed a glass of tea from the fridge and went to sit down to watch TV.

Brian had not spared any money on his creature comforts here. Taylor eased himself back in the recliner and watched the end of *Battlestar Galactica*. As the credits started, he flipped through a few channels before settling on a news program.

Not long after Taylor began watching, Rayla's picture popped up in the corner of the screen. The anchor related a story of a dangerous woman that had escaped hospital custody. When his image appeared on the screen as an accomplice in her escape, his heart sank a little.

Not much time now. Brian is a good friend but once he's back from London in a couple of days, we will have the police at the door! He flipped through the channels, found the That 70s show marathon he had been watching back in his own home, and moved to the couch before drifting off to sleep.

Taylor awoke the following day to the smell of cooking bacon. He stretched out and pushed his legs up over the armrest of the couch. The stiffness in his legs from sleeping with them bent all night eased. Peering over the sofa, he looked to the kitchenette and saw Rayla cooking breakfast.

He immediately turned the TV to a local channel to wait for the morning news to start. A nature program was on at the moment, so he left it there. Then, with a growl in his stomach, he stood and started to walk over to the kitchen island to see what Rayla had cooked.

"You're finally up; I thought the smell of food might rouse you. Would you like something to eat?" Rayla asked.

"Yes I would, thanks." Taylor smiled at her, leaned in over the stove, and breathed in the aroma. "We were on the news last night; the police have my picture circulating on the news, and by now it's likely all over social media. Though the chances are unlikely that anyone will find us here until Brian gets back. To be safe, we will have to decide what your next move is."

"I don't believe it will be long before I have regained my strength to use a larger amount of power. It will be taxing on me, but I knew that coming here. Once I have recovered, I can take us back to my world," Rayla retorted.

"No, no, we already went through this." Taylor felt anger begin to bubble inside of him. "I don't believe you are from another world, not even a little." He could not explain the extraordinary things she could do; but another world? A loud screech sounded on the TV announcing an emergency broadcast, and Taylor paused to watch.

"Hi, I'm Karen Daniells, and this is Channel 12 news. We interrupt this program for a special report. There has been a break in the escape of the woman with a mental health condition from the Saint Joseph's hospital in Denver. She and her accomplice, Taylor Burke, who helped break her out of the hospital, have been reported—"

"I hear someone coming up the driveway," Rayla said as she paused cooking.

"... a gas station near Eagle just outside the Sawatch Range and were seen heading toward Glenwood Springs on the I70 West. Police have begun searching for their vehicle."

Taylor turned off the TV and stopped to listen for a minute. He started to panic when he heard car tires crunching on the gravel in the driveway next to the cabin. He had phoned his friend Brian, who owned the cabin, on their way here yesterday. "No one will be back up there until next summer, so knock yourself out," Brian had said. "Get some of that R and R you were talking about." So who, then, was coming up the driveway? The cabin was too remote for the oncoming car to be a random driver. That was one of the reasons that he had chosen this place. With Brian in London, there was only one possibility.

Taylor's heart pounded faster as he opened the curtains of the window to peer through. Two officers were getting out of a police car in the driveway. He stepped back, allowing the curtains to fall. Rayla had faded from his mind; she had walked away from the window, collected her sword, and gone into the bathroom. Taylor heard the water start running, but he paid little attention to the noise in his present state of panic.

As Taylor stepped back from the small cabin's window, his heart began thudding against his chest intensely. The sound of water running hung at the back of Taylor's mind, seeming to come from miles away. Everything in that moment had become surreal—the cabin, Rayla, the past few days.

Taylor was jarred from his dazed state by the police officers knocking at the door. Neither Taylor nor Rayla had turned the lights on in the cabin, giving less proof of occupation. He wondered if the truck outside would make the officers curious, or if they might disregard it and leave before discovering them inside.

The sound of a second knock was more persistent. Taylor knew the police in rural areas were quick to notice out-of-place things. He remembered from a previous trip; the officers had stopped by unannounced after seeing the smoke rising from the chimney. *I should have remembered that,* floated through his mind as he glanced at the fire burning in the fireplace.

"Why is she running water?" Taylor said aloud to himself as Rayla's strange actions began to sink in. He headed toward the bathroom, still in a panic, wondering how to get out of this situation. The gleam of water on the floor caught his eye, and he pushed open the door to find Rayla standing in front of the sink as it overflowed.

"Rayla, what are you doing?" Taylor said in a hushed, panicked tone.

"Taylor, we are in danger if we stay here," Rayla whispered as he approached.

"I realize that! You need to be quiet; can't you hear the knocking?" As he spoke, the knocking became a pounding.

"Sheriff's office!" one of the officers shouted. "We see

the smoke coming out of the chimney, and I know the owner is out of the country. Open up!"

"They will hear water running and see it soon enough," Taylor continued. The sound of his boot sloshing on the wet floor as he walked toward the sink finally sounded an alarm in his head. Taylor should have been aware of what the sound of the running water and the pool on the floor meant. He jolted himself to a stop short of her, but the realization had come too late.

She raised her arm and placed her hand on his chest, an action that seemed to take forever while Taylor stood frozen, staring at her. "I know," she agreed. The Orb that hung from her neck turned from its usual deep gray to shine a deep purple. "We need to return to my world, Taylor. It isn't safe here any longer." She closed her eyes, and through her hand, his entire body felt the jolt of the Orb's power, prickling like a thousand needles. Everything went white, and his body numb.

Chapter Eight

DAEMOR

THE REFUGE

"Wake up, Taylor."

The voice of a young girl brought Taylor out of his slumber. He opened his eyes to find himself in bed in a strange, dimly lit room. "Welcome home..." he thought he heard the girl say—her footfall echoed as she left the room. Taylor's eyes focused on the ceiling, walls, and floor, all of which were of hewn rock. Braziers sat attached to the walls, pitch torches the source of the light in them.

He felt so drained that he found it hard to move, but he tried to sit up to get a better look at the room. Every muscle in his body screamed in pain, and he fell back. He relaxed as much as his muscles would allow and, with extreme effort and pain, turned his head toward the glimpse he had gotten of a doorway. As he did, the young woman he had saved, the one he had come to know as Rayla, appeared through it with a tray in her hands. She placed the plate on the side table and touched his forehead.

"Where did the girl go?" he asked.

"I'm not sure who you mean. You should sleep now, Taylor, the journey you have taken requires a great deal of rest to recover from," he heard Rayla say.

She has taken me, even though I said no.

He fell back to sleep, and when he next awoke, Rayla sat cross-legged in a chair at his bedside. She wore a long white linen dress, pulled down over her knees. She had pinned her hair back, exposing her olive-skinned face. The smoothness of it, her small nose, and her pouty lips once more struck him with awe. Taylor had never had a woman take his breath away like she had; it was a surprising sensation.

"It's good to see you have recovered," she said, "It has been four days since we arrived. I was beginning to worry."

"What do you mean four days since we arrived? Where are we, Rayla?" Taylor asked. He knew the answer but did not want to admit it. Those few days in the cabin had taught him something about her, but it had never seemed real.

"Let's just say I have taken you on a journey of sorts," Rayla replied.

"By that do you mean you kidnapped me?" he asked, trying to keep his voice level.

"That is a bit harsher than I'd put it, Taylor," she replied. "As I tried to tell you, you were always going to end up here. I had never expected it to be this way, though."

God damn it! She did kidnap me.

"What is that supposed to mean? You brought me here

against my will. How could you do that?" Taylor asked, his voice becoming hoarse.

"I never had any choice; you belong here," she replied coldly.

"I should have never helped you," Taylor shot back.

"I doubt you could have done otherwise, it's not in your nature; that is part of why you're the one to fulfill the Prophecy," Rayla retorted. "You can't but help those around you; the children at the camp, your parents and aunt and uncle, your friends when you were younger, whenever your wife was in need, and especially in her death. I saw it all when I touched you before emerging through the water. You can't bear it when those around you are in danger."

"Screw you!" He turned his head away from her. In his vulnerable, weakened state, fear was building in him.

Rayla stood, "You need to rest now, Taylor."

I've done the right thing. You will see it soon enough. The FBI wouldn't have been kind to you, Taylor, those so-called officials, and you belong here.

Rayla stood and watched sleep take him over again. She thought of the men that had come for her at the lake in Taylor's world. They had detected the massive amount of energy the doorway through the lake and the Orb had emitted. So much so it had caused them to panic, to try and get to her through him.

There had been more than one of the flying machines with guns that day. Only one had approached, leaving the others to hover off in the distance. She had scanned those men, and as she brushed against their minds, hers had flooded with images of death. War machines that killed and destroyed. One among them had a deep anger that made her shudder. Horrified, she watched through the man's eyes as he fired his weapon and killed innocent people; women and children. Rayla had retreated in horror, wondering *how* could he do such a thing? The others had done terrible things, but he was the worst of them.

She remembered back to waking in the hospital back on Earth. After she had scanned the nurse in her room, a second person entered, flooding it with angst, then anger. She recognized him as the man from the helicopter, that she later came to know as agent Sadue from the FBI. The others who had touched the Orb in the hospital had dark thoughts, the brutality was in them all, as it was in Taylor, but this man and those like him were hateful beyond her imagining.

She left Taylor to sleep, but at the door, she stopped to look back at him. *He's going to be angry for a while. I'll have to get past that before he listens. But he will come to understand in time what I have done.*

Chapter Nine

DAEMOR

GLYDANE, THE CAPITAL

Sitting on his throne in the central chamber of the Legislative Assembly, Tarak looked about the room. This building had been an architectural wonder before he had come here. It was still a wonder, but it had deteriorated in the years he had ruled. The well-being of these people and the state of their city was of no concern to him. It had never been, but the man in front of him was; a smile spread across his face. "Godry, what is it that this man did again?" he asked.

The gaunt man at his side smacked his lips, a tic caused by the magic, and an annoyance. Tarak's corruption of this man's mind was total, causing some inconsistent behaviors. "He slaughtered every man in several villages, he and his men defiled the women there, and ... he took a large amount of livestock." Godry smacked his lips again nervously.

"What is your name!" Tarak barked. Godry cowered, but the man he addressed gave only a slight sign of fear. When he did not speak up right away, Tarak clenched his fist, and the Orbs' power flowed across the room. Lashing the Power around his body, tightening it like a rope, Tarak pulled the man forward. This time Tarak got the response he desired. The man's wild eyes shot around the room, looking for help where he should have known none would be offered. "Ahh, that is more like it." *The stink of these people is wretched. Their inability to wield magic disgusts me.* "Speak your name!" Tarak demanded.

"Captain Wynfor, my king," the man said, his breath labored.

Tarak released him, and the man dropped like a sack, gaining his feet quickly, knowing that showing weakness could get him killed. "Wynfor, what was the meaning of this break in ranks? What was it that you and your men hoped to do?"

"The villages couldn't make their quotas, my king. I had thought to add their livestock to the kings'. The women we took will be valuable additions to the slave stock or the brothels for the men." Wynfor stood straight, waiting to see if he was to meet his death.

"What of the crops?"

The Captain spoke in a rush, "We left the men under twelve alive and the girls under nine, tasking them to make sure the crops came in at harvest in exchange for their lives."

Tarak leaned back, "And did you take any for yourself, slaves or stock?"

"I took only what right I had! And made sure that my men did the same. I took one of each, and the men were allowed to choose one." The Captain stood taller at each word, showing he did not regret the move.

Smacking his lips, Godry spoke under his breath, "He didn't ask your permission, my king."

Tarak's gauntleted hand came up fast, hitting Godry in the mouth, knocking his front teeth free; "I didn't ask your opinion." Godry dropped to the ground from the blow, sobbing on the floor.

"Taking initiative in my name and following the edicts of the right of claim were good steps for you, Colonel Wynfor. Let us see how long you can please me."

Wynfor stood straighter at the offhanded promotion, "Thank you, my king. I will make great strides to prove my position."

Tarak smiled, "Indeed, you will. I have a problem that needs some attention. The Orb Bearer named Rayla sneaked into the city library some days ago. The book she took may cause a bit of trouble. She managed to escape me after I sliced my sword across her back. The amount of energy she was using could only mean that she has slipped to another world. She would never stay away long, though. Her precious people mean too much to her.

"You're tasked with finding her when she returns. Bring her and those useful for making examples out of. We can always use more slaves, and butchering a few will show what resistance leads to. She may not have returned alone. Make sure you bring anyone that isn't of this world."

Wynfor had stood there listening on edge, and when Tarak paused, he interjected, "I can find her, my king!"

Tarak pursed his lips, "I doubt that! I have left those two meddlers and their merry followers alone too long. I thought that chasing them off would give me peace.

However, the book of Prophecy she took had hints of where "He" might come from."

Wynfor stood confused, "What would you like me to do, my king?"

"Find the place those two Orb Bearers have been hiding!" He shouted, losing his temper at the incompetence of the people in this world. "They think they're so smart. That I don't know that they have spies in my court. Once I have extracted the information I need from them, I will summon you once more. Then you will be tasked with joining Mina, my Seer, and finding them."

Tarak watched his new Colonel back away and leave. "GODRY! Stop your whining. I need you to gather a few of my court members."

Tarak had deliberately lapsed in making sure that those in the council were corrupted by the Power. Warping these people during his time here had done a great deal of damage and had turned many of those in Glydane dark and loyal to him. However, he had understood that he would need to let the Bearers feel like they had influence in the council some time ago. Thus, he had allowed new councilors from the outer areas of their civilization to join. Ensuring that some of them were open to the Bearers' influence meant he would have the opportunity to track the resistance back to their Refuge. He laughed to himself. *I going to destroy you and your precious people, and make you all pay!*

Ultimately, of the ten men Tarak had suspected of being spies for the Orb Bearers, none had proven to know anything of consequence. It had turned out that it was not one of his men passing information on at all; it had been a long-time servant woman in the service of one of the councilors. She had paid; he had broken her mind, extracting what he had wanted. She now sat on the floor, drooling as she stared at the wall. With no will of her own, she would do whatever he commanded her.

"What a bore," he said. That had gotten old a hundred years ago. "Jump out the window." The woman stood, walked to the nearest window, and leapt out of it, falling over a hundred feet to her death. He smiled a little, "I haven't done that in a while." He turned about the room, looking for that sniveling man. "Godry! Where is my new Colonel?" The gaunt man stepped out from behind the throne, his fingers dripping with blood. The man had taken to eating the dead at some point. He could see that Godry had dragged a dead body behind the throne. *I think I might have told him to do that.* He smiled to himself. *Kind of clever of me.*

"I'll fetch him, my king. May I finish eating?"

"NO! Get him now!" Tarak's impatience was growing with Godry. Had he bent the man's mind too far? Godry scurried off, and Tarak called to the servants in the room. "Clean up this mess!" The other bodies of the council members he had killed during the interrogation lay sprawled on the floor. The first man he had ripped apart with the Power to show the others he meant business. He had not even interrogated the man. The last standing councilor had been the one to lead Tarak to the spy. He had still killed him though. The servant that was passing information had always left their letters in a temple collection box. *I will have to kill the holy servants there!*

He had left the temples and the holy ones to symbolize hope. People without hope lost interest in living; he had seen it as a boy on his world many times. Feeling hopeless, they withered and died. Tarak needed people here that would labor and serve to make his little civilization run. Besides, torturing someone who wanted to be dead held no pleasure.

He sat at the throne in time for Godry to enter with Wynfor. "Ah, there you are. You must have been close."

Godry, eager to please, spoke, "He was—"

"I was waiting outside the antechamber," Wynfor interrupted. "I heard you had gathered those you suspected. I arrived in time to hear some of the screams, though." A wide smile formed on Wynfor's face.

"I see that my methods of extraction are of your liking." Tarak smiled. "Very good, this will serve you well, as you will need to be brutal in your discovering and capturing of the Bearers and miscreants that follow them."

"I look forward to my Right of Claim in recovering the people you have lost to them" The colonel stood straighter. "Is there a direction in which I should begin my search?"

"The servant girl knew the rough area where they hide, in what she called the Refuge. Quaint, don't you think?" Tarak jeered and Wynfor gave a slight laugh at the joke. "You commanded a small force as a captain, I assume?"

"I had one hundred men in my service. Not as small as some."

Tarak tapped his fingers on the arm of his throne. "You will need more. The Colonel you served under, you will kill him and take his men. I have sent word that you're to meet with him to collaborate in finding the Bearers. I'm sure he suspects something with your promotion. I'm curious to see if you can dispatch him without getting yourself killed in the process."

Wynfor stood taller, "My men are crafty, and I'm good with my blades. It won't be a problem!"

"Good, good, it's obvious he has gotten soft if his men think they can do as they please. Remember that."

Wynfor smirked despite himself, "I will, my king!" He bowed low and excused himself.

Tarak took a deep breath, "I wish you were here to see this, Mother. I'm making them pay as I promised. Once I have finished here, I'll find those who captured me after I left our world. I'm going to cause them pain as none of them could have imagined for what they did to me." He took a breath, thinking back to his mother in that silly hat she had found, and wore to make him laugh. A small tear fell from his eye before he set the servant in the room ablaze for having seen it.

Chapter Ten

DAEMOR

THE REFUGE

As the next few days passed, Taylor spent his time recuperating. He had only spoken to Rayla once more, and she had briefly explained his fatigue. "The Orb I wear allows me to move through the portal without significantly impacting my body. I haven't ever brought someone through with me, but others that have traveled through with Bearers have often needed many days to recover."

Since then, Rayla had stopped in but had not been forthcoming about any of Taylor's questions. She simply checked on him, then left. He saw no one else aside from a young woman that brought him food, drink, a bowl of soapy water, and a cloth for him to clean with. One morning, his muscles felt more at ease, and he could sit without much effort. He found Rayla seated at his side once again as he did so.

"You're feeling a bit more recovered by the looks of you," Rayla sat forward. "Perhaps it's time to tell you the answers to some of your questions."

"Do you think? I have been here for days!" His fear turned to anger as he spoke.

"As I said, I didn't have a great deal of time on your world. Prophecy has already begun fulfilling itself here on mine. Your authorities were literally at the door. If things had been different—if the military hadn't detected my presence so quickly, if I wasn't injured when I arrived, I could have spent time explaining your role in saving my world," Rayla explained.

"So, you want me to believe that I'm on a different world?" Taylor scoffed.

"Yes," she replied, "and I need your help; my people need your help."

"That's ludicrous," Taylor countered. "What do you take me for? A fool?" He was angry at himself, too, that he had not paid more attention to what was happening in the cabin. But his anger was aimed mainly at her. He had seen her do things in the few days after saving her. She had escaped from the hospital by changing her appearance, teleported them from his apartment to the parking lot to avoid the agents, and somehow prevented them from being seen as she and Taylor drove right by them. She had even changed the paint color of his truck right before his eyes. But taking him to another world was something he could not believe.

Rayla sighed and, with an unbelievable speed, was beside him. With a seemingly impossible strength, she grasped his hand and pulled him to his feet. The Orb flared to life, though he did not feel the tingling he had before. Instead, the walls, floor, and ceiling quivered and shifted into the night sky. The stars shone in the warm air of summer. "From what I gleaned from touching you, you're quite good at orienteering using the stars. See if you can work out where you are."

Taylor stood a moment looking at the night sky, his reality shaking apart. When he looked at his feet, it looked as though they were hovering about a hundred feet off the ground. However, he could feel the ground beneath his feet. He took a breath and stamped gently on firm ground.

"You can feel at ease. This is a simple projection of my mind. You're still in your chambers."

"These stars aren't familiar to me, and if we were in the Southern Hemisphere, I'd know. I spent a year in Peru."

"That's right, they're the stars I see every night on my world," she replied. Rayla let go of his arm, and the room flashed back into form. "Taylor, my people desperately need your help!"

Taylor's legs wobbled, and he sat down in a chair at the table in his room. "I don't feel well. This is a lot to take in. This is not real! This can't actually be real! And why do you keep saying your people need my help? I'm a nobody!"

She sat across for him and waited patiently, "But you are a somebody! This all started with a misinterpretation of the Prophecy," she began. "In the Prophecy, it was said that a man from a distant world would help save us when my world was in great turmoil. The trouble started when the flying craft crashed on my planet. The crash and the stranger inside the ship caused an uproar. Many believed that he was the man in the prophecies, showing that the prophecies were at the point of beginning to be fulfilled. However, the Bearers of the Orbs had reservations about the truth of the stranger, as did The Octaves, the keepers of the prophecies.

"Fear can cause people to act in strange ways. Those that thought this crashed survivor to be the prophesied savior would not listen to reason. A split in the leadership of my world began; it was the Orb Bearers and the Octaves against several leaders who thought it would be wise to help the stranger. He would need to recover to protect us if he was the savior. Those proposing to help him won the debate and sent help.

"The Orb Bearers always had a hand in leading my people, but with so many clearly not willing to listen, they could do nothing. Our planet had been at peace for generations, and the thought that it would be broken in their lifetime made them panic. We had not used weapons of battle in so many years. Many feared the idea of war and the destruction of our civilization. In the end, only a few thousand people agreed with the Bearers.

"The situation only worsened when the stranger recovered. He soon learned of the prophecies and began conspiring against those who opposed him. The Orb Bearers started having horrifying visions of what he was to do to our people, and they tried to warn the leaders. No one listened.

"Concerned, they began organizing an escape for those that stood with them. We have remained in hiding since then; seven generations have existed in our hidden society.

"A few months after the escape, one of the Bearers, Zoltec, was captured while leading a hunting party into the forest. All but Zoltec escaped, for it was him that they were after. We later learned that he was taken back to Glydane and put to his death. The Orb was given to the stranger in a ceremony, and he named himself Tarak, King of Daemor; there was no stopping him after that." Rayla was becoming a bit concerned with the look on his face. He was just staring at her, shock setting in. "Taylor, are you okay?"

"I'm not sure ... I feel a bit strange for sure, " he replied. "Please carry on."

Rayla tried to read any open thoughts Taylor was having, but all she could pick up was deep concern. She carried on, "He started creating an army to enforce his new laws and destroy any remaining opposition. Those he enlisted became horrible and twisted people overnight. It was a common occurrence for people to just disappear, later to be seen in the ranks of Tarak's army. Those that were once good and kind people would be completely different. Turned to become a twisted and evil person, much like his initial followers. Tarak created an army of thousands of monsters in only a few years.

"From the beginning of all of this, Tarak had begun manufacturing primitive weapons; swords, daggers, crossbows. He put out the call for blacksmiths to come into his employ. Paying them generously with tax money he commandeered for his own purposes and continually raised taxes to meet his growing needs. His army was well-armed from its origins. Most people in my world hadn't seen a weapon other than in a book. Within one hundred years, he returned my world to what it had been so many thousands of years ago.

"Neighbors could no longer trust each other, even after generations of family camaraderie. Those who opposed him or were unwilling to do as he commanded were turned into slaves or were later seen in his army changed people. Whole villages at a time were destroyed, and the people in the villages were killed or taken into service. He took my world into utter chaos. And as cunning as he was, he treated his top advisors and army well. They were given almost total domination over my world; if they wanted it, they took it. He turned a once-civilized people into savages.

"After only two years, those in my world under his reign started to become afraid of Tarak and his army. Many had lost good friends and relatives to him through death and slavery. Those not graced by his protection hoped that there would be an end to the tyranny. It was, however, too late; Tarak the King had become too powerful and his armies too strong.

"Our Refuge has grown as the years have passed, and we have allies in his army willing to help however they can. We even have a few of his personal staff in coalition with us. People's lives are hard now, and though we have sympathizers everywhere, most are hard-pressed to do anything. Most of my people have little and wish not to lose anymore by helping us. While Kalamar has wisdom enough to keep us safe, we are no match for this man's cunning and brutality. We have no leader that could show us how to take a stand and certainly not enough people to make a stand against his army. You see, everyone but the Bearers thought the stranger, Tarak, was you."

Rayla paused, and there was a look of concern on her face. "It looks like you might need time to sort out everything I have shown you today," she said.

Taylor nodded; he felt shaken to the core, but he still could not grasp what had happened. "How very astute of you."

"You're free to leave your chambers when your strength returns. The Refuge is quite extensive, and the people here are hospitable. Mind you, watch the markers on the walls, so you don't get lost."

Taylor stayed in his room for the next two days out of anger and fear. In return for his help, Rayla had betrayed him and brought him here against his will. This was not the first time Taylor's trusting nature and high sense of justice had stung him, but it was the worst. *I need to work out how to get out of here.* Rayla was not going to let him off the hook in her delusion.

As he brooded about his situation, still a bit shaky on his feet from his abduction through a supposed portal, he wondered if Rayla had drugged him with something that could have made him this weak. One morning, he found his steps were easier to take, and he felt the energy to move about. Instead of brooding, he would leave his room. He wanted to see if he was indeed free to wander, and to see what lay outside his room.

Taylor sat at the small table and stared at the door, summoning up his courage. Would he find hostile forces outside his door?

He stood and walked to the door, unlatched it, and peered outside. At first, he was hesitant as he walked out of his room; the cavern seemed empty. The corridor that he stepped into was not hewn as his chambers were, but a natural cave. Braziers hung at the walls and lit the corridor. To his right, the cave ended a short distance down. To his left, the cave wound away until it turned about a half-mile down. The cave was wide enough for at least five people to stand abreast, and the roof was just out of reach for Taylor to touch. The floor had been worked flat and smooth. "This must have taken a lot of work to carve out," he said aloud.

With a deep breath, he started down the passage. After

a few steps, he heard voices and realized other people occupied rooms a short distance from him. None of them paid particular attention to him as he walked by. The doors to their rooms stood open, and some of the occupants sat eating alone, while others contained families. He saw people of many different races here, to his surprise, none more prevalent than others. Rayla had not brought him to a third-world country of one ethnicity. Listening to their conversations, trying to decipher where he was, Taylor found that while they were not speaking a language he knew, it was familiar somehow.

No one tried to stop him at any point; the odd person in the corridor nodded to him as he made his way. He thought the passage would lead him out at first, but when he reached the first intersection with markers on the wall in a different language, he realized then that there would be more to it. He discovered that the Refuge Rayla had told him of was enormous. It was a natural cave formation with several passages and corridors. With a little chipping and digging, it had become a comfortable home. As Taylor found sections of commerce, markets, and residential areas, the archaeologist in him became intrigued.

There were several caverns dedicated to an assortment of markets. Taylor found the first filled with artisans, weavers, and clothing makers. While he wandered through, the merchants smiled and offered him their wares. These were pleasant people. Where was he, though? Rayla could have taken him anywhere, even a remote island.

No currency changed hands that Taylor could see; people took what they needed and carried on. The crowds voices in the cavern were amplified, until a passerby knocked a metal bar over at a smithy's cart. A loud clang rang out, and everyone stopped to look for a moment, those close covering their ears. As everyone began shopping again, the language tickled a familiarity in the back of his head still.

He passed into a different chamber, and the smell of food hit him. His stomach growled, and he realized he had been walking for what must have been a couple of hours. Checking the markers at the entrance of the chamber, he noted them and carried on. As he walked through the area full of food carts, he stepped up to a merchant, "May I have one?" he gestured to one of the several fruit varieties in the elderly man's cart. It was one that he recognized from the trays of food that appeared outside his door every few hours.

The merchant looked at him confused, then took one of the fruits and handed it to him. "Qubul," he said, nodding and flourishing for Taylor to grab another.

"Qubul," Taylor held the fruit up, repeating the word. The merchant made a confused look at Taylor. "Not the name of the fruit, I guess." The man shooed Taylor away as other customers approached his cart. With reluctance, he bowed his head to the man and wandered off. *At least the food is free. I think.* He looked back, and the merchant had indeed dismissed him. *I wonder if this is a type of communal living. Everyone here contributes to the greater good.*

As he walked through the market, a small boy drew his attention. The boy seemed out of place; his clothes were different than the others, formal and pressed. The boy's eyes seemed like they might pierce right through Taylor, but he disappeared as someone walked between them. Taylor thought it strange but carried on, placing the happening aside. His wanderings took him through one of the several residential areas, where children ran up and down the passages. The doors to the homes in the passage stood open as they had in the area of his chambers, indicating to him that this was an invitation for visitors to stop in at their leisure and have a warm drink. *Why are there so few adults in their middle years here? It doesn't make sense with all the children around. And where are all the men?*

Chapter Eleven

One morning, after several days of not seeing Rayla, he awakened to the sound of a little girl's voice again: "Taylor, she's coming. WAKE UP!" The door into his chamber slammed shut as he sat up bolt upright. A moment later, there was a pounding at the door, and he unlatched and opened it to find an unimpressed Rayla.

"Slamming the door in my face now, are you?" she said with bitterness in her voice. "A bit childish, don't you think?" She pushed into his room and invited herself to sit at the table, taking the chair facing the door. "Why don't you join me," she gestured to the chair on the other side, attempting to smile. "I'm sorry I lost my temper the other day."

With the latch still in his hand, he looked outside and back to Rayla. "I didn't slam the door."

"Right. It did it on its own." She paused and looked at him. "Are you going to join me?"

As Taylor closed the door, shutting out the light from the hall, the room dimmed. Rayla snapped her fingers, and the braziers flared to life, adding to the lamplight at his bedside. He thought they were brighter than usual as he sat down, his back to the door. As he did so, the latch clicked, and the door swung open. "That is odd; I secured the latch." *Who is this little girl that I keep hearing?* "Is this place haunted or something?"

"Not in the slightest." Rayla replied, "This place is old, and things need replacing every once in a while. How are you feeling today?"

"Considering that I'd be, right now, finishing off my hiking trip if I were home, after which I'd head to the tropics and begin working at my passion? NOT great!" he replied. He stood, closing the door—this time giving it a jiggle to ensure it was closed. When he returned to the table, Rayla was frowning at the door; she turned to him.

"Still a little bitter, I see; in time, that will change," she smiled. It was more genuine this time. "I saw that you were out exploring the Refuge yesterday. I'm glad that you have left the comfort of your room. What do you think of our little home?"

Taylor thought for a moment of this woman that seemed an enigma. She had kidnapped him and brought him to a strange place. Yet, she had not hindered his movement, though she had been watching him. "It isn't what I would call little. What would happen if I found my way out of here? What would stop me from running to the nearest town? Would you stop me? You have been watching me after all."

Rayla's smile turned to an all-knowing expression, "You would have to walk for weeks to find an actual town, and it might be disappointing to your standards. This world is in shambles compared to what it used to be. I wouldn't let you get farther than a few days before I stopped you. It isn't safe to go into towns or cities here. Besides, there is no way you can get back home and no way for you to contact anyone there. This room is at the farthest point from the exit you could be. Without knowing what markers to follow in the passages here, you wouldn't likely find your way out of the Refuge for a couple of weeks."

"I noticed the markers, quite ingenious. So, we are in a second-world country, then? If there is no way to call home or get back there from here." Rayla shrugged. "You are impossible! You can't keep me here like this." Taylor turned away in a huff.

"Even if you got there, you wouldn't be able to communicate with anyone. My people speak a different language."

Her comment about their language sparked something in him. "I have some questions. The language here has a familiar sound to it, but I can't quite put my finger on how."

Rayla nodded, "There are some similarities in the root words of some of your and my peoples. I don't understand how that could be myself. Our peoples would have had to have come from the same world."

"Hmm, riiight—I noticed that there are different races here. However, everyone in the common areas and the markets spoke the same language. It sounds so familiar." Taylor scratched his head and sighed.

"The journey getting you here was an exhausting one for you," Rayla began. "It would have been for anyone. As the days pass, you will feel more rested, and your mind will be clearer. Don't fret over something so inconsequential. Perhaps a good soak will do you some good, and it will wash away that smell you have going on. Afterward, some sunshine would likely do you good too."

Taylor grimaced, "I'm fine, thank you."

"It will clear your head and ease any aches you have." Rayla stood, "I'll send Marita with a change of clothing, and she will take you to where you can clean up. When you're ready, she will show you the way outside. That will do away with you needing to spend the next couple of weeks finding your way out." She smiled at him, "You aren't a prisoner here."

"Ha! You take me to an undisclosed location in a different country where you say the population is hostile. According to you, there is no way for me to get back. Because I'm 'on another world,' your world. Once I fulfill your 'Prophecy,' are you willing to take me back home?"

"Even if I had the strength to open a portal now, which I do not, I wouldn't take you back. You belong here!"

"A prisoner it is then," he turned away from her in anger.

"Puh," Rayla breathed deeply, "if you will excuse me, I have a few things to attend to. So you're aware, I have told the others in the Refuge that you are a woodsman that has lost your family and home to Tarak's men. It's a familiar story among my people."

"I suppose telling them you kidnapped me wouldn't be wise."

Rayla ignored his jest, and walked out of the room, leaving him at the small table. He sat stewing; this was almost too much to bear. *How do I get out of here?* The moments passed while he stared into the brazier across the room. A sense of hopelessness filled him as he wondered if he would ever see his home again. A few minutes later, a knock at the door startled him back to reality. When he answered the door, a woman in her mid-twenties stood in front of him.

She wore the same type of dress as Rayla, but with a

floral pattern, and was beautiful in a different sort of way. This woman was in deep contrast to Rayla, with her pale skin and long red hair, green eyes and a lightly freckled face. Marita, he presumed, stood with a wicker basket full of clothing and motioned for him to follow her. Impatiently, she turned and began to walk away without him. Surprised by the woman's direct actions, Taylor closed the door and followed. She led Taylor through a different series of passages Taylor had not yet been through. If Taylor was to make a guess, they were headed straight to the heart of the mountain.

The air moistened and warmed as they walked further in, and Marita stopped. Before them, the passageway widened into a small chamber. At its sides, benches stood hewn out of the rock. The chamber was partitioned off by a curtain at the other end, steam pouring out through the sides from behind. She waved him toward the curtain and handed him the basket. When he did not move right away, she shoved him toward the curtain. Reluctant, he walked across the chamber and opened the curtain, and a wave of steam hit him in the face. It was hot but not scalding. He stepped through and let the curtain fall behind him. As it fell back, he had a moment of panic that Marita might have left him to find his way back. He pulled the curtain aside to see if she had gone. To his relief, she sat on one of the benches etched into the cave wall. She looked at him incredulously and waved him back in.

Taylor let the curtain close and walked forward in the steam-filled passage. He strolled on cautiously, only able to see a yard ahead of him. The steam cleared after a short distance to reveal a large open cavern. A steaming pool of water covered a quarter of the floor on the far side. Across the rest of the stone floor lay sparsely placed, large metal basins, some occupied by men and some by women. A natural hot spring!

Taylor removed his clothing and proceeded to a basin that an attendant had freshly poured. He eased his way into the tub, immersing himself up to the chin. The tubs were large indeed, and the heat of the water was soothing. His aches and pains seemed to melt away, as Rayla had suggested. While he soaked, his mind did its best to reason things out. However, he could not understand why Rayla was making such a big deal of hiding the truth about where they were. The people here proved that he was somewhere else; the tongue they spoke, how they lived, this massive underground city. In frustration, he put it out of his mind as best he could and focused on relaxing in the tub. It did not last long, and he finally gave up and returned to his basket. Strangely, someone had taken his old clothes, leaving him no choice but to wear the ones Marita had brought him.

Dressed in his new clothing, he found Marita outside the curtain. She led him back through the passageways and stopped at the exit to the cave.

"It has been very nice meeting you," Taylor said to Marita as he reached out to shake her hand. Puzzled, Marita looked at his gesture. "Right, you don't have a clue what I'm saying," he withdrew his hand. "You may not understand me, but I'd like to thank you for your kindness. Next to Rayla, I think you're the most beautiful woman here." It was then that Marita tilted her head, smiled, and nodded to someone behind him. Taylor filled with dread and turned around, finding himself face-to-face with Rayla.

"It's amazing what someone will say when they think no one is listening," Rayla said with a wry smile.

Taylor stood flushed, unable to speak. *Ugh! How much worse could my luck be?*

Rayla patted him on the chest, "Join me for a tour if you like." She walked toward the exit of the cave. "Coming?" Taylor turned as she motioned toward the vine-covered entrance of the cave, illuminated by light filtering through. "The afternoon sun should be warm by now."

Taylor followed her out, and as he broached the vines, the light blinded him for a moment. Rayla, acting on instinct, took hold of his hand and guided him forward. Once they had stepped a few paces into the sunlight, his eyes adjusted, and he could finally see. Taylor looked back over his shoulder toward the cave entrance out of curiosity. Even as close to the opening as they were, he found it quite impossible to tell the cave entrance was there.

Rayla let go of his hand and spoke, "If you're wondering about the entrance, there are many people we call Shard Carriers who are here among us. They have shards of broken Orbs worked into jewelry, created by the men who set the Orbs into their pendants. One of the Carriers is quite gifted at creating hidden places. She maintains the wards that hide the entrance into the Refuge and many of the footpaths that lead here from other areas."

Quite amazed at the illusion, Taylor allowed his gaze to linger there as he walked. Unaware Rayla had stopped walking, he bumped into her, knocking himself off balance as he ricocheted off her. He stumbled a couple of steps before he righted himself. "Sorry about that," he apologized distractedly, lost in the scene that unfolded before him. A large meadow spread out before him almost out of a storybook, wooded at its far edge. Beyond, the small forest was surrounded by snow-capped mountains.

Taylor had exited into a paradise; to his left was a small

lake surrounded by tall, strong-looking trees that bore beautiful red fruit. The grass was bright green with a freckling of various colored flowers that left a sweet fragrance in the air as Taylor and Rayla walked upon them. As far as the eye could see, there were rows of mountains, each covered in lush green trees. The sun shone high above them, bringing a deep warmth to the air. The moon that hung in the sky was smaller than it should have been, and bright in the daytime sky. An illusion of light played tricks on his eyes, creating what looked like a ring around it. "That is odd," he muttered in a shallow voice. His legs wobbled a little at seeing this, and he felt nauseous.

He took a big breath in and looked into the meadow before them where children played, running about, chasing each other. Focusing on their laughter, he managed to not puke. By the lake, adolescents sat talking amongst each other. A few adults mingled at the meadow's center, presumably parents, enjoying the afternoon sun.

"It's beautiful, is it not?" Rayla commented from beside him. "We are blessed to have this as our home."

Taylor had trouble forming words and nodded instead. Between nausea and the scope of this place, he was feeling overwhelmed. "Taylor?" He heard Rayla say.

"Yes, it is quite beautiful." he finally managed.

"Are you alright?

"I'd like to be alone, please!" he snapped, not willing to confront the possibility of where he was and what had happened. The sight of the place had lulled him into a false sense of awe. What he needed to do was to stay ready to escape from here. "I'd like to have some time on my own out here," he said as he walked away. He glanced back to see Rayla was clenching her jaw and her fists. *Good!*

Taylor walked toward the lake, bypassing several young

women with their children at the waters edge. Some were lying in the afternoon sun, while others played with their children in the water. He strode to a small boulder at the side of the lake and sat on it. He watched in silence as the children played, and noticed there were many more than would account for the adults there. Several unfamiliar bird songs and the sun's warmness drew his anger away. His mind went blank as he looked up at the mountain they had exited. It was not large compared to the others surrounding it. However, it was still substantial enough to house the vastness of the Refuge.

He gazed and wondered at the work it would have taken to build and that it could not have recently been done. There were no piles of rubble lying about, and the meadow was a lush green and overgrown. That meant several years had passed since the chipping of the caverns had stopped. He was jostled from his thoughts by the shouting of a woman. Taylor guessed she was her calling for her child. His several summers as a wilderness instructor at a kids' camp snapped his awareness into place. With the many families about enjoying the sun and the cool water, Taylor was reminded of the summer camp where Lilly and he had met as counselors. The sound of water and children's laughter brought him peace. He noticed a young girl of maybe ten out of the corner of his eye, standing on a log that hung over the deep water to his left. The girl had managed to walk along the log to its end, which was suspended a full ten feet above the lake.

She looked ready to jump from the log into the water. She bent her knees to jump, but she lost her footing as she straightened. Falling backward, her whole body landed with a *thud* on the log, causing her head to snap back, knocking soundly on solid wood. Her body slipped into the water in what seemed like slow motion. He heard a couple of panicked cries. Taylor, without thought, began running toward where she had slipped under. He rushed into the lake, and when the water was deep enough, he dived in and swam frantically.

Taylor pushed hard to reach her; once he was there, he dived under the crystal-clear water and saw her body just under the surface. There was blood trailing in the water, and she was still. Pumping and kicking wildly, he reached her, and with the girl in hand, he thrust toward the surface, breaking free and gasping for air. With the limp girl under his arm, Taylor worked hard to get to the water's edge.

There was a crowd at the shore as he laid her on the grass. A woman pushed him to the side, almost knocking him over in an effort to check on the girl. She began crying, "Māta laqad!"

He tried to push her aside but was held back by a man that looked saddened too. "She isn't breathing! Give her to me," he said. The woman ignored him as other people reached them, looking suspicious. "She isn't breathing; let me do CPR!" Taylor pulled free of the man and pushed the shocked woman aside. He cleared her mouth of water. "There is still time! It has been only a couple of minutes, and the water is cold." Taylor said to her and began giving her mouth-to-mouth, and then slammed his fist on the little girl's chest.

He could hear shouting, and as the girl coughed up water and started breathing, chaos broke out behind him. "Tanaffus hiya!" He heard the woman say—a wave of shock rippled through the crowd.

Rayla rushed through the crowd and burst into tears as she dropped beside the girl. Rayla went white as she saw the blood on the ground at the girl's head. "Taylor, what did you do!?" she inquired, shock in her voice.

"She wasn't breathing," he uttered.

As she looked around at the closing crowd, alarm filled her face. She grabbed hold of Taylor's arm while she held the girl, and everything went white.

Chapter Twelve

With his body stiff and his head pounding, he opened his eyes to see Rayla holding the girl. She had her sprawled on her lap, and her hand was on the back of the girl's head. There was the familiar glow of the Orb at her chest, and in the dim light of his chambers, he could see that the blood in the girl's hair was disappearing. There was an incredible amount of concentration on Rayla's face, and she was putting a concerted effort into what she was doing. Suddenly, she slumped forward as the girl opened her eyes.

The girl began to cry and sobbed, "Mama...."

Taylor realized he was in his bed, and they were on the floor. "How did I get here? How did we get here?"

Rayla looked up at him, "She needs rest! I'll be back to speak with you shortly. Please stay here."

She took the girl with her, and the door opened and swung closed of its own will. When he tried to open it, the door would not budge. Returning to his bed, frustration filled him, and fatigue overtook him as his eyes slid closed, and he fell asleep.

As Rayla made her way through the corridor, Daphne weighed heavily on her heart and her arms. Bringing Taylor here was having unexpected consequences. She had been wrong to let him wander so early before he believed that he was indeed in a different world. There were things here he would not understand, ones that could get him or her killed before he fulfilled Prophecy.

Daphne had settled, and she had fallen asleep with her head on her shoulder. Rayla's heart hurt for her. Taylor's actions were likely something common on his world, but what he had done was unheard of here. She was going to have to lie to her people to cover for Taylor's ignorance. Daphne was going to be the object of much talk in the coming days. Coming back from the dead ....

With Daphne resting in bed, Rayla made her way to see the woman who first checked the girl. She heard the talk before she got to the woman's home; the door was wide open, and candles were lit outside to ward off unwanted spirits. Her people had always let the dead be. Doing something as Taylor had was unheard of in her society. An advancement that old tales had blocked. There were stories centuries past of men and women turning to beasts after they died and came back. This girl was nothing to be feared, but she would have to show them. The people praying stood shocked as she approached; Rayla nodded and entered the home.

"What of Daphne?" the woman inquired, fear in her eyes.

"Abigail, please let me speak with you," Rayla implored as she joined her at the table. "It's not as you think."

The woman's lips quivered, "She was dead!"

"You saw me touch her after she woke?" Abigail nodded. "She wasn't dead, I promise you. I checked with the Orb; she was never dead."

"But, her heart didn't beat when I laid my hand on her chest."

"The water was cold. It made Daphne's heartbeat slow. All the man did was shake the water from her so she could breathe. That man saved her! But he didn't bring her back to life."

Abigail looked at Rayla, beginning to accept what she was saying, "Then Daphne isn't dangerous? She isn't saytan?"

"No," she confirmed. Abigail sighed in relief. Rayla looked toward the door and found that the others had been standing close enough to hear. "If you were listening, then you know that it was all a mistake. Make sure the news spreads."

With the lie set, Rayla found her way back to Taylor. She released the ward on the door and stepped inside without knocking. Taylor lay there asleep; shifting him would have only drained him in a small way. He would only need a small amount of sleep. She sat at the table and poured some water, sipping it slowly. *How do I convince you that you're in a different world? You have explained away everything you have seen. Even the moon and its ring in all its splendor haven't persuaded you.*

She waited for Taylor to wake as she thought. *What would convince someone that they're on a different world?* As she tapped her finger on the table, it occurred to her that everything here was similar to Earth. What she needed was a contrast he could not dispute. First, though, she would need to make sure the mess Taylor had made was cleaned up. He would not be able to fulfill the Prophecy if no one trusted him.

There was a noise out in the corridor, causing Taylor to stir, though he stayed asleep. Rayla pursed her lips, "Ghost, my ass!" She stood and walked to the door, "Kerisa—" She yanked the door open to find Abigail standing there, laying an offering of flowers at Taylor's door. "Oh, I hadn't thought ... Hello Abigail."

Abigail straightened, "She may not be my daughter, but I have cared for her many times in your absence. I'm sorry that I wasn't watching her closely today. This man has saved her, and he deserves the recognition."

Rayla smiled, "I'm sure Taylor will appreciate it."

"I told many in the food commons that they needn't fear him. That you confirmed Daphne didn't drown. And the others present while we talked confirmed that you had said it."

Down the hall, a woman and her small child walked toward them, flowers in hand. Rayla took a deep breath. *Can I contain the lie?*

"Thank you, Abigail," Rayla closed the door as she stepped back into the room. Taylor was sitting up in his bed, looking at her curiously. "I thought you'd never wake up." Finally, she had come to understand what she needed to do.

Rayla's voice had slowly seeped into his mind as he woke; she was in the hallway outside speaking with someone.

"I was so tired that I couldn't stay awake. How long was I out?"

"A few hours, very long hours on my part, but I have managed."

Taylor swung his feet over the edge of the bed and stood, clutching the back of his head. "I don't understand. Why the need to bring me here after saving the girl?" The look of conflict on her face told him that the answer was likely going to be complicated.

"I have been very busy sorting out a mess you inadvertently caused. Breakfast should be along soon, shall we sit?" Rayla sat down casually. He joined her; his head was still splitting. "I can dull the pain a bit," she said. The Orb she wore glowed a brilliant blue; she reached across the table to touch his forehead. As she did, a warm tingle moved through his head, and the pain lightened. *Is she using some sort of dermal painkiller?*

"The dead here don't come back. In our oldest tales, those that did became monsters. Fearful of the old tales, my people never developed techniques to bring back the dead."

Taylor listened, unsure of what to think of the monsters Rayla was making up, of the unbelievable story that she was telling. "Why bother weaving this story? I don't believe any of it!"

Rayla looked at him for a moment, "I suppose you don't have to believe me. That isn't essential; you do need to understand that the people here believe it. You did something no one here would ever attempt. I need to keep who you really are a secret for now. People knowing you're from a different world could get you killed."

Taylor thought on that a moment. Nodding, he agreed, "People will do the oddest things when they believe something to be true. So what of me saving the girl then? Is my life in danger?"

"Luckily no, you aren't in danger. I have gone against my morals and spun a lie to conceal what you did. Many fear what the other possibility could mean. It's spreading quickly that Daphne wasn't dead at all, but that you simply emptied her mouth of water, allowing her to breathe. Against odds, you have become a bit of a hero. People have begun leaving you offerings of thanks outside." Rayla sat back and sighed.

"This is the oddest place on Earth I have ever been," he remarked.

Frowning, Rayla set herself forward, "You aren't on Earth! And I intend to prove it. For now, though, I need to sleep; the task of showing you will take a great deal of energy, even if I only manage for a few moments." She made to leave, but at the door, she turned. "If you go out, be cautious. I'm not sure my lie has spread everywhere. And don't cause any more trouble."

Chapter Thirteen

Taylor sat for many moments, thinking to himself about what she had said. *How do I trust someone that has kidnapped me?* A knock at the door of his room brought him back to reality, and he moved to answer the door. Marita stood with a tray of food for him, and after he took it, she smiled at him. She walked away before Taylor thought to say anything. "Thank you!" he shouted after a moment; she did not turn back.

He ate like a wild animal to satiate his hunger, which he could not explain. In the end, he ate twice as much as he usually could. Afterward, he took his chances and walked out into the Refuge. Many people nodded their heads in acknowledgment, whispering, "Batula." Which he took as akin to "thank you," and nodded back.

When he returned to his chambers, he found that many more people had left offerings for him. The day was late, and though it was odd, he found himself tired once more. He crawled into bed, fell asleep, and dreamed of the young boy from the market days earlier. The boy stood at the end of his bed with a young girl. Both were strikingly beautiful and bore an uncanny resemblance to each other.

The following days were filled with strangeness. Taylor had indeed become a hero. He suspected it was something these people needed. "Heroes fill gaps where people lack faith in something greater," his grandfather had often said. He did not see Rayla for many days; he wondered if she was sorting out how to keep her ruse up.

During her absence, he had thought of taking his chances in the woods several times. If he found a river and followed it, there was a good chance that he would find at least someone living near the water. Rayla had made it seem a hostile territory. Taking the chance of meeting someone of a harsh nature might be a chance he would be willing to take. Or not!

The boy and girl had appeared only once more in his dreams, sitting at the table watching him. It was odd, but he knew stress could do strange things to the mind.

Several days later, Rayla appeared at the door as he finished eating. He had found the food commons a few days previously and taken lunch there, but everyone kept looking at him.

"I believe that I have a way to show you that you're *not* on Earth," Rayla began. "Are you sure that you're ready to see the truth of where I have brought you?"

Taylor looked at her in disbelief, "I don't see how you could achieve something so outrageous, but sure, dazzle me with more of your tricks." He scoffed to himself a little as he took the last bite of his toast, "Perhaps then you will be able to let go of this delusion." *I can't be on another world, I can't be this man she believes me to be! She has done things I can't explain yet. But her taking me to another world?*

Rayla stood and walked to the door, "Coming?"

He followed her through the now-familiar passages, where people smiled at him and nodded. He smiled despite himself; life here was odd but comfortable. Outside, he followed her through the meadow, past gardens and a line of trees, through a field containing bunches of tall hay tied together. She led him into the wood at the other side of the field, then followed a well-worn path for several minutes before Taylor heard what he thought was the sound of rushing water. Moments later, they stepped into a glade with a raging river running through it. A hundred yards or so upriver were two waterfalls fed from two different rivers, emptying into the larger river before them. A plateau of rock midway down stood between the waterfalls, untouched by the water.

Rayla continued up the path and then did something unexpected—she stepped right into the water a few feet from the falls. "Kalamar always did like a view! He placed several stones in the water so he could lounge between them. Follow my step; the pathway is made of pillars. If you misstep, you will end up downriver, alive if you're lucky."

Stepping with care, he followed her as they made their way to the bottom of the dry plateau in the middle of the river. The falls were not large—ten feet across—and they met to face each other. The two rivers had worn away the rocks into an unnatural V-shape so that they almost faced one another. An elaborate stairway led up to the top of the plateau, which stood roughly four yards above the water.

Rayla took the stairs to the top, and Taylor followed to a lush green space above. She veered off to the side of the plateau and walked to the edge of the waterfall, where she stopped only a step from it. She looked back toward Taylor. "It's time you see where you are."

Taylor looked around, confused, "This is very beautiful,

but how is this supposed to show me that I'm on a different world?"

Rayla clenched her teeth, "I have realized that this world is much like yours. By many, it would be indistinguishable from yours. You're sure you can handle this?"

He laughed snidely again. "Yes, I can handle it," he mocked.

She took a deep breath and closed her eyes, and the Orb at her chest began to glow. The air started to shift around them into a slight breeze. She put her arm out straight, palm toward the falls, where a small point of blue light formed and hung inside the waterfall in front of her. Then in a flash, it expanded, opening to the size of an oval door he could have walked through. The surface gleamed a moment and then became clear.

Taylor looked into it and could see a reflection—or what appeared to be a reflection anyway. The image was not of that as a mirror would show, but instead, it was of them from behind and a few feet back. Like someone had placed a camera beside the waterfall behind them, and there was a projector somewhere unseen. "A trick of some sort? Where is the camera?" He turned to Rayla. She had dropped her hand and was smiling.

"No! It's a portal, Taylor."

Taylor scoffed and looked back to see where the camera might be hidden. To his amazement, he saw a second oval mirror hanging there in the opposite falls. But this one showed a frontal view of them, reflecting what the other portal should have. Rayla smiled at him from the other mirror, then walked toward him and stepped through it. Slowly he turned his head back to the first oval and could see that Rayla was no longer in front of him. She stood with her back to him on the other side of the portal. He watched as Rayla walked away from him in that portal, and toward his back, he could hear her footsteps.

"Whaaat ... !" He shoved his palms into his eyes and rubbed them. Taylor froze as she tapped him on the shoulder. When he turned about, she was still smiling at him. "it's a trick!" His mind worked furiously, trying to find a more logical answer.

"It's no trick. It's real."

Taylor shook his head, "No, it can't be."

Rayla sighed, "I had hoped that something local would have done."

She raised her hand again to the portal, and the surface shifted. The image inside was now one of the desk in Taylor's living room, the desk Lilly had sat at to study. His whole body trembled; he looked back to where the other oval mirror had been, and it was gone. Rayla, too, was shaking, but out of effort, it seemed. She reached in and grabbed the picture of him and Lilly off the desk, and as she brought it through, the portal snapped shut.

"Here," she shoved the picture at him. As he took it, she dropped to her knees, unable to stand.

With shaky hands, he touched the image of his deceased wife, then looked at Rayla. "How?" was all he could manage.

"Because you *are* on a different world!" She said weakly.

When he looked up and around, something changed for him. The day moon that hung in the air was indeed smaller! And the ring was no trick of the light. The evergreen trees at the side of the river with the weird red berries, the odd language, everything snapped into place. There would be no way a vast population of people could be living here like this without it being known. "I'm on another world!"

"YES!" Rayla replied.

For the second time in as many weeks, Taylor had to help a weakened Rayla out of the woods. Back home on Earth, he had built a stretcher to carry Rayla. This time supporting her as she walked sufficed. "I'm on a different world," had left his mouth several times.

As he approached the meadow of the Refuge, people began to notice him helping Rayla. Some wore worried looks on their faces, others shocked. Taylor started to become a bit nervous when he heard someone say, "hāmail kura ánqanda Rajul," words that almost made sense to him.

Rayla laughed under her breath, "They think you saved me."

Taylor laughed with her a moment, mostly out of nervousness, "It seems I'm making an impression on your world." The sound of "your world" felt odd in his mouth.

"Let me rest by the water. I just need a few minutes. I'm beginning to feel a bit better already."

He had noticed during the walk back she had needed less of his help. Shifting her weight to stand on her own, she lowered herself slowly to the grass at the lake's edge. "Join me," she patted the ground beside her. Taylor dropped down beside her, his head swirling with questions. He looked at the photo in the frame he held. "I think that proves that you're where I say we are."

"You have," he nodded. "You struggled to open and maintain it, I noticed. You managed only a second or two. How is it that you came through to my world or pulled us here in such a small amount of time?"

Rayla wiped the sweat off her brow with a slightly shaky hand. "With much difficulty is how. Traveling in such a way uses up a lot of my strength. Using the Power takes some of your personal energy, but not in a significant way for most things. Some things take energy in the likes of a light stroll, others like pulling a cart full of goods across a field. Opening a portal is the most exhausting thing I have ever done. The Power in the Orbs is limitless, but our bodies have limitations. Running too much through it can kill you."

"How is it that you have come to possess the Orbs?" Taylor asked.

"The story goes generations back. First you have to know more about this world. I will tell you of it another time. As for me, this was given to me by my grandmother, who raised me in secret after my parents and younger brother's deaths." Rayla's voice shook just a little as she spoke of her family. "My grandmother kept the Orb safe while I was a child after my parents and brother were murdered by Tarak's men.

"When I was twelve, my grandmother took ill suddenly, leaving her incapacitated. She asked me to retrieve a pouch from her dressing table. She warned me to not wear the Orb until I was an adult. It needed to touch my skin to imbue its power, and it would have an effect on my aging. She instructed me to leave the Orb in the leather pouch and always keep it with me. Lastly, before she died, she instructed me to keep it hidden."

Rayla sniffled as she took a deep breath, then spoke in a firm voice. "I set fire to the house to hide any sign of my presence there. Her home was far off into the woods, and I knew no one would get there in time to stop it from burning to the ground. Then I walked into the woods, living in the wild for five years, the Orb in its pouch at my side. By the age of seventeen, I stumbled across the Refuge, and their leader, Kalamar, an elder that bore an Orb himself.

"I chose to stay with them, though I kept having an Orb secret for two years. When I finally told him that I had an Orb, he shrugged, saying, 'I know, my dear, you should have put that thing on ages ago.'"

Rayla paused, looking to see if Taylor was still following. He turned his head toward her, curiosity in his eyes. She continued, "I donned the Orb for the first time that day, and I have never once removed it.

"Kalamar visited almost every day following our conversation, teaching me the entire history of our world known to him. From the beginning, some prophecies warned of a war that would break our civilization apart."

Rayla yawned, "You've been very quiet since I started telling you the history of my world."

"It's a lot to take in," Taylor pondered.

Rayla yawned again, "I imagine it is."

Taylor had been working his way to asking a question in the back of his mind. Now seemed an appropriate time. "So after a time, you could take me back to my world then?" he asked.

As he spoke, a shadow fell across them from behind. Taylor turned to see Abigail standing over them. She bent and whispered in Rayla's ear. She smiled at Taylor as she stood and left them. Standing a few steps away, the girl he had saved beamed at them and then took Abigail's hand, walking with her.

"She wanted me to say she's sorry for causing you so much trouble," Rayla related, ignoring his question. "She wanted to whisper so you wouldn't feel sorrowful over your loss."

"What do you mean by my loss?"

"I couldn't very well have someone wandering around who didn't speak or understand our language. So I told the people here you suffered a hit on the back of your head, and now all you remember is the language that your village speaks. Our common tongue has gone from you." Taylor looked at her stoically. "I can't take you back, Taylor. I don't have the strength, and you must fulfill Prophecy here."

Taylor stood, angry with her, and stormed off, walking toward the Refuge.

Chapter Fourteen

The following day, Taylor awoke to a knock at the door. He turned up the wick of his bedside lamp, illuminating the room and strode groggily across the room to unlatch it. It would be, of course, Rayla standing there when he opened it. Anger bubbled inside him at how she had abducted him and taken him to a different world. She had no right to bring him here, nor did she have any right to keep him here.

However, that had not stopped him from coming to like the people here. They had no part in Rayla's actions. The incident with the girl had thrown him off somewhat, but knowing he was on a different world had given him a different perspective on things. When he had gone to Peru, he had understood well enough to allow for the customs there. There was a great deal of superstition there; not knowing it could get you in trouble with the locals.

To his surprise, when he grumpily opened the door and growled, "What do you want!" a shocked and frightened Marita stepped back. "Oh, my. I'm so sorry!" He raised his hands in apology, motioning for her to keep calm, as she looked as though she was about to cry. "I don't know how to apologize in your language. Damn it!" Strangely, the Dali Lama popped into his head. Willing to try anything at this point, he looked her in the eyes and pressed his hands together in a slight bow.

Marita stepped forward, drew back her hand, and slapped him hard across the face. She stood back with her arms crossed, anger on her face. After a moment, she walked off, and a few feet away, she stopped and waved him to follow. Walking for what Taylor guessed to be twenty minutes, Marita shot him many angry glances. After a time, she led him to a corridor containing residences.

Up the corridors stood Rayla, chatting with a small child. The young girl nodded and ran off, her golden hair flowing behind her. Marita walked him to Rayla, nodded to her, and shot Taylor one last perturbed glance.

Rayla watched Marita go with a puzzled look on her face and then turned to him, "There is someone who would like to talk to you. If you follow me, I'll take you to him."

"Please lead the way."

She looked at him, "Whatever did you do to Marita? I have never seen her give someone such a foul look."

As Taylor recounted what happened with Marita, Rayla burst into laughter at his description of the Dalai Lama praying. She laughed so much so that tears streaked down her face. When she could finally contain herself, she stopped walking. "Whew, that is something. So not only did you frighten the daylights out of one of the kindest and gentle people here ... you asked her to have sex!" Rayla couldn't contain her laughter and burst again.

"I asked her to make love?" Taylor said awkwardly.

"Oh no, you didn't ask her to lie with you in joining. You asked her to have wild sex with you." Rayla managed to contain her laughter this time. "No matter, you can explain it to her yourself in a week or two." Laughing sporadically, she led him through several different passages.

In an effort to change the subject, she began talking about the caves. "For the most part, these caves are natural, which I'm guessing you already know. The founders began adding on here and there to make rooms for individuals and families to live as our community grew. I have heard that you have eaten in the enormous cavern we call the food commons. I have seen you wandering around. I hope that you have at least enjoyed exploring."

She paused and looked over at him as they walked, but he avoided her gaze. He was still angry at her for what she had done.

"When Tarak took over, people didn't have a place they could go to protect themselves from attack. Kalamar found these caves a couple of years after Tarak started his reign of destruction. He took it upon himself to be in charge of the escapees, moving everyone around at first. Making small camps and moving further and further from civilization with each new campsite.

"Each time, they would have to move due to Tarak's men closing in on them. My people were pursued for over a year before Kalamar decided to run as far as possible from civilization. They traveled for a full circle of the moon before a hunting party stumbled across this place. They chased an animal much like a deer on your world into these caves. They became lost inside here while they searched for it. Tracing their path back out took several hours.

"Until we made this our home, our people's safety was quite hard to direct. There were pockets of those that followed the Orb Bearers everywhere. Only a few hundred people, mind you, but it was a burden to those who knew wilderness survival, with so many not used to the wilderness.

"It also made it very hard for Kalamar to organize any resistance in those first years. Unfortunately, by the time they had settled here, it was too late to do anything of impact. Tarak had his hold on most of those of influence," Rayla stopped in front of a large door. On it was an inscription that looked like a title of some kind.

She became silent, having failed to get him to talk to her. Taylor did not mind that she was leaving him to his own thoughts. The natural formations of the caves in themselves were extraordinary. This would have been a dream place for those that lived off-grid back home. This society was self-sufficient, had its own commerce, and seemed happy to be here. He followed her through the natural passages in the rock for what seemed like an hour before she spoke again.

"Here we are," she announced.

The large door was the slightest bit more ornate than the others he had seen. He could not remember seeing any doorways in the passage since they had rounded a corner several minutes back. To the side of the door was a small metal plaque with strange writing on it. Taylor reached forward and ran his fingers over the engraved inscription. "What does it say?"

"It reads, 'Kalamar the Elder,'" she replied. "He is, of course, the man I have been speaking about. He stepped down from most of his responsibilities twenty years ago. Our best estimate is that he's three hundred and ninety years old now, though he won't confirm it. He knew the world before Tarak very well, and I think it stings him to remember what we once were. He had borne the Orb many years before Tarak's arrival. A very long time to live, considering our life span is only a little longer than yours."

As Rayla finished her sentence, the door opened, revealing a tall and distinguished man. He stood over six feet in height; his hair and beard were long and gray, his skin a tanned color, and his body was old and wiry. The gray linen robe he wore draped to his feet, and its sleeves were long enough to cover his hands.

"Telling stories again I see, Rayla," Kalamar said in a soft gruff voice. He waved them in and muttered under his breath, "always telling stories." He walked off, not waiting for a response, calling back to them, "So this is the man we have long waited for. He doesn't look like much." The old man made his way over to a small round table in the middle of the room, where he sat down. "Are you coming in or not?" Kalamar said, sharpness in his voice.

"Don't take any offense. Kalamar is much friendlier once he has had his afternoon nap." Rayla said sarcastically as she led Taylor to the table and directed him to sit. Taylor looked around the room; there were plenty of shelves filled with books and little trinkets. Papers that looked as if they had fresh ink-covered a small portion of the table. On the far side of the room hung dried plants.

"You are a healer?" Taylor inquired.

"Of sorts, I guess. I fix scrapes and scratches and make a potion or two to cure common ailments. There isn't much need for me here in that respect, though. Although we live a simple life here, we have evolved into a species far superior to yours in many ways. For example, our immune systems are much more robust than yours, and from what I understand from Rayla's time in your hospital on your world, our bodies heal faster."

"But you live not much longer than the people of my species?" Taylor asked.

"It isn't uncommon for our people to live well over one-hundred and fifty of your Earth years. I'd say that is substantial! We choose to work hard on our world; we do everything by our hands and backs. As a result, the land provides us with all we need, unlike your lazy people. Preferring to sit in front of your entertainment while you eat and drink things that are bad for you. Though Rayla did say it was rather hypnotic," Kalamar glared at her from under his brows.

Taylor rebutted, "So, it seems that your people are also susceptible to the wiles of my world. Even one of your Bearers."

Kalamar glared at Taylor, "I understand that most of your world's population has less of the basic necessities than we do. I also understand that those with wealth in your world stand on the backs of the have-nots. Our lives are simple here. Before Tarak came, our technology wasn't much more advanced than the Roman period of your history. We had developed rudimentary technology, machines with gears, and the ability to smelt metal. But we lived here in complete harmony and peace, unlike the majority of your planet. The one exception on your planet is the Tibetans. Their history is much like our own." Kalamar paused, adjusting his old body.

"There isn't yet a cure for wear and tear on the body, on either of our worlds. Until recently, most didn't live past forty years from what I know of your world. If I recall, machines do much of your work, and take much of the hard work out of things, extending your life as fatter, lazier people. That rubbish you call medicine, extending your life while keeping you sick the entire time."

"How do you even know any of that?" Taylor asked.

Rayla looked at Taylor, "I showed him some of the things I saw on your planet. Including what the Orb collected for me when I was unconscious." She turned to Kalamar, "But I didn't really see everything in that great of detail."

"I might have had a little peek into Taylor's thinker while he slept—nothing much, some small details you might not have thought to look for," Kalamar made an innocent face.

"Kalamar, how could you do that? That is such an invasion," Rayla said.

Taylor looked at her angrily, "Says the woman that invaded everyone's privacy she came into contact with on my world."

Rayla stiffened as Kalamar gave her an all-knowing look, "I was barely conscious when they were touching me. But, you know how the Orbs seem to have a mind of their own sometimes."

Kalamar's face changed to one of understanding and irritation, "Yes, yes, I do at that. Dang blasted things."

Taylor felt anger rise in him, "How very convenient that the two of you can explain away your behavior due to the Orbs. The two of you are a pair of hypocrites."

"Now, I'll not be dressed down by the likes of you," Kalamar said, standing up.

"ENOUGH, Kalamar!" Rayla chastised. "I haven't brought Taylor here so that the two of you could debate whose species is more evolved."

Kalamar exhaled, "Yes, my dear, you're right," he replied as he left the table. Taylor thought that for a man of three hundred and ninety, Kalamar moved well. At one of the bookshelves, he removed an elegantly carved wooden box and returned with it. "This is the reason I have asked you here, Taylor," he said as he placed the box on the table, sat, and then slid the lid off. As the top slid off, a bright golden glow emanated from within.

Kalamar reached inside with his old wrinkled hand and removed an Orb identical to Rayla's by its silver chain. As he held it up, the Orb levitated toward Taylor, pulling the chain taut. "I have never heard of them reacting so intensely. They do seem to always know when their new Bearer is about." Kalamar released the Orb's chain. It hung in the air for a moment, then levitated towards Taylor. Finally, it glided to a stop at eye level with him.

"I guess that says it all," Rayla said in amazement.

"That's trippy," Taylor said out loud without thought. *If I just held it a moment, that would be okay! Whew. I can feel the Power emanating from it.* Overwhelmed by the pull of the Orb's power, he reached out and plucked it from the air, looking at it for a moment. The glow of it mesmerized him, and without thinking, he let it fall into the palm of his hand and wrapped the chain around his wrist. The force of its energy pulsated through him. *Holy Moly, this thing feels amazing! What a high.* The Power of the Orb moved through him and rejuvenated his body from its place in his palm.

"I haven't been able to wear it at all since I used it to have a little look inside your skull. It simply wouldn't allow it. It's yours now; take care with it. It's a tremendous gift," Kalamar asserted. "Go now. I must rest."

Rayla and Taylor, awed by what had happened in the last few minutes, took their leave of Kalamar. Taylor walked back through the passageways of the Refuge with the Orb in his hand. He would not don it, even though there was an urge to do so. The possession of an Orb was not in line with his desire to return home.

"Would you like to go outside for a while? It's about midday now," Rayla broke the silence. "It should be warm out."

"I could use a little fresh air," Taylor replied. "A little sun on my face wouldn't hurt either; it has been a while."

"I have a question. No one here but you speaks English, yet Kalamar speaks it perfectly. Can I assume he learned that from his invasion of my mind?" Taylor asked hotly.

"No, actually," Rayla began. "Before I left, Kalamar voiced a desire to be able to speak directly to you. Once I returned, I went to him and taught him English with the help of the Orb. Which I'm assuming was before he visited you. You will find the Orbs can help you do many things that will, as they say on your world, 'blow your mind'." Rayla stopped at the door to his quarters. "I'll leave you to it."

Before she could walk away, Taylor halted her. "If the Orbs are so powerful, why don't you use them to defeat Tarak?" he asked. *There has to be a way for Rayla's people to win this on their own.*

"Indeed," she said. "Kalamar tried some time after Zoltec died, but he soon found out that the Orbs' power can't be used against one another. With Kalamar being so old, combat was out of the question. He barely escaped with his life."

"Then, why not you?" Taylor asked. "You came to my planet wearing armor and that magnificent sword. Can't you fight?"

"I'm glad to see you have such faith in me, Taylor," Rayla said. "Although I can hold my own in a good sword fight, Tarak is almost two heads taller than you. I have also seen him best warriors with better skills than I."

"Well, I haven't exactly been practicing my swordsmanship lately," Taylor said sarcastically.

"Don't worry, you will have plenty of time for that. If you aren't too tired, you should take in some sun. We find our moods benefit from it." She walked off without another word.

Chapter Fifteen

Taylor watched Rayla walk down the corridor, doing his best to puzzle out his new gift and new reality. The pulse of the Orb he held in his pocket flowed through him. The feeling was almost too much to handle, but he also had trouble letting it go. With a deep breath, he let go and the feeling faded, but he still felt connected to it. There were a few offerings off to the side of the door. These had dwindled in the last couple of days. Abigail still left one every day, the girl waving from the doorway. Taylor had begun to leave his door open. He had learned a partially open door meant, "Come in if you need something." No one had entered, though; some waved or nodded if he looked out.

Pushing his door open, he found a tray of food on the small table and a vase of flowers beside it. When he had completed his meal, the sun's vitality seemed like a smart idea. Slipping on his boots, he followed the markers that would lead him outside. At the exit, he parted the vines and stepped out and to the side so that his eyes could adjust. Shading his eyes with his hand, he could see the sun was hanging in the mid-afternoon sky. He drew in a fresh breath of air and started into the meadow, looking for a place to walk and stretch his legs.

To the right, a glade flowed up along the side of the mountain below a ridge. Walking for almost an hour through a trail that arced back to the glade, he found a large slab of stone protruding from the ground and sat down upon it. As he sat there, enjoying the sun and the beauty, a voice brought him out of his daze.

"Young Taylor, we meet again," a familiar old voice called. Taylor turned to find Kalamar walking toward him. "Found one of the best places to sunbathe, have you?" he jested. "I find this spot especially nice this time of day. One of the benefits of being an old man is that most allow me exclusivity to it." Kalamar came to stand beside him," I see you haven't put on the Orb yet."

Taylor instinctively put his free hand over the pocket where it lay. "No, I have not," he submitted.

"It won't do you much good there," Kalamar said and took a seat close to him on the large stone. Stretching then closing his eyes, he let the sun fall on his leathery old face. "Do your people often stare at others when they don't know what to say?" Kalamar smirked at him as if he had scored another point in a battle of wits.

Taylor had indeed been staring as he worked out the many questions he had and which were the most important. Before he could say anything, though, Kalamar spoke.

"Keep the Orb on you, hidden, mind you. People here are a bit touchy about those." Kalamar scooched himself up the slab, lay down, and got comfortable. "Good for the old bones and the thoughts too." He closed his eyes and seemed as though he might fall asleep.

"I have a question for you," Taylor said.

"Get on with it," Kalamar replied, shifting a little to get more comfortable.

"You said that the Orb enhances the mental ability of whoever wears it. Why not use it to build a weapon to destroy him?" Taylor inquired.

"Why not indeed!" he replied. "You're talking about advanced technology. Those types of things don't exist in this world and never have. Nor do the tools to build them. It's not like we can saunter into the city and start buying things that don't exist, is it? All aside from that, Tarak is the problem. You're talking about those bombs your species has built, thinking you're so smart. There are many innocent people, including children, that are in his grasp.

"The problem with war is that you have to live with each other after it's all finished. Over a hundred generations ago, we turned our species into civilized people that lived in harmony until Tarak came. Can you imagine trying to rebuild a civilization led by people that fought for life and peace by killing bystanders, including innocent children?

"We must stand for our morals and principles and hope that goodness will prevail in the end. We have always fought Tarak's soldiers straight on, and never if innocent people might be hurt. Once we have eliminated Tarak and all three Orbs are back in hand, we will become that civilized world again! We can't do as you suggest. Unfortunately, the only way to defeat him is in hand-to-hand combat. Men armed with swords will be the way this goes, as brutal as it is." Kalamar's expression softened, and he looked off into nothing. "Now, I wish to finish my nap in peace."

Taylor left Kalamar to his sunbathing and walked toward the lake. When he reached it, he saw Rayla speaking with two young men, one tall and fair, the other stocky and dark-skinned. She nodded to them when she saw Taylor and walked in his direction.

"I'm glad that you took my advice. Did I see you talking to Kalamar?"

He ignored her comment about taking her advice, "Ah," he turned back, looking toward the stone. "Sort of..."

"Since you're about, come, I'll show you my favorite place to sit." Rayla walked to the opposite side of the mountain Taylor had taken and followed a well-worn trail along the mountain's base. The path began to wind its way up in a gentle slope. For several minutes they climbed before coming to a split in the trail. One direction continued up the mountain; Rayla veered to the right, taking the second path leading to the trees. The way meandered, eventually coming to the bluff above the meadow.

The trail followed close to the edge of the bluff, and the forest hugged the trail; its thick foliage created a dense, impassable wall. As they walked along the path, Taylor peered down the sheer drop off to the lake. "That is a long way down," he said under his breath as he sidestepped as close to the trees as he could. Further on, the path opened up to a small clearing above the bluff, where Taylor joined Rayla as she sat down on a rocky outcrop a few feet back from the path. The view from there was beautiful; he could see the whole of the meadow, lake, and mountain ranges from where they sat. In the meadow below, more children had emerged from the Refuge to play in the sun. As he looked around, Taylor noticed one of the mountains in the far-off distance.

"That is where we must go to fight Tarak," Rayla explained.

"Screw you and your war. I'm not going to fight for you, Rayla."

"Haven't you listened to anything Kalamar and I ... " Rayla began.

But Taylor turned his back to her, put his hands in his pockets, and ignored her as she lectured him. Without thought, Taylor rolled the Orb in his pocket into the palm of his hand, clutching it. It pulsed, and a sense of calmness swept through his body. He could still hear Rayla in the background. Her voice was shrouded, yet Taylor's mind felt clear and sharp.

" .... we need you Taylor! We have been under Tarak's tyranny for over three-hundred-years. We have remained hidden most of those years here in the Refuge." Rayla stared at him.

Taylor stopped her, "Wait a minute. That is ludicrous! Now you expect me to believe this man has lived three lifetimes. Over three hundred years old indeed. Am I going to get to live three hundred years or more? Is he some kind of hunched-up old man using his cane to whip everyone's butt? Ha!"

Rayla looked at her Orb, "It's one of the things that comes with being an Orb Bearer; unnaturally long life for as long as you wear it. It keeps you the same age as when you put it on.

Taylor looked at her, taking stock of her explanation, "Say I believe you. You have one, Tarak has one, and I have one. How many Orbs are there?

"There are three of this size, there are a handful of smaller ones among my people, here in the Refuge—

Taylor cut in, "You have several here, and yet you can't manage to uproot this man from power! Why could your people not stop him all those years ago?"

"When he came here, my people had been at peace for thousands of years. There were no weapons here, aside from those in museums," she responded. "My people couldn't fathom hurting another for gain. As for myself, I have come to be quite excellent with a blade, but I have never once taken a life. We use them as a defense, and on occasion, I have used wounding strikes on opponents. I can't kill my people, nor can I kill Tarak."

"And I can! How highly you must think of me." Taylor shot back. "I've never killed someone. I've hunted most of my life, but killing a human? With a sword?" Taylor mimicked stabbing someone with a sword awkwardly, mocking her, but it got the point across. "Jesus!"

Rayla frowned, "I see you're still unconvinced of the magnitude of your importance here. Your people war with each other all the time on your planet. You will save my people Taylor."

"Right, so what are we talking about, some big-armed bullies that walk around with sticks whacking people to keep them in line? While Tarak sits on a throne eating pastries?"

At this point, Rayla gave Taylor a look of anger that made him sit back. Through gritted teeth, she spoke, "How dare you make light of the pain my people suffer."

Rayla closed her eyes and took a deep breath before putting her hand on her Orb at her neck, "You have seen that I can do wondrous things with these." Taylor nodded his agreement. "Tarak somehow seems to be able to do things no one here ever could. He can influence people in ways we don't understand and has a power that is impossible. There was no way to stop him once he had an Orb. I can influence people's decisions if the idea isn't against their nature. It isn't something I do light-heartedly, mind you. Tarak can completely override someone's ability to think for themselves. Even overwriting the person that was once there.

"The takeover was quick for Tarak; he's a brutal man with brutal tactics. My people were in a golden age of peace. He enlisted artisans and blacksmiths to start making weapons. At first, they were crude, but as time passed, these men he twisted refined their craft. Swords, bows, and axes came first, giving them great advantage. At first, he called them peacekeepers, though there was no need. He said that these men would keep our people safe when the prophesied war came. As time passed, he began using the men to take advantage of our people. Finding out where any resistance was and doing away with those behind it. Calling them, 'supporters of the war'. He diverted resources to support his ever-growing army—food, metals and wood for armor and weapons, textiles for clothing, and beds for barracks that sprung up everywhere."

As Taylor listened, he thought of Hitler and his ability to take over Germany and then half of the continent of Europe. "This is all interesting, but where were you and the other Bearers during all of this?" he said pointedly.

"I wasn't alive then, but the other Bearers were secretly laying escape plans. Both had gone into hiding, creating an underground escape system. Literally, I might add. They used the Orbs to make a system of tunnels. I heard seeing it was astonishing. They manipulated the soil, pushing it to the side to create tunnel walls of rock.

"I came by mine through my grandmother. Its previous owner, Aleasei, tried to rally a small group of citizens to help others escape. They all died horribly, except her. She fled into the woods, my grandmother, ten at the time, at her side. My great-grandmother had been one of those gathered to rally against Tarak; my grandmother had followed her.

Aleasei rescued her from the oncoming soldiers before running into the woods. In a final stand, she gave the Orb to my grandmother, telling her it would show her its next Bearer, and bid her to run as fast as she could. My grandmother said she would never forget Aleasei's screams when Tarak caught up with her. Those screams set my grandmother's feet to move as fast as she could."

"So, you aren't three hundred then?" Taylor murmured snidely.

"No, as far as I can recollect, I'm one hundred and sixty-three."

"Oh, well, that is super believable since you look all of twenty-two."

Rayla seemed to not bite at Taylor's taunting. She was keeping it cool today. How did she expect him to believe all this?

"It wasn't long before his army was everywhere—the accounts we have say within ten years. Once they were all in place, he took over the entirety of my civilization, small as it is. Those who opposed him and wouldn't do as he commanded were turned into slaves, or later seen in his army, changed people. Entire villages at a time vanished, the people killed or taken into service. He took my world into utter chaos. He turned my people into savages. This is the man you must save us from!"

Taylor put the cup down and looked at her stoically, "Just me by myself?" he scoffed, anger at her for kidnapping him flared to life again.

Rayla didn't give an inch on her position. "No, there are some that would help. Our Refuge has grown as the years have passed, and we have allies in Tarak's army willing to help as they can. We have a small militia that the civilian population supports. It will have to be enough.

"While the other bearer and I have wisdom enough to keep us safe, we are no match for this man's cunning and brutality. We bred the violence out of ourselves generations ago. The most pressing argument was what seeds to plant. I'm not a military tactician; I don't know about war. I have led a few skirmishes against small groups of soldiers to help innocent people escape. I have no way of knowing what to do. Kalamar is no better than I; he's a gentle spirit and fighting Tarak took great courage. Since that time, he has withdrawn from us and kept to himself. We have no leader that could show us how to take a stand, and certainly not enough people to stand against his army. My vision showed that you're meant to be this leader!"

Taylor looked up at her, "You want me to lead a small force of your people into a battle when I have no tactical training, and you want me to lead a battle for you. I'm not sure how to even respond to that." Taylor shook his head, "No! Take me back to my world."

"My people need a leader, and that is you," Rayla declared. "I have seen it in my visions of Prophecy." She turned and stormed off.

Chapter Sixteen

"Mommy!" the voice of a small child cried, bringing him out of the hypnotic state. He turned toward the voice and saw a familiar, fair-skinned, petite girl, with long blond hair flowing behind her in the breeze, running towards them. This was the girl he had saved from the lake. Once she was close enough, she jumped up into the air toward Rayla. She caught her, and they embraced. "Where have you been, Mommy? I missed you this morning!" her daughter asked as she leaned back and looked at Rayla.

"I had to show that man right there around the Refuge," Rayla nodded toward Taylor.

The girl looked at him, "You look familiar."

Taylor looked at the girl curiously and stepped forward, "I know that wasn't English, but I understood what she said."

Rayla smiled in surprise, "I could see you gripping the Orb in your pocket. it's helping you understand us." Rayla spoke in her native tongue, amazement on her face at what had just happened. "It's unbelievable how soon it has begun to work for you. May I see it?"

Taylor pulled out the Orb, and to their surprise, it glowed brilliantly. "I have never heard of its symbiotic process working this quickly or intensely." Rayla put the little girl down, "You go back to the caverns now, Daphne. I'll be along soon."

Daphne smiled at Rayla and turned, skipping her way down the path. She stopped a few feet away and turned to them, "Do you promise?"

"I promise, now go on," Rayla said in laughter as the girl disappeared into the trees.

Taylor stood a moment unsure what to say, he had never considered Rayla might have a child. "I hadn't considered she might be your daughter. I don't know what to say," Taylor stared in Daphne's direction.

"We all have different sides to us; she has brought out a part in me that I didn't know existed. I found Daphne as an infant after Tarak's soldiers killed her parents and left her there to die. I had seen many orphans in my time here, but I had never rescued anyone myself. Daphne was in a situation similar to mine when I was her age. But without a grandmother to care for her, as I did. I brought her here, where everyone has helped raise her, but I have been her mother since the day I found her.

"When I was a little younger than Daphne, my grandmother found me wandering in the woods. Seeing how hungry and filthy I was, she scooped me up and ran for my family's home. A few strides from it, she found my father's murdered body, and inside the house, my mother's naked body lay in their bed. She had been raped and beaten before they slaughtered her like an animal." Rayla's voice shook, and a tear ran down her cheek before continuing. "She was nineteen years old when they killed her; my grandmother couldn't understand how someone could have done such a thing to such an elegant and kind woman. My sweet little brother lay beside her on the floor, a sword driven through his heart."

Taylor stood in shock, "That's horrible. I'm sorry you had to go through such a thing. Having a parent die is a hard thing. I can't imagine my whole family dying like that."

Rayla wiped the tears from her cheek, "You will notice most children here are orphans. There are about three hundred in all, most young females under eleven. They outright kill the boys under that age, not wanting to have to take the time to raise them to be men in their army. It also prevents them from turning into men looking for vengeance. Girls younger than eleven are left to die after Tarak's soldiers kill their families as a final cruelty. The teenage girls are taken as slaves but often end up in the sex trade for Tarak's armies; the boys at that age are enslaved or put into service for his troops.

"Among my people, raising orphans as a collective has been a practice since before recorded history. Once the children are old enough, they can decide what role they wish to play in our community."

Taylor turned back to the meadow, "I have seen quite a diversity in the ages of the people here," he commented. "How many people live here?"

"There are about six thousand people here in the Refuge and another twelve thousand in the outlying villages," Rayla answered. "Our resistance network has rescued more and more people as time has gone by. Tarak's armies are getting increasingly barbarous as the years pass. The people that we bring here are primarily women and children. In fact, that is what our population consists of for the most part. Of the people residing here, only a few, no more than seven hundred, are adult men under seventy. Many of those have grown up here, but we get the odd male refugee. The male population makes up a quarter of our militia.

"And the rest of the militia come from the villages?" Taylor asked.

"Not at all, actually. The few men there are needed to help protect the village and maintain the farming. I might add that the majority of our militia are women, well-trained women. When the fall of our society started, and refugees were forced to hide with Kalamar, men were scarce. The women took on protecting the camps; after all, there's no fiercer opponent than a mother protecting her family. Besides, there is a good deal of upkeep in the buildings we reclaimed from the ruins. We let the men do the heavy lifting for that part."

Taylor perked up a bit, "Did you say ruins? What kind of ruins?"

"When Kalamar first settled my people here, they discovered several small ruins in these mountains. Some of the larger stone buildings were still intact; they became the neighboring villages' sites over time. We don't know how they came to be here, but I imagine it was before our written record during the dark ages." Rayla paused, "Perhaps you could have a look at them and tell us what you think. That is what you do, is it not?"

Taylor smiled to himself, "I will consider it. Why don't you carry on with your story."

"After the initial creation of his army, the men brought into service no longer changed as once was common. Kalamar speculates that it's unnecessary. Tarak's darkness has polluted the population that lives under him. That his power no longer corrupts his troops enables us to place spies in his army and the cities. Even though it takes them from their families, men and women from here and the surrounding villages volunteer for the duty. My friend Careed is such an example. We also have friends and allies in most cities, and some in Tarak's army have given their loyalty to us. Tarak's evil grip still holds the majority of his army, though. Most of his men are third and fourth-generation soldiers; it's hard to break the chain.

"Where once Tarak's men would have enslaved a whole family, he now does as with Daphne's. Tarak no longer needs to enslave as many of my people; he has accumulated enough in his service to produce the food, supplies, and servants required to run his army over the years. Sometimes, rarely enough, though, one or two family members still escape, the man sacrificing his life so his wife and children may flee.

"Through the years, we have had to create five more settlements in the mountains close to here. There is a messenger system to keep in contact with each other. This allows us to have the latest news."

Taylor, only half-listening, was thinking about the ruins Rayla mentioned. As he peered out over the lake, something struck him. "Rayla, when you arrived on Earth, you were wounded. It doesn't seem likely that that happened here. I remember seeing structures far off behind you when I saw you in the lake. Very dilapidated crumbling structures. Were you exploring ruins before you came to Earth?"

A saddened look came over Rayla's face, "No, that is what remains of our capital city. The years of neglect have taken its toll." Rayla looked off to the lake and thought of that moment all those days ago. "The lake where I called forth the Power of the Orb to open the portal was outside of Glydane. Tarak ambushed me there, but I escaped, if only barely.

"I thought someone had followed me out of the Central Library to pursue the book I had taken. It was the last of the early histories of Daemor, written after the Orbs were found. Everyone knows the stories, but few have read first-hand accounts. The portal opened, and I saw you there as Tarak broke through the trees. He was within striking distance in an instant, and I felt his blade slash open my back as I reached through and took hold of you on the other side of the portal."

Rayla took in a deep breath as she looked him in the eye, "I have sent for the leaders of each community to come here to meet so we may discuss what our next move is."

"What is it that you need to discuss about your next move?" Taylor inquired.

"With you here, we can begin discussing how to start moving against Tarak," she said firmly to him.

Taylor filled with fury. "This isn't my war!" Taylor shouted at her. The Orb changed its glow as he held it to a shimmering blue. Taylor felt peace and calm flow from the Orb, curbing his temper, but it was not enough to overcome what he felt. He turned and walked away into the forest.

"Wait, Taylor, you can't just go off into the woods," she called as she watched Taylor storm off.

"Watch me!" he called back to her as he shimmered and vanished from sight.

"Damn you, Taylor, you can be so stubborn," Rayla said to herself.

"It will take time for him to adjust, Rayla," an old frail voice said from behind her. Rayla turned to find Kalamar there. "You shouldn't have brought him here if he didn't want to come," he paused. "That vanishing trick is quite brilliant, especially in an argument. I often thought of doing that many times in the last years after witnessing our two gifted little guests do it. I just never had the ability."

"Great gods, I hate looking for those two; minds of children with the Power of us," she growled. "And we discussed bringing him here."

"Yes, those two can be a hoot," Kalamar said, "but you should find him instead."

Rayla ignored his jest, "He's like talking to a thick-headed beast. His thoughts are so primitive at times, and the rage he generates is awe-striking."

"That is what will make him the greatest adversary against Tarak we could have. Should he choose to stay and help us," Kalamar countered.

"I thought you said I shouldn't have brought him here?" Rayla questioned.

"Yes, but he's here now. You might as well do your best to persuade him to help us. He's the one best chance of leading us to our victory," Kalamar replied.

"It's going to take a great deal of work. I don't think Taylor has the will to fight for us," she said in frustration.

"Yes, indeed, it will be some work; he's quite different from us. Even after our predicament, our people are far more evolved than his. We have ten thousand years of cultural evolution on him, and most of those years in peace. Tarak may have destroyed the way of life here, but we bred the violence out of ourselves. Even our best fighters pale compared to what I saw of his people when I looked into his mind. Violence isn't anything that comes naturally to anyone here. We simply don't have it in us.

"His people are still warring with each other as we speak. He was born into violence. The times of swords and shields are but two hundred years in his past. There are some among his people that would kill their neighbor or friend to better themselves. His people are full of warriors; his very soul is still full of violence. Anger is in his blood, and you must find a way to bring it out so that he can be of use to us. Even better if he has the tactics of war in his mind." Kalamar paused and took a deep breath. As he did, he looked up to the sun, "Ahhh, it's time for my afternoon nap! You should go find your 'thick-headed beast' and calm him down. He's of no use to you if you're the one he's angry at," Kalamar turned and began walking off but turned, "Also remember Prophecy has its surprises. We may not yet know all the roles he must play to bring about our salvation.

Rayla sat down for some time before she set out to find Taylor. He was not in any danger walking off some of that anger ...

Chapter Seventeen

The nerve of that woman! How can she be so single-minded? Taylor walked through the trees on the path he had taken from the clearing. The trees of the mountains here were giant, with needle-like leaves. Twenty people at arm's length would have struggled to hold hands around some of them. He had seen the likes as a child, called red cedars and Douglas fir, while visiting Canada in a park called Cathedral Grove. His dad had been a sci-fi nut and one summer had sought out the area where the second *Star Wars* film had been shot. Taylor had thought it fun walking through the woods as a boy pretending he was on another world. The thought was a little disconcerting now.

The enormity of the tree's canopy meant only ferns and small brush thrived on the forest floor. The forest's similarity to the memory of Taylor's childhood made him feel safe to a degree. He breathed in the fresh air with relief, but sucked in a tiny bug up his nostril. He paused and rubbed his nose a moment before noticing he could not see his hand or himself. "What the—?" His hand flashed back to

being visible, as did the rest of him. "That's interesting...."
He shook his hand, trying to make it invisible again,
without any success. "That's annoying." *Almost as much as
Rayla. How can I make her understand I'm not fighting for
her? She seems not to hear a word I say.* Taylor's anger
bubbled again. "Damn it!!!" Taylor shouted, its sound
muted by the trees. He picked up a large branch and bashed
it against a boulder to the side of the trail several times.
When it broke, he noticed that his hand had become invisible again. *Very interesting!*

With his anger out of his body, he breathed a sigh of
relief. *That felt good. I need to put some distance between her
and me for a bit.* Without hesitation, Taylor did what
always helped him think; he ran. The Orb's energy flowed
into him as he ran, the trees rushing past him in a blur at
one point. It did not seem Taylor would tire at all. It felt
amazing to feel his body working, the tension washing away.
He ran along the trail for several minutes, pushing harder
and harder until he finally felt his strength waning. As he
slowed to a walk, Taylor noticed that the trees were thinning, and the path steepened. His anger only at a simmer
now; he could take in his surroundings.

As he walked, he caught a glimpse of color in the trees
as a bird flittered about. The brightly colored birds here
looked more like tropical birds on Earth. They seemed out
of place here. As the trees thinned more while he walked,
they changed to more of a spindly variety, with long, broad
leaves, and there was more light on the ground, giving
shrubs a chance to grow larger.

Taylor looked down at his hand, now visible again,
where he gripped the Orb, and opened it. Where Rayla's
Orb was set in gold with silver inlay and a gold chain,
Taylor's was the reverse. He had wrapped the chain around

his wrist without realizing he had done so. With most of his anger gone, he became immersed in his thoughts of the Orb. His surroundings moved to the back of his mind as he walked. Until a sharp, rigid voice broke his thoughts.

"What have we here!" the voice said, "I think we have found ourselves a playmate, Vaz." Taylor looked up to see two uniformed soldiers step onto the path before him. Both were heavily muscled but a head shorter than him. The one who had spoken had blond hair and the other black. Their uniforms were cloth, with a metal chest plate, armor at the forearms and lower legs. To finish off their gear, each was armed with a bow, short swords, and long broad swords at their side. Taylor stopped dead in his tracks, stunned at their sight, unsure what to do. These were soldiers from Tarak's army, not the local militia. These soldiers were not supposed to be here.

"Might I ask what you're doing in these parts of the forest," the blonde-haired one asked in a brash manner.

"Go on, speak up! What are you doing here?" the other asked, sharpness in his tongue.

Terror swept through Taylor, and without a thought, he turned and ran as fast as he could into the woods, the soldiers in pursuit. Again for a second, the trees blurred, but fearful about his lead, he turned his head and looked to see if the soldiers still followed. Weighted down by their armor, they had fallen behind, but in his haste, as he looked back, he stumbled. Surprised, he could not get his arms up in time as he fell, and he smashed his face into the ground, hard. Pain flooded through his body; blood gushed out his nose. *Get up!* He thought to himself. *I have to get up. They will catch up to me any moment now.*

Taylor tried to flip over on his side, but excruciating pain shot through his abdomen when he did. He rolled himself over onto his side and looked down to see that a small piece of a tree branch protruded there. Taylor felt at his back in a panic, and his fingers fell upon the other end of the tree branch. When he brought his hand out from behind his back, it was soaked in blood.

"It seems our playmate has hurt himself," the black-haired soldier said as they caught up with Taylor. Both breathed hard with the effort of catching him.

"Yes, I guess our little game is over," said the other, as he lifted his sword above his head as if he intended to slice Taylor in half.

Fear spread through Taylor, and his heart pumped more adrenaline into his body. As the sword came down, Taylor threw his hand up and screamed, "NO." His hand jerked to a stop with his arm stretched out, with the Orb clenched in his other. Tingling energy rushed from the Orb, up his outstretched arm and out of his palm. Taylor heard the audible sound of the soldier's bones breaking as a significant force hit him. The soldier was hurled some fifty yards back before falling to the ground.

The other soldier stood there in shock for a moment before he came to his senses. He looked at the sword in his hand, dropped it to the ground, and began backing up as he gathered his wits and reached for the bow at his back. He clumsily pulled a handful of arrows from the quiver, and as they fell to the ground, he managed to keep one in hand. It shook as he tried to nock it.

Many thoughts ran through Taylor's mind as he tried to comprehend what had occurred. Had he really killed the soldier with the Power of the Orb? The sound of the bow's string stretching set off alarms in his head. He needed to do something before the soldier fired his weapon, but what? He turned his head wildly around and looked for something to defend himself with. Finally, his eyes fell upon a large stone. Taylor looked back to the soldier and saw the arrow drawn and aimed at him.

One thought ran through Taylor's mind—*Stone!* He reached for it and threw it with all the strength and accuracy he could muster. It scored a lucky hit, striking the soldier square in the forehead, but it ricocheted off. The soldier stood motionless, positioned as he had been when Taylor reached for the stone. *It should not have done that! Why is he so still?* he thought, before he noticed the color of the soldier's skin was wrong. Taylor took a moment to stand, then hobbled over to the motionless man. His mind worked to tell him the impossible truth, but he could not believe it. The soldier did not move in any way; it was unsettling. He faltered in his step and reached out toward the soldier's arm to keep from falling. Taylor breathed in surprise. This man's flesh was hard to the touch. He had somehow turned this man to stone.

Taylor dropped to the ground and lay there for a moment. His mind whirled. *I need to do something before I go into shock. Otherwise, I'm going to bleed to death.* Something strange happened to Taylor in that moment of crisis. An odd clarity came over him. He knew better than to remove the branch, but he could not seem to stop himself. With a quick jerk, he pulled it free, and he let his hand and the branch fall to his side. He took a sharp breath in; the pain from the wound was almost unbearable. Instinctively he placed the hand that clenched the Orb over it, and as the Orb touched his side, a brilliant blue hue flared from it, calming him, and the pain from the injury stopped.

Energy poured from the Orb, out through his hand, and into the wound. At the same time, the energy moved up his arm into his torso. The Orb's power was simultaneously healing the damage inside and outside. The warm tingle of the energy lasted only a moment, but when he moved his hand away, the wound had closed over, leaving only a scab. The tingling subsided as the Orb's glow lessened, and a dull pain filled the damaged area.

How can this be? Taylor thought to himself. He felt the wound on his back and found it too was covered over. He tried to sit up, but the newly healed wound protested any large movement, so he lay there in thought. With a blood-soaked, shaking hand, Taylor held up the Orb and looked at it. It was also covered in his blood, though he could see the blue pulse emanating out from the uncovered parts of the Orb. "What are you?" he said out loud. Every ounce of strength had been sucked out of him during the healing process, and unable to hold his hand up any longer, he rested it on his chest and passed out.

Taylor awoke disorientated as raindrops fell upon his face. Nightfall was coming, and he thought he had dreamed the whole thing for a moment. But as Taylor sat up, the pain in his abdomen reminded him of his wound. In the fading light, his eyes fell upon the soldier he had turned to stone. Reality settled in; he had killed these men. The thought hung there in his mind; an ache filled his chest at what he had done. *They tried to kill me! It isn't like I meant to kill them.*

Dropping back down again from exhaustion, the pain in his wound diminished. Yet, his heart still felt the sorrow of what he had done. He lifted his hand and opened it to expose the Orb, which still had a slight glow. *Thank you for keeping me alive.*

Taylor felt exhausted, but he managed to check himself over—the wound had healed substantially overnight. The Orb had repaired his body while sleeping, allowing him to regain a small amount of strength. He tested his strength once more and sat up; the Orb's light increased, and the pain dulled enough for him to manage. He still felt weak but was able to stand. He ventured a few steps with wobbling legs. He would manage, but it would be slow going. If he could sort out which way to go, that was.

In his attempt to escape the soldiers, he ignored the direction he ran into the woods. One of the skills he wished he had developed more at this moment was how to track. The puddles on the ground meant the rain had fallen for some time before it had woken him. The more clear tracks would have washed away hours ago. He reasoned with the basic survival skills, which told him the best way to get back to the Refuge was from the bottom of the mountain.

When Taylor had left Rayla yesterday, the lake had been at his back. Finding a stream might lead him to the meadow. Either way, it would be a long trek. He hoped the Orb would keep him alive long enough to make it there. The pain as he moved told him his wound still needed to heal more, and the cold sweat told him he had a fever. That likely meant infection had set in, and the Orb was not yet combating it. He was now in a race against time. If the infection spread into his blood before he reached help, he would die out here.

The moon had come out, and it illuminated the way for several feet ahead of him. He ambled his way down the mountain slope, wandering through the trees at the quickest pace possible. He used the trees for support in spots that became too steep as he moved between them. After three hours of walking, he heard the sound of water running off to his right side, bringing him hope. He leaned against a large tree's base at the steam's edge and rested. His eyes slid closed while he considered the Orb's power. It was wonderful and awful to think what could be done with the Orbs.

As he fell asleep, he understood what the Orb's power could mean for him. With an Orb in his possession, he would no longer need Rayla to take him back to Earth. Once he had recovered and worked with the Orb enough, he could, in theory, return to Earth on his own.

He stood after what seemed like an hour, somewhat recuperated, and continued his trek down the mountain, following at the side of the stream. When he finally reached the bottom, the sun had begun to rise. The journey had taken a toll on him, though, and beyond fatigued, he dropped to the ground and passed out once more.

Chapter Eighteen

Taylor dreamed he awoke to find himself home on his couch. For a few moments, he relaxed and found peace before a gentle touch at his shoulder, caressed him, soothing him. Taylor welcomed the larger sense of calm the touch brought him. As the hand lay upon his shoulder, he could not place how or why, but the touch felt familiar.

The hand rested there on his shoulder for a moment. The urge to see who was there overcame him. He turned his head and looked up. To his surprise, Rayla stood there. This woman of both inner and outer beauty and power, had worked her way into every part of his psyche. Her hair hung down on her shoulders, and she wore a white linen summer dress like she had when he first awoke on her world.

"That first night at your home, this is what I wanted to do to you," she said and leaned in, pressing her lips to his with passion.

Taylor's heart burst with joy, and he kissed her back in pleasure. Out of nowhere, Rayla slammed her fist into his thigh. "Ouch," he shouted, shoving her away. "What was that for?" he asked. Rayla looked at him with innocence in her eyes.

"Wake up!" Rayla's demeanor changed to anger, and she slammed her fist on his thigh again, sending pain through his leg.

Taylor flinched and reached down to his thigh, "Ahhh, what the hell? That hurts. What is your deal?" he pushed himself back into the cold hard surface of the couch.

"Taylor, wake. Up!" she exclaimed.

"What?" Taylor asked, confused. Rayla smiled innocently again, then lunged forward and slapped him across the face.

Taylor shuddered awake and opened his eyes to a soldier staring at him. The man slapped him once more before hovering over him and staring intently. Still not quite awake, Taylor rubbed his face where the soldier had slapped him. Shocked and unable to think what to do, he stared at the soldier in the same uniform as the two soldiers Taylor had run into yesterday. Except that this man looked older and rougher. As Taylor's mind cleared, fear kicked in, and Taylor backed himself up against the boulder behind him. As panic set in, the familiar sensation of the Orb's power came to life.

"It seems that our lost boy is found," the soldier said in a stern voice, "And alive to beat all."

"Relax, Taylor, he's a friend of the resistance," a familiar voice said. Rayla stepped out from behind the soldier, and Taylor's fear eased. "This is Colonel Careed, my friend I mentioned. He has journeyed here to bring news of Glydane." She knelt beside him in alarm when she saw the blood all over his shirt and pants. Concern spread across her face as she became frantic and checked him over for injuries.

"Run off and got lost, did you?" she was saying, her

voice becoming increasingly agitated as she spoke. "And you injured yourself in the meantime. This is a lot of blood Taylor. What happened to you?" She lifted his shirt, which revealed the scab there. The scab flaked away when she touched it, showing the scar underneath. "This wound looks as if it's completely healed. How did you manage this?" she asked, more to herself than Taylor.

Taylor sat up and pushed her hand away, "What does it look like happened! The Orb sealed the wound; it must have completely healed it this morning while I slept. At least the pain is all but gone now."

The Orb in Taylor's hand flashed brightly, the scar faded away, and the Orb's light faded back to a dull gray. Rayla sat back on her heels and looked at him in bewilderment, "Taylor, it took me years to learn how to use the Orb in this way."

"I wasn't even aware that I was using the Orb. It just sort of happened on its own," he replied. "Like teaching me your language. It started doing extraordinary things when I ran into two soldiers. I outright killed one and turned the other to stone."

Rayla sat up straighter, and Careed perked up. "Soldiers! Turned one into stone!" she said in amazement. Rayla looked at Careed with worry, "You ran into soldiers? And killed them!" Taylor nodded to her. "Impossible! There are no soldiers in these parts. Besides, even I can't turn things to stone." Rayla stood up, her bewilderment increasing, "How is it possible for you to do these things? You have only been in contact with the Orb for a few days. It took me a month to connect with my Orb and years before I reached my full potential." Rayla stood there and looked between Taylor and Careed.

Colonel Careed, of course, understood the surprise in

her face. "We don't have time to take this further with him, Rayla; leave it for now. We had better find the soldiers Taylor ran into. We will need to find clues as to why they're this far into the mountains. Them being there means trouble for us, and likely soon."

"You're right, of course; this could mean that there could be more on the way," Rayla agreed. "There is no reason for Tarak's men to be out here unless they were looking for us. Not even deserters would come this far out." She looked down at Taylor and asked, "Are you able to walk? Can you show us where they are?"

"I think so," Taylor replied while he slowly got up. "I followed the stream down the mountain. We should be able to retrace my steps from there." At that moment, Taylor realized there were several other members of the search party back a few yards away. Two young men in the crowd laughed to themselves. One of them, a tall tan-skinned man, looked at him and nodded. "I can show you," Taylor said as he walked in the direction he had come from the night before. He was still exhausted, but he would manage.

"You can thank Tae for leading us to you," she gestured to the young man that had looked at him.

Taylor's stomach growled loudly, "I'm starving! Does anyone have something to eat?"

Tae stepped forward and handed Taylor some of the dried meat from a pack.

"Hey, that is mine," another young man interjected. He was the opposite of Tae, short and stout.

"You don't need it, chubby," Tae said poking the other man's stomach. The man frowned before Tae said, "Now Zem, you should be kind to the man; he has been lost all night. He likely hasn't eaten for hours."

Zem looked at Taylor then nodded, "Yeah, okay, but

you're making breakfast when we get back." He hustled ahead.

Tae smirked and nodded to Taylor. "He's gets grumpy when he gets hungry." He walked off to catch up to Zem.

Taylor nodded back his appreciation, and ate like he had not had food for days. Luckily the others had been back far enough not to hear the conversation with Rayla and Careed. Taylor was not sure that her people would have readily accepted Kalamar's gift to him. After Rayla dispatched the rest of the party back to the Refuge, she and Careed followed Taylor. They walked near each other, but no words were spoken between them. Both looked deep in thought about Taylor's story. Rayla broke the silence only once, muttering loud enough for Taylor to hear that half the camp had gone out and looked for him. The journey that took Taylor all night injured, now took only a couple of hours to complete. Upon their arrival, Rayla and Careed looked over Taylor's attackers in awe of what he had done.

Careed shook his head as he inspected the soldier's uniforms. "Damn!" he cursed, "These are scouts in Tarak's army. This means that more will be coming this way or are already nearby. I've been away too long. I would have known this was coming had I gone back sooner. You should get back to the Refuge. I need to return to Tarak's headquarters. I have been away for several weeks. This has either been recent or kept secret. Otherwise, I would have heard news of this before I left."

"I'll trace the trail the scouts left as best I can and see where it leads. But with the rain, their trail will be hard to follow. If I don't cross paths with other scouts, I'll head for Glydane," Careed said. He bid goodbye to Rayla and left at breakneck speed down the mountain.

Rayla examined the man Taylor had turned to stone.

"How is it that you did this? The man himself is stone, but his clothing and belongings aren't changed."

"Well, I'm not quite sure," he replied. "All I remember is looking at the stone I intended to throw at him. But when I threw it, it ricocheted. And the other one...." He raised his hand and pointed to the soldier that lay several yards down the path. "All I did was raise my hand to protect myself, and I felt a great force leave my hand. Throwing him back." Rayla looked up at him, and Taylor noticed the agitation in her face. "You're angry?" he asked.

"Not angry; I'm frustrated!" Rayla raised her voice.

"*You are* angry. I can feel it," Taylor said. "You're angry because of the pace at which I have connected with the Orb. That I don't want to help you is what infuriates you."

Rayla looked surprised now. "Why ask if you already know?" she said as she turned to make her way down the mountain.

Taylor was at a loss for words. He stood for a moment and watched her go. When Rayla did not slow down, he followed after her. Minding his distance, he stayed behind her a few paces in thought. *This woman is infuriating! I'm the one that got hurt, which wouldn't have happened if I wasn't here. Now she's cross with me for being able to wield my Orb better than her? So what if what I did with the Orb is pretty outstanding? I'd happily give her my ability with it if I could. And then she could save her people.* It hit him then, where her frustration came from. Her people were in peril, but she could do nothing more than she was. *Yet, here I'm doing amazing things with my Orb, and I'm unwilling to help.* The moment of clarity was sharp, and he felt sorry for her for just a moment, but that was still not enough to make him sympathize with her cause.

The walk back to the camp was long and silent. He

tried to talk to her twice with no success before giving up, deciding to enjoy the walk instead. He no longer felt any pain or discomfort, and the Orb lay muted against his chest. As he detached himself from Rayla's upset, he lost himself in the forest that surrounded him. The trees and the fauna here were quite similar to Earth. There were a few unusual plants, but he would have thought he was in the Rockies back home if he did not know any better.

They returned to the meadow in the late afternoon to a large group of riled-up people. The search group that Rayla sent back had related the news of Taylor being found. From the look of hope mixed with unsureness on their faces, the rescue group members had heard some of the talk of him killing soldiers and had told the tale. A small crowd of curious community members stood waiting to greet Taylor and asked how he had single-handedly stopped two soldiers with no weapons. At least none of the party had overheard enough to put the Orb in Taylor's hands. Some offered their thanks for saving their Refuge from discovery by the scouts.

Several minutes later, Taylor finally gave his thanks and returned to his room in the Refuge. New clothing was laid out for him, and a fresh towel sat to their side. After being out in the woods for the last two days, he would be glad for a bath and new clothing. He picked up his towel and change of clothes, then strolled out the door to the bathing area he knew. Taylor took his time in the tub; no one was there, so he enjoyed the heat and allowed it to relax him. The exhaustion he felt from healing was still heavy on him. Taylor dried off, dressed, and went to the meadow, where he lay in the sun to rest.

Chapter Nineteen

Rayla had fumed all the way home. She could not believe the audacity of Taylor. When they had returned, she took the first opportunity and slipped off on her own. She needed time to process the day's events. While in thought about Taylor and what he had managed to do with the Orb, she fell asleep, exhausted from the day looking for him.

In the morning when she awoke, her anger still burned. With all that Taylor had already done with the Orb, how could he not see to help them? She was sure that if he trained, he could wield a sword. He was physically capable enough. After all, if he had instinctively used the Orb already, surely he could use it to learn swordsmanship.

Taylor's abilities with the Orb amazed her, but she was unsure how it was possible. How could he already use the Orb with such proficiency? She had sneaked into the main library over the years, and had read almost all the written histories of the Orbs. Not one mentioned such a thing had ever occurred. Finally, after she lay there with her thoughts for a time, she arose, collected her clothes and bathing supplies, and went off.

As she walked through the passages toward the closest hot spring, she started to feel motivated to talk to Kalamar. She bathed, dressed, and went off in search of him. At this time of day, he would likely already be about somewhere. It took her a while to find him as she searched the usual spots he loitered about. Finally, she found him outside in the meadow, where he basked in the morning sun. Rayla sat beside him but was quiet while considering how to begin her conversation.

"What is troubling you, Rayla," Kalamar asked as she sat in silence beside him.

"You know me all too well, old friend," Rayla turned to him. "It's Taylor. I find myself angry and yet hopeful about his abilities with the Orb. He has so much potential but is unwilling to help us. It has taken me years to master the Orb's power, and Taylor is doing the impossible with it in only days. And all this from a man whose world is still so primitive it's on the brink of destruction."

"Yes, I can see your frustration and understand it. Taylor is everything we had hoped for but is a very reluctant hero. I find it interesting that you have become jealous of your savior." Kalamar turned to look into her eyes and raised his bushy eyebrows. "Tell me, has jealousy taken the place of the love you feel for him?"

Rayla looked at him, surprised, with her jaw hung open. Kalamar smiled, "I knew when you first told me of the champion in your visions. The way your eyes glittered." Rayla blushed and turned to hide her face.

"Do tell me, how is it you can be jealous of Taylor? He must master the Orb if he is to do what he must. He must, in fact, go through a metamorphosis. The Orb mustn't be only a tool as it is for us but be part of him. Therefore, he must have a special gift for it. Prophecy has led you to believe in an idea of him, a story if you will. But our stories of who people are and who they truly are can often differ very much."

Rayla took a deep breath and exhaled, "But how is it that his connection is so strong with the Orb already? If I could understand why perhaps I could be more efficient with my Orb. I wouldn't have to spend my energy convincing him to help!"

"If you were able to do that, you'd be the one fulfilling that part of the Prophecy, not him. It doesn't matter how, but that he can. He will fulfill the Prophecy. Forcing him to believe as you do is fruitless. He must come to it on his own."

"I hate that you always have the right thing to say, showing me that I'm so wrong. But you're right; I'm being foolish." Rayla turned back to Kalamar as a tear streaked down her cheek. "It frustrates me that I have to lead him to his fate. I thought that when I found him, he would be a warrior already like I saw him in my visions. The man I saw there was my equal, and this man is not. Events will take longer now that I must force him to stay and teach him to fight."

"And what of your love for him?" Kalamar asked

"It still burns strong in me. It may be that is what fuels my anger," Rayla said. "I know Taylor has feelings for me, I can sense them, though they haven't grown into love yet. Yet, they grow stronger each day, as does the conflict within him. He fights his feelings for me because I brought him here, but he still feels them."

"And remind me again, what did your visions show you regarding Taylor with you?" Kalamar inquired.

"I felt his love for me in my vision of him. A love that makes him a fierce fighter in the end. He will fight out of love for me in the final battle." Rayla looked at him, saddened.

A knowing smile on his face, Kalamar did not push further—not all things were for sharing when it came to prophecy. "Prophecy is a tricky thing. Seeing only parts of the actual event and none of the events which lead there. I prefer staying away from interpreting them. So many have tried to decipher how they branch off into several different outcomes. A small thing happens, and Prophecy isn't triggered, collapsing the entire branch. Or there are dark and light branches depending on how certain situations turn out. Even with all my studying, I have failed. The only people that have ever been remotely successful are those with the prophetic gift like yourself. The Orbs bestow gifts as they see fit, you have yours, and I had mine.

"I do know that Prophecy never plays out as you might expect. Not to mention, some are not so bound by Prophecies. For instance, you see many outcomes to the Prophecy about Taylor, where at one time there was only one. Do you not?"

Rayla smiled to herself, "Is there nothing I can hide from you?"

Kalamar looked at her endearingly, "Don't be so hard on yourself. No one expects you to be perfect." Kalamar placed his hand upon her shoulder, "Another thing you must remember is that it isn't so much his people that are primitive, but the social structure they exist in. Taylor's world is caught in a place of brutality brought on by greed. Our brains are no bigger than theirs, and we think no faster than they do. If you replaced their social structure with one more evolved as we had, they would be no different in time."

"You have opened my eyes once more with your wisdom," she replied. "I feel better talking with you. I must have patience with him and myself to see this through. I must speak with you of the soldiers Taylor encountered."

"Indeed," Kalamar replied with a concerned voice, "Our Refuge is in danger. It's hard to believe there were soldiers this far out. I feel that it would be best if you and our scouts began looking deeper into the mountains for a new home." Kalamar stood up, not waiting for a reply, "Also, it would be wise for you to take Taylor with you when you go. The more people he becomes friends with, the harder it will be for him to leave. And it would be better that he falls in love with you, sooner rather than later." Kalamar paused, "It seems he has already found a new friend to keep him company." Kalamar pointed down to the meadow before disappearing out of sight.

Rayla followed his gesture and saw Taylor with Daphne as she ran about the meadow while they played. Kalamar took his leave, and she sat there for some time and enjoyed the sun while watching them. As the sun rose toward midday, reminding her she had plans to make, she stood and made her way through the meadow toward them.

Chapter Twenty

Taylor had carried and chased Daphne around the meadow for over an hour. The amount of energy she had was boundless. He finally stopped, breathless. "OK, Daphne, that's about all I can take. For now, I have to rest for a bit," he said, hunched over as he tried to catch his breath.

"Alright, you can rest for a little while. But remember you said you'd spend all day with me," Daphne shouted behind her as she ran off to play with a group of children nearby.

"It seems you have found a new friend, Taylor," Rayla said as Daphne ran off. "You're very good with her."

"Well, I love kids; they're great to be around, and she's pretty special." Taylor sat down on the grass, "Children are so full of energy. To them, life is an amazing discovery. It's one of the things that made my job at the summer camp so enjoyable."

"Daphne has been a wonderful gift in my life," Rayla said. "She is the one thing that keeps me going sometimes. Just being around her energizes me and fills me with love."

Rayla's face lightened as she spoke, and she smiled to herself.

"You have a strong bond with her," Taylor said.

"As much as if I had birthed her myself, I couldn't imagine living without her. Not being able to have children always saddened me before she came into my life. She has changed that for me." Rayla lifted the Orb from beneath her shirt and looked at it. "It's important for you to know that, once you have put this on, having children isn't possible while you wear it."

Taylor took out the Orb from his pocket and held it up, "The things this Orb can do are amazing, but I'm still not the person you're looking for. I will have to sort some things out when I get back, but I'm still going back."

Rayla stayed silent for a moment and, with an earnest look, began, "I have realized that I can't keep you here if you don't want to stay. I'll take you back as soon as I'm able. Traveling to your world and back drained me. It takes a toll on a person using that much power. It will be at least a moon cycle before I recover enough to journey again. I was curious if, during that time, I could ask you a favor that may keep you here for a short while longer."

Taylor gave her a look of hesitation, "An offer of peace with strings attached; I should have guessed."

Rayla ignored the jest and carried on, "Tarak is closing in on our Refuge. We are no longer safe here. My people will have to find a new home." There was a hint of fear in her voice. "We must move quickly, and we have several tasks that need tending to. My people will need to pack up their lives for the next few weeks. Not an easy task, considering we have been here for so many years.

"We will be doubling the guards that keep watch over our Refuge. Colonel Careed will do what he can to get us information, but it will be weeks before we hear from him. I'm dispensing as many of our scouts as we can afford to look for any sign of Tarak's men in the mountains surrounding the Refuge.

"With that done, we will need to begin looking for a new home. We are forming parties to begin searching further into the mountains. Considering your skill with the Orb, I wondered if you would accompany me as part of the search parties. And an extra pair of eyes would be of great use."

Taylor thought for a moment as he looked her in the eyes. Had she finally come to her senses? Could he count on her to honor her word? With Rayla conceding, he began to consider the present opportunity to explore an alien world. Besides, what would he do here for the next month while he waited? Watch the people here pack? Rayla had mentioned ruins in the mountains here. A chance to look at them on the way would present itself. At least there could be some appeasement in his passion for history, albeit not his own. "I can agree to that," Taylor replied.

For the next week, Taylor hardly saw Rayla. She had a daunting list of preparations to deal with, including their journey further into the mountains. He watched her as she rushed about for the first two days organizing people; by the end, the whole community had mobilized.

Alternatively, Taylor chose to spend his time engaged in one of the things he loved best. He explored the outlying areas of the Refuge and searched for hints of an ancient civilization. While he investigated the Earth-like area around the Refuge, he managed to find the remnants of foundations of buildings close by. Strangely, they did not fit with Rayla's story of her planet. The foundations were ancient, setting them back before the time Rayla had said was the dark times before the Orbs came. The building techniques were far too advanced for that period. It just did not make sense.

Taylor noted the footings had metal pins that held the stone blocks together, something a primitive society would not have been able to accomplish. He also found stone architecture with precision holes cut into them. The surface was smooth and polished, with no tool or blade marks, something that could not be done with the most advanced technology on Earth, suggesting that a technologically advanced, powered device had been used. He found further contradictory evidence as he explored and began to wonder if there was more to Rayla's story. He did not have concrete evidence, though, so he decided not to tell Rayla what he had seen.

There were other options to be considered, and he had not wanted to look foolish. Rayla's civilization changed a considerable amount over a short time after the Orbs and the shard jewelry were made. One could almost say that it became full of mystery and magic. One of the initial Shard Carriers could have developed a skill with masonry and architecture in those times. The time of the hundred years of change could have spurred a city out here to be lost and forgotten in the thousands of years that followed. People had lost information about their origins on Earth, after all. Still, the ruins did seem very out of place.

On his way back from his daily excursion, Daphne would often find him. They would then spend the rest of his day playing games. As the days passed, sometimes Daphne brought a friend or two, and once or twice, several children played games with them. It was always Daphne that sought him out first, though. By the end of the week, Taylor woke up excited about his day of exploring and his time with Daphne.

Taylor saw that the men here did their best to accommodate their scarcity. But a lot of children went without a masculine influence. Rayla had explained one day when she had come to gather Daphne that the lack of positive male role models in her society was a blow to her people. Men and women had been equals on her planet before the fall of their civilization. They were two parts of a whole that came together and raised their children in a balanced way.

When it came to raising children, the mother and father had always reflected mutual love, respect, and care for one another. They embraced each other's aspects and never took the premise that one was better than the other or could replace the other. The divine masculine and divine feminine formed naturally in all romantic relationships. It was an honoring of the sacredness of life. It had been common for siblings, parents, and friends to provide additional image-making. This allowed children to grow into their identity without prejudice. They did their best to provide for the positive masculine and feminine roles, but the men were spread thin with their numbers. Rayla hoped one day that her people could be whole again.

Rayla had found it so strange in Taylor's world that it did not seem there had ever been a balance between the sexes. It had made sense to her why Earth's civilization had not evolved further than it had with such indifference. To not have that balance that was once so prevalent here, had caused a hole in Rayla's community and the larger society.

What Rayla had said resonated with Taylor. He had once spent some time working with a female shaman to understand a different archaeological perspective. The shaman had told him that, as a lesbian feminist that had been raped, she had spent many years healing herself. And in the more recent part of her healing, she realized that she was still about hearth and home and receptive-creative no matter how masculine she was. Even if she did not like it, she eventually embraced it. She had also recognized that men were an essential part of life, and she had strived in her community to bring the men there into balance, as she had become.

Taylor had already noted that the men here were quite involved with the young. There was mutual respect between the women and men in the community that Taylor had never seen on Earth. The men and women here appreciated the qualities of their opposite sex.

The weeks passed quickly, and one morning, Taylor awoke to a knock on his door. He found Rayla waiting in the hallway, wearing traveling clothes, a cloak, and the hiking boots he had bought her back on Earth.

"We will be leaving today to search for a new home for my people. It's just after dawn. You should get dressed, fill your travel pack, and meet me in the food commons for breakfast. Oh, and don't forget your travel cloak," Rayla flourished hers, "The rainy season is coming, and it leads up with ... rain." Rayla smiled excitedly, turned, and walked off down the passage, not waiting for his reply.

"Sure thing," he muttered to himself, "Aren't you peppy this morning!" He dressed and looked over the odds and ends he had picked up at the small market area for the journey. Rayla had also left a package containing supplies for the trip at his door each day. He busied himself and packed the gear he would need over the next few weeks.

With everything in hand, he looked to the side table of his bed last. There sat the Orb where he had placed it the night before. He had taken to putting it in his pocket during the day, but he left it at his bedside in the evening. He had fallen asleep with it in his pocket one night after Kalamar had given it to him. The dreams he'd had were strange and off-putting. He found himself a child in the dreams, always concerned, even afraid that magic would get him. Rayla had told him she often had dreams of a sort. The Bearers all did. It was her opinion that they were the memories of past Bearers. Or maybe even memories of those where the Orbs had come from.

Taylor pocketed the Orb, left his room, and made his way through the passages to meet with Rayla. He spotted her at a far corner table in the food commons and joined her after collecting a plate of food. "Your plans are complete? For where we are going to search?" he asked.

"Indeed they are," Rayla nodded; she had yet to eat anything on her plate. "We will all leave in different directions into the mountains. I have assigned you with my group if that is alright with you." She looked Taylor in the eye and waited until he nodded in agreement. "Good; I also thought that you'd like a chance to say goodbye to Daphne."

"She's already in the meadow, waiting expectantly to see us off. Daphne is playing it tough, but she's a bit of a mess this morning with my leaving and with yours." Taylor felt her meet his eyes to make sure he understood what she was insinuating. Daphne had become attached to him. "We will be leaving in a couple of hours. I'd like you to meet me in the meadow in an hour to give me a hand with the final preparations. Perhaps you could spend some time with Daphne before then."

Parting was always hard for children, Taylor knew. He had seen it with every group at the kids' camp. Rayla was looking after her daughter's feelings, and Taylor understood the importance. "I'll look for her as soon as I'm finished here, and I'll see you in an hour."

"Great," Rayla said as she pushed her plate forward. "I never can eat when I'm leaving the Refuge for more than a couple of days. There is so much to do, and I always start to worry about Daphne the day I leave." She smiled at Taylor. "I should go." Rayla left him to eat his meal and headed out of the commons.

As Rayla left, Taylor noticed that the commons were now full of commotion, unlike when he had entered moments ago. It was full of those who would go today as part of the search parties. Sparse families ate together as their children shed tears at the departure of their father or mother. Several other people with packs, those with no families, ate with each other. Most of the people in the commons were women, emphasizing their percentage in the population. Many women here were experienced trackers and hunters, and vital to the search parties' success.

Taylor finished his breakfast, slung his pack over his shoulder, and left in search of Daphne. He found her in the meadow, where she sunned herself after her morning bath. "Taylor!" She jumped up, "I was wondering when you were going to get here." She hugged him as he knelt down; her wet hair brushed up against his face and dampened his cheek and shirt. Daphne lifted her head from Taylor's shoulder and giggled when she saw his damp face. "Sorry," she said as she wiped the dampness from his cheek with her sleeve. "You look sad, Taylor. What is wrong?"

"Well, Daphne, Rayla has told me that we are to leave this morning to look for a new place for all of you to live. I think I'm going to miss you." Taylor said as he realized he had started to become attached to her too.

A small tear rolled down Daphne's cheek. "I'll miss you too," she said as her little chin quivered. She wiped away a tear, stood taller, and smiled, "But you won't be gone forever because you have to come back and get us. Right?" Daphne asked.

Taylor brushed a second tear from her cheek as it leaked out and felt a slight pang of heartache. "You're perfectly correct. I'll be back in a short time. In fact, I'm already looking forward to coming back." He smiled at her, "I still have a bit of time. Shall we play a game of tag before I go?"

Daphne smiled happily and playfully pushed him back; using her hands on Taylor's shoulders, she threw him off balance. "You're It!" she said as she ran off into the meadow as fast as possible.

Her laughter brought a smile to Taylor's face as he hopped up and chased her. Taylor was so wrapped up in enjoying his play with Daphne that he lost track of time. That was, until he noticed Rayla watched them from a distance. "Look, it's your mom," Taylor pointed, "I need to help her with a few things. Why don't you play with some of the other children for a bit?" Giving her a big hug, he left her to play.

The meadow bustled at this point, filled with community members with different wares on tables and in carts. The party members and their families stood off to the side. After joining Rayla, she introduced him to the people they would travel with. Taylor recognized some of them from his time there. After being introduced, Rayla spoke for all the party members to hear. "Gather anything else you might need. I have asked our community to provide what they could. We leave as soon as everyone is ready," she gestured to the tables and carts and the bustling meadow. The party members collected the last of their supplies: food, extra clothing, waterskins; the selection was well thought out. After everyone was satisfied, their packs were complete, and they gathered back into their groups.

Five hundred and forty-nine seasoned explorers stood in the meadow in formation—fifty-five groups of ten search parties in all. Rayla and Taylor stood in the only group of nine among them. Rayla reasoned that with Taylor and her as Orb Bearers that it would make up the difference. Kalamar stepped upon the stone podium in front of them all and raised his hand. All in the meadow fell silent as Kalamar spoke of the importance of their journey.

"We find ourselves in a predicament we haven't seen in almost two hundred years. Our Refuge has been found, and we must begin preparing to move ourselves to a new home. It's of the utmost importance that you take every measure to ensure it.

"We are relying on you to do this enormous task and do it in the quickest of measures. If you fail, the consequences will be dire. We have likely only two full moons to find our new home and abandon the Refuge. You're some of the best hunters and trackers we have. Go now. May you be gifted with speed and luck!

After Kalamar finished, the parties divided and took to different directions into the forest of the mountain.

Chapter Twenty-One

Rayla and Taylor's group traveled together with two other parties for the next three days. They were empowered by Kalamar's words and trekked out, speed in their steps, stopping only for rest and food. Friends and comrades bid their goodbyes on the fourth day, and the other parties moved off into the mountains on their separate paths.

On the fifth day, the nine awoke and prepared to continue, dividing into pairs and one group of three. Each party would search in a specific area of the mountains in a designated direction. Each would search for thirty-five days, a full moon cycle, and meet back where they stood. Once everyone had returned and revealed what they had found, they would decide to either return to the Refuge or continue their search. They broke camp and wished each other luck as they left.

Taylor found himself relaxed and enjoying the wilderness while he and Rayla traveled. Taylor had been an active hiker for his entire adulthood. His certification in wilderness first aid had allowed him and Lilly to spend many weekends in the deep wilderness. It still astounded him at the similarities here to Earth. He saw only slight differences in plant life. The birds were still out of place with their bright colors, though.

Rayla had resigned to leave Taylor to his own thoughts. She took that time to work through her own feelings about her people and Taylor's place in Prophecy. The days passed quickly as they explored and found themselves almost at the end of the first part of the journey.

Taylor had thought a great deal about Rayla's motives during that time; she worked to save her people and her daughter. Taylor had often considered in the last few days what he would have done with an Orb's power to save Lilly that day she had died in the river. Rayla had taken him against his will, which was unacceptable, but when people felt their loved ones were in danger, their ability to rationalize changed. Unfortunately, or not, primal instincts often replace reason. Taylor had not forgiven Rayla, but in the days he had walked beside her, he had gotten to know her and been able to let some of his anger go.

"What's your favorite food?" Rayla had asked as they walked one afternoon.

"That's a strange question. How would you have a comparison?" Taylor replied.

"Hmm, I guess you're right there. I did have a limited sampling on your planet. Do you like spicy foods? Salty or sweet after dinner?" she inquired.

"I do like Mexican a lot, which is spicy. Hot tamales are amazing. I like cabbage rolls... which is meat wrapped in cabbage...." Rayla gave him a strange look. "It's a leafy plant that grows in a ball." Rayla made a face like she had no idea what he was saying. "It's savory. And as for dessert, I like a little of both. How about you?"

"I like ocean food! Glydane lies beside the ocean, and there is an abundance of creatures that I like to eat. We make something like your butter, and we slather it over the food. As for dessert, I prefer cake." Rayla paused in thought. "What was your childhood like?"

"Right into the deep questions today, I see." Taylor looked over at her, and she shrugged nonchalantly. "My dad was an academic, so he was always about learning. But we had fun with it, or at least he tried. He told me that my mom would have made it fun had she been around. She disappeared when I was almost four. Most of what I know of her is from stories. She apparently had much more of a sense of humor and adventure than my dad.

"When I was little, we spent summers at my dad's parents' farm helping out. Which my mom had loved; she grew up in the city, you see. She was a champion martial artist, a real spitfire, my dad liked to say. He thought that I got my spirit from her. I have fond memories of her, holding her hand in the park, lying in bed with her, her chasing me in the backyard as we played.

"My dad told me once as a boy that she craved seeing the open countryside when we were at our home in the city. Before she disappeared, my childhood was pretty happy. Her memory inspired me to become a pretty good athlete. My dad and I moved to the guest house at my grandparent's ranch after she went missing. He took a job teaching at the local elementary school so that we could spend more time together. Not to mention that my grandparents needed help at the ranch. I did a lot of hard work there, and we played hard too; hiking, hunting, fishing, camping. Not a lot more to say; that's pretty much it."

Taylor realized at that moment that as the days had passed, he had begun enjoying Rayla's company. With her need for him to stay here gone, Taylor had found it easier to relax around her. She had started to teach him about small game and what plants were suitable for eating. He felt a little joy as he learned how to survive here. While the plants here looked similar, much of the edible plants were vastly different. Taylor woke each day and looked forward to the hike as he explored, and even his conversations with Rayla. And with that joy, the days started to go by faster as their deadline to turn back approached.

Taylor's time exploring around the Refuge and as he hiked at Rayla's side had ignited his drive as an archaeologist. As they walked, he was discovering a lost civilization and learning about it. He found several more ruins along their way, and he had begun to show Rayla. If there had once been inhabitants in these places, there was potential for it again. All they needed was to find a location that would accommodate all her people. Taylor knew that there were basic environmental requirements necessary; accessible water, food, and land for planting and dwellings for a community to thrive.

During their search, the ruins they had come across were many thousands of years old and had been unsuitable. Changes in the river flow had flooded two of the locations. Further down the ravine, the river at another site that had once flowed deep was only a trickle now. The last site they found three days ago had been lost to landslides that left only slight signs of buildings at the outer edge.

Taylor noted that as they had moved on from the mountain of the Refuge, the ruins had become much less advanced, though they were of a newer era. The ruins closer to the Refuge had been constructed of stone. The ruins' buildings had degraded and fallen in on themselves over time, but the evidence of the architecture had been still present. The foundations in the last location had been made of stone, with only the bottom layer left intact. Taylor speculated that the upper part had been constructed of wood, long since disintegrated. There was only enough stone to build a two or three-foot foundation, and the construction was rudimentary at best. This meant the people who created them did not likely have the skills to create the exquisite architecture around the Refuge. Something had happened to that once great civilization and the technical skills they knew.

"Many things don't make sense about your planet," Taylor said one morning. "The ruins are more consistent with a cataclysmic event. Where your people became unable to maintain their level of sophistication."

Rayla looked at him as they walked, "I can't tell you why that is. This study of ancient life isn't something we have here. I'm sorry I can't help you figure this out."

"I have been considering that perhaps one of the Orb or Shard carriers created them," he speculated. "But I don't really know a great deal of their history. Could you tell me more about them?"

"The information that I have been able to find is sparse, but I did find some literature in the library once. It's said that in a time when our land had fallen into chaos, a strange burning object fell from the sky into a farmer's field. The mass, the size of a large bear, found its way by means of the farmer's cart to a blacksmith's forge where, with hammer and chisel, the smith discovered a strange metal threaded through the rock.

"As the man worked away at separating the metal, four large Orbs, each the width of a plum, and seven small ones were nestled in the hollow interior, lying amongst the shards and crystalline dust of other shattered Orbs. One large Orb was broken into two pieces, and when the smith held one half of the Orb in his hands, it began to glow. A warm feeling spread into him, filling him with a sense of peace.

"The blacksmith enlisted a fellow craftsman's help, and together they melted some of the metal and created two rings for themselves using the broken halves of the Orb. After putting the rings on, they felt guided by the Orbs and created two pendants for their wives, made from smaller Orbs. Over the next few months, the smith and the craftsman created exceptional quality jewelry with the shards, and a magnificent sword with the remainder of the extracted metal and the last five small orbs. As if by fate, a different traveler bought each piece as they completed it. They all said they had felt drawn to stop in the small town and then visit the craftsman.

"The final three large Orbs were fitted into simple gold and silver bands and attached to a chain. As the craftsman finished the settings, each Orb guided him to find the person who would bear the Orb of Power. His own Orb in his ring began to show him visions that the blacksmith and himself would travel searching for the Bearers of the Orbs of Power. Their wives accompanied them, each bestowed gifts by the Orbs they wore to help them on their journey; the blacksmith gained foresight and his wife a gift for alchemy, the craftsman gained intuition, and his wife the gift of telepathy.

"The four traveled vast distances over many years to find the Bearers, until they bestowed the Orbs of Power to a genuine and kind-hearted knight, a girl aged five, and a teenage boy born slow of mind."

"Hmm," Taylor thought a moment. "That gives me some context and suggests your world fell into chaos from something better. But still, the buildings could have been from the time of the first Bearers. Is there anything in your texts that would support that?

Rayla frowned, "Maybe, but all I could find in my reading was bits and pieces of the first Bearers. Octave, the knight, became a great warrior and advisor to the king he served. He influenced the king to begin constructing what eventually became Glydane, our capital city. Finally, he thought to retire from his work as the king's counsel and removed his Orb. However, he discovered that his increased abilities gained—intellect, the evolution of self, and spiritual growth—remained. It was a significant loss when he died in an avalanche at one hundred and ninety-seven years old, looking still like a man in his forties. He had long since passed the Orb on to the next Glydane, knowing it was time for someone new.

"When asked why she waited to don the Orb, the young girl Mazze said the Orb had instructed her not to. She grew to the age of twenty-seven before she donned her Orb and soon urged the construction of a great library, stating that knowledge was a key to becoming a better people. She became a great scholar and, eventually, a great leader. Living to the age of two hundred and forty-seven, she spent the last sixty years of her life without the Orb. Her passing was fifty years after the accidental death of Octave.

"The last of the three to receive an Orb, the boy Egeldor, found great intelligence and became a renowned sorcerer and healer. Egeldor also became a champion of peace, quelling many battles, and he used his prophetic gifts to lead many leaders to the right path. However, his best-known Prophecy was that the Orbs would be the downfall of the civilization he helped create. He also prophesied that a man from another world would save them when their world was again torn apart by war.

"The Orb, through Prophecy, showed him visions of the future that disturbed him so much that he left the civilized world. Before the other two passed away, he entrusted his Orb of Power to Octave, the knight, and Mazze, the scholar, who had become trusted friends. No one could ever find Egeldor, and it isn't known when or where he died. Thus, all three did many great things individually during their time with the Orbs. However, none compared to the foundation of the leadership of The Orb Bearers that they built together."

"But no mention of other cities?" Taylor rubbed his chin in thought. "Could Egeldor have built them when he left?"

Rayla shrugged, "There is a chance, I suppose, but it's not likely." They both fell silent and continued exploring.

Chapter Twenty-Two

Late on their fourteenth day, they found a site that met Taylor's criteria. It was a large clearing at the base of the mountains, where a river raged to the side. He had seen plenty of game in the last couple of days, fulfilling their hunting needs. The small brook they followed had joined a large river coming down from the mountain above. There were the remnants of several old foundations, and the land to build upon was plentiful. The brush and small trees could be further cleared when Rayla's people were ready to plant crops. After only a short time in the area, Rayla discounted it as feasible. Taylor was disheartened and argued his points, but Rayla would not budge on her decision.

Taylor awoke the next day to the smell of meat cooking. "I thought you were going to sleep all day Taylor. It's already well past dawn. This trek must be wearing you out," Rayla jested with a smile.

He rubbed his eyes, sat up, and stretched. The disappointment of yesterday still lay heavy on Taylor's mind. It had been too late to carry on from the clearing after they had explored it. So, they had set up camp by the river. Taylor looked around at the area and still wondered why Rayla had dismissed the site. "Other than this place, we have not seen any sign of a site that would be suitable for a new home. What is it exactly that you're looking for?" Taylor asked.

"It's a combination of things; for instance, the area needs to be defensible." Rayla stood and gestured, "Look down the valley in each direction. The direction we came from was a rougher terrain, with trees for cover on each side of the stream. This would allow an enemy easy access to march a force of men through it without us noticing first. The other way down the ravine has no vegetation and is even terrain. I can see straight down the ravine we are in for at least a day's walk. If you have a closer look, though, it splits in two directions a quarter day's walk from here. The route that cuts off and takes a sharp turn creates a blind spot.

"While we can see a great distance straight, we can't see around the ravine's bend. This means posting outlooks at the curve and further up it. Otherwise, someone could sneak up on us and be only a quarter day's walk from here. Posting militia to guard these routes uses up valuable resources, a hurdle we could overcome, but there is still more to consider. The ravine walls are shallow here, allowing for an open attack position from above us. An attacker could literally walk down the embankment with ease.

"Last of all, you may have noticed that we have been walking down a slight slope, and the ravine widens and levels out here. Then further up, the ravine narrows and has a slight rise again. If you look at the riverbank, you can see the ravine walls have no growth for several feet upward. The embankment has been worn away by water over time during the rainy season. This area is a flood plain! When I checked the walls on the other side of the ravine beside the ruins, they were recently worn there too. Even though the ruins are on higher ground, it's still part of the flood plain. The erosion of the walls by the ruins' site is five to six feet up the ravine wall. I'd say that the ruin site only floods every thirty to forty years when the more significant rains come. But it's likely enough to have swept the buildings downriver when they were still standing.

"The flood plain aside, each of the problems has remedies. Unfortunately, my people don't have the luxury of time or militia staff to manage them all. It would be disastrous if Tarak were to find us again before we were prepared. Did your ancestors not build fortifications like this in your history?" Rayla asked.

Taylor had not considered the necessities needed to defend the area Rayla's people would live in. She had just exposed how ignorant he was on this journey. The flood plain explained why the place had only shrubs and no standing trees and why the foundations' enormous stones had been worn. He felt a little stupid. Had this been a dig site at home, he would have been laughed at. He felt the sting of his ignorance and only managed a nod of his head in response.

"My people traveled further out into the mountains, all those years ago to the Refuge, to help evade detection. Discovering the Refuge was unbelievable luck. We have sentry posts throughout the area, allowing us to send warnings of attack to the Refuge and the surrounding villages. Your running into those soldiers saved us considerable trouble. We have the foreknowledge that Tarak has found us. The Refuge would have only been defendable for a short time. Our best defense there was not being found. We must again move further into the mountains for our home's new location, hoping Tarak's men won't find us. But the area still needs to be defendable, and in a reasonable amount of time after moving our people there. Natural boundaries are essential for slowing Tarak's men down should they find us, and the more confined the entrance, the better.

"Eighteen thousand people take a great deal of time to move, and that is a lot of traffic through a single area. If Tarak's men find our Refuge before we can cover our tracks, the trail we leave behind will lead them straight to us. If we are unprepared because our new home isn't defendable right off, it will undo us.

"There are two Shard Carriers among us that can combine their magic to cause rapid regrowth of any plant. I have asked if they will stay behind and cover our tracks. But the trail that eighteen thousand people make will take them at least two months to regrow enough to hide our escape. So you see, there isn't just one piece of the puzzle I need to think of, but all of them," Rayla finished.

"I hadn't considered all of the details," Taylor said solemnly. "I see why you're so well-respected. You have great merit as a leader. This will be a lot more work than I had considered!" Taylor got out from under his blanket, moved over to the fire, and held out his hands to warm them. The evenings and mornings had been colder in the last few days. If the weather was similar to Earth's, the season had changed. He took the plate of cooked hen Rayla handed him and ate.

"It will take a miracle to accomplish," Rayla said under her breath.

Chapter Twenty-Three

"We should pack up and get moving, Rayla suggested after they had eaten. I have been thinking, we should follow the bend in the ravine. It leads back in the general direction of the rendezvous point."

"Sounds good to me," Taylor agreed, still feeling the sting of his ignorance earlier on.

"After you." Taylor gestured for Rayla to go ahead of him.

"This ravine might enter some territory I hadn't intended to explore," she ventured. "But it will be worth our time seeing as we have had such hard luck so far."

"We have indeed," Taylor agreed.

The ravine meandered through the bottom of the mountains for another day, before it came to an abrupt end at the bottom of two mountains. It took two days of climbing to find a pass through. Rayla guided them to the bottom of the mountain pass as the sun began to set. She stood looking at the darkening sky, "I should be able to judge our position from the stars once it's a little darker. If you collect a bit of wood to build a fire with, I'll find us some dinner."

"A steak would be nice!" Taylor joked.

"I'll see what I can do," Rayla retorted.

Taylor busied himself building a rock ring and collecting wood in the twilight. With the wood gathered, he pulled out his tinder box and flint, and worked away at making the fire. Rayla pushed through the brush as the flames came to a roar, a long stick fashioned into a spear in hand. There was something at the end of the spear, but Taylor could not distinguish it until she was at the fire. At the end of the spear, two of the most enormous spiders Taylor had ever seen. Their legs still wriggled as they worked to free themselves.

"I'm not eating that," he grimaced.

"Where is your sense of adventure?" Rayla chided. "They're quite tasty, and they're rather meaty." Rayla jabbed the butt end of the stick into the ground and leaned the spiders over the fire so they would start cooking. "They taste better if you cook them alive."

Taylor grimaced at the meal when it was finished cooking. Rayla had pulled two large leaves off a tree and used them as serving plates. "You're really going to—" Taylor began.

Rayla took a big bite out of the spider; there was a bit of a crunch. She chewed and swallowed. "Go on. You will like it."

Taylor took a reluctant bite. The crunch of the shell was a little odd. But then the meat of the spiders' flavor kicked in. "It's spicy! And... it does taste a little beefy. It's almost like a taco without any fix'ns."

Rayla wore a knowing smile, then continued to eat the rest of her meal in silence. "All done. I need to get an idea of where we are, if you will excuse me." Rayla took a few steps away, turned her back to the fire, and looked up at the stars. "We are a little off track. As I had guessed, the pass has put us in a region that wasn't assigned to be searched. But we should be able to get to the meet-up location with a little extra effort."

They had yet to find any site that would accommodate their needs, only days from the rendezvous. Both were weary of the journey, with their hopes dashed, and were ready for its end. Both had voiced small hopes that the other parties had had better luck. If they had found ruins where neither of them had expected to, the others might have too.

As midday approached, they stopped, ate foraged roots, and filled their water skins in the stream. Rayla squatted down, washing her hands, which Taylor had learned meant she was ready to move on. The thickened foliage forced them into the stream at times as they continued. The tall, thick trees blocked much of the sunlight and kept them in the shadows. When they came to an impasse along the river, they were forced to more challenging ground. The extra effort left them to their thoughts, and an hour passed without words between them.

Taylor's mind wandered back to the dream he'd had of kissing Rayla. He played the moment in specific detail through his mind; how she smelled, her touch, the warmth of her lips on his. The dream shifted, and they were in bed underneath the covers. She lay propped up on her arm beside Taylor, her warm body pressed against him. She leaned in and kissed him; the daydream felt so real that he felt himself becoming hot. While the encounter unfolded in the fantasy, Taylor noticed a strangeness in his mind. As if someone was there in his daydream, yet there was more.

Suddenly the dream took on a life of its own. Rayla no longer did as he fantasized in the dream. Rayla leaned back and smiled at him, "You have interesting fantasies, Taylor. Though it's a little one-sided."

Taylor snapped out of his daydream as he understood what had happened. He'd heard Rayla's voice in his head. "Really, Taylor, you shouldn't broadcast your thoughts!"

Taylor looked up the path where Rayla stood. She wore a wry smile on her face. "I, I, I," Taylor stuttered, quite embarrassed.

"You're entitled to your fantasies, no matter how steamy they are. But remember, there is more to me than my body!" Rayla said. An aurora of self-confidence emanated from her before she turned forward again.

"HOLD IT RIGHT THERE!" A voice demanded as two large masked men stepped out from behind the trees. Both held their swords raised in an attack stance. Taylor jumped in surprise, and a jolt of fear raced through him.

Rayla passively looked over the two young men; one was tall, lanky, and dark-skinned, and the other was shorter and stout, with white hair and reddish skin. She let out a breath of exasperation. "You two are a constant nuisance. Tae, don't you ever tire of your pranks?" Rayla asked. One of the men relaxed and shrugged his shoulders. "As for you, Zem, couldn't you for once greet someone with civility?"

Zem laughed and lowered his sword, "We caught you off guard, Rayla! Is someone distracting you?" Zem asked and nodded toward Taylor, "I haven't ever seen you drop your guard so much. Maybe you should pay more attention to the surroundings you're traveling in—rather than the man you're traveling with. The Rayla I know wouldn't have let us sneak up and ambush her."

Rayla rolled her eyes. "I heard you some distance back.

You two move through the forest like a pair of thundering beasts. And it's not too late for me to give you a lesson in manners." Rayla replied, pressing her lips together.

"I see you still lack a good sense of humor as always," Zem said as he reached out his hand and greeted her.

Rayla smiled at him, clasped his hand, and shook it, then greeted Tae with a handshake as well. The whole thing seemed like a jest that had occurred frequently. Rayla's voice became more at ease, and she said, "You're lucky I heard you two snickering in the bushes. Otherwise, you might have gotten a dagger in the chest." She paused and looked at the two of them as a thought occurred. "What are you two doing out here? There isn't supposed to be anyone out in this direction."

With his initial fright passed, Taylor realized who the men were, now that they had exposed their faces. They had scared the wits out of him when they jumped out, and he had lost control for a moment. Taylor took a deep breath while they talked, and recalled a moment when he had felt at peace. The rolling hills of his grandparents' ranch and the sound of his mother calling him floated into his mind, a memory from a time when he was around four. The simple recall of her voice brought his mind into a state of ease.

He was glad they had not actually rushed them. He might have done something terrible to them—something he would have regretted. Tae broke his thoughts, patting Taylor on the shoulder.

"Come, we have something to show you," Tae said in excitement. They led them a short distance through the woods and connected with a different game trail. After twenty minutes on the path, the trees thinned while the trail itself began to hug the embankment of the mountain's base. The trail started sloping downward, and after a few minutes of walking, they found themselves only a few feet up from the bottom of the ravine.

As they rounded a sharp corner in the path, they found themselves at the entrance of a large clearing and the end of the ravine. The trees dead-ended there, and the game trail they were on continued to wander down into the cleared area. It briefly met up with the river that flowed from the ravine and off into the unseen. The river itself flowed to the left of where they stood, along the mountain's sheared-off side, where it emptied into the large lake. Mountains continued encircling the cleared area, each sheared-off, making an unnatural-looking barrier. Taylor took a moment and looked out into the ring of steep cliffs that surrounded the area.

The embankment turned into a thirty-foot-high wall of sheer granite to their right, and vines covered it from top to bottom. The clearing itself was overgrown with small trees, which struck odd to Taylor. The trees there should have been much more substantial. It looked as if, in recent years, the area had been logged, or a fire had swept through.

They walked along the wall a little way into the more open area before Tae stopped at the base of the wall.

"Here we are! So what do you think?" Tae asked as he gestured toward the wall.

"This is exactly what we need!" Rayla exclaimed.

"No, about that!" Tae gestured toward the cliff face.

"I think it's a wall of solid rock, which makes this place very hard to get to. No one would even consider climbing down the mountains anywhere along the edge. It looks as though there is a plateau at the top here. I could use the Orb to get up there and get a better view of the area." Rayla said with joy in her voice. "The two of you have possibly saved our people."

"She doesn't see it!" Zem said to Tae dramatically. "This looks like a normal rock wall, but watch this." Zem walked up to the wall, pushed through the vines, walked right in, and dramatically back out.

"A cave?" Taylor said aloud. "That is going to save us?"

"Not quite." Tae said as he gestured inside, "Why don't you have a look for yourselves."

Taylor and Rayla walked through the vines to find themselves in an archway. Zem and Tae followed in after them and picked up burning torches off the floor they had left at the entryway. Tae handed Taylor and Rayla each unlit torches, which ignited when Rayla's Orb flickered.

Tae looked at Rayla. "I love that! The hallway is about twenty strides long, and there is an unusual metal door at the end, like no other I have ever seen," Tae said excitedly.

"Why do you have two extra torches?" Taylor inquired, frowning at the two of them.

"You see," Tae began, "I thought we ought to leave a couple of lit torches here at the entrance. So we wouldn't get lost while we explored, which was Zem's job. But he got very excited—"

"It was exciting," Zem interjected, "Very exciting."

"And so," Tae dropped back in, "he forgot to light them before we walked into the cave."

Taylor nodded his understanding as he stretched out his torch to better look at the construction of the entrance and hallway. The archway was six feet across and was, in fact, a doorway to the passage. The metal frame of the archway was heavily reinforced and cast in one piece. He moved the torch to the side of the passage, and sure enough, there was a massive, foot-thick metal door. He could see no bolts or locking mechanisms, contrary to the door's construction. He looked a little closer and saw what he was looking for, the bars of steel set in the door: Bars that slid out to fit inside the frame it hung in, locking it. "This shouldn't be here ... it's too complex." He moved the torch about, looking for a mechanism to slide the bars out of the door. "How is the lock activated? That is the question," he said aloud to himself. "Not that I could open it as it is with the hinges rusted in place. The door has been that way for some time, by the amount of rust." When he didn't find a way to release the locking bars, something dawned on him. "Is this electric? How could that be?" He looked over at the others —Rayla, Tae and Zem had not said a word to him since he began rambling.

The others stared at him, bewildered at what he was saying. *They haven't seen technology of this sort. They have no idea what I'm talking about. Though it speaks to the other ruins I have explored here.* He moved the torch about the wall beside the entryway and found what he looked for. There, on the wall, was something akin to a panel. It was a large oval shape, and set into it, there was an impression of a hand. The panel itself was a dull gray from the grit and dust of years gone by. Taylor pulled a handkerchief from his pocket and started to wipe the dirt away. To his surprise, the grime came free quite quickly, and the panel was not hard, but soft and impressionable. Once cleaned, it was a silver color, with a slight backlit glow.

Chapter Twenty-Four

"That is unbelievable, Taylor," Rayla said excitedly.

"How did you know that was there?" Tae asked.

Taylor thought a moment before he said anything. Tae and Zem did not yet know he was from another world, nor that he had an Orb. "It just seemed like it should be," he said. Curiously Taylor reached out and placed his hand in the impression in the panel. There was not much chance it would work, but the dull backlight meant it had power. As his hand touched the surface, something unexpected happened. It began to glow a blue color and became a thick, liquid-like substance. It flowed up out from the panel to surround his hand. It all happened so quickly that Taylor had no time to act. Once the substance had covered his hand, it hardened and trapped it inside.

Rayla gasped, "Careful, Taylor, you don't know what might happen."

A constant eerie hum began emitting from the panel, which caused Taylor tremendous anxiety. His hand was stuck, and he had triggered what could only be described as a magical security system. He expected any minute for something dire to happen. He turned to the others to see Tae and Zem standing there; their mouths hung open in shock. Rayla grabbed hold of Taylor's arm and started to pull. When his hand did not come free, Rayla tugged on his arm with all her might, one foot up on the wall for leverage. The panel stopped humming suddenly, and the substance receded. They tumbled back to fall on the floor. With a thud, Taylor landed on top of Rayla.

Everyone was still for a moment as a clicking sound began. To Taylor's surprise, globes of light appeared from bracers attached to the passage's wall. The lights were dim but began to shine brighter after only a moment, illuminating the hallway. The floor was covered in debris, and there were visible signs of habitation by animals, though they were old.

They were jarred back to reality as the door's mechanisms engaged and worked to close it. Taylor jumped up and hastened the others to run outside before they were trapped. But before they could act, the door gave a loud grinding noise of effort then ceased. The door had resisted any movement due to the years of being weathered. The blue hue faded from the panel, and all was silent.

Rayla stood up and brushed herself off, "Taylor, what did you just do?"

"I'm not sure, but some of the things I have seen on our travels are starting to make sense." Taylor got up and looked down the long, stone corridor to the far end where the other door was. "Shall we continue?" He did not wait for their answer and walked away down the passage at a slow pace. Rayla followed immediately, while Tae and Zem took a moment and discussed if they should follow. In the end, curiosity won them over, and they both rushed to join them.

When Taylor reached the door at the other end of the hall, he found the panel he suspected would be there. He cleaned it and placed his hand upon it, and the same rush of magical liquid formed around his hand. But instead of emitting a hum, the liquid receded immediately. The panel began to glow slightly brighter, pulsing as it did. Taylor looked at Rayla. She shrugged her shoulders and gave him a curious look.

Taylor leaned in for a closer look, and as he did so, the same liquid metal shot out from the panel. It enveloped his head from below his eyes, up and around to the base of his skull, holding him fast. A series of bright lights flashed in his eyes, and the liquid metal receded. Momentarily blinded, Taylor stumbled back and bumped into Tae. A chime sounded, the door's locking mechanisms released, and the door swung open.

Taylor stood there a moment as he recovered, the spots in his eyes still limiting his vision. Sunlight shone into the hallway as the door opened, helping Taylor's eyes adjust. Rayla led the way this time, stepping over the threshold and taking several paces into the long grass that grew beyond.

Across an immense field lay what had once been an expansive city. Now though, it was mostly a pile of rubble and stone, with the exception of a small portion of the city that had a few partially standing buildings. Within that area, Rayla could see that there stood one last building stood intact in its center; a sizable dome with a shining glass top.

As Taylor stepped up beside her, she felt her heart quicken. Just his presence made her fill with joy. "Are you able to see?" she asked.

"Yes, and I can't believe what I'm seeing," he responded, his voice full of excitement. "This is unbelievable!"

"This city may be in ruin, but it was a fortified one," Rayla said in awe. She pointed up, "The granite wall we just walked through encircles the city three-quarters of the way around."

"And the wall joins to the side of the sheer face of this enormous mountain," Taylor finished Rayla's thought. "The builders of this city cleared half of the mountain away to create the groundwork for it."

"I can't believe it," Rayla declared, "I don't believe our luck."

"Ehem," Tae cleared his throat. "It took us almost all day to find the entrance. If I hadn't had my shards with me, I would have never known to look for it." Tae pulled back his hair and exposed an ornate earpiece made of silver, with several shards of crystal inlaid into it so they touched the skin of his ear. "The moment I stepped into the field outside, I knew there was something profound here. When we saw the door, we knew we had to find you. The earpiece led me straight to you." Tae paused and looked around. "We figure that this has been here for some time. And by the look of the overgrowth on the buildings, this place has been abandoned for a few hundred years. How can that be, Rayla? How would we not have known the people that built this city were here?"

Taylor interjected himself into the conversation, excited to share his knowledge, "If you look further back to the mountain wall, they carved the buildings right out of the stone. They have seen hard times, but it's still amazing work. I have seen similar work before, but never on such a large scale on Earth. Every building here is carved right out of the rock. This would have taken generations with thousands of people. And look at the lines of the buildings that are still standing. They're perfectly straight! Oddly, the decay of the buildings and the growth of the trees and vines aren't consistent throughout the city." Taylor pointed, "See there at the far side of the city, the buildings are completely collapsed. And the trees growing there must be at least a thousand years old from their size. But as you move in toward the center of the city, the deterioration of the buildings decreases, as does the size of the trees. From an archaeological standpoint, I'd say from the deterioration that the outer city was abandoned several thousand years ago. Yet, this field and the inner city have been abandoned less than two hundred years."

"Taylor!" Rayla scolded.

In all his excitement, Taylor had dropped his guard. When Tae and Zem gave Taylor a strange look, he knew he had said too much. Their civilization had crumbled, and no one much cared about studying old cities. They were too busy trying to stay alive. Tae stepped forward; the shards in his earpiece glowed bright green—he was using magic to see the unseen. A surprised look spread across his face. "You have an Orb!" he said, "Kalamar's Orb."

Taylor sputtered and tried to explain. Tae lifted his hand and motioned for Taylor to stop his panic. Excitement swept across Tae's face and he said, "You're him! From the Prophecy. Thank the stars." Tae swung his arm back and swatted Zem, who stood with his mouth open, "Close your mouth," he whispered.

Zem did so and stepped forward with his hand out,

"About damn time you got here. Tae and I have talked so many times about what it would be like when you finally came. I just never expected to be one of the first to know."

Rayla sighed in relief, "The two of you need to keep this to yourselves. Not everyone will be so welcoming. And Taylor, perhaps you could contain your excitement when it comes to dusty old cities and not out yourself."

Taylor smiled awkwardly, "Sorry about that, but it has turned out OK." He shook both their hands, and they stood a little taller and took on more of a presence of maturity. Taylor continued, "I studied ancient places on my world. However, there were none the likes of this. Back on Earth, this would be a find of a century. I could spend my whole life exploring this place." Taylor looked around in bewilderment.

Rayla took a big breath and exhaled loudly;

"Made of metal, stone, and glass,
Horseless carriages,
Light to ever last,
A place of beauty for all to die,
Lost and forgotten,
As time went by,
A hundred lifetimes or more to wait
Till disease is gone,
And so is hate,
Then again, we shall return,
Beauty found,
and much to learn.
To seek the knowledge therein bound,
Before the time of the return,
Beware the time of forbidding,
Or become one of the Delwirn,

> When a hundred lifetimes have come to pass,
> Go to the dugout mountain,
> And through the bounded gate at last,
> The city's guardian will lie in wait,
> Use your hand upon the plate,
> To bring her at last awake."

Rayla recited the nursery rhyme without missing a word.

"Could it be, do you think?" Zem asked. "The actual lost city?"

Taylor looked at Rayla in confusion, "Do you care to elaborate?"

"It's a rhyme we say to our children." Rayla looked at him and then to the city in front of them. "Everyone here knows it, that you'd become a sickening beast if you went in before the time of return. It was said that the curse would eventually fail, and we could enter again. But I always thought it was a myth."

"Well, let's hope the time of return is now. Or the doors have opened for us to walk into our deaths or worse from the rhyme," Taylor replied.

"One would hope, though, that a magical security system wouldn't have let us in if there was still a curse about," Tae added, eager to explore.

"Let's look around and see what kind of condition the less deteriorated parts of the city are in. It looks as though there is a direct path that would be easy to traverse." Rayla pointed across the field to a roadway that seemed less overtaken by nature.

After following the path through the city streets for

several miles, its buildings and roads started to appear to be in better condition. Buildings here were intact, though the exteriors were faded and aged by time. Little or no debris was seen here in the streets and sidewalks, and the vegetation was small, indicating it had only been growing a short time. Eventually, the road changed to one of perfect condition, almost as if its stones had been freshly laid.

Their journey along the cleared road ended at the tall polished dome in the city's center. It was frozen in time and showed no signs of decay or deterioration like the other buildings here. Its height rose above the others, and it was topped with clear shining glass, as freshly cleaned and repaired as the roadway that had led them through the streets of the decaying city. So too was the set of stairs it ended at. The stonework could almost have been said to shine. All thirty of the steps led to the entrance to the building before them.

Chapter Twenty-Five

Taylor and Rayla walked up the steps and to the large wooden doors, each bound with iron, set into an archway. He pushed on one, and it glided open, allowing light to penetrate the darkness within. Rayla stepped to his side while Tae and Zem hung behind them. When Taylor's boots touched the floor inside, balls of light came to life above braziers at the walls. All of them stopped, shocked at what they saw. With the giant room illuminated, he could see that there were ornate murals of strange scenes, twelve in all. None of the scenes resembled anything he had seen or heard of here or on Earth. Rayla guessed these were different worlds by the buildings, animals, and plant life. In front of each were small obelisks, roughly four feet high. It made the archaeologist in him ache. *What are those doing here?* The obelisks sat atop a raised platform directly in the center and flowed out from symbols that looked alchemical in nature.

Taylor looked down to the floor at his feet to see similar symbols spread throughout the room. The design, in its entirety, brought his eyes to the center of the room, where a single spiraling staircase flowed up to a second floor.

Rayla broke the silence, "It's breathtaking! What do you think this room could have been used for? Some sort of museum?"

"Whatever the purpose, the stairs at the center seem the likely place to go," Taylor said as he began walking forward.

"This is quite possibly the most interesting place I have ever seen," Rayla said as they walked. "The great city pales compared to the architecture and the wonder here in this building. These murals are massive! I can't even imagine what it would have taken to paint them."

She looked over at Taylor when he did not chime in. He was lost in what he saw. The gleam in his eyes suggested that he was studying this place far more astutely than she was. "Honestly, Taylor, don't you ever look at something for its beauty?"

Taylor looked at her, "Those obelisks shouldn't be here!"

She watched as he pointed to the stone shapes in front of the murals. "How do you know that the ob-i-lasts shouldn't be there?" she asked.

Taylor looked perturbed. "No, I don't mean they shouldn't physically be there. The concept shouldn't be present in this structure. We have them on from Earth! The symbol occurring here also is highly unlikely. And it's o-be-lisk."

Rayla thought, "Perhaps it's the other way around. Perhaps they should not be on Earth because they exist here."

Taylor looked a little like she slapped him for a moment. "Point taken!" he nodded and halted at the stairs. A small smile spread across his face. He looked at her, then took the first of many stairs. "I hope you don't mind being watched."

Rayla glanced around the room, "Do you see someone?" She had her hand on the pommel of her sword in an instant. Her Orb began to glow.

"Because of all the stares! Get it?" Taylor laughed at his joke.

"Jesus, Taylor!" She cursed. "It's a good thing I like you. Your sense of humor is even poorer than Zem's sometimes. Which I didn't think was possible!" she said as she glanced at him sideways.

"Hey!" Zem shouted from behind, "I'd never say anything so lame." Tae laughed but did not say anything.

"'Jesus Taylor?'" Taylor frowned. "That's a little colloquial, don't you think? Lilly used to say that to me. She thought I was corny too."

"I know!" was all she said as she followed him up the stairs. She could hear him mumbling to himself. He stopped after a few moments, and they climbed in silence.

At the top of the staircase, they found themselves under the glass dome. This would have been a great way to view the city. It still provided a great view, but the city looked a little worse for wear. "It would have been beautiful here when the city was still intact," she said aloud.

"It was!" A woman's voice said.

As they stood there frozen in surprise, the Orbs at her and Taylor's chests flared to life, fiercely glowing a bright blue hue. The same light caught their attention as it emanated atop a pedestal a yard high, a few paces ahead of them in the room. There, encased in a small six inch glass dome roughly across, sat an exact duplicate of the Orbs Rayla and Taylor wore. She took a sharp breath in surprise.

As Taylor and Rayla stood there staring at the Orb, a woman materialized at its side. Tall and thin, she had long blonde hair, green eyes, and wore a long, elegant, blue and white dress. The woman turned to Taylor, "Hello, my name is Milthra. Welcome to Naeim, your ancestral home, Legatee Ximen. Though I'm surprised to see someone of your lineage here. Your people left this world long ago."

Milthra turned and looked toward Rayla, "And who might you be?" Milthra lifted her hand toward Rayla; it began to glow a purple hue.

Concern began to rise in Rayla, but not soon enough. A ray of purple light shot out of Milthra's hand and enveloped her. The light held her tight for a moment, and a tingling sensation swept through her. She could see out of the corner of her eye that Tae and Zem had drawn their swords. But a ray of light had enveloped them too, and they stood frozen in place. Taylor stood with a look of shock on his face. He was frozen in his spot in fear, though, not from any sort of magic.

The beam of light stopped suddenly, and all three were released. Rayla drew her sword, and Tae leaped forward, lunging his sword into Milthra. But instead of causing her harm, Tae and his blade went right through Milthra without as much as a cut. He regained his balance and turned quickly into a protective crouch. Zem hunkered down, sword out, angled toward Milthra.

Milthra smiled wryly, "I can't be wounded in such a way. I no longer have a physical form." She turned toward

Rayla, "I have been expecting you too, my dear, and both of you are long overdue. Welcome home, Legatee Amakhosi." Milthra turned to Tae and Zem in kind, "As have I waited for your peoples." She addressed Tae, then Zem "Kiosh and Murcer. Fitting that you two would be together; your houses were ever intertwined."

Rayla could see that Taylor had relaxed, but he had a puzzled look. Tae and Zem were still in protective stances, confusion on their faces. "How is it that you think you know us?" Rayla asked.

"I have been here for longer than you could understand," Milthra began. "This once-great city was home to many, including the houses of your ancestors. I'm a creature of magic, a wizardess if you will, though my people called us the Incoa. My job here was to maintain and protect this city. The magic Taylor used to gain entry here told me of whom he was. As it did with you just now."

Taylor spoke up this time, "And why did you say that my line had left long ago?

"Your ancestors once helped stand guard here in the city," Milthra replied. "The general you descended from left for another world, called Earth, hoping to get to his wife and bring her back to safety before the curse that was spreading from world to world, destroying the Navaden, reached there. He never returned. Against all odds, the curse appeared here as well. I managed to save a few from becoming Delwirn—men and women changed to primal beasts. All those that weren't affected had to leave here. I sent word using magic to the other world that no one should come back."

Taylor took her answer in, "So the people of this city fled? What happened to the infected?"

"I sent the uninfected out of the city walls, hoping they could survive in the wilderness long enough to return here." Milthra replied. "I had told them to return after the quarantine was complete. But they never returned."

Taylor's understanding of the universe had been turned upside down in the last weeks. He could not deny that Earth's mythology was full of stories of magic. Some people even believed it still existed. Rayla, Tae, and Zem all looked at him questioningly. They had taken Milthra's answer wholeheartedly, where he could not. Other, more apparent questions needed answering; he would ask more about this curse later. "How is it that you're incorporeal yet able to affect us physically?"

Milthra turned to the pedestal and the Orb that glowed there. "I was once mortal as you are, but my duty to our people called me to a higher purpose. I was aligned with the Vidre," she paused, "what you call Orbs, and its magic, where I now reside. I may appear to you as a specter, but my magic is very real.

"I see that you both have an Orb fashioned around your neck. Just like the magic of your Orbs can interact with the world around you, so can mine. Wearing an Orb was most forbidden in my time, however. It had unforeseeable consequences for Navaden and gave too much power to Vidreians. I understand why you can wear one Taylor, due to your magical bloodline. But you, Rayla, it should have absorbed your spirit."

"It should have what now?" Rayla asked.

Taylor spoke over the top of her, "How do you mean magical bloodline?"

Milthra turned to Taylor, "There are two types of life in

the stars: magical, referred to as Vidreian, and non-magical like the people I came from before I chose this form, called Navaden. They have battled for dominance since discovering each other. You're a mix of the Vidreian and Navaden bloodlines." She turned to Rayla, "However, you, Rayla, are Navaden through and through and shouldn't be able to use its magic. May I examine it?"

Rayla was reluctant. She was, however, intrigued by Milthra and what she was saying. She stepped closer to Milthra, "May I?" she motioned to wave through Milthra. When she nodded, Rayla passed her hand through Milthra and back again. *That is eerie! What harm can she do if she doesn't have a body? I'm not sure what a wizardess is, but if it's anything like the Power I wield, then she shouldn't be able to do anything against another Orb. I hope.* Rayla nodded her head for Milthra to inspect the Orb.

Milthra lifted her hand, and a ray of light emitted from it to touch Rayla's Orb. The beam of light lingered briefly and then stopped. "Interesting! These Orbs are changed. How did you come by them?" Milthra asked.

"They fell from the sky many thousands of years ago. My people have been using their power to help us rule in peace since the time of their settings."

"And how many are there?" Milthra asked inquisitively.

"There are three whole, one broken, and several shards and smaller Orbs," Rayla responded.

Milthra moved over to Taylor, and he nodded, giving her permission to scan his. "Interesting; again, this one is changed. And you, Tae, I sense that you have several shards. May I?"

Tae pulled back his hair, and Milthra examined the earpiece. Milthra frowned in sadness. "Pieces of an Orb," she frowned, "what a shame, the aligned spirit will forever be in turmoil. And where is the other Orb?"

"That will take some explaining," Rayla sighed. She related their tale and plight from Tarak.

"Then the Orbs led you home for a good reason. My city is in ruins from long abandonment. But it can be rebuilt. The water is still flowing here, there is plenty of game with grazing areas, and there was once plentiful land outside the wall for farming that can be retaken. You must bring your people back here so I may help protect them."

"When you say 'help protect them,' what did you mean? How could you protect Rayla's people?" Taylor asked.

Milthra's face turned serious, "With my and the city's magic, I could once lay entire armies to waste. But now, with my city destroyed and its magic with it, I have become bound to this Dome. I can no longer move past its walls. However, you would be safer here inside my walls."

Rayla had a curious thought, "Is there a way for us to use your magic at the Refuge? We wouldn't need to move all of my people if we could recreate your city's magic there. One of us could carry you."

"Could that work?" Zem stepped forward, "I'd be willing."

Milthra frowned, "It doesn't work that way, but thank you, Zem. It would be horrific for the person with spirit to hold me. The only way for me to protect you is for you to return here. I still have magic enough within me to keep your people safe inside the walls. With a little rebuilding, you will have a home here. It will take some time, but if all traces of your Refuge are hidden, along with the course you take here, Tarak would be hard-pressed to find you before I finished securing the city."

"That could be made possible," Rayla speculated. "The wards keeping the Refuge hidden could be maintained from a few miles away. We could leave Ria, the woman that creates the wards, with a small group of experienced trackers at the hunting camp. If Tarak's men find the Refuge, they would have plenty of time to escape."

"Moving all your people here, through the mountain range, and into the city will take some work, Rayla." Taylor speculated. "With your years of our ancestors living here, did they ever create an easier way to get through the mountains, Milthra?"

"There was a smaller settlement close to where you described the Refuge. But the road to there would be long gone by now. You will have to follow the original path you took to my city through the mountains. A hard trek for that many people." Milthra declared.

"I have been thinking of how to accomplish that, and I may have an idea or two," Rayla said. "I just need to work out all the moving pieces."

"It's settled then!" Milthra said excitedly. "I can't wait for my city to be inhabited once again."

The party took their leave of Milthra and talked of her, the city, and their next move. Rayla spoke of the organizing it would take to get their people mobilized. Zem interrupted her as they approached the wall. He pointed up, "I saw something I thought interesting. I could see the top of the wall at one point while we explored. I thought I saw what appeared to be lookout towers along the wall. If they are as I suspect, we could hold off a whole army from in here like Milthra said."

"They're indeed lookouts," Taylor spoke his thoughts aloud. He recalled having seen the same structures. "There are crenels and merlons on each of them."

"What are crenels and merlons?" Tae asked in confusion.

"That will take some explaining. I'll tell you while we set up camp," Taylor replied.

Rayla had gone silent as they spoke; she gazed off toward the field, and her face betrayed her thoughts. As she stood there, she worked on a solution to all the moving parts of getting her people here. "There is enough room here for everyone at the Refuge, the villages, and more," Rayla said to herself as she looked back at the city.

While the sun fell behind the mountain behind the city, they hurriedly set up camp. While they worked, Taylor did as he promised and explained that crenels and merlons were the gaps and uprights on a castle wall, which enabled soldiers to shoot arrows and hide. He then carried on about machicolations.

"So you'd drop stones on peoples' heads? Through holes above a doorway?" Tae said, part in shock and part in admonishment. "That's terrible and brilliant at the same time!"

"REALLY TAE!" Rayla scolded, "I know that you have a hate for Tarak's army, but we could never consider such a thing."

Tae did not retort, but Zem gave him a nod of confirmation that he understood. By the time their camp was set up and the cook fire started the sun had moved behind the mountain, and all at once, it was dark.

Chapter Twenty-Six

When the sun rose over the mountains at dawn, the four of them awoke and broke camp. Rayla moved quickly and finished before the rest. "We should eat our rations as we walk and get back to the Refuge as fast as we can. We can't be certain how long our people there will remain safe from Tarak."

"You're quite right," Zem said as he quickened his step, "There is no time to waste."

They had only a few days to collect the rest of their party and meet at the other groups' rendezvous. As the four of them trekked back through the mountains, Rayla kept them at a steady pace. "I hope that we can reach the rendezvous point before the other groups do. Taylor, you and I will continue on while Tae and Zem stay there to tell the others of the ruined city."

On the morning of the third day, they reached their first rendezvous, where the other five members of their party waited for them. Everyone happily greeted each other, then sat to speak. Tae excitedly filled them in about the ruined city they had found.

While the other members of the party were well-rested and ready to move on, Tae and Zem were not. The four of them ate a warm meal for the first time in three days, and both Tae and Zem slept for a short time. Meanwhile, the other five busied themselves and broke camp, during which Rayla explained her plan to return as fast as possible.

Strangely, Taylor did not feel he needed to rest at all. As the journey had progressed, Taylor had noticed that he needed less sleep and physical rest. Taylor joined Rayla, where she sat at the edge of the camp on a large boulder. "How is it that the Orb alleviates our need for rest?" Taylor inquired as he held it at eye level, inspecting it. It was more of a statement than a question.

She looked over at him and acknowledged what he already knew with a nod. "It isn't like when you were injured and it was able to heal you. It was using your own energy to do that. When we aren't using the magic within the Orbs, the latent magic does things we aren't in control of. I'm assuming you have noticed a decrease in your appetite?" She waited for Taylor's acknowledgment, then continued. "The Orb can help our bodies absorb more nutrients and energy from food at an accelerated rate. Typically we eat a great deal less due to the high energy absorption. But to warn you, we are well known for our appetite when we have work to do. Like healing or traveling."

"These are unbelievably powerful tools. It makes me wonder how they came here," Taylor looked at the Orb speculatively.

A voice interrupted Taylor and Rayla's conversation, "Are the two of you ready to go?" Tae said as he stepped in front of them.

"Yes, we are." Rayla jumped off the boulder and looked back at Taylor. "Coming?"

He followed her and joined the other party members as they walked through the forest. Wilderness survival came naturally to these people in their mountain homes. They quickly followed the trail they had left a month ago. Tae walked beside Taylor, talking about how it would take a long time to recreate what had been accomplished at the Refuge. Their hunting parties frequently used the area they walked through. Over the years, his people had learned the places in the surrounding mountains to find quarry, a practice spurned early on in the founding of the Refuge. Kalamar and the first settlers had hunted exclusively close to their new home for the first few months, exhausting the game there.

The game was plentiful enough if they rotated the hunting to different areas, though. Three to four parties went out daily, hunted overnight, and returned with the bounty the next day. Twelve thousand mouths ate a great deal, but Taylor had seen the game that they brought in. Large animals, akin to a moose, had to be parted up to be carried home. The parties often brought in giant flightless birds that Taylor thought looked like emus.

In the meadow back at the Refuge, Rayla's people tended gardens in the meadow to the side of the lake. Taylor had not initially noticed the gardens because they were tucked behind a row of trees. From the gardens, a short walk back through the trees and behind the lake, were several small fields of grains and hemp for clothing and rope. Still, what the Refuge had for food was not quite enough. The smaller hidden communities in the mountains had abundant space for crops and supplemented what the Refuge could grow.

Tae went silent suddenly, smiled, and thanked Taylor for the conversation. He dropped back to walk beside

Zem. *As lovely as he is, Tae is a strange fellow,* Taylor thought.

The party walked late into the evening before setting up camp. With the fall of darkness, it had become impossible to see the path they followed. They ate a cold supper of dried meat and hard bread while they talked excitedly of returning home with the news of the ruined city. Exhaustedly the party turned in for the night, all of them falling quickly asleep. When dawn broke, everyone promptly packed up and started the day's journey. Now in the more familiar area of their home, the party walked with ease. They reached the rendezvous point by mid-morning and found the other parties waiting for them. At least, what was left of them.

After they relieved themselves of their gear, Rayla and Taylor met with the two parties' leaders away from the camp. The first leader, Maud, reported that she led her party for seven days, searching the area assigned to them before one of their members was lost to an avalanche. Eleven days later, two more group members were lost in the night, attacked by mountain panthers. The area proved to be fruitless, and they returned without finding a location. The other group had also found nothing but had returned intact to wait for the others.

By the time the debrief was complete, the sun sat high in the sky, and everyone was ready to eat. Hunting parties had gone out earlier that morning and had returned with several rabbits. The midday meal sat prepared for them, and they collected their plates and sat with the group. Tae told the story of how he and Zem had found the city as he ate.

Everyone's interest piqued at how Taylor had opened the door.

Taylor sat on a log and listened to Tae's story, amused at how he lured everyone in. Rayla had sat on the opposite side of the fire from him. She had joined Maud and consoled her over her dear friends' death. Rayla hugged Maud, and she sat back and wiped her tears away. Rayla smiled at her before she stood and slowly worked her way toward him.

Taylor had spoken a few words to the others around him but had otherwise remained quiet and introspective. Staring into the fire, he had sat alone while he thought to himself. What had transpired since Rayla had brought him here played through his mind. Indecision about what he would do when he returned to the Refuge had set in. Lilly's death had left him an orphan of sorts; his father had passed during his second year at college. His friendships had been strained in the last year, and his connection to home seemed lessened.

The people here lived hard lives under the threat of death or slavery, yet they were still full of dignity, morals, and civility. It brought forth in him his innate sense of justice and the need to help. His anger toward Rayla that had blinded his sense of justice now waned, which had allowed him to see the full scope of Rayla's peoples' need for him, and hers as well.

Aside from Tae and Zem, no one else here could find out that Taylor had Kalamar's Orb or where Taylor was from. If things became complicated, it would cost them valuable time. Who he was would come out eventually if he chose to stay. Perhaps sooner if he was not more careful with the secret. He had barely managed not to use the Orb when Tae and Zem had surprised them.

"Do you mind if I sit and keep you company for a while?" Rayla asked, which snapped him out of his thoughts.

"No, not at all," he said, "Please sit." He moved over to make a spot for her. Those that listened to Tae cheered as he completed his story. Zem clapped him on the shoulder in camaraderie. A thought occurred to Taylor, "Zem and Tae, do they ever leave each other's side?"

Rayla smiled at Tae and Zem for a moment before her face saddened, "They came to us at the same time from a village that was raided. Neither of them was much older than eight. The two of them grew up as playmates, and their families were close. The day their village was raided and their families were killed, the two were out exploring the countryside. Had they not been, they would have suffered the same fate as everyone else in their village.

"Upon returning home, they were faced with the horrors their families suffered before they died. Days later, a passing traveler found them amongst the remains of the village. She brought them to us dirty, scared, and unwilling to be separated.

"For the longest time, they would only speak to each other. They were raised in the same home to help them adjust. They eventually warmed up to others, but your observation is mostly correct. They do leave each other's side but never for long. They're devoted to each other and love one another very much. Tae is due to marry next spring. I'm interested to know if he moves out or she moves in. Zem's girlfriend is already there morning and night. We might have to assign them larger quarters if they all start living together.

"When they were old enough to pick up a sword, they learned how to fight in unison. You wouldn't know it, but the two of them are a deadly combo. I believe that they look to one day exact vengeance for their families."

"Every day, I see more of how much Tarak has taken from your people," Taylor said solemnly.

"His grip reaches far," she replied. "You seem rather preoccupied this evening."

"I've been thinking a great deal about the city we found. How could something like that exist here, and your people know about it only in remnants of an old rhyme?" Taylor asked. "None of it fits within your people's history, even if the wizardess says your people are from there. That my ancestors were supposedly from there is shocking and stranger still. The city's degradation was so different throughout the city, meaning she maintained it for thousands of years. Why do that if your people didn't return when they were supposed to? It's all a lot to take in."

"I don't know how to answer any of it. The city, Milthra, our history, it's a mystery to me as much as it is to you," Rayla replied.

Taylor thought of the archaeological anomalies on Earth and the ancient alien theories that abounded as the global community became more connected. He had not put much salt in it before being abducted by an alien and brought to her world. A human that was intelligent and interesting, but still an alien. "Why, on such a large planet, would they build only one city? On my world, civilizations less advanced built many cities. It occurs to me that I have never asked. Are there no other people on this planet that could help you?" Taylor asked.

"In our golden age, we explored the seas. Nowhere else did we find other peoples. This is the largest landmass on my planet. For comparison, this continent is half the size of your 'Americas' on Earth. The other continents we discovered were small and few. it's written that some chose to settle on a few of the smaller islands, but because my people flourished here and wanted for nothing, most stayed here. As time passed, the islanders became distant, preferring to rule themselves. It has been many generations since we have had contact. I have hope that they at least remain free.

"Even still, we in our golden age never took to creating machines the likes of what your people did. We always used simple technology and our bodies to thrive. You explained to me on our trek that your people's population exploded with the invention of electricity. Without electricity here, our population never grew to the size yours has, and neither will have theirs. They wouldn't be of use to us in this war, and I'd rather spare them the horror of it." Rayla sounded saddened and worried as she spoke of the troubles they faced. They sat in silence for a moment before Taylor looked up to see Tae standing there.

In his youth, Tae had not yet learned to discern the mood of those around him. "We are eager to get moving Rayla, the others have packed their belongings. When do we leave?" Tae was bursting with excitement. He had made it known that he would be happy to be in the first group to go back to the city. He wished to explore it and make sure it was prepared for when the others came.

Rayla stood and smiled at him, "Let's get moving. We have at least eight hours left of sunlight. And two days' worth of travel to tackle." Tae moved with delight as he encouraged everyone to hurry with a cheerful voice.

The group moved swiftly through the woods, now on the well-worn path toward home. After so long away from their family and loved ones, they were all eager to be back with them. The day passed quickly, and that evening, fatigued, no one lit fires. They consumed cold meat and hard bread for dinner, and afterward, rolled out their bedrolls and settled for the night. For so many days, Taylor had camped with Rayla that, without thought, he set up his bedroll beside hers. Rayla's mood had lightened as the day had gone by, and she smiled as he lay down beside her. Strangely, she had chosen a tiny nook tucked away from the others in a grouping of trees. Taylor had needed to put his bedroll so close it touched Rayla's.

Chapter Twenty-Seven

"Thank you, Taylor, for helping us with the search," Rayla spoke in a quiet voice as they lay there. "We would never have understood what we had found, least of all gotten through the door, if not for you. Your knowledge of the like is something that none of us have. You have been of great help. I was hoping that perhaps, you could go with the first party there. To see what else you might discover," she paused hopefully and awaited his answer.

Taylor had come to feel more and more distant from his life back home in the last few days. His connection with Daphne, Rayla, and some of the people here had become important to him. The excitement of the city's discovery spurred his desire to uncover history, even if not his own. "I find myself as excited as Tae about the city. I'd like very much to return to the city and explore as much for myself as to help your people."

Rayla smiled to herself for both the fact that the Prophecy had taken hold and that the man she loved would stay. What would transpire for them, according to

Prophecy, still troubled her, though. She left the conversation there, and in the silence, they drifted off into sleep.

When Taylor woke in the morning, Rayla's head was snuggled on his chest while she slept. He felt a pang of joy in his heart with her there, something that had not happened in a long time. Taylor found himself thinking of his daydream of Rayla just before they had bumped into Tae and Zem. With so much going on, he had not thought of it since. Rayla had been there in his fantasy, actively participating. He was not sure what that meant, but he thought she felt something for him. What that was, was yet to be revealed.

Taylor felt Rayla stir. She lay there a moment before she moved slowly to sit up, doing her best not to wake him. But Taylor met her eyes when she looked down. Her cheeks blushed, and she gave him a small smile. "Sorry," she said, her cheeks showing embarrassment.

Taylor paused briefly before saying, "Ahhh, no harm done here," as he smiled awkwardly. She smiled at him with less embarrassment, and without saying a word, she stood, collected her things, and excused herself.

Taylor waited a moment to allow his heart to slow; the moment of embarrassment had made his heart rise into his throat. He packed up his gear and joined the others to find they were packed up also, and their eagerness grew as they got closer to their home. The party would reach home later, and it was unlikely any of them would rest until they were there. Rayla walked up to his side, hard bread in hand, and nudged him to take it. As he ate it, he understood that they would take breakfast this morning as they walked. There would be no stopping today.

Rayla set them at a steady pace at the front before she fell in beside one of the other women in their party. She gave Taylor a fleeting glance only twice the entirety of the morning. He felt conflicted by the way they had woken up together. Had he forgiven her? Had love overcome his anger? He sensed she felt conflicted, too, but her reasons were unclear.

In the mid-afternoon, Rayla broke off from her conversation with the woman she spoke with and walked alone. Taylor took a deep breath; he felt like a young teen working up his courage to talk to a girl he liked. He quickened his pace and approached her. "The terrain is beginning to look more familiar," Taylor said to her as he attempted to strike up a conversation.

Rayla gave him a small smile, "Yes, we are about three finger widths from home. I can hardly wait to tell Kalamar of the city. He will be relieved that we have found a new home for ourselves. Even more, that it's so well fortified." She smiled to herself, "And Daphne, I can't wait to wrap my arms around her. I'm sure she will be glad to see you as well, Taylor. She grew quite attached to you; honestly, she could talk of nothing else. You and her adventures in the woods were ever the topics of her chattering."

Taylor smiled, "I'm looking forward to seeing her." He paused and looked thoughtful, "I'll miss our alone time once we return and the chaos of moving your people begins. You're an interesting woman Rayla. There are many facets to you that I hadn't seen when you first brought me here."

"I think I'll miss it too, Taylor," Rayla replied, and the two continued without a word. The others fell silent with them in anticipation of their loved ones at the Refuge, which lay only a short distance away.

Tae broke the silence as he entered the clearing above the Refuge when he screamed, "Look, smoke overhead!" He pointed above the trees toward the Refuge. Within an instant, the whole party ran in panic toward their home. Rayla moved at an incredible speed; her Orb shone brightly as she outran them all. Taylor had seen the fear on her face, fear for Daphne, he thought. A woman's shriek echoed through the mountains, and Taylor thought he could hear steel against steel.

As they ran through the clearing, the path leveled out at the bluff, where Rayla had introduced Taylor to Daphne. *Taylor*, she thought and glanced back over her shoulder to see he trailed a small distance behind. She righted herself and headed for the lookout. There she would be able to see the source of the smoke, the smoke that hung about in the air that she could taste in her mouth. The noise of the battle below told the story, but she denied what her ears told her. Rayla reached further into the Orb and used more of its power, and willed it to make her body move faster.

As she approached the large oak a few feet from the lookout, where the grass became taller, she tripped on what she thought was a tree root and fell. She hit the ground hard but was back on her feet in only seconds. Blood ran from the deep gouge on her elbow, down her arm, and dripped from her fingers. Pain shot through her arm for an instant before the Orb dulled it. She was in such a panic to get to the edge of the lookout; she almost did not notice the legs of a body, not a root, she had tripped over.

Taylor skidded to a halt just before the man that lay there. With shock in his eyes, he knelt down. The look on Taylor's face brought the body that lay there fully into Rayla's awareness. Hurriedly she stepped back to the man that lay face down in the dirt. Her mind raced as she began to recognize him. Taylor turned him over as she knelt and revealed Kalamar's kind, elderly face.

Tears rolled down Rayla's face, her hand came up to cover her mouth, and she sobbed in heartache. A broken arrow protruded from Kalamar's chest. Here, under the oak, one of his favorite places to sit, they had shot him as he sat relaxing. He had lain down here and died. Rayla placed her head down on his chest in sorrow, and to her surprise, he took a shallow, ragged breath in. She leaned back as he looked up at her and placed her hand on his cheek. Her heart sank further as she felt the last of his spirit seeping out of her old friend. She sensed his final feelings of failure at not being able to save the people he had protected for so long. To her astonishment, Kalamar opened his mouth and spoke.

"Raayyllaa," he said in a weak voice. He caught hold of her eyes and projected his thoughts to her. *They waited until mid-morning when they knew we would all be out working in the gardens and fields. I thought it was safe, Rayla, that we were safe. His men waited, Rayla. Like they knew, we would all be out during that time.* His eye's clouded over as he exhaled, and his spirit slipped away.

"Hold on, Kalamar!" She said, crying fiercely, "I can heal your wounds, don't die yet." The Orb beneath her shirt glowed as she placed her hand on his chest.

"It's too late," Taylor said as he placed his hand on her shoulder.

"No!" Rayla shouted and pushed him back.

"We have to help the others," Taylor said as he pulled her around to face him.

Rayla had been so enveloped in Kalamar that she had not noticed the others run past them. She had not heard the screams of the people below. Nor the cries of her party as they reached the bluff and saw the horrid sight that awaited them. Rayla rose fluidly, turned, and ran as fast as she was able. Losing Kalamar was almost unbearable, but it would be nothing if she lost Daphne.

Taylor jumped up to follow her toward the meadow and ran as fast as he could. He worried about Daphne and her safety. The smoke, the party's screams, and fighting below could only mean one thing. The Refuge was under attack! At some point, unknowingly, Taylor had taken the Orb from his pocket and wrapped the chain around his wrist. He held the Orb tightly in his hand as its power flowed through him and made him aware of Rayla's panic for Daphne. As he followed the lookout path, Taylor caught sight of a horror scene as he broke through the trees into the meadow.

Smoke billowed from the entrance of the caves and brought to light what Taylor feared. In the meadow were soldiers on horse and foot that corralled women and children as they separated them into groups. While most of the militia had fallen, a remnant of the Refuge's defenses still fought at the furthest side of the meadow.

An army of Tarak's men, at least a thousand strong, occupied the meadow. And the trees at the edges of the meadow were filled with movement of still more of his men. A solitary man sat atop a large horse off to the side of the attack. A ring of soldiers surrounded him. He held one end of a chain that led to a collared man at his side. Taylor instantly recognized Colonel Careed at its end. Careed could barely stand upright, beaten and broken as he was.

The battle and the screams of the Refuge's people disoriented him for a moment, until he glimpsed Rayla as she ran at breakneck speed into the melee, her sword drawn, screaming in rage. He stood there, frozen and unsure of what to do. He had never witnessed a scene of such brutality. There was so much death and blood everywhere. Tarak's soldiers walked among the wounded on the field of battle and killed the men there. Still others of his men dragged off women from the crowd and raped them in plain sight.

Taylor searched desperately for Daphne. Finally, he caught sight of her out of the corner of his eye as she ran toward the lake. His heart leaped with fear for her and brought him out of his shock. His body felt heavy and wooden as he urged it to move toward her. For just an instant, his vision blurred, then cleared as he ran found himself running in a different part of the meadow. Somehow, he had transported himself across the meadow to where Daphne had been.

Chapter Twenty-Eight

His fear peaked when he realized she was nowhere to be seen. He peered back over his shoulder and looked frantically for her. Instead of her, though, he saw a horseman, sword raised to strike. The horseman rode straight for him and quickly closed the gap between them. He tried to quicken his pace as he cut toward the lake to dodge his pursuer, but his body refused to move faster. His body felt slow and strange, and the Power of the Orb seemed distant and unable to help him. He squeezed his hand where the Orb lay only to find it not there. "Mommy, where are you!" he heard himself scream.

At that moment, the horseman sped past and swung his sword at Taylor. The strike narrowly missed him as he ducked, and the sword swung just an inch above his head. He skidded to a stop at the edge of the lake, exhausted and unable to run anymore. He hunched over and breathed heavily as he stood over the reflection in the water. What he saw caught him by surprise. Where his reflection should have been, he saw Daphne's. Taylor was somehow seeing through Daphne's eyes, knew her thoughts, and felt her feelings. While he stared down at Daphne's reflection, what he felt physically and emotionally made sense. His inability to move faster or access the Orb, and the desire for Rayla's comfort and protection.

Confused in all that had happened, he had forgotten momentarily of Daphne's predicament. The figure that appeared in the reflection behind Daphne brought him back. She turned to a horseman with an arrow nocked in his raised bow. Fear swept through her anew. At that moment, Taylor saw himself across the battlefield. The soldier released the shaft, and time slowed. Daphne's voice shook with terror as she screamed, "TAYLOR!"

As the arrow sank into her chest and through her heart, Taylor felt her pain as she shuddered. He felt himself leave Daphne's body, and he jumped as he felt his consciousness slam back into his own. His eyes snapped open, and he looked toward the lake to search for the spot where Daphne had fallen.

His eyes landed upon Rayla with Daphne cradled in her arms. The soldier that had shot Daphne lay dead only feet away. Taylor ran across the field toward them as he dodged through the newly arrived search party members engaged in battle with Tarak's soldiers. He saw that men and women from other search parties burst out from the trees from different directions while he ran. The smoke had hastened their return, and with swords drawn, they rushed into the fight to repel Tarak's men. Taylor reached Rayla and Daphne, dropped to his knees before them, and with a shaken voice, asked, "Is she alive?"

Rayla shook her head, "She was only a child," she choked out to him as she closed her eyes tightly. Tears leaked out their sides and ran down her cheek. Rayla held Daphne to her chest for a moment before her eyes opened, pure hatred in them. She laid Daphne down, took hold of her sword from the ground beside her, and stood. She wiped away her tears while her anger caught hold of her. With a tightened grip on the pommel of her sword and the Orb that glowed at her neck fiercely, she shouted a war cry as she ran toward an unmounted horse and leaped into the air, landing on its back. With her sword raised, she raced into the battle.

Taylor watched as she rode off into the meadow and the full-out battle. He surveyed the brutality of it and was aghast. Both sides had taken casualties, but the losses on the Refuge militia side were far more substantial. Taylor could see several children's bodies among them, children that would be of no use to Tarak. He looked back down at Daphne's lifeless body, and anger started afire in him, which turned to rage.

The rage rushed through him as he looked up from Daphne to the battle. The Orb that had hung loosely off the chain at his wrist swung into his hand. The fullness of its power surged into him. He lifted the Orb to his neck as the chain came to life and wrapped itself around his neck of its own volition. The click of the clasp told him it was secured, and he let the Orb fall to his chest and stood. Power flowed from the Orb, and he knew suddenly how to kill in the most excruciating ways.

A warhorse from behind screamed and drew Taylor's attention. He reacted instinctively and flowed into a defensive crouch to face the warhorse. The soldier atop held his sword up for a striking blow, his eyes wild with bloodlust. Taylor felt the Orb's energy react as it glowed fiercely, working to protect him. Taylor threw his hand up and without thought, created a burning hot wind that emanated toward the horse and rider.

It blew toward the soldier and across the upper part of his body. The wind melted and stripped away the horseman's armor and helmet, and along with it, his skin. When the wind subsided, the soldier sat erect on the untouched horse, his muscles singed and his blood baked to them. The soldier screamed in agony through his lipless mouth. Taylor left him there; a quick death was too good for him, for any of them. What they had done was inexcusable; they would all die in the most horrible ways he could imagine.

He walked directly toward the battlefield, focusing his attention on the first soldier he came upon. As Taylor broke the first bones in the soldier's feet, the soldier screamed in surprise. Comforted by the scream, he moved slowly up the soldier's body, breaking the bones one at a time. The soldier crumpled to the ground, convulsing. Taylor took care to leave the soldier's spine intact so that he would feel every ounce of the pain.

Taylor continued toward a pocket of Tarak's soldiers that stood back and watched the battle progress. Not understanding that Taylor possessed an Orb, they thought him a fool. The soldiers drew their swords, thinking to make a little sport of him. For these soldiers, he thought of an excruciating death. Locating all of their nerve endings, he seared them with white-hot heat. He watched as the soldiers fell to the ground and screamed, convulsing in agony. Death would come to them when their brains could no longer manage the pain.

As he walked toward the prisoners, each of the soldiers close to Taylor fell to the ground, engulfed in flames. Cries of agony rang out from them as they rolled about—their bodies on fire which would not extinguish. Taylor walked through the battlefield and thinned Tarak's soldiers' numbers as he left a scene of carnage behind. He skinned several of them, others he simply pulled apart. Taylor dealt death to every one of Tarak's soldiers he could see, each death unbearably painful and slow. The soldiers began to notice the wake of death that followed Taylor a few minutes after starting his rampage. Panicked, they began to run.

While Taylor destroyed Taraks' army, Rayla ran toward him from across the battlefield. "Taylor, you have to stop. The Orbs shouldn't be used in that way," she implored him.

The sight of her drew him out of his killing momentarily, long enough for him to stop and look around at the people there from the Refuge. Even with the rage that still gripped him, he could see the fear in their eyes, fear toward him. He allowed Tarak's soldiers to break free of the Refuge's people. Once they were, he cocked his head to the side and tried to think of a less brutal way to kill them.

He fell short; however, the pressure he used to burst the soldier's hearts caused them to crumple to their knees screaming in pain. The collective sound was so loud that those around him covered their ears. The exception to the killing was the officer that held the chain of Careed's collar. He would be important, Taylor thought, and need to be interrogated. Taylor closed his hands into fists and broke both of the officer's legs. The pain caused the man to let go of the chain leading to Careed's collar as he grasped his mangled limbs. Taylor took one more liberty and flipped one of his hands, which tossed the officer in the air. He landed several feet away, unconscious.

Taylor collapsed after that moment; an unfathomable ache filled his heart, tears sprung from his eyes, and a heart-wrenching wail erupted out of his mouth. The Orb turned black and sent dissonant waves of displeasure into his mind that already barely coped from all the death he had caused.

Taylor shook as he cried in the field, surrounded by the blood of the enemy. His wail ended as he sat and stared up at Rayla.

Rayla knelt before him, "The Orb is making sure you know the price of what you have done." She had been stricken with fear for Taylor as he had killed Tarak's men in his rampage. She had never considered that he might kill her people using the Orb. It had taken past Orb Bearers years to bond strong enough to the Orb to be able to kill with its magic. In all her visions of Prophecy, he had wielded a sword as a master. *How could I have been so foolish!* Her single-mindedness in Taylor helping her to save her people had just put everything in jeopardy. Concern flooded her for Taylor and what he would feel in the coming days.

The accounts of men and women going mad during the wars after the Orbs were created rushed into her mind. There was a price to pay when using the Orbs to kill in such a way. In the early days, men and women had gone mad when they'd wielded the Orbs to kill. It had taken a thousand years to stop the warring on her planet. In that time, some had used it in battle as Taylor just had, trying to protect the innocent. Even with their good intentions, they had still gone mad. The Orbs would allow themselves to be freely used in defensive magic. As it had in protecting him from the soldiers he had encountered in the woods. But to kill as an offensive measure always had a cost.

She could not remember anyone in all the histories who had killed so many in one blow. It was likely madness would take Taylor and shorten her time with him, something Prophecy had not shown her. He crumpled into her arms when she knelt in front of him and sobbed while she cradled him. She felt the toll of the pain and torment he felt before he passed out from the exhaustion of what he had done.

Rayla laid Taylor down and called to militia members nearby to carry him to a spot untouched by the battle. There she set up a triage for the injured and cordoned off a separate section for the women who had been raped. They would need extra care from their community for their bodies, hearts, and minds. The healers sprung into action to care for the wounded; others among the survivors stepped forward to help them.

Tarak's army had been efficient in its taking of the Refuge. Her people had taken casualties, and much of the militia lay dead and injured. However, many of the civilians of the Refuge had remained unharmed. She gathered those left in their militia that were still fit for duty and set them as sentries around the perimeter—an action more for everyone's comfort than protection. If there were more soldiers, Rayla's people would not be able to repel them. It would be hard to know if any of Tarak's force was still hidden in the woods until they searched it. She held a small hope that Taylor's actions had frightened them off if there were any lurking about.

The uninjured mobilized to extinguish fires and manage the younger population of children still alive. Kalamar had always insisted that those in the Refuge be prepared for such a situation. Even in his death, he again helped her people. A moment of heartache for him filled her.

She collected herself and then gathered a large group of her people to prepare the dead. It would be a painful task that would require a great deal of work for those left alive.

She left them to their work and walked to where Daphne's body lay; tears flowed freely down her cheeks. When she reached Daphne, she looked down at her and then back to the serene lake. *Here, beside the water, is the perfect spot to create the funeral pyres. Many tears will be shed today and in the days to follow.*

The smoke that rose toward the sky caught her attention from the corner of her eye. It billowed from the Refuge and the crops the soldiers set ablaze. It would be seen for miles and miles and by anyone in the area. That included any divisions of Tarak's men. The smoke from burial pyres would be inconsequential. They would cover their tracks after the death ceremony was complete. She looked back down to where Daphne's body lay. I *will build yours, my darling.*

"The soldiers were dispatched to the villages as well." A hoarse, weak voice said from behind her. "They will have Niea," Careed said. "The Colonel said he would make sure she was alive but broken when I next saw her. She will have lived horrors in the last two days."

She turned to him; he was so beaten and bloodied he could barely stand. The collar sat askew around his neck, and its chain trailed behind him. "Was it you? Did you lead them here?" she asked.

Careed shook his head in response, "There was a third soldier in the woods that day when Taylor wandered off. I was so shaken and worried that they might have found Niea's village. I took no time to look for evidence of other men. Before going back to Glydane, I rode to see Niea that day and spent the evening with her. That third soldier followed me to the village before he continued to a base camp two weeks' hard ride from here." Careed collapsed to his knees, and Rayla knelt to meet him in the eyes. "Colonel

Wynfor dispatched men to intercept me while mobilizing his army."

"Once there, I was imprisoned in a caged wagon to watch helplessly as we moved closer and closer. I watched as the scouts reported back each day. Each evening, Wynfor had me brought to him to have me beaten and taunt me about what he knew about the people here, in the villages, and, more specifically, Niea. That third soldier from the woods told the Colonel of my visit with her. Scouts first brought our people's locations, and later information about the daily movements within the Refuge and the villages." Careed paused to take a breath. He looked like he might pass out.

Rayla felt sympathetic for him and reached out her hand to touch the collar around Careed's neck. She created a flow of power from the Orb into the mechanism that kept it closed. It clicked and dropped to the ground. Relief spread across his face as he took in a deep breath. The Orb still glowed as she lowered her hand to his chest and placed it there. She guided a flow of energy through him. Her ability to heal was not great, but she could repair enough of the damage for him to be comfortable. With a sigh of relief, Careed relaxed. He would be in less pain. The healing, however, brought on exhaustion for the healed. The rest of his wounds would need to heal naturally over time.

"Thank you, Rayla," Careed said before he continued. "The army's base camp is now only a day from here. Wynfor picked a perfect place to dispatch men here and to each village with ease. Timing the attacks at the villages in unison so that no one could alert their neighbors. He planned on capturing as many villagers alive as possible, wanting to make examples of them. He left the Refuge as his last attack, wanting to come here himself. The scout that day saw what Taylor did and knew you'd be amongst the people here. Wynfor hoped to catch you and Taylor as prizes."

"Could you lead us to the base camp?" Rayla asked. Careed nodded. Exhaustion was taking him. "Good! Get some rest. I have some planning to do."

Chapter Twenty-Nine

Rayla planned her attack on the base camp in her head while she coordinated her people. There were fires everywhere, inside and out of the Refuge. She gathered several parties of people and sent them off in different directions to fight the fires. The fields that were ablaze she would deal with herself, before the whole valley was on fire.

Rayla ran swiftly down the path in the woods that led to the fields. The smoke thickened, making it hard to breathe. The Orb's glow brightened at her chest while she filled herself with the Power. She weaved flows in intricate patterns that kept the air around her clean and chilled. Simultaneously, she cleared the smoke from the path ahead and exposed the burning trees at the end.

She used the Power to weave a void of air around the trees at the end of the path and extinguished them. Then she created a bubble of life-giving air around her and stepped inside. What she saw distressed her. The field burned, as did a good portion of the forest surrounding it. She considered creating a void as she had done at the entrance around the field and trees. It would strain her magic beyond anything she had done before. But left unabated, it would kill her people. She was left with no choice.

Rayla walked into the raging fire wrapped in her bubble of air until she was at the fire's center. With determination in her heart, she took a breath and drew in as much power as possible. Then she created a void outside the weave of air around her. With all of her might, she shot the void outward, and within an instant, it reached the outer edges of the burning field. There it stayed, however, pulsing as she poured every bit of available magic she had left into expanding the void, but it still was not enough. She screamed in frustration, she needed to put the fire out, or the valley would be consumed in minutes and her people with it.

Rayla fell to her knees and struggled to push the void outward. The weave of magic started to shift and warble; she was losing the weave; her magic was failing. She knew if that happened, she would not be able to do magic for several hours. In that moment of panic, it came to her. She realized that she need not push more. Rayla released the weave sustaining the void, and the air rushed inward from all directions within an instant. It gathered debris with it, burning branches, embers, stones, and dirt, all of it speeding toward her. As the air rushed in, she saw that her ploy was successful. The fierce wind created from releasing the void was so forceful it uprooted trees out a quarter mile, the wind extinguishing the last of the flames. At the last moment, she hardened the walls of her bubble of air, turning it into a shield so that it could protect her.

Branches, dirt, and debris crashed against the shield she had woven. A thunderous boom followed as if acknowledging what she had done, and she sighed in relief. When it had subsided, smoke filled the area, and she stood. Her legs shook as she walked back to the lake, her protective weave still around her. She made her way back to where Daphne and Kalamar lay. She felt her people's eyes on her when she entered the meadow, watching her, in awe of what she had done. Clear of the smoke, she released the weave and called upon a group of four people. She walked past and sent them to retrieve Kalamar's body and instructed them to place him beside Daphne.

Rayla's actions and the crack of thunderous proportion brought many people in her community back from panic and shock. Some of the prominent members walked toward her to commend her. But as they approached, she forestalled them and said, "I'm in no need of praise. I did as was needed. We have work to do; move the soldiers from the lake and pile them in heaps. We will burn them later. Once that is complete, let us collect our dead and prepare them for their journey. We begin building the pyres at the side of the lake today." She left it to them to organize. The community would come to its senses when the prominent members had begun their work.

Rayla made her way through the meadow to Daphne's body and looked down at her daughter once more. She took a moment to grieve before gathering wood and small sticks to set Daphne's pyre. She worked meticulously for two hours, and when it was completed, she lifted Daphne onto her arms. Her limp body pressed against Rayla's chest and caused her heart to ache like never before. As her eyes filled with tears, she placed Daphne's body upon its final resting place.

Rayla had walked through the pyres the community built the following morning. It surprised her, as she stood in the meadow, how her community had come together to care for the dead. With the help of the horses from the army, the soldier's bodies had been moved, and the funeral pyres completed the evening before. In all, there were nine hundred dead men, women, and children, all laid out. It was a saddening sight for all those there, and several cried with grief for their loved ones. The meadow continued to fill as the people of the Refuge gathered. At the sun's rise, they started the parting of the dead ceremony in their traditional way. The sun's rays would light the way to the next life for them.

A single arrow shot into the air signaled the fire bringers to light the pyre with their torches. A family member or friend lowered their torch to the kindling at each pyre. The fire caught, and the sending began. Rayla watched as the flames took hold of Daphne and Kalamar's funeral pyres before joining the others that watched from the meadow. In only moments, the fire engulfed the dead. Everyone stood and watched as the flames consumed those they had loved. Their pain burned and raged within them as the fires that released their loved ones to drift away with the smoke.

Everyone remained until the burning was complete as they consoled each other. Rayla fell into a trance while she stared into the flames, in the thought of her daughter. She drifted through her memories of Daphne and felt the love between them as each one passed. She slowly found herself thinking of her memories of Daphne and Taylor in the meadow. While she replayed them, she felt a presence in her mind. Taylor's familiar feel brought her gaze up and back to the bluff, where he sat. Taylor looked intently at her before he looked away to Daphne and watched her body burn.

She had not tried to approach him; what he had done was as worrisome, as were its possible consequences. As he sat there, he held a look of uneasiness but, thankfully, not one of madness. *I'll look for an opportunity to broach the distance between us you're creating,* she thought. *With luck, you will come to me first.*

Rayla left Taylor to his grief, as she wished to be with her own, watching the pyres of her people burn. When the last of the embers of Daphne's pyre went out, she took a deep breath and committed to putting her pain away as best she could. Her community needed her to lead them, with Kalamar, their wisest elder, gone.

Rayla needed to deal with the matters that pressed them most. Getting her people to the ruined city as fast as possible was paramount. However, Careed had brought news of prisoners from the surrounding villages. She could not leave them. Seeking out the scouts, she dispatched them to the five villages. Careed, upon his insistence, she sent to Niea's village in hopes she had escaped. She sent the last and best scouts to the location that Careed had given for the base camp. All were to return in a day to report their findings.

With the parting of the dead ceremony complete and the fires out, Rayla set those able to pack up what rations and supplies that could be found. She knew that it was likely that a good deal of their stores would have been destroyed by Tarak's army. What supplies his army did not need would not be left behind for others to use. Moving her people would be a struggle without the proper food stores and supplies. There was hope, though; an army the size Tarak had sent would have brought a lot of supplies.

Wynfor had been boisterous while Careed was his prisoner and told him the entirety of his plan. There were little more than five hundred guardsmen and soldiers left at the base camp. He had dispatched spies to each of the villages to gather information on them. He knew their routines and that few men lived there among the women and children. Besides, Tarak knew that those in the villages were farmers, not warriors. Fifty well-trained, well-armed men to attack at night was all he needed. They were to slaughter any that could not make the trek back to Glydane and capture the rest as prisoners. He had brought the remainder of his men to sack the Refuge.

Word had spread fast of the raids on the villages, and already members of her community had stepped forward, voicing the desire to join the militia. Everyone was required to train in basic soldiering as an adult, even though being in the militia was optional. Rayla would have a smaller force, but she had the advantage of surprise on her side in her attack on the base camp. As her community began to salvage what they could from the Refuge, a plan started forming in her mind.

Due to the maze of the cave system of the Refuge and the interruption of the attack, some of the inside areas had not been ransacked. Rayla had a temporary headquarters set up for her in a small meeting room in one such place. Once the rescue was planned and executed, she would spend many hours preparing to move to the ruined city here. Those with usable living quarters returned home, and a large dining hall became their temporary shelter for those whose homes were destroyed. Rayla had the healers commandeer one of the smaller meeting halls as an indoor triage and moved the wounded inside out of the weather, to add to their troubles, the autumn rains had begun.

The following day when the sun had risen, the first scouts started to return with their report. What they found came as no surprise to Rayla. The villages were full of carnage. The young women and any children able to make the trek back were missing, and the rest lay slaughtered. Careed's arrival at mid-morning brought first-hand accounts of what had happened. Two survivors from Niea's village, a girl of eleven, Dazan, and her six-year-old brother Kenwick, told their grim tale. That their house rested on a hill at the village's outer edge was the only reason they were spared. They had heard, then seen, the invaders from their hilltop home long before the soldiers found it.

Their parents had made sure that they were well hidden by the time the soldiers reached their home. Both parents had confronted the soldiers outside, knowing they were sacrificing their lives. The children had stayed hidden under the floor in the woodshed for two nights before leaving their hiding spot. Dazan had searched in desperation for any survivors, including her best playmate Niea. No one was to be found. She had explored all of the places Niea and she had secreted away in during hide-and-seek. And Careed had searched again. Not finding her was confirmation that his daughter was among the captured. While Dazan told the story, Rayla saw Careed's sadness and fear for Niea in his eyes.

As the day moved forward, Rayla had come to a standstill at the side of the lake. She felt Careed's approach; his anger was radiant enough that she could feel him from paces away. She ignored his presence for a few moments; it had been a long day. She looked up to the sun and saw that it still hung at least four finger widths from the horizon. "I can't wait for this day to end, Careed. What is it?" Her voice was a little curter than she had meant it to be.

He did not answer right away; she knew the edge in her voice gave him pause. "We have yet to deal with Wynfor. Taylor did a good deal of damage to him, and the healers won't tend to him. If we leave it much longer, he'll be dead before he can tell us what he knows."

Rayla sighed; Taylor, losing control like that, had scared her beyond anything she had ever experienced. He had gone too far. Even in his restraint with Wynfor, he had done a lot of damage. The leg bones had stuck out in places, and much of them were shattered below the knee, more like pulverized. "I don't have it in me to do much more damage to anyone. What is it that you wish?"

"You could look into his min—"

"I will *not* do that!" She shot back. "I have no desire to become like Tarak, and that would be a step toward a slippery slope." Just as it was with Taylor.

"Then let me question him! I have every right to know Tarak's plans with our people." Careed breathed heavily as he spoke, anger in his voice.

"You mean you deserve retribution, more to the point!" The words were not harsh or accusing, but a matter of truth. "You do deserve that, but I fear your need for it will blind you." She paused. "But who else in this place is capable of extracting information from a man so dedicated to Tarak's cause, I wonder? Certainly not any of our own here, and Taylor is out of the question. He avoids my every approach. Let us go then and see what you can find."

She found herself in a small room in the Refuge before

she knew it. Wynfor sat in a chair or, more precisely, was propped up and tied to the back. His legs were angled in strange directions, and someone, likely Careed, had roughly bandaged the man's legs to stop the bleeding. The look on Careed's face was of a man looking to get even; she could have even said he wore a slight grin.

Careed took a bucket of water from the floor and splashed it in Wynfor's face. The man sputtered then eyed Careed, the pain from his legs only betrayed by his eyes. The bucket crashed into the Colonel's lower legs, and he howled with pain. Shocked at Careed's actions and the screams of pain, Rayla started; her heart raced. She could not be here; this was a mistake.

"Perhaps you should wait outside. You have seen a good deal of death today." The voice was far off, but she heeded it and turned and left at Careed's suggestion. With the door left ajar, she waited outside while scenes of horror went on inside the room. It seemed like hours passed, though she knew it was a trick of her mind. At last, she heard Wynfor start telling his tale.

"He sent me out blindly to look for you," he sobbed. "I only had a small lead to follow, and we got lucky, that is all. Tarak has no idea where you might be."

"How did you get this information?"

"He tortured half of his advisers, men he suspected might be traitors." Wynfor gulped for air; the man would not make it much longer. The pain Careed was inflicting on Wynfor would be with the man as he died; Careed knew that.

"But in the end, it was a servant girl passing information to the Priestesses in the Temple," Wynfor gasped.

"And what of the girl?"

Wynfor laughed at this, "He tore her mind apart, taking

the information. She was drooling in a corner before he told her to jump out the window." Wynfor was building strength in defiance now as Rayla sobbed outside. "And the Priestesses, oh how they screamed, you'd have lik-," Rayla had heard Careed loose his knife from the sheath and the Colonel's voice cut short.

Rayla's salty tears touching her lips. "Oh, dear Ilauna. I'm sorry you met your end in such a way."

The door opened fully, and Careed stepped out. Without a word, he embraced her, and she collapsed into his arms, crying for her people. An interesting turn of events, as she had often comforted this man as an orphaned boy with scraped knees and bruises.

"Thank you, old friend!" She pulled away and wiped her tears. When she looked at him, she saw no satisfaction in his face where she thought there would be. "At least we know we are undiscovered still. We have a rescue to mount and our people to relocate. Let us get moving."

Chapter Thirty

It was midday when the last of the scouts finished returning, all of them telling the same tale. After the final reports arrived, Rayla left her little command post to walk in the meadow. She allowed her mind to wander as she strolled through the corridors and to the outside air. Before Rayla knew it, she found herself sitting on the boulder up on the bluff, where she had always found the most peace. She took in a deep breath and did her best to focus on all the plans she had made. The slight breeze rustling the leaves in the oak behind her, the one Kalamar had died under, bringing Rayla thoughts of Kalamar and Daphne. The two of them had been the only ones she had become close to since the death of her old friend Neala. The loss of a father figure and a daughter both in one day had left her feeling hollow.

"I miss her too," a voice startled her back to reality. Taylor stood beside her, silent for a moment. "I can hear them," he nodded to the people below. "Ever since the battle, I can hear them. Their thoughts are like little conversations in my mind. I can hear yours the loudest of all."

Taylor's words were emotionless as he spoke; he stood looking stoic.

What would it be like to hear all of that in your head? Rayla could not imagine what he was going through. Running that much power through your body to murder often had odd side effects, aside from madness. Rayla felt concerned for him but chose not to say anything.

"They're scared of me, you know, all of them. Your people are grateful, but I still scare them. And no wonder." He paused and looked down at her, then at the Orb around her neck, and said, "They know now that I carry an Orb, Kalamar's Orb. That scares them too." Taylor took his Orb in his hand and held it in front of him. "I see their faces when I close my eyes, the soldiers I killed. The Orb shows them to me, so I can't forget what I did. My dreams are filled with the battle and watching the soldiers' souls twist in pain as they leave their bodies. Their faces linger in my mind after I wake.

"I thought it might break me in the hours after. At its worst, I sat alone in the meadow and stared off at nothing. I was doing my best to not close my eyes and see their faces, when I felt a presence at my side. I looked over, and this little girl of maybe three or four stood beside me. She had this odd look of peacefulness to her. She wasn't hurt. She wasn't afraid of me. I felt the Orb's power flash through me, and I began seeing part of the battle as the little girl saw it.

"I felt her body struggle to break free of the older girl that held her back as she tried desperately to get to her mother. She watched a soldier drag her mother off by the hair. I felt the screams at her throat as she tugged harder and harder to free herself. The pressure of the older girl's fingers holding fast to keep her safe sunk deeper into her arms. It was then that she saw me as I walked through the battlefield toward her mother. Soldiers fell dead before me again and again. And as I walked past the soldier that dragged her mother off, I reached out and touched his arm. He crumpled to ash, and I felt the girl's joy at her mother's release from the bad man. Even more so as her mother stood and ran toward her. Then her tears of relief as her mother wrapped her in an embrace.

"It was at that moment that I felt all of her emotions toward me. She felt love and gratitude that I killed the soldier and saved her mother. A heaviness lifted in me at that moment. I felt freed from the burden of what I had done. The girl smiled at me, and with her mother holding her hand, they walked away. I felt your people's fear of me when I looked around, but I also felt their happiness. Their happiness that they and some of their loved ones were saved."

Rayla did not respond; how could she say something back to that? Taylor had not just crossed a line; he had run miles past it. To have killed that many people under normal circumstances would have been tormenting enough. But to kill with the Orb meant that the pain was amplified tenfold. Rayla hoped that the little girl's shared memories, and the love she felt for her mother's savior had hinged him back into reality firmly enough.

Others who had done less with the Orb's power had become brutal killers, not caring who the victims were, friend or foe. She would need to trust her visions of him saving her world. Like Kalamar had told her, Prophecy was a tricky business to interpret.

"I'll see to getting your people to the ruined city. But I'm no longer sure what I'll do after we are there. The man you brought here a few weeks ago no longer exists, and I'm not sure I could return to his old life. I have heard the whispers of an attack on the base camp. I'd like to join you. Though I don't know that I can endure the pain of killing with the Orb so soon. If only I had listened to you and taken the time to allow you to teach me to use a sword."

Taylor's last words were a good sign. She thought he might still have both feet on this side of sanity. "Follow me," she said and jumped off the boulder and led Taylor down to the meadow. However, instead of beginning a lesson in the sword as Taylor had expected, she led him into the Refuge. She meandered through the maze of hallways into a remote area that Taylor began to recognize. Due to the remoteness of Kalamar's quarters, the door stood untouched. The soldiers had not followed the passages this far down, thinking them unused. She pushed the door open and stood a moment before she entered.

Taylor felt the sadness that emitted from Rayla, which had heightened as she stepped across the threshold. He followed her in and to the corner of the room, where a chest sat. Rayla knelt down and opened it to retrieve a large item from inside. When she stood and turned toward him, she held a sword sheathed in a scabbard made of silver, inlaid with gold, with brightly colored jewels set throughout it. On the hilt of the blade at its end, Taylor could see three small Orbs set there.

The steel of the sword rang as she drew it from its sheath and held it before him. She looked at him, "This is the most exquisite sword ever crafted here. It was forged by the blacksmith that crafted the jewelry and the settings for the Orbs. Passed down through the generations of leaders,

Kalamar kept this sword proudly. It's the truest blade I have ever seen in action. Kalamar said that you become as one while wielding it—not an extension of you but a part of you. I only ever saw him wield it once, in a rescue mission. He seemed to move with the grace of the gods. It was like nothing I have ever seen.

"He had always thought to use it against Tarak before that day. But after the lives he took in that one instance, it unnerved him to use it on our own people. The smaller Orbs are somehow different, we don't understand why but they don't cause repercussions such as you felt, but he always found killing our own distasteful. The thought of a sword that could kill with such ease and grace was unacceptable to him. After the rescue mission, he placed it in that chest, never taking it out again. I'm giving it to you. If we are to survive, we will have to prepare to begin warring with Tarak's people and killing our own."

She slid the sword back into the scabbard, stepped forward, wrapped the belt around his waist, and buckled it there. "This sword can enhance the abilities of the wielder. If I impart some knowledge to you, I know you will be able to negotiate the battlefield. It will take some time for you to comprehend all I have shown you." She led him to the small table and sat down as she gestured for him to sit in the chair across from her. She placed her hands on the table with her palms up. "Put your hands down against mine and close your eyes."

Hesitation filled him as he placed his hands against Rayla's. He was not sure what she was up to. Rayla had not always been forthright with her end goal. "OK. Now what?" he asked.

Rayla smiled to herself and felt some amount of success. *A few weeks ago, he would not have trusted me.* "I must tell you that this will join us in a way that can't be undone. However, there isn't time to teach you the theory of sword form." When their hands touched, a flood of emotions rushed into her from him. Not only trust, but love had begun to influence him—love for her. Her heart leapt, the vision of Taylor passed through her mind. The love that they would share was coming to fruition, as was Prophecy.

"Good, now open your mind," she whispered in a soft voice. "Allow your consciousness to flow into mine, see what I see, and feel what I feel."

Rayla felt Taylor open his mind and let go of any resistance toward their consciousnesses merging. The jumble of their thoughts confused him at first, and she felt his panic about losing himself start to build. She wove a calmness through his being and steadied him. It gave him the emotional balance necessary for him to allow their merge to complete. A peace fell over him, intimately intertwined as they were, separate yet not. She could see a flood of stronger memories of Taylor's life, playing with his mother, fishing with his dad, and his first kiss with Lilly. The two were as one. She could feel every part of him and he of her. "I'll show you now, Taylor, my knowledge of combat," visions of Rayla's past began to flow from her mind into his mind's eye.

Taylor found himself looking through Rayla's eyes on the battlefield, her emotions hot with fear and anger induced by the small force of Tarak's men before her. These were once her peaceful people, turned by Tarak to be murderous and cold. Lifting her sword, she let out a piercing war cry before running toward her foe. Her comrades followed beside her. Rayla led him through different scenes of battle, skirmishes, and ambushes she had been in. Taylor felt her knowledge of swordsmanship imparting to him with each memory. He accumulated years of experience in battle with a sword within seconds. The feeling of her mind and his merged as such was unimaginable. He was living parts of her life as if they were his own.

Something happened that Taylor had not anticipated in living those moments of her life. He also felt the pain in her heart in striking down the soldiers in Tarak's army. Her rage at what they had become, and in turn, what they had done to the innocent. It was subtle at first, and then persistent while the memories played on. Woven into her rage were the turmoils and struggles of what she had done to protect her innocent people. All her worries for her people that she was protecting. Taylor had a window into Rayla's consciousness, her mind, and a side of Rayla he had not come to know yet. Then her love for Daphne filled him, mixing with her heartache at the young girl's death.

The memories stopped as sudden as they had started, and all was dark. Out of the blackness, Taylor heard Rayla's voice. "This was the only way I could think to prepare you in time for the attack we are heading into. If there was another way, I'd have chosen it. Know that our souls have become as one Taylor, and from this time forward, our souls will be entangled. We are joined in life and in death." Taylor's eyes snapped open.

Chapter Thirty-One

The dream had come again, as it did so often. Tarak could do many things with the magic, but he could not block this dream he often found himself in.

"Mommy? Mommy?" a young boy's voice called out from the corner of the darkened outpost.

His call fell unanswered among broken, dusty consoles and blank screens, broken glass, old bones, and wiring. Tar shook his mother vigorously again. She had taken ill after a venomous rat had bitten her, the poison working its way through her veins. She had been sick ever since.

She had looked him in the eye only the night before and said with a shaking voice, "I'll be alright."

He had known better, though, and now her skin was pale and waxing. She felt stiff all over.

"You can't be dead, Mommy," he sobbed, "I don't want to be alone."

He stuffed his palms into his eyes to stanch the tears, but it was futile. He collapsed onto her chest and *sobbed*.

"I love you, Mommy," he said with a tiny, squeaky voice as his tears wet her shirt.

He sat up and looked at her, and as he did, her words rang in his ears:

"If something ever happens to me, you go as far into the shafts as you can. And you stay in there until you're almost too big to get back. There are those here who will take advantage of you so young as you are, but no one will ever find you in the shafts."

"I'll do what you told me to do. I'll hide!" he promised through his sobs.

He covered his mother's face with her blanket, and as she disappeared beneath it, he knew he wouldn't ever see her face again. He stood and wiped away his tears.

"Rotten Resistance! It's your fault!" He mimicked his mother. It was what she had said whenever they had no food or were out in the cold rain.

She and many others blamed the long-dead Vidreian Resistance and their virus. Their magically created bioweapon had killed most of the non-magical Navaden, the technologically advanced and otherworldly invaders that had built the outpost. The virus had twisted their human forms, mangling their organs inside, until death took them or they transformed. His mother had shown him the surviving Navaden descendants once.

"Come with me, Tar," she had said one day. She led him to the sparse woods and pointed to a group of hairy beasts that walked upright. "There, Tar, you see them? That is what the invaders became when the virus arrived. They're so unintelligent that we cannot even train them to do simple tasks. Fitting punishment for what they did to us."

Leaving his mother's body, the boy collected some old rations; the tetra-packs crinkled as he pushed them into his bag. He had found the packs a few days before in a storage locker down one of the shafts. It was a good thing the Navaden invaders had made things to last.

"These rations are so old; your grandfather's grandfather would have thought them so," his mother had said with a silly grin.

The thought of his mother's smile reminded him of the time they had found a closet full of tattered uniforms.

She had put on a round hat with a little brim, "Do you like my hat?" she had said. It was too large for her head, so it had drooped over her eyes. She had worn it all day to lighten their mood. The sight of it had made him burst into laughter every time he looked at her, and she had laughed with him.

The outpost had been one of the last ones standing after the long-ago intergalactic war between the Vidreian and the Navaden. The Navaden had come for the crystalline giver of magic they called Vidre. The whole of the planet had been strip-mined to extract it, until it was desolate, and the people of Kardain were left with a world without any real magic. Some Navaden had stayed behind to take care of the people here.

At least, that is what his mother had thought. Old Malc had said otherwise. "The Vidreians were slaves here for the Navaden. But at least they had food and shelter back then." Malc had said emphatically. "As things are now, we have less than nothing."

The outpost had lost power generations ago. He and his mother scavenged for food, clothing, and flashlight power cells. They rummaged through the over-picked buildings on the outskirts of the base.

"If you're out in the open, stick to the outskirts, Tar," she

had constantly reminded him. "Going too far into the base on the roads can get you killed. Those flying machines vaporized more than a few that did not heed the warnings."

Knife, flashlight, batteries, water collector. That's it. He collected the last few items for his pack and was ready to move on. His mom had figured out that the shafts in the walls and ceilings led to everywhere in the outpost. His mother had not been much more than a child when she had given birth to him. When he was only four, his mother had grown too big to fit through most vents, so it had become his job to "get the loot," as she had called it. And he had been good at it.

Life had become dangerous for them over the last year. A new gang had shown up at the outpost from the nearby colony, and in an attempt to flee, the boy and his mother had followed the tracks in the underground tunnels. They found a stairway that had led up into the base, and an old office room, a few blocks inside the dangerous part of the city, had become their home.

"Isn't there anyone that can beat those bullies?" he had asked her of the gang.

She had taken him by the shoulders and looked him in the eyes, "I don't think so," *she said with a sad look.* "There are too many of them. We need to stay hidden."

He fretted over the situation again as he stood over his mother's body. *That rat would never have bitten you if the gang hadn't come,* he thought to himself. With his things packed, he took one last look at his mother's shape under the blanket before he climbed into a cold shaft. He shivered, but he kept going, crawling for days. He had found a lucky strike of two nutrient bars in a small storeroom.

One day while working his way through the maze of shafts, he heard the distant murmurs of a man's voice. A voice of which he followed down several shafts, to find himself above a large control room. *There shouldn't be anyone here. No one could have gotten in this far through the streets.*

"And to think that Renoslan sent me here ..." he heard the voice say.

"Hello? Hellooo?" Tar called as he peered through a grate in the middle of the room, leaning on it to get a better look. The grate gave way with his extra weight, and he dropped to the floor below with a thud. The room was lit by a slight glow. After his eyes focused, he could make out that in front of him sat a pedestal. Atop the pedestal sat a glass dome with an orb resting inside, pulsing a brilliant blue light.

A voice called to him, "Are you okay?"

"Yes ... Where are you?" he asked curiously. "I can't see you."

"My name is Sailock; I will tell you about myself. But first, please introduce yourself. What is your name?" the voice asked.

"My mommy called me Tar, but it's short for Tarak," he replied.

"You cannot be more than eight years old," the voice said.

"I'm six, but I turn seven in a month," he replied, still looking about for the man belonging to the disembodied voice. A ghostly image of a tall, distinguished man dressed in formal robes appeared. Tar gasped and shrunk back.

"It's quite alright," Sailock assured. "I'm a magical being of a Vidre orb. Abandoned by the Navaden and the resistance after the virus reached this outpost. I'm desperate for some company after my centuries of solitude."

Tar eased a little. "Malc told me there used to be those

like you, those captured by the Vidre. I had thought he was lying. What does it feel like in there?" Tar's stomach growled, and he paused, looking around, "Do you have something I can eat? I ate the last of my rations yesterday."

Sailock was silent a moment, "Tarak, I think we may be able to help each other! I would like to know what happened to my people. I could teach you the wonders of the universe and, eventually, how to escape this world. All I would ask in return is you bring me news of those who created me, and the resistance I became part of after my transformation."

"But you have food?" Tar asked.

"But of course! I can tell you where there are more ration packs," Sailock replied.

I will have vengeance for you, Mother! If only you knew that one of the resistance would be raising me in exchange for help that I will never give.

"Okay," Tar said.

When he opened his eyes, his heart was afire with rage at what they had done to his mother and what they had done to him. He needed to make them pay. "Wynfor! Godry, where is Wynfor?"

Chapter Thirty-Two

Rayla sat there before Taylor, her face calm and breath even. She opened her eyes, and a small smile spread across her face, but she said nothing. What he felt of her thoughts and emotions swirling in his mind dissipated; in a sudden whoosh, her consciousness left. When it was done, he realized he could still feel a small part of her in the back of his mind. Some part of her consciousness had stayed with him, residing in him, as had a piece of him within her. He found he had a heightened awareness of her, and in closing his eyes, he knew precisely where she was.

Rayla stood, "We must hurry now. There isn't much time." She left the table and gathered together medicinal plants they might need.

Taylor remained where he was and worked to grasp how to make sense of his thoughts and feelings. There was an emptiness within him now, like a piece of him was missing. It could not have been more than a few minutes of being connected as they were, and yet it had a drastic impact on his way of being.

"Taylor? Are you alright?" Rayla asked him. He sat a moment and looked up at her, unable to form words. "It's alright, Taylor; the Famsha can be difficult the first time." She helped him stand. It took a moment to sort himself out before he helped Rayla with the rest of the supplies. She ushered him to follow her lead to the meadow when she felt complete in what she had gathered.

As they moved back through the passage, Taylor stopped at an odd corridor that looked in disuse. He had not noticed it on their way toward Kalamar's quarters, but some twenty soldiers lay dead in there. Most looked twisted in odd ways. "What is this, Rayla? They look unnatural in the way they lie," he inquired.

Rayla stopped short. *It appears my wards are about. There is no time to explain the likes of those two,* Rayla thought. *They will reveal themselves to Taylor soon enough.* "It was likely one of the Shard Carriers. Some of the larger pieces can impart great gifts, and fear can make the most timid do terrifying things."

Taylor took her at her word, and they carried on. To their surprise, when they exited the cave into the meadow, there stood two hundred and twenty women and men of the militia. All were adorned in Tarak's dead soldiers' armor as they waited for Rayla to lead them into battle. They were not a force that could attack straight on, but there were other ways to defeat a foe. She knew that their time to attack in surprise was running out. Colonel Wynfor and his men, who now lay dead at the other side of the field, would have not immediately returned. They would have taken time with the sacking of the Refuge and with the women. It had been four days since the attack, and the other soldiers at the base camp would soon expect the return of Wynfor's forces.

Good blades were hard to come by, and Rayla had a suspicion that the armor had started with acquiring swords and axes as an upgrade to their own. Somewhere along the line, though, one of them had gotten a notion. She suspected she knew who, as Careed, dressed in Wynfor's armor, came up to her. There was a lot of unease and tension in him hidden by the smile there. Niea would have been in the hands of Tarak's men for several days now.

Careed still walked with pain but managed, "What do you think? A worthy disguise?" Careed said as he waved his arm toward the women and men in formation behind him.

"It's brilliant, Careed!" Rayla agreed and a wry smile of her own formed. She walked to the front of the formation and began addressing them. "We need to move fast and without delay. Our friends' lives depend on us getting to them as quick as possible. It has been over eighty years since we have attempted an assault on Tarak's army. The small raids on little camps and wagon convoys will be nothing like we do today. We will be outnumbered, but with your great inspiration, the armor you're wearing will create a great advantage of surprise." Everyone stood tall with the compliment, eager to begin the rescue.

Rayla took a moment and looked around. She saw that many in the meadow had stopped what they were doing to listen to her. She was now the leader here, and as such, they gave her the full dues of leadership. Even though the preparation for their migration to the ruined city was essential, when a leader spoke, it was always something to listen to, especially if they had been alive a few centuries longer than you.

What Rayla had to say could, in their eyes, be paramount to their people's survival and wellbeing. Many civilians had armed themselves with the dead soldiers' weapons; the armor would be cumbersome, but the blades were worth the effort in saving. Someone had begun making piles of swords and other weapons in the meadow. With the wrath of Tarak's men fresh in their minds, they started cheering for the militia in a brilliant sendoff. What the militia was about to do was necessary for their people.

Those who stayed behind had a large amount of work to do. This sendoff would empower them for that. With luck, Rayla and the militia would be back in a few days. She hoped that things would come together as swiftly as she thought with the rescue and the move's preparation. The additional horses taken from the army had made a significant dent in moving the dead soldiers. For the last two days, her people stripped the fallen soldiers of armor and weapons. They had begun burning the bodies immediately after the sending of her people. These soldiers were Tarak's men, but they had been hers before that. They deserved to be sent by fire at the very least. Spots smoldered in the meadow where the fires had consumed the dead soldiers already. The last thing they needed was for a disease to spread through the Refuge before they began their journey.

It surprised Rayla, but well over two thousand of Tarak's men had been in the meadow and hidden in the woods, many of which had died when Taylor had crushed their hearts with the Power. The scouts she sent out initially had found men almost a mile back toward the base camp, dead with their hearts ripped out. Taylor had not missed one of them, which unnerved her. He lived up to his people's reputation. She was beginning to see why he would be so successful in defeating Tarak's army. She shivered at the thought that he had killed so many with the Orb.

Nothing in the Prophecies alluded to him being sane when he saved my people. Nor do any of the different outcomes I saw in my visions. Rayla felt hopeful. Maybe there was even a yet unseen way for him to save her people. Some of the outcomes did not end well for her or Taylor.

Taylor looked at her inquisitively while half-dressed in armor from one of Tarak's men. Rayla realized she had inadvertently allowed her gaze to linger on him too long. As she thought, a look of concern had spread across her face at some point. The same worries Rayla had shielded him from in their merging now swam in her mind. She smiled at him and redirected her attention to the militia before her. She raised her voice so everyone could hear:

"These last couple of days have been a blow to our people. We have lost many of those we loved. But we can't falter now. There isn't time to mourn those we have sent off on their journey to the afterlife. I have known many of you since you were born. I know what you have lost. We must rise above our grief and save our friends and family that Tarak has taken prisoner so that we might move forward to our new home and to safety. I know what I ask is hard, but it's essential to our survival. It's time we get moving! There is still enough time in the day to make it partway there. Gather whatever else you need for the next days to come. We move for the base camp as soon as everyone is back here and ready."

Those in the field, civilian and militia alike, stood taller and roared in unison, "RAYLA, RAYLA, RAYLA ..." After a moment, the militia followed her toward the base camp.

Chapter Thirty-Three

"Godry! Godry!" Tarak screamed, his anger bubbling inside him, the magic that trickled through him feeding it. "Where are you hiding this time?" The man's quirks were infuriating; keeping him alive with magic had its costs, as did the many weaves he had put in his mind. "Where are you?" his voice shook with rage.

It was then that he spotted him, hiding halfway under the bed. He still wriggled, trying to get further in. "What are you doing under there?" Tarak reached down with his meaty hands, grabbing Godry's leg and ripping him out from under the bed.

Godry shielded his head with his arms and screeched, "Please Master, no more changes to my mind, please don't beat me either. I was only scared."

"Scared?" Tarak boomed. "Of what? I haven't struck you in years."

"I saw you were in a bad temper. I was worried."

"Get up! I have a council today. And I wish to check for word from Wynfor." Tarak had not felt settled in days.

Where is Wynfor after all? How could he be taking so long? He had gotten up some time ago; one of the menservants lay in his bed staring up at the ceiling, his mind broken, and his wife huddled in a corner. Her mind was not broken. Yet.

The dream of his mother always brought him into a killing mood. Neither Wynfor nor Mina had sent word still. "Hurry up, Godry, we must see to the council. Why do you just stand there?" Tarak implored.

Godry did not move for a moment. "I thought you might want to get dressed for the occasion. Instead of going in all your glory."

Tarak looked down at his naked body, "Ah, yes, I believe some clothing would set the mood better." He paused, looking thoughtful. "Something formal but fear-inspiring." He set the web around him, and a dark leather suit of armor set upon him; a well-defined breastplate of thick leather mimicked his every muscle; at his waist, he had two razor-sharp daggers at each side. A mace formed in his hand, and a smile set on his face.

Now for a bit of blood to let them know I mean business. The woman screamed as Tarak destroyed her husband's body with the heavy weapon. He left her there and walked through the passages, leaving carnage interspersed from there to the council chambers. Some backed away when he entered the room, hoping to run, but the doors slammed shut tight, locked with magic.

Tarak had regretted reducing Godry to ash immediately once he had done it. In his rage that Wynfor had neither returned with nor sent word of Rayla, Kalamar, nor the stranger, he had gone on a rampage killing anyone he saw.

At first, the people in the legislative assembly had not understood his temperament. Turning to rush away, seeing the wrath in his eyes, he had burned them with rage.

The next day, he could find no one; not on the residential floors, not in the guest quarters. The staff had gone missing; even the stables were empty of horses. "Have I burned them all?" he thought.

He instinctively went to shout for Godry but stopped short. "Godry, you hadn't left my side for over one hundred years," he mumbled.

Godry had been First Councilor when Tarak had arrived; keeping him alive that long was a parlor trick in the vastness of what he could do with the Orb. The pile of ash before him stung a little more than he liked. The man was loathsome, and torturing him had given Tarak pleasure at one point. But with Godry there for all those years, he had come to depend on the man.

With a huff, Tarak walked through the ash and toward the docking bay of the warehouse at the ground level. He had not been down there in years, but a soldier had raced in just before he had ignited Godry. "Your chariot my king, there are lights in the chariot—" Tarak had crumpled the soldier into a heap of flesh. "How dare he interrupt me incinerating you, Godry."

"Please, my king, it hurts." Godry had pleaded, steam rising from his skin as it baked.

"Stop your whining!" Godry had burst into flames at his shouting, burning so hot that he was ash in seconds.

With a quiver in his lip, Tarak returned to what the guard had said.

"My chariot! Simpletons!" Of course, they had known in principle what his ship was when he landed here. It was in their Prophecy. But after taking over the world, he had needed to dumb down the population. Outlawing reading and writing for the masses had done the damage he wanted within twenty years. After that, he had set his Clerics to disseminate the information he wanted them to know.

His boots knocking against the stone echoed as he walked through the halls leading to where his ship was stored. It was more of the size of a large pod—he could have walked its length in forty steps—with only a cockpit and cabin with room enough for two to rest. It had not fit well through the small doors of the loading bay. He'd had new ones made, but there was only enough room in the bay for the ship to fit tightly inside. It was a shame that it had taken so much damage in the crash. The automated defense of the Starport above this backward world had fired on him, which was strange. He had hoped for a warmer welcome here.

Swinging the loading bay doors open, he saw the red flashing light through the broken-out window in the cabin of the stolen ship, which made him hesitant at first. "No, matter! I can easily dispense with my old captors if they have found me," he boasted as he stroked the Orb. "Besides, it will save me having to search the cosmos to locate your previous owners after I have burned this world." He patted the ship and then entered through the door. Excitement rushed into him when he saw that the signal was from the ground, here on Daemor.

"What luck could this be? Someone has activated the distress signal from the old base here." He stood in triumph, "You can take your time, Wynfor! I have other things to occupy me."

Tarak burst the loading bay doors open with the Orb. Splinters flew in every direction. "I need a pool of water!" He shouted and stormed toward the fountain at the other side of the legislative assembly. The display screen showing the location of the beacon had been shattered. He had not been able to make out the exact location, but he had an idea of the general area.

"Drat, my luck; of all the greatness of my bloodline and the Orb I possess, the one thing I'm not great at is slipping through those damned portals." He needed water as Rayla did, but he could only go short distances, unlike her. He could sense water a day's walk away and could port there. He could do this two or three times before needing to rest for the day. It would take him several days to get there, but he would be there soon enough.

At the front of the legislative building, people crossed to the other side of the street to avoid him. *A wise choice!* he said to himself. When he had almost reached the fountain, he realized that he wore his dress robes. "Gahh, these won't do!" He took a breath. He would need to be calm to see this through. If he got over-excited at the prospect of what might still lie in the city, he might lose sight of the other goals he had here. Getting off this planet was important, but so was destroying these people. He had promised himself he would eradicate all the Navaden for what they had done to his people. "And the other Orbs! I will take them as my own. I'll be a power to be reckoned with once I have those in hand."

A smile slowly worked its way across his face; with calm back in him, he could think again. He sauntered back up the littered steps to the main doors. He could take his time now. Whoever had turned on the beacon in the city had blundered. How could someone be there, much less turn on the beacon? It seemed impossible! But there it had been on the screen in his ship. "What a lucky day!"

Chapter Thirty-Four

They walked along the trail created by the invading army that afternoon. Everyone chose to stop only once to eat and rest before nightfall brought their day's trek to a close. They set a loose camp, arose at dawn, and continued to work their way through the woods toward the base camp. Taylor had not spoken to Rayla since the Famsha. From his presence in the back of her mind, she knew that the deaths of the two thousand men he had killed still haunted him. Taylor, from what she had gleaned, had put most of that away in a room inside of his mind. He locked his feelings away to deal with at another time.

She had no advice to offer him, and no one alive would. The Famsha gave her a better chance of saving him, but there was no guarantee. He was not unstable from the killing, but he was not stable either. In all the lessons she had learned from Kalamar and the healing literature she had removed from the Great Library, it all said that you could only bring someone back from insanity if they wanted to come back. Even with the assistance of another Orb, it could not be forced. In most cases, those that had gone insane from using the Orbs to kill did not want to return to their right mind to live with it.

At midday, a signal call sounded and gave everyone pause. All halted while Rayla replied to the scouting party she'd had Careed send out to watch over the base camp. Careed had told the scouts to set their camp inconspicuously outside their quarry's location as a precaution. They would have kept tabs on Tarak's soldiers and waited for the rescue party to arrive. Careed's last message was to expect him and the militia to come disguised as Tarak's men, and Rayla's presence would signify that it was them.

Rayla sent the expected signal back and quickly took the scouts' reports. Afterward, all but the squad leaders went to rest for the remainder of the afternoon. With Taylor at her side, they led them off for a meeting.

The twelve leaders sat in a small clearing in a circle and waited for the plan to be laid out. Rayla stood and spoke. "It's time we discussed how we are going to proceed."

"I say that we attack at first light," Jaken, a tall skinny man suggested.

Huden, a wise, boisterous, and broad-shouldered woman, spoke in a hushed, angered voice, "No, I say under cover of the dark! It will mask our identities. They will only see men they believe their comrades. We will attack when they least expect it."

Careed stepped forward, "I have a plan if you will only listen."

"What does it matter what you think! You were one of them," Huden said hotly, still full of anger at the loss of her son.

Fury raged through Careed. He unsheathed his sword and stepped toward Huden. He had the blade at the woman's throat before she could even reach for her own.

"Do you forget that I was once a boy in the Refuge? That I gave up a great deal to join Tarak and be a spy for our cause? My daughter is amongst the prisoners, Huden. I should slit your throat for speaking to me that way."

As he finished speaking, Taylor was at Careed's side, putting his hand on Careed's blade. A kind look from him dissuaded Careed from carrying out his threat. Taylor had gained a great deal of respect for what he had done in saving many lives. Their thoughts had told him as much in the last two days. Many of Rayla's people had begun to believe he had earned the right to hold the Orb, and Careed was one of them. Taylor had saved Careed that day, which gave him the chance to save his daughter from a life of slavery. Careed sheathed his sword and stood back.

"Huden is right about the attack. We must wait," Taylor said. "We are all tired and angry. We can't fight like this. We must be well rested before we attempt our rescue. I also agree that we use the dark as cover, but not this night. We should rest this evening and tomorrow morning. We will march later in the day, allowing us to cool our tempers and go with clearer heads and our wits about us."

Rayla stepped forward to Careed and, using a hushed tone, she spoke. "Cool your temper. These men are your allies." What Taylor had just done brought hope to her heart. He still had care in him, and that was important if he was to stay sane. "You all mustn't forget, Careed has been with us for a long time, longer than most of you have been alive. He's a well-seasoned soldier, and he knows how to plan an attack. We must listen to him."

Careed had chosen a challenging path in life, being a soldier in Tarak's army. He had not moved up in the ranks by being idle in the tyranny that Tarak's men caused. His warnings had saved them many times, but he'd had to kill innocent people to gain ranks. The lives he had saved far outweighed those he had killed, but it had taken its toll on him. There was no mistaking that Tarak's taint had stained Careed, but he was still as true to their cause as the first day he volunteered.

The angry look on Careed's face withdrew. His daughter being taken had begun to wear on him. The thought of what horrors she might be facing dug into him. "Thank you, Rayla and Taylor." He nodded to them, taking the opportunity to begin telling the plan. "Rayla and I have discussed our strategy as we have been riding. We all know we have no chance of standing against them in a battle. We will approach the camp tomorrow after the sun has gone down and most are asleep. I will lead our party in, on my mount, in my disguise as the Colonel.

"Rayla will trail behind tethered to my horse, feigning to be our prisoner. Taylor will follow close behind me, ready to help should something go wrong. Once we are in the camp, those appointed to kill the watches will begin the attack in silence. Our disguises will hopefully disarm most we encounter until it's too late. Understand we must kill all the soldiers in the camp. No one must escape. Word must not reach Tarak that they have found our Refuge.

"I have seven loyal to me among these soldiers in the camp. Two of them were part of the guards posted on me after my capture, allowing me to instruct them to dispose of any messengers sent out. I had hope of escaping with them and the others to warn you, but the opportunity never presented itself. However, my request to kill the messengers puts us in a good position. With my departure as the Colonel's prisoner, they will, by now, have left the camp permanently to watch for messengers. I'll sneak into the camp tonight and get word to them to join us in the attack.

"Once we have dispatched everyone in the camp and freed the prisoners, we can begin taking stock of their supplies. It will be a few weeks before anyone notices their messengers are late. And a month before they re-deploy soldiers here to investigate. Tarak's army is arrogant, and they will never suspect things have gone so afoul. With luck, we will have two full months before another of Tarak's companies reach here. We will meet further in the morning to discuss the detailed attack plan.

"For tonight, we will split up into our squads and disperse into the woods. This will allow us time to act should any of Tarak's soldiers wander from the base camp and stumble upon a squad. You are each of you well-trained to blend into the woods. If there was a time to excel at that, this is the night. Each group should post a lookout for precaution, and it should go without saying, but keep a cold camp tonight."

With those final words, he stepped back and left it to Rayla. She thanked him, then sent everyone to disperse with their squad and set out their bedrolls for the night. Like before, on their search for a new home, Taylor set his bedroll next to hers. He slipped into his covers and fell asleep without a word. She knew through the Famsha that he still held the calm within him. However, the ever-bubbling turmoil was still present in the room inside his mind.

After the lookouts secured the area, they gathered the squad leaders in the morning. Careed addressed them, "I was able to speak with two of my men last night and get a general layout of the camp. This morning Rayla, Taylor, and I have been discussing our plan."

"Those of you who lead marksmen with bows will be our first strike. At last light as the moon begins to shine and shed its light, you must kill all the guards in the outlying areas and take their place, the ones that will not be missed right off, then move in slowly with our approach. Kill any other soldiers you see on the outskirts of the camp. Do this with extreme accuracy, but do not take out the three men guarding the prisoners or the two at the base camp entrance. Remember, missing a target means a chance for them to set the alarm.

"Once you have completed your task, hide the bodies, and replace the guards with your own men. The rest of you put away your bows and ready your swords, and come in closer to the camp if possible. We will ride in, as we discussed last night. Once the guards on duty inside are dead, we will begin moving to the tents." Careed began drawing a map in the dirt, allowing the squad leaders to follow the plan.

"The soldier's tents are off to the left here as we enter, and the supply wagons are to the right. There are two men in each tent and two hundred and seventy-five tents. Have your men form groups of three, then disperse themselves to the doors of the tents at the front of each row. Each group will have to dispatch the occupants of three or more tents. Be silent, be swift, and be deadly.

"The moon should be high tonight and give us a fair amount of light in the clearing they're in. Once everyone is in place, I'll wave a torch as the signal to begin the attack. With luck, none of the soldiers will set off an alarm, and each team can move swiftly to their next quarry. Give your men explicit instructions to kill the occupants quickly and quietly. No funny business with revenge; it could cost everyone their lives if we have to fight the entire camp.

"Once all the soldiers have been dispatched, meet back at the center of the camp where the prisoners are. Remember, do *not* approach them until our mission is complete. We don't want the prisoners to bring any unwanted attention to our presence because of one of your squad members going to look for a loved one. I know it will be challenging, but the prisoners won't be safe if they start a commotion. After we meet up at the center of the base camp, we can begin setting the prisoners free and look for our loved ones.

"I expect the prisoners to be in rough shape, and some will need medical attention. With that being said, Rayla, the sight of you should put our loved ones at ease. Our two Orb Bearers will be leading the party of healers that have accompanied us and protect them if necessary. They will move to the supply wagons at the entrance once we are in, using them as cover. From there, they will approach the center of the camp as close as it can be deemed safe, until it's time to free the prisoners."

"Is everyone clear on the plan?" Rayla asked. They nodded before she continued, "Go back to your squad and relay the plan. Rest up for the remainder of the day."

The squad leaders dispersed, and Taylor, silent throughout Careed's brief, gave her a reassuring smile. "It's a good plan. It will work!" he said to her. "I sense your worry, but I have watched and listened to these men these last two days. They're well trained and ready to do what it takes."

"It's a good plan, but it's hard not to worry with so much at stake. My visions have always reassured me of Prophecy, but they never showed me the truth of what would lead up to the last battle with Tarak." Rayla paused, taking a breath, "Let us get some rest. it's going to be a long night."

Chapter Thirty-Five

When the sun was down and the full moon cast its light, Careed mounted his horse and tied Rayla's tether to the pommel of his saddle as planned. He dug his heels into the horse's side and guided it forward. The squads followed in behind. Two horsemen with torches joined Careed at each side. Their torches cast a flickering light on the trail before them. The militia wove their way through the sparse trees in the basin Wynfor had chosen for the base camp.

When the moon was high in the sky, they came upon the first signs of the base camp. Torchlight flickered through the trees, denoting the entrance ahead. Careed secured his helmet, dropped the visor down, and hid his face from the guards that would recognize him as a fraud. They rounded a bend in the trail and saw two guardsmen at the end of the path that led into the camp.

That the guardsmen stood to attention on their approach and saluted, a good sign for them. The two recognized the Colonel's armor and had taken for granted who wore it. The two looked surprised to see them return at such a late hour. Careed had speculated with twenty-five hundred men in the camp, there would be plenty of men that did not know one another. He had instructed the men beside him to leave their visors up to allow their voices to carry.

"Why are there so few guards posted?" The man to Careed's left spoke out.

The two guardsmen looked at each other in confusion and snapped to attention. "All the fugitives in this area have been captured or killed, sir," one said. "The commander didn't think that more than the two of us at the entrance and the night watches were necessary..." he spoke with conviction.

"There is no one left to attack us, he figured," said the other as he shrank back. Wynfor was a cruel man and apt to take his disapproval out on the closest man available.

Tarak's men were even more confident and arrogant in their position than Careed could have hoped for. Over the years, he had seen it become common among the lower ranks to be more complacent. No one in fifty years had dared challenge these men.

He signaled the archers behind him with a raised hand pointed toward the two guardsmen. Two arrows sailed through the air, passed him, and hit their targets with remarkable accuracy, killing them in silence. They fell to the ground. Two women dressed like foot soldiers ran forward, dragged the bodies into the dark, and returned to take the soldiers' places.

Careed took off his helmet, hung it from his horse's saddle, and tossed the end of Rayla's tether to her. There were no more soldiers posted between their current position and the tents as far as she could see. With a nod from Rayla, the squad leaders dismounted from their horses and joined their squads where they stood in formation. "Now," Careed said to the men at his side in a hushed tone. They waved their torches, and the militia swiftly crept into action toward the tents.

Rayla removed her loose tether and nodded to Careed as she moved toward Taylor. He hopped down from his horse and joined her, walking toward the healers. When the group was ready, they crept to the closest position to the prisoners that would not alert anyone. Taylor could see that the healers were tense, many knowing what Tarak's men would have done to the prisoners. All were silent as they waited for the battle to be over and to begin their part in the rescue. There were still dangers to be wary of as they waited; they could be discovered, ruining the militia's element of surprise.

The women and men of the militia, now would-be assassins, moved into position for the strike. Careed could see everyone was in place with the high moon overhead, and he gave the go-ahead. The militia moved in unison and with absolute precision as they slipped into the tents of their intended victims. Careed patiently waited for his men to come back out. The first assault went off without a sound, and they moved to the next quarry and carried out the following two assassinations without incident.

Meanwhile, Taylor, Rayla, and the healers moved with caution through the supply wagons. They used the caravan as cover and were able to approach the center of the camp unseen. Taylor kept a keen eye on the assault as they snuck through the wagons. The uncertainty of the mission pushed his nerves to the edge. At first, he had wanted to be part of the attack, but the thought of using the Orb in battle had become too tempting. Taylor was not sure the desire to use the Power would not overcome him, even with the knowledge of how to use a sword to fight. His stomach turned at the thought of the pain the Orb would cause if he chose to use it in such a manner. A split in him formed, one that wanted to use the Orb for killing, the other setting off a dire alarm that he should avoid it at all cost.

Taylor took a breath as they edged closer to the last few wagons that separated them from the prisoners. He watched the assassins as they moved in for the fourth and final assault, but his concentration was broken when he heard a man's voice.

"I told you to be quiet," a gruff voice said. Taylor heard the distinct sound of a firm blow to flesh and the thud of someone falling to the ground. "Get up," the voice demanded. The sound of sobbing became a wailing cry.

Taylor turned to see a soldier step out in his underclothes from a wagon in front of them. His outstretched hand held a young woman in a tattered and dirty dress by her hair. Her feet dangled above the ground; the tips of her toes stretched down to look for footing. Taylor saw the fear and pain in her eyes. Her face and exposed skin were covered in bruises and minor cuts from being beaten. Taylor understood what had happened and that it was likely not the first time. His chest tightened with sorrow for this woman, and anger filled him from the injustice. Her beastly-sized abuser clenched a knife in his other hand—the cause of the fresh cuts on her thigh.

The soldier saw Taylor and Rayla before they could find cover. His eyes widened as he shouted, "Intruders! Intruders!" at the top of his lungs. His shouts roused the sleeping soldiers; the assassins had not reached the rest of their targets. Half-dressed men poured from the tents, and a battle for their lives started.

Taylor disregarded the battle amongst the tents; he

kept his focus on the soldier before him. Rage filled him and flowed into the Orb, triggering its power and bringing it to life. The Orb turned a deep black, a void that drew in all the light around it. Taylor raised his hand toward the soldier and closed it into a fist while he created weaves of power around the man. The man froze in place, and Taylor directed a second flow of power to the man's throat, crushing his windpipe. The soldier's screams became but a gurgling sound that barely escaped his mouth.

Taylor moved the flow of power toward the soldier's hand and arm that the girl dangled from. The weave moved quickly from the soldier's fingertips to his elbow, burning it all away to ash. The soldier writhed in pain as Taylor used the Power to cauterize the wound so the soldier would not bleed out. The girl fell to the ground in a heap as she cried. Rayla was at the girl's side; her Orb shone purple as she used her limited healing abilities and comforted her.

Taylor strolled over to the soldier and took the knife from him. He reached down with his other to pull the string that held up the soldier's underclothes, and they fell to the ground. An angry smile spread across Taylor's face. The soldier's eyes went wild with fear and understanding of what Taylor had in mind. With a firm slash, he gelded the man, then released the weave that held him; the soldier fell to the ground sobbing. Taylor left him there to bleed and likely die.

Through the Famsha, Taylor had felt Rayla heal the girl as best as her skill would allow while he contended with the soldier. He knew the Famsha told her of his rage even as she looked out of the corner of her eye at his face. The soldier deserved the pain he currently felt, but fear rose in her about how far Taylor would go. She reached up and caught

Taylor's arm, spinning him toward her as he walked past and said, "Taylor, you cannot use the Orb for killing again."

Taylor removed her hand, a wild look in his eyes, and stepped back to unsheathe his sword. Then he looked down at her and the girl she held in her arms, and his face softened. "I don't need to." With the sword lifted in the air, he ran off into the battle among the tents.

At first, Taylor felt clumsy with the sword as its power merged into him during the battle. He knew the forms from Rayla, but putting them into practice was something entirely different. The first soldier he engaged cut him deep in the side, and he faltered. Tae and Zem rushed to his aid.

"Are you OK, Taylor?" Zem asked.

The wound began to close, and he stood. "Just getting my bearings." Taylor looked him in the eye and dove back into battle. Tae and Zem fought at his side for a few moments before they became separated. As Taylor fought, he began to feel more comfortable, but took cuts to his thigh and arm, deep ones, before he fully connected with the sword and its power. One now with his weapon, he walked through the tents, cutting a swath through Tarak's men. No one could touch him. The tip of his blade whistled as it moved through the air with each strike.

The feel of the whole thing brought him a sense of justice. He did not think of killing with the Orb. The fullness of his connection with the sword took over, and its blade sang as he killed with it.

The battle was more lengthy than Careed had hoped for. While sleeping, men make easy prey; those that had awoken to the alarm fought heartily. It lasted almost an hour, with the militia taking some losses. Those able collected the wounded and helped them to the rendezvous point in the center of the camp. They stopped short of being seen by the prisoners, pausing to hurriedly remove their stolen armor. They knew their people would be frightened by the armor of Tarak's men. When they were done, they continued to free the prisoners.

Chapter Thirty-Six

After Taylor ran off and the battle ensued, Rayla stayed where she was. She had killed many soldiers during the battle at the Refuge. The blood that had stained her hands that day made her stomach turn. Killing was not something that her people took to well, her least of all. Tonight, she had committed to saving people's lives, not taking them. Rayla soothed the girl Taylor had saved. She removed her travel cloak and covered her for warmth and security. Rayla kept tabs on Taylor through the Famsha, worried for his life and for his sanity. Once the battle ended, Rayla lifted the girl in her arms and made her way to the rest of the prisoners, healers in tow.

She arrived at the camp center to see the prisoners unguarded, and made her way to the first caged wagon. The Orb's power enhanced her vision and enabled her to see many in similar conditions as the young woman she carried. Some huddled themselves around their sleeping children protectively.

As Rayla approached the prisoners, some noticed her and cried out in joy. The locks that barred the doors of the prison wagons shattered as she wove flows of power into them. She laid the girl down beside the first door to swing open. Rayla untied a woman from inside and bid her to care for the girl outside. Then moved on, from woman to woman, and freed them. The healers spread out to the other prison wagons and joined her in her task. The women began helping each other, and when all the prisoners were free and out of the wagons, Rayla used her small healing ability on the worst of the wounded. She would not be able to do much for those close to death, but for them, she could at least ease the pain. At the same time, the healers cared for the others.

Throughout the night as Rayla healed, she felt Taylor's thoughts several times through the Famsha. He had chosen not to return to the center of the base camp from the fighting. Instead, he made a camp far out on his own to work through the heaviness he felt.

The night was a restless one. Rayla's people were free of Tarak's soldiers' threat for the moment, but there was still much to do. All that were able among the militia helped with the freed prisoners, the wounded, and the children. Exhaustion abounded in her people; they had endured a great deal in the last few months, some more than others. Still, this was no time to rest. Tomorrow they would need to begin sorting through the wagons and prepare those unable to walk for the return trip.

Posted watches worked in rotations as a precaution, while Rayla continued healing late into the night. After the worst of the wounded were cared for and settled, those not on duty went to sleep. Rayla found an unoccupied tent and lay down to rest. Her last thoughts as she drifted off were of the turmoil Taylor felt inside.

When Rayla awoke the following day, Taylor sat at her

side, calm and quiet. "Has anyone ever managed to get past how the Orbs punished when they killed with it?" he asked.

Rayla sat up to face him and replied, "Once, but not much is written of how he did it. When people inquired, he said that the Orb had forgiven him." She reached out and took his hand, looked him in the eye, and continued, "You're much different from any who have carried the Orbs before you. If there is anyone that could duplicate that task, it's you." Rayla shielded her feelings from Taylor that he might not, hoping only to empower him.

"Last night, when I used the Power on the soldier at the wagon, it felt sickeningly sweet. It was hard to stop and not kill him with the Orb outright. But at the same time, I felt desperate to control myself, to make myself stop. The memory of killing made me feel sick, and knowing what the cost would be afterward was enough to stop me," Taylor, confided as a tear fell down his cheek.

Rayla's heart sank. This was what drove those that killed with the Orb mad. There became an internal conflict. The Power to murder with the Orbs was irresistible once used; the feel of the Power was intoxicating. But that only lasted for a short time, as the pain from the Orb afterward was almost unbearable. As the murdering continued, the pain became so intense after each use that it crippled for days, weeks, and then months. Magic always had its costs, but those that used the Orb to murder paid an unimaginable price. Left with the knowledge that only killing again would stop the pain, if only for a few moments, they killed again, leaving them caught in an endless cycle. After a time, this drove them to madness. She felt the divide in Taylor through the Famsha as his feelings flared inside him.

"I managed the rest of the battle with only the use of my sword, but I wanted to kill them with the Orb, all of them. I channeled that need into my sword," Taylor said with euphoria on his face.

"And it was a sight to be seen for sure. I've never seen anything like it," Careed's voice broke in. "I think you even cut one of them in half. If it weren't for Taylor, we would have had many more casualties." He sat down to address Taylor. "I owe you a debt of gratitude. The young woman you saved from that brute was my daughter Niea. She told me what happened, and I'm very grateful that you're here." Taylor stood and nodded to Careed, accepting his appreciation before walking off.

Careed sat a moment before he turned to Rayla. Wondering what bothered Taylor was written on his face. When she said nothing, he changed the subject to the other reason he sought her out. "We need to begin returning to the Refuge as soon as possible. It will take us some work to get back with all of the wounded." Careed stared off toward the wagons and continued, "It's a shame we can't return with the supplies here."

"Actually, I believe we can," Rayla said as she stood. "But first, we need to care for the wounded. I healed the most critical, but many won't make it through the next few days without attention. I think that I know someone that may be of help in that." Rayla set off after Taylor.

After catching up with him, Rayla walked at his side. *How do I say this to him? He's losing his grip on his sanity, and bringing him back is of the utmost importance.* Taylor turned toward the woods, in the direction she knew his camp to be. She spoke in an urgent voice, "Taylor, I need to talk to you. I need your help."

"I'm not sure I can do anything at this point. We have defeated Tarak's men here. Who's left to kill?" he said stoically as he kept his pace toward his destination.

"Stop, Taylor," Rayla said as she grabbed his arm and spun him around to face her. There was a faint glow from the Orb under her shirt.

"I thought we couldn't use the Orbs against each other?" Taylor asked, shocked.

"I don't intend you harm Taylor. As long as I bear you no ill will, I can use it to protect myself." She fixed her eyes to his and continued, "I don't need you to kill anyone, quite the opposite. Many of our people need healing. With your many leaps in talent with the Orb, I had hoped you might present with an aptitude for healing too."

Rayla paused when Taylor looked at her, puzzled, "Remember not so long ago when you had that wound in the forest? When you ran into those soldiers?" Taylor nodded his head, not sure where Rayla was leading. "You healed yourself that day, with no understanding of the Orb. You weren't even conscious of doing it. Others can be healed with the Orb consciously in much the same way."

"How do you think I could heal someone with so much death around me?" Taylor said back to her. "All I recall from that day is a fleeting thought passing through my mind. That I needed to find someone to help stop the bleeding. The healing just happened."

"Exactly, it took no effort; you did it without thought," Rayla replied. Taking his hand, Rayla led him back to the area where the wounded were. She knelt at the side of a young woman not much older than Niea, pulling him down with her. "I have a small amount of ability with healing. I'll show you how by beginning to direct the weaves into her. All you have to do is mimic them."

Gently, Rayla directed her voice to the woman that lay there and asked, "Serin, can you hear me?" Serin did not respond; she had been beaten unconscious, it seemed. Out of one of her arms, a bone protruded from her flesh. Rayla took Taylor's hand, placed it palm down upon the woman's chest, and left hers to rest on top of his. Rayla opened herself to her Orb's power and allowed it to fill her. Then she let the flow of the Famsha between her and Taylor swell, but took care not to be overwhelmed with his guilt.

She began a sending to him, *Let me show you how it works for me. Focus on Serin's forehead, above the crest of her nose. There is an energy center there that will allow you into her being. Her body will tell you of its pain, and from there, you can heal her.*

Taylor followed her instructions from the image in her mind of where the energy would be located. Taylor allowed the Power of the Orb to fill him and tried to concentrate. Unsure of what to expect, Taylor felt a hopelessness come over him after nothing had occurred in the first few moments. *Can I not help the woman? Is that power beyond me?* As sadness filled him, something strange happened. An overwhelming desire to help the girl overtook him, a counter to the feeling that drove him to kill.

A flash at his chest drew his attention to the Orb, which only a second before had shone black; it now emitted a white light. At once, every part of him was different. He felt serene instead of angry. There was a determination where hesitation had been. He closed his eyes and took a deep breath, and when he opened them, Serin's brow had a tiny pinprick of fluttering white light where there had been nothing before.

The light began to draw him in to look deeper. Taylor refocused his energy, which triggered the Orb's power. *Not that way!* resounded through his mind from Rayla. But the caution was too late. The light at Serin's brow shot out and enveloped him. Her thoughts, who she was, and what she felt were like an open book. Her sorrow flowed into him; its immensity was like nothing he had ever experienced. He felt his consciousness lurch forward and enter her mind through her energy center.

He felt Serin's agony of being run down by a warhorse, and later to be dragged and beaten. It was so intense that he thought he might pass out. The pain of her body aching at every point from being beaten struck his heart. His presence in her consciousness triggered a flash of memory, with Taylor trapped inside to feel all of it.

A soldier that had walked past her stopped and stepped back as she crawled toward her home. Terror ripped through her; she screamed, "NO, PLEASE!" She summoned all her strength, and tried to stand to run away. But she was too late. The soldier, with all his might, kicked her in the side. She flew into the air like a rag-doll, landing on her back. The soldier dropped to his knees and straddled her chest, pinning her down. He reached down, placed a hand across her throat, and tightened his grip so she could not breathe.

With the lack of air, she began to feel faint and weak. She tried her best to fight back, scraping at his flesh and hitting him, angering the soldier. He used his free hand to pull the dagger from his belt and jab it into her thigh. Pain flooded through her and she jerked in surprise. He used the force of the blade as he twisted it to disable her further. The hand at her throat tightened, and she lost her ability to breathe entirely. Taylor could no longer separate himself from Serin. He, too, felt the terror, the pain, the emotional defeat.

The soldier looked at her and said, "Ahh, I remember you!"

Tears filled her eyes and horror filled her heart in recognition. Her clenched fist swung wildly up, catching him in the jaw in one last defiant effort. He retaliated in a fury, grabbing her wrist, and twisting it sideways until her arm snapped at the elbow. Serin fell unconscious from the pain, but not before Taylor recognized the soldier. He was the one that he and Rayla had stumbled upon tormenting Neia. Taylor felt satisfaction that he had let the man bleed out.

Chapter Thirty-Seven

Everything went black for an instant before Taylor found himself in an earlier memory.

It was just dawn as she lay in bed, slowly waking. A panicked scream from outside her house brought her heart to a race. "SOLDIERS, RUN!" echoed through the village. She jumped out of her bed, still in her nightclothes, and ran for the front door to bar it. But the door burst open before she could reach it.

A soldier stood in the doorway, a dagger in his hand; the same man that Taylor had felt strangle her, just moments ago. Serin stopped in her tracks, the back door only a few paces away behind her. She saw a broad, sickly smile spread across the soldier's face before she spun and rushed for the door. She heard the thundering sound of the soldier's boots coming for her as she swung it open. She had made it out! Suddenly, she felt a sharp pain in her arm, and the man's dagger flew past her into the brush in front of her. Blood dripped from the cut it had made as it grazed her.

As she ran for her life, Taylor felt her heart pounding and the pain in the bottom of her bare feet. There were small sharp stones along the path; the smell of smoke was in the air. Taylor was not only a voyeur in this memory but part of it, unable to distinguish himself from Serin. They ran as fast as they could along the path. The village came into view; houses burned and their people were being slaughtered.

It was then that she heard the sound of hooves on the ground behind her. The impact of the horse knocked her to the ground, stunning her, and her body ached. Scrambling to recover as the soldier rounded his horse, she rolled over to see him looking down at her. He had caught up to her. With a sickly smile on his face, he reared his horse up, and its front hooves came down upon her. Landing on her arm and side, her arm snapped, the bone breaking through the skin. Several of her ribs broke on the other side of her torso, where the other hoof landed.

The soldier looked down at her in satisfaction and rode away. Tears filled her eyes; she lay broken, sobbing for only a few minutes before she passed out. The screams of her family, friends, and fellow villagers haunted her as she faded.

"Taylor, Taylor!" *he heard a distant voice calling his name.*

"Memories can be a dangerous place to go," Rayla's voice said. "In your mistake, you have learned to know what being violated as a woman feels like. Keep it as a reminder of what women go through and what they fear daily. But also let it remind you that entering someone's memories can have a cost. You can do nothing for her soul. Separate yourself from her mind. Repairing her body is the best and only thing you can do for her. I'll show you the weaves I use to heal."

He took a shaky breath, the horror of what had happened breaking his heart. He refocused. Only seconds had passed, but he had experienced much in that time. As

Rayla worked on the wound at Serin's side, he saw the weaves moving to knit the flesh back together. When she finished, he took over and started to imagine the flows healing her wounds. He felt the Orb's energy flow through him and out of his hand into Serin. Rayla withdrew her energy as Taylor took over the healing process. When she was satisfied he was capable, she removed her hand and sat back. Taylor needed to come into his capabilities on his own, like those before him.

In his mind's eye, he pictured Serin's injury wholly healed. Quicker than he could imagine, the tissue knitted together, and the wound vanished from sight. Taylor looked at the deep cut in her thigh and imagined the tissue knitted together. Again the weaves formed and did their work flawlessly. The wound closed together seamlessly within an instant; the infection there healed with it. He moved his intention to the bone in her arm, and it slid back into place, mending the broken skin closed. With the life-threatening wounds healed, his concentration flowed to the large cut on her arm; as with her other wounds, it responded to his will with ease.

Lastly, Taylor healed the bruises that dotted her body. As he finished, Taylor was left with only one regret. He wished that he could take away Serin's trauma of being hunted down, trampled and strangled. That, however, would have to occur naturally and would take time.

Taylor took a breath and withdrew the Orb's energy from Serin, then closed his eyes and remained in his own thoughts for a moment. When he opened them, Taylor was met with Serin's tear-filled eyes. His hands shook; her memories were fresh and sharp as they played in his mind. She took in a deep breath as the connection dissolved. Even though they were Serin's memories, Taylor would carry them for the rest of his life. No being should have to live through that, no one.

"Thank you," Serin said, and began to cry.

Leaning in, comforting her, Rayla said gently, "You will need rest still, Serin. Your body will be tired from the healing and your captivity. The energy rush your body received from the healing will only last a few moments." Serin abided Rayla, closed her eyes, and fell fast asleep.

Taylor's sense of anxiety, anger, and horror at what he had done had diminished. It wasn't as though it hadn't happened, but there was a sense of balance. He had saved this young woman's life and repaired the damage to her body. She would still need to work through what she had gone through, but it would be without the pain in her body. *Could this be the answer to the killing?*

Taylor stood as Rayla did, and asked, "I don't feel her in my mind as I did with you. When you passed your knowledge to me ... what you did was different?"

"Yes, our connection is deeper and in both directions. You, in a sense, saw Serin's memories, felt them, experienced them. But she did not experience yours, nor mix with your mind. The connection I created to impart my knowledge went both ways and connects the soul. What you did healing her was a one-way connection, serving to deliver energy and aid in repairing the body."

Taylor thought about what Rayla said, and it made him consider what she had shared in their Famsha. It was hard to let someone know how you felt, let alone your unfiltered feelings and deepest thoughts. He was unsure why she had shared such a deep connection with him. He had come to understand that Rayla was driven to save her people and not always forthright in her intentions.

Rayla had kept her feelings locked away and hidden

from Taylor during the Famsha. But Taylor had gleaned something in Rayla's heart when they were joined. Tucked away in an attempt to hide them, Taylor suspected were feelings for him. In that well-protected space, love had shone through for an instant before she had locked it away. Something that surprised Taylor, leaving him to believe that Rayla felt more for him that she let on.

"Taylor?" Rayla said, snapping him out of his thoughts. She paused to see if he was listening. "Would you like to carry on, helping the other prisoners? It can be a lot to take in for the first time."

He nodded to her with a smile and said, "I can indeed."

Rayla walked to a man lying on the ground only a short distance away. Taylor's heart sank, recognizing Tae. His injury was substantial, an arrow protruding from his chest, and his shirt was soaked in blood. Tae's face was pale from the blood loss, and his breathing was ragged, he was near death. Tae had been one of the unlucky ones to be surprised when the alarm had been raised.

Zem sat there beside him, pale with fear. It appeared as though he had not slept since his friend had fallen. Taylor thought Zem might fall over at any minute.

"I think that Tae might die! Rayla, can you help him?" he pleaded, hopeful her small ability with healing would be enough.

"I can't heal such a wound, but Taylor might be able. Let us step away so that he might try," Rayla answered. She took Zem's hand to usher him back.

Tae's breath was shallow, but he opened his eyes and nodded to Taylor, "It almost went off without a hitch."

Taylor knelt, placed his hand on Tae's chest, and held his gaze for a moment. There was only a tiny amount of life lingering, "I'm going to help you now. Be still," Taylor shifted his attention to Tae's brow. Without the light enveloping him, Taylor had better control of the Power. This time he directed the energy flow out of his hand and into Tae's chest. His mind's eye saw inside Tae where the arrow had pierced his lung.

Taylor saw that Tae's chest cavity had filled with blood. The sight increased the urgency for Taylor to set to work. He wrapped his free hand around the bolt in preparation to pull it out. Where Siren's injuries had been substantial, they had not been immediately life-threatening. Taylor felt nauseous as his nervousness rose. He had to think about what he was about to do. Taking the arrow out would cause Tae to bleed out if Taylor did not heal him quickly enough.

Sweat dripped from Taylor's brow; he wiped it away. Taylor used the Power to dull Tae's pain. Then he created a weave that formed a stream of blood, drawing it out from the lung and around the arrow. It was an easy enough weave. But it took some thought to maintain as he urged the lung to take in air. The flow of blood seemed endless as Taylor worked against the clock. In actuality, it ceased after only a few seconds.

With that done, he pulled the arrow out slowly, mending the tissue as he did. Again, it took a great deal of concentration. Taylor shook with the strain. The whole process took less than two minutes to complete, but it felt like hours to Taylor. As the last of Tae's lung knitted together, he quickly sealed the first bit of the wound on the interior of Tae's chest. With that complete, Taylor jerked the arrow from his chest and hastily sealed the wound on the surface. He barley finished in time; a few seconds longer, and Tae would have died.

Rayla looked on in amazement. She could not find words for what Taylor had done. She had felt his struggle with so many weaves at once, but nevertheless, he had done it. Never in the histories had a Bearer ever been capable of healing like he had done. Taylor had yet to cease to amaze her in the abundance of the gifts he had with the Orb. Taylor stood as Tae opened his eyes and took in a deep breath.

"Thank you, Taylor," Tae managed as he found that he could breathe with ease. Exhausted, he closed his eyes and fell fast asleep.

With color returning to his face, Zem shed a tear before wrapping his arms around Taylor in a bear hug. "Thank you, Taylor," he choked out with joy. He released Taylor, met him in the eyes, and said, "I don't know if I can ever repay you for what you have done." He smiled and sat back down beside Tae.

As Taylor stood there, that same sense of peace washed over him. Using the Orb's power to heal was defiantly easing the need to kill that came from it. Something unexpected was occurring as well; his body felt refreshed and rejuvenated, and he felt ready to use his new gift elsewhere. He turned to Rayla, "Who's next?" He carried on to the next person and knelt beside them; the Orb flared to life with a white glow as he healed them. He carried on to the next after that, and to the next, and so on as he healed with increasing ease.

In the early morning hours, after he had spent the night without rest, Rayla stopped him. "At some point, the Orb won't be able to recharge you, Taylor. You will need to rest, and if you choose not to, overwhelming exhaustion will suddenly overtake you. It had taken some many days to recover when they pushed on further than their bodies could manage, falling into a deep sleep from which they couldn't be woken."

"One more," he replied, relishing the peace healing brought him. The Orb flared to life once more, and he began picturing the wounds in the man before him healed. When he was finished, he stood. Abruptly his head spun and caused him to sway back and forth. Taylor dropped to his knees and almost passed out. The Orb's power withdrew from him without warning, leaving him almost unable to remain upright as exhaustion overtook his body.

Rayla rushed to his side, an angry look filling her face as she scolded, "I warned you, Taylor; you're lucky you're still conscious." She called two of the militia nearby and had him carried to an unoccupied tent, where she left him to sleep. The tent's previous occupants had been removed and piled off to the side of the camp, as had the rest of the soldiers. The tents now held the wounded militia and recovering captives.

Chapter Thirty-Eight

While Taylor slept in the early morning hours, Rayla and Careed took stock of what supplies were in the wagons. There was much more than Rayla had anticipated or hoped for. They now had seventeen covered wagons, seven full of food, two chuckwagons, two full of military supplies and mending tools for armor, and one full of feed for the horses. Plus, five empty covered supply wagons—likely full of food at the beginning of the journey. These would likely have been refilled from the stores of the Refuge and surrounding villages, but now they would be perfect for the wounded and children. There were also roughly one hundred horses they had gathered after the battle.

As the two of them leaned against the back of the wagon they worked on, Rayla could see Careed had several thoughts running through his mind. Rayla was still looking into the wagon, in awe at their finds. Careed took in a deep breath, "This is better than the best-case scenario, but how do you suppose to get it back? Wynfor had several thousand men clearing the path through the mountains."

Rayla looked over at Careed and smiled, "Daven, Kerisa! You can come out now." She shouted. She paused and yelled again. "Daven, Kerisa! I mean it."

Righting himself and stepping away from the wagon, a puzzled Careed scanned about. "Who are you calling to?" he asked.

Two small figures materialized out of the nothingness right before them. Careed jumped back, startled, and began to draw his sword in fear. Rayla grabbed the pommel of his sword halting him, a look of caution on her face. She guided it back into its scabbard and looked at him with a grimace.

In front of them stood two children, a boy and a girl, both about eight years old. Their striking resemblance made it evident they were brother and sister. Each sported fair hair, bright green eyes, and delicate facial features. He thought them very beautiful.

"I thought I said this is no place for the two of you. Why did you follow us?" Rayla barked.

"We are quite old enough, Rayla," the young girl replied. She raised her chin to the side in defiance.

"She's quite right. You do always treat us as children," the boy said matter-of-facty.

"Careed, meet Daven and Kerisa, two of the oldest residents on our planet." He looked at her with disbelief, and his mouth hung open. They both wore smug looks as they stared at him. Rayla continued, "After five years of Tarak's rule, their grandmother realized that he was on the hunt for Shard Carriers. She slipped her deceased husband's ring on Daven and hers on Kerisa, knowing that the two halves of the Orb in the rings would protect them.

"She bade them goodbye, knowing that as long as the children wore the set of rings that had once been whole, they would never age. The rings were heirlooms passed down through her family for generations. She and her husband wore them in their youth—" Rayla frowned as Kerisa cut in.

"For over one hundred years, they had adventures, which I can tell you about later if you like. But you see, they really wanted a baby. Grandmother said it took ages to talk Granddad into it. But she did, you see, and within a couple of months, their baby was born, which is strange, really. Because most babies take months and months to be born. Anyway, after taking them off, the rings, they had our mother.

"We, Daven and I," Kerisa motioned to Daven, "took the regular time to grow in our mommy. She had a mysterious husband, our father, of course, that no one knew. She died in childbirth, our mother did, and Grandmother raised us. That's how I know the story. She told me it all the time because I really liked hearing about the mystery of my father and mother's love. When Grandmother put the rings on us, she knew the effects the rings would have on us. But she said she would collect us before any time at all. She told us to run into the woods and keep going until we saw no sign of civilization.

"And we did, waiting for several years in a little hunting cabin with our spectacular rings to care for us." Kerisa lifted her hand to display the ring with half of an Orb set into it. "I tell the story much better, don't you think? Rayla's such a poor storyteller. Daven has the other half of the Orb. Show him, Daven." Kerisa insisted.

Daven breathed, "You're doing it again, Kerisa. Stop being so pompous. I've been telling you for a hundred years, people don't like it." Daven tucked his hands into his pants pockets.

"That would make them well over three hundred years old," Careed said to Rayla in disbelief.

Interjecting before Rayla could answer, Daven said, "Older actually, we don't always live—" He stopped short after a kick to the shins from Kerisa, and became tight-lipped at the reminder that he was about to say something that was a secret.

Continuing, Rayla chose not to acknowledge the engagement between Daven and Kerisa. "They wandered into our Refuge a few years before I came here. As far as we can tell, Kerisa is correct; the Orb halves in the rings are from the same Orb. It's the only explanation for why they don't age. The rings also work much more effectively when Kerisa and Daven work together. These two have had a lot of time to refine the Power of the Orb. They have a lot of little tricks in their arsenal, like being invisible."

"Stop, stop. Stop," Careed said. "I don't understand how it is that I lived in the Refuge for so many years, yet never saw these two in my time there."

"Because we didn't want you to, silly! Why would we talk to children." Kerisa had her nose in the air and a tone of superiority in her voice. "You were so much more fun when you first came to the Refuge, Rayla," Kerisa said, then turned her gaze to look at Careed. "She used to play hide-and-seek with us, you know. We laughed and talked for hours. Now all she does is pine for Taylor." Kerisa pointed into her mouth and made a barfing sound. It was quite a display.

"Oh please, Kerisa," Daven said as he looked at her. "All you have talked about for days is Taylor and how handsome he is. 'Wouldn't I look beautiful on our vow day in a long flowing dress?'" he said while he made his voice high with a silly look on his face so Rayla could see. A kick to the shin from Kerisa, but harder this time, caused Daven to yelp.

Reddening in the cheeks, she replied to Kerisa as kindly as possible. "Some of us had to become grown-ups." She looked at Daven, winked, and continued her story, "Their grandmother told them to not take the rings off for any reason."

"And we have not!" Kerisa butted in proudly.

Rayla frowned, "I have a job for the two of you since you're here. We need a roadway built to lead us back home. I'd consider it a kindness if you helped us make our way through the trees?" Rayla asked, using a pleasant tone.

Daven perked up and spoke eagerly, "I'd be happy to! I like doing things for you, Rayla."

Kerisa glared at him hotly, "Now who has the crush? Hmmm?" She jabbed him in the chest so hard Daven had to step back to keep his footing. Daven's cheeks began to redden.

"You will also have to make sure everyone gets through the roadway safely," Rayla said as she fixed them both in the eye.

"Alright, but Taylor has to escort me on the way home," Kerisa bargained and shifted her eyes away nonchalantly.

Rayla nodded in agreement, then replied, "He's recovering in one of the tents. I'm sure he would be happy of the company."

Kerisa brightened and turned, "Come along, Daven." She grabbed his arm and tugged at him. He rolled his eyes and allowed her to pull him along behind her.

Chapter Thirty-Nine

Rayla knew that Careed had seen the Orbs do a great many things in his time. Daven and Kerisa were something else, though. She watched as a shiver ran down his spine. He stood there a moment and did his best to comprehend what had transpired. Unable to come to terms with Daven and Kerisa's existence, he asked incredulously, "Why leave them like that?"

"I don't think you understand. The two of them choose to be like that and won't have it any other way. They have lived like that for so long that they cannot consider anything else. They're both super-intelligent, have great wisdom, and are unbelievably powerful. Due to the Orb though, they have remained the same maturity since their grandmother put the rings on their little fingers. Not even I could manage to take them off.

"We tried once, despite knowing how much pain it would cause the person who tried. The four men that volunteered all passed out from the pain after a few minutes of restraining them and trying to remove their rings. All four of them, hard, seasoned soldiers, woke up the next morning as six-year-old girls—Kerisa's just punishment for them that Daven was happy to oblige. Kerisa and Daven can together do things they shouldn't be able to. It's a mystery that will likely never be solved.

"She said that she and Daven could play rough too. No amount of convincing ever changed her mind to return them to the men they were. Imagine waking as a thirty-something man in a six-year-old girl's body. It was a great deal for them to get over. One of them is Serin's mother, if you can imagine.

"Kalamar once tasked me to try and convince her and Daven to take them off. I spent months with them, playing and talking like she mentioned. In the end, they knew all along what I was up to. She wanted a girl to be her confidant, and Daven already had a little crush on me. That they liked me and the Orb I wear at my neck is likely why I'm not six years old and at their mercy."

"Why allow them to stay with you if they're so dangerous," Careed asked.

"Because they're children, and on a good day, like today, they're a real asset to the community. I found them hiding under their beds in their room, terrified after the battle. They still have the emotions of children. Can you imagine Niea at nine, facing soldiers?"

Careed shook his head, "I hadn't thought of it like that."

Rayla carried on, "You have to play their games if you want something. They don't like to be outsmarted or caught. That is what all the pretense was about just now. Kerisa wanted to reveal herself, not be revealed. Before we marched here, I told them to stay put. I wanted to check on them after Taylor and I saw several dead soldiers in the passage to their quarters. I knew they would disobey me. They're still obstinate even after all these years.

"I'd step carefully around them. Kerisa once used her half of the Orb to fill my bed with stinging oak while I slept. She thought I was out of line when I jumped into the lake with her in my arms after refusing to bathe. She smelled awful; she hadn't bathed in a month. Even Daven had started giving her a wide berth. When I asked her why she wasn't bathing, she said, 'I simply do not feel like it.' And turned and walked away."

Careed stood mulling over his thoughts, "She sounds.... difficult."

"Difficult falls short of what it's like dealing with her. Anyway, we should begin loading the wounded and the children into the wagons after second meal. Tell our people to pack up whatever they think would be helpful, including the tents if we can manage it. We will need to find drivers for the wagons; ask around and see who has experience. In the meantime, I'll start to work on getting Daven and Kerisa to begin making a roadway. With their power, they should be able to get us home in three or four days." Rayla paused, realizing that Careed had his own troubles, "How is Niea?"

Careed's face saddened for a moment before he spoke. "She speaks little and has yet to get out of bed. I didn't want to bother you or Taylor, so I had Mazy, one of the healers, speak with her. I thought it could help Niea to talk about what happened. Niea wouldn't speak to Mazy. Wynfor said he would rape her first and instruct his men not to damage her when they took their turn with her. She would be used for as long as possible and that she should grow to an old woman being raped each day as punishment for my betrayal," Careed went silent, a tear rolling down his cheek.

"I'm sorry for what happened to her, Careed. I wish we could have made it back from searching for a new home sooner." Rayla said, care in her voice. "Talking with a woman and a friend is more comfortable in matters like this. I'll visit her in your tent when I finish with Daven and Kerisa."

Taylor awoke to a cold little hand on his forehead, and when he opened his eyes, a little girl stood hovering over him. "Hi! I'm Kerisa, and that is my brother Daven on the cot there. Are you feeling better?" Kerisa chirped. The young boy on the next cot to him had a striking resemblance to her. "Rayla said I should come to look after you." Taylor's gaze stayed on Daven long enough to see him roll his eyes. *This is the boy I saw in the market the first day I left my room. And her voice sounds like the little girl's voice in my room I had been hearing.*

Kerisa smiled at him, a smile he recognized from many girls at the kids' camp. As far as crushes go, this girl had a serious one on him. He could remember seeing her before but only in a distant way. "Have we met?" Taylor inquired.

"No, we have been hiding since the troops came, but you bumped into me in the meadow once. While you were playing with Daphne. You said, 'Hi,' to me." She smiled at him, "Do you need anything?"

"I don't think so. Do you know where Rayla is?" Taylor asked. He was about to get out of bed when he realized that he lay naked under the blankets. Frowning at Kerisa, he asked, "Do you know where my clothes are?"

The girl's cheeks reddened, "Oh, there at the bottom of

your bed, on the chest. We will go outside and wait until you're dressed."

Daven took Kerisa by the shoulders and directed her toward the exit. "Come on, Mooney."

Kerisa gasped, "I'm not mooning over him." As they exited with a big smile on her face, she cheerfully said, "Bye!" before she directed her voice to Daven. "You're so rude to me sometimes."

Daven ignored Kerisa as they exited. He instead announced a cheerful, "Hello Rayla!" then cautioned her, "You should wait; he's dressing."

Rayla paused in front of the tent and replied, "I was looking for you and Kerisa, Daven. Are you ready to begin making a roadway for us to get us home?"

The words were barely out of her mouth before Daven answered, "Yes, of course, we are. You're coming with us, right?"

Kerisa let out an exasperated sigh, annoyed with her brother, before directing her voice toward the tent as she spoke to Rayla. "Do not forget your promise that Taylor would escort me."

Rayla smiled at her, like a parent would smile at a needy child; "I didn't forget, and I'm sure Taylor will be happy to escort you. And yes, Daven, I'll come with you for a short while. Are you decent, Taylor?" Rayla called into the tent impatiently.

Taylor stepped out of the tent, fully dressed, and peered at Rayla questioningly. He inquired, "Did I hear we were going somewhere?"

"Yes, we are!" Kerisa said. She stepped over to Taylor's side and slipped her hand around his.

Rayla feigned a smile and replied, "I see you have met Daven and Kerisa. We will be escorting them to the camp exit, toward the path we used to enter the camp the night before last. These two carry an Orb between them, giving them equivalent power to ours. In different ways, of course. They have agreed to make a gateway home, wide enough for the wagons to fit through. So, we will load the wounded in the empty wagons and bring the supplies back with us. Kerisa has asked if you would escort her along the way. I didn't think you'd mind."

Taylor could feel Rayla in the back of his mind as she coaxed him to agree. He played along and led the way to their destination. A resounding, *I'll tell you later,* echoed through his mind. Kerisa held his hand as they walked. If this got them back to the Refuge faster, so be it. He could put up with a little girl's crush for a few days. *Who is this girl?* he asked Rayla, using a sending to her. She did not answer, to his annoyance. He would have words with her later.

Kerisa gripped his hand tightly while she looked up at him and asked, "Is there a special someone waiting back at home for you?" As Rayla followed in behind Taylor, Daven stepped in line with Rayla and smiled at her, content to just be at her side. Daven seemed the more pleasant of the two.

Taylor felt Rayla's amusement at his current situation at the back of his mind. He thought he even felt the broad smile on her face. She enjoyed the situation a little too much for his liking. He directed his attention back to Kerisa, "I was very happily married back on my planet. She died a little over a year ago, while carrying our unborn child."

"That's really sad. Mommy died giving birth to us." A tear fell from her cheek, and she gave Taylor's hand a slight squeeze before loosening her grip. Taylor felt a tingle in his hand as she did so.

"KERISA," Rayla shouted from behind them.

Kerisa let go of his hand immediately and sidestepped a pace away to continue at his side. Taylor felt anger flow through Rayla at whatever Kerisa had just done, an emotion he knew she did not take on lightly. He left the incident there in an attempt not to embarrass Kerisa, but put it on the list of things to ask Rayla about it later.

It was silent between them as they walked across the camp. And after only a few moments longer, they reached the exit. From there, the soldiers had marched through the forest, weaving their way through the trees. The lines of men had created a wide swath of trampled plants on the forest floor.

"It's up to the two of you now," Rayla said to Kerisa and Daven.

The twins strode up to the center of the exit. They joined hands so that the halves of the Orbs in their rings touched each other. Concentration filled their faces, and the rings began glowing a familiar purple hue; something powerful was about to happen. The path in front of them shimmered, and a twenty-foot stone archway appeared; it reminded him of the Arc de Triomphe in Paris. Through it, Taylor could see a familiar meadow. Taylor remembered this meadow; it was on the far outside of the Refuge where the gardens were. The twins had made a portal that would take them directly home.

"That's something else!" Taylor exclaimed in amazement. "Why didn't you do the same to bring us here?"

"While the two of them have some unique abilities," Rayla began, "they aren't always reliable. We wouldn't have done well if only half the militia made it through."

"And what about now?" Taylor emphasized.

Rayla jabbed her finger into Taylor's chest, "That's why you're here!"

Taylor rubbed his chest where Rayla had jabbed him, "Ow!"

Rayla grimaced, "Sorry! I didn't mean to poke you that hard. Will you be okay?" Rayla made her lip quiver in jest.

Taylor frowned, "Yeah, don't poke me, though."

"Okay," Rayla pouted, making a face as if she might cry.

"Haha," Taylor brushed her off. "So I'm her reason. That is nice of you. So, what is with these two? Some answers would be great."

"Everyone in our history that could create a doorway needed to move through water. But not these two. However, it requires a great deal of them. By the time we get the caravan through, they will be exhausted for the day. As far as I can tell, they can make a roadway about two days' walk for a column this size. The shorter the distance, the longer they can hold it. I've often wondered how far they can extend a roadway for just the two of them. I doubt I'll ever know. They're very tight-lipped about what they can do with their Orb."

Tae stepped up to them, Zem at his side. "We will go on ahead and let everyone in the Refuge know that we are on our way back as planned."

"Thank you, Tae!" Rayla said to him as he stepped through.

Chapter Forty

The militia readied to leave through the archway back to the Refuge as Taylor and Rayla stood chaperoning the twins. Rayla took in a long, drawn-out breath before she tackled the subject on her mind. "She tried to bind you to her. You would have felt a tingle in your hand, I'm imagining. That was push-back from your Orb. Once the Orbs sensed each other, they would never allow something of that magnitude, for any purpose, to happen to their Bearer."

"What does binding someone mean exactly?" Taylor inquired with concern.

"You would have been hers to command, Kerisa becoming your master, or Dominus. Without fault, you'd have had to obey her. Though, binding would have had quite a different outcome were she an adult. You would have become her partner of sorts, but without love. The bound person feels an overwhelming devotion to their Dominus, which often become sexual due to their need to please. With Kerisa, however, you'd have been locked in a bond governed by a child's love for the remainder of your days."

Taylor paled at the thought and asked, "How is it that she's allowed to walk around free?" Anger bubbled in him for the first time since the healings he had performed. Taylor closed his eyes and recalled healing the night before, which calmed him. The memory kept him from falling back into the madness that rushed forward.

"It's an archaic practice that hasn't been accepted for generations. And to have an Orb Bearer bind someone without asking was met with swift justice. It only happened once, and the other Bearers beheaded Gilinda for it. The binding takes away the person's free will, creating the Devoted. It's a practice that was used before my people achieved peace. It was, however, the best way the Bearers knew to protect themselves. A Devoted would protect the Bearer at all costs.

"To bind someone that hasn't volunteered is akin to rape. Gilinda had already been driven mad by killing with the Orb. During an attack, she saved a group of children from certain death by taking the raiders' lives with the Orb. She killed more than twenty of them by setting them on fire. A few years after the incident, Gilinda sought out one of the girls—who was in her teens by then. The girl didn't have a chance, thinking Gilinda had come to check on her well-being. Knowing then that madness had taken her, the other Bearers were forced to act swiftly. Even with the knowledge that the girl would kill herself upon Gilinda's death."

Rayla paused and caught Taylor's gaze, "Binding someone isn't to be done lightly. But Kerisa has never shown any interest in being with anyone for companionship other than Daven. She is irresponsible to a large degree, but she has never done something so out of character. I'm frankly quite surprised that she would even consider it, let alone try it."

Taylor frowned but did not respond. There were many things that the Orbs were capable of that were downright dangerous. How someone would think that a child could handle one was quite impossible to grasp. "You will have to tell me how those two came to have their rings." He did not wait for a reply before turning back to the camp. His anger bubbled again, and he felt the need in the Orb to kill start to overwhelm him.

Taylor used the flurry of commotion in the camp to distract himself and stay calm, distancing himself from the madness. The militia moved about, hitching the wagons filled with food, supplies, and tents, then loaded the wounded into the empty covered wagons. Taylor watched the grace with which they moved. Her people were efficient in working together in everything they did. With the pace at which Rayla's people moved, the camp was packed up and ready to go within a couple of hours.

Meanwhile, Taylor and Rayla stood behind Daven and Kerisa as they stood holding the roadway open. Rayla and Taylor, both bored, watched people walk through the gateway. Each of them held a weariness in them from travel, capture, or the fatigue of helping the wounded, elderly, or young. Those in the militia with no assigned task had started gathering the freed prisoners who could walk and escorting them.

Taylor turned his head and saw that Kerisa and Daven had moved to sit under a large tree, their packs off to the side. Both ate hard bread from their bags and sipped wine, of all things. They talked to each other in a whisper so as not to be overheard. "They're an interesting pair to watch," Taylor said, still a little unnerved by Kerisa's actions earlier.

Rayla nodded, "Yes, they are, intertwined as two of them are. It's hard to imagine them separate. They have been children for over three hundred years! Yet they have more knowledge and experience than you and I put together." Rayla paused. "I have spent many a year contemplating what it would be like for them. To spend all those years in seclusion with only each other. One day children who played as they should, and the next day, Orb Bearers, told to secret themselves away in the secluded woods for an eternity. I wouldn't likely take off the rings either! After all that time as a child, the thought of change would be frightening.

"I imagine you have noticed Daven has a crush on me. He asked several years back if we could ever be together. I told him grown women require the maturity of a grown man to be happy. Unknown to me, he told Kerisa he wanted to grow into a man and for her to grow into a woman. The conversation didn't go well. She refused and wouldn't hear any more of it.

"Conflicted in wanting to be a man but unable to cope with growing old without her, he waited until the evening to slip off his ring and tried to slip off hers while Kerisa slept. He knew the rings recognized them as Bearers of the Orb and would allow him to remove it. However, after wearing that ring for hundreds of years, its movement woke her.

"Kerisa was so furious that she stopped speaking to him for six months. As punishment, Kerisa took his ring before he could grab it and told him to enjoy being a man. You can see he looks slightly older than her if you look close enough. She left him standing there in terror, moved her things to another chamber the following day, and avoided him. After several failed attempts to try and get her to forgive him, he stopped eating and hid away in his chambers.

"He almost died of starvation. After not seeing him for almost a month, Kerisa's curiosity got the best of her. She found him unconscious in his bed and no more than skin and bones. She sounded the alarm for help and slipped his ring back on him. The Orbs have amazing abilities, but with Daven so depleted, the Orb had no energy to use. It took a few weeks before he was able to recover. She stayed by his side the whole time he was recovering, feeding and bathing him, sleeping with him in his bed. She keeps an ever-watchful eye on him now."

"How did no one notice his absence?" Taylor asked, "Everyone in your community is very close with one another."

"They weren't well-liked in our community when they first lived here. For obvious reasons, most people avoided them like death itself. They eventually stopped interacting with anyone but a handful of people. Kerisa has, over the years, sought out different young girls for company, keeping herself hidden from everyone in the girl's life; Kerisa is perceived as an invisible friend. Coupled with the fact that it wasn't uncommon for them not to visit me or anyone else for months, no one thought anything of it," Rayla replied.

"Huh, invisible friend, you say? A few things around the Refuge make a bit more sense," Taylor glanced at her sideways.

Rayla smiled, "Would you have believed me if I had said, 'Oh, don't worry about the strange little girl's voice in your room at night. It's only our three-hundred-year-old narcissistic children that can warp reality?' Having a conversation about three-hundred-year-old children that are tricksters isn't easy." Rayla's smile turned wry, "And, it may have been a little fun watching you squirm."

Taylor smiled with impudence, "Aren't you the prankster!"

Rayla and Taylor fell silent as they sat and ate hard bread and cured meats from the soldiers' stores. They drank from their waterskins and talked for a little while, waiting for everyone to move through.

Taylor saw Careed at the bulk of the militia's lead as they approached. His daughter, Niea, was at his side. In the flurry of all the healings he had performed, he barely remembered visiting Niea. By the time he had reached her, Taylor was quite exhausted. Tarak's soldiers had obeyed his orders, and Rayla's ability to heal had been enough for Niea.

When he had touched her arm to check if her body required more, the Orb had shown him the growing seed in her womb. She would be a child giving birth to a child, and it broke Taylor's heart to think of it. Taylor was torn; how could he tell her? Was it his place? No matter when she found out, it would not be enough time for Niea to mentally heal any of what had happened to her.

Careed nodded to Taylor as he and Niea broke ranks and approached. Careed spoke leisurely, "Things are going well. If this holds, we will be through in only a couple of hours."

"Would you like to sit with me, Niea?" Rayla motioned, "The twins are occupied enough with their task. They won't complain about us visiting."

Careed creased his brow at the twins, and then a look of understanding washed across his face, "Yes, Niea, I think you should rest some before we continue." He looked to

Taylor, "Perhaps the two of us could help check the wagons at the end of the column. If you're up for it?"

Taylor smiled in greeting to Niea and said, "It's good to see you, Niea."

Smiling back, Niea replied, "And you as well."

Careed cleared his throat as a cue to Taylor to come with him. Taylor followed him off through the column leaving Niea with Rayla to speak alone. Niea was the youngest among many women to have a seed in their womb whom he had healed. There would be a rough time of healing ahead for the women in the column that had been assaulted—especially those that would become mothers. Careed's hopes resounded loudly in Taylor's mind that Rayla could help begin Niea's process of healing some of her pain.

At midday, Taylor watched the last wagon move through the gateway. Rayla hastened Daven and Kerisa, "OK, let's get through to the other side, so you two can close the gate and rest. It's a dangerous time for our people. We will need the two of you to help us get to the ruined city with your gateway." They all stepped through the portal, and the twins turned to face it. The two did not seem affected by the use of their power, but when the twins let the stone doorway dissolve, they both let out deep breaths. Rayla led them to a large tree, where she left them to rest. Then she walked to join Taylor a small distance into the meadow.

Taylor stood and watched the wagons come to a halt. By his best judgment, the column of Rayla's people stretched roughly a mile. The column had moved at a good pace, especially if you considered the number of people on foot. "Looks like they might fall asleep," he said to Rayla as she walked toward him, pointing to the twins.

"They do," she replied. "Oddly, they pushed hard today, which is unlike them. I'll need to keep an eye on them when we move to the ruined city."

Rayla walked to the front of the column to find many of the Refuge's people there. They were greeted happily by those they had left behind. Their partners hugged them with tear-filled eyes; children rejoiced at the return of their mothers and fathers. Rayla took the opportunity and slipped off in the commotion and chaos to her quarters, where she sat amongst Daphne's things. Having yet to grieve for her, the loss of her daughter flooded into her. Rayla broke down and cried tears that she thought might not stop.

While the others celebrated, Rayla's sadness and need to be alone filled Taylor as she took her leave. On returning, Taylor had stood at Rayla's side and listened to her give Careed charge of what was left of their small militia. Rayla explained that it allowed her and Taylor time to take stock of supplies from the Refuge and what the wagons had brought back with them, something which needed to be done in preparation for the journey to the ruined city. It was a farce, though; Rayla needed to be alone and could not manage that with all the responsibilities she bore. Rayla had barely held on to her emotions as she walked away. Coming back here had drudged her bottled feelings up. Taylor waited late into the night before he made his way inside toward his quarters. He found Rayla there, asleep on her bedroll at the side of his bed.

Chapter Forty-One

When Taylor awoke the following morning, he heard the whisper of Rayla's mind. She was, from what he could muster, a mixture of annoyed, pleased, and angered. It was quite a combination to comprehend. Since he had joined with her, Taylor understood that women were a complex web of emotions that he was likely never to grasp.

The Famsha led him to Rayla in the meadow by the water, quarreling with Kerisa and Daven. "I don't need you two showing off or whatever it is you're doing. If you exhaust yourselves before we get there, we have to wait for the two of you to recover. You will *not* get us any further by pushing that hard. In fact, it will take longer if we have to wait a few days while you sleep."

"What's all the commotion about, Rayla?" Taylor asked with concern as he approached.

"As I suspected yesterday, these two are pushing harder than they should in making the gateway." Rayla replied in almost a shout, "I'm not too sure what they're up to, but it's most unlike them. It's almost as if they have grown a heart between the two of them."

At that, Kerisa crossed her arms, turned her back to them, and made a hurt-sounding "humph." Taylor was not sure what to say; Daven had his chin up in dismay, and his eyes flittered between the two women that meant the world to him. Taylor knelt down behind Kerisa and gently turned her around. "What is with the two of you? Neither of you has ever really cared about the others in the Refuge."

Kerisa stamped her foot, "Perhaps I have grown to like some of these people, and I want to give them a fighting chance."

Taylor was not sure of Kerisa's motives; from her reputation, this was quite unlike her. "Kerisa, everyone is tired and weary. We are all pleased you're helping us, especially me," Taylor embellished, and she smiled happily at him. "We need you to make sure that we all get there, including the two of you, as quickly as possible. So, if you just take a little more care not to overdo it, we will all be happier for it."

Kerisa eyes moved fluidly from Taylor to Rayla before settling on Daven. To him, Kerisa ordered, "All right, Daven, you will have to be a little more careful." She turned back to Taylor and gave Taylor a nod of agreement. Kerisa took a slumped Daven's hand and led him off back to their room. The two of them looked exhausted still. Taylor felt for Daven; he would likely never find a happy middle ground between Kerisa and Rayla.

"I have never in the time I have known her seen her act more peculiar. She's doing her best to impress you, Taylor. All of her behavior in the last couple of days points in that direction. I just don't get it. She despises men or, at least, has until now."

"I believe you may be right. Kerisa definitely has taken a liking to me," he sighed and continued, "I have been the object of a lot of crushes working at the kids' camp. Though none of those girls could have destroyed me with a thought."

Rayla raised an eyebrow and nodded in agreement, then put her hand to her stomach. "Would you like to get some food?" she asked him, a smile on her face. "I'm famished."

"I'd like that!" Taylor replied. Taylor recognized the smile on Rayla's face. It was one that Lilly had given him when she was feeling especially in love with him. It amazed him how much perspective could change the thoughts and feelings you had for someone. *Now that I'm no longer here at Rayla's bidding and I have seen the love that lies inside of her for me, my feelings have changed for her,* he realized as he walked beside her. She smiled at him, and most unexpectedly, his heart swelled. *I think I might love her.* Somewhere along the line, he had found forgiveness for her. Where anger once lay in his heart, love now grew. He smiled back. *I hope her feelings have grown for me too. I feel like I'm falling for her more as each moment passes.*

As they finished packing a few days later, Taylor wove through the caverns on his way back to his room to turn in. Rayla had walked at his side, silent since the two of them had entered. Neither of them had spent a great deal of time inside the Refuge since returning. Each of them had chosen to work long hours preparing to leave, and they had set up one of the newly acquired tents instead of returning each night to sleep in their quarters. Rising early and working late, Taylor had a suspicion that Rayla avoided her grief so she might carry on getting her people to the ruins.

There was an eerie hushed tone to the place. People here were saddened to leave their homes, and after several days of packing provisions, they were exhausted. Most had gone to sleep early; some had not even offered words between each other. Taylor supposed they did not look forward to the month-long journey through the mountains either; they would start out exhausted in the first place. As Taylor approached the branch in the caves that led to his quarters, he offered to walk Rayla home.

"I'm not ready to go back there yet. Do you mind if I come to your quarters?" She asked.

Taylor had not considered that there would be reminders everywhere here of the loss Rayla had endured in the last few days. Most of all, in her quarters where Daphne's memory would be sharp with her belongings in every room. "I'd be happy to have the company." Taylor gestured for her to continue walking with him to his quarters. When they entered his room, Rayla sat at the table and was quiet for a moment. After her silence continued, Taylor joined her but stayed silent.

"I have too much to do before I face what lies in my and Kalamar's quarters," Rayla said with sadness. She lifted her hand to her mouth and stifled a yawn. Her eyes were heavy from the turmoil of the last two months.

Taylor's room had been tidied by some unknown occupant of the Refuge. Likely as a thank-you for killing the soldiers. Rage filled him as he thought of that day and what they had returned to. He pushed it down and away and refilled himself with calm.

The person that had tidied the room had left dried meats, cheese, and a skin of water. Taylor reached toward the middle of the table where the food was and divided it into portions. He gave half to Rayla, took the other half for himself, and poured both a glass of water. He watched as Rayla ate woodenly, and as she finished her food and drink, Taylor motioned to the bed. "Why don't you lie down and get some rest; I can sleep on the floor."

Rayla stood and walked over to the bed and stood with her back to him. "Would you lie with me?" she asked with sadness in her voice.

Taylor understood her request from the Famsha. Rayla needed comfort, and those that would have provided her with it were now gone. As Rayla lay down and curled into a ball, Taylor felt her love for him flow through the Famsha. Only for an instant, but it had been there. Taylor laid down beside her but left a space between them out of chivalry. Rayla reached back and pulled his arm around her, so Taylor had to move closer. Moments later, Rayla fell fast asleep, and Taylor followed soon after.

Chapter Forty-Two

A crippling sadness in his heart hit him as he sat eating his breakfast. Rayla had gone, but her presence was sharp in the back of his mind. Rayla was in her quarters, curled up in Daphne's bed, as Taylor sensed from the Famsha. Rayla's thoughts and feelings were wide open to him, an unusual occurrence. It took a moment to separate himself from Rayla's feelings. There was a pull from her that he come to her amongst her need to be alone. He understood the mourning process and the often turbulent emotions that came with it. Using his better judgment, Taylor gave her the time she needed as he got ready to go.

When Taylor left his room, he walked toward Kalamar's quarters. Rayla had cried for a long while in Daphne's room before staunching her tears. She moved on to mourn in Kalamar's quarters.

Pain washed over his heart as Rayla emoted her sadness. The volume of it had gotten harder to keep out. When he reached Kalamar's quarters, the door was open. Rayla stood at Kalamar's workbench, where he had made medicine.

Rayla turned; tears fell down her cheeks. Without thought, Taylor walked across the room and embraced her in his arms. Rayla collapsed into him and shook and cried for her loss.

Rayla held a cloth doll curled in her arms at her chest. It was tattered and worn from years of play and being held while Daphne slept. Taylor felt her sadness, as well as his own, for the girl he had befriended. They stood for some time, and Taylor supported her while she let go of so many days of the withheld grief. At one point, the pain he felt from her was almost unbearable. All at once, it stopped, and she lifted her head from his chest. "Thank you, Taylor. I don't know what I would have done had I lost you as well. I wasn't certain you'd come back from all the death." She paused and put her head against his chest once more, "I love you. I began to love you as my visions started. It has only grown with you being here."

Taylor was not able to say anything back right away. It had been hard letting Lilly go that day when he laid her ashes to rest. But his time here with Rayla had shown him that the woman he held in his arms was where his heart now belonged. "I know." He said, "And I love you." Rayla leaned back, and Taylor placed his hands on her cheeks.

With tears streaming down her face and a shaking voice, she said, "I want you to stay here with me. I can't bear the thought of being without you."

"I can't think of a place I'd rather be than here with you," Taylor said. "I am beginning to find that you fill my heart with joy at every moment I am with you." Taylor leaned in and gave her a gentle kiss on the forehead. She curled back into his chest, and they stood for a moment longer before Rayla pulled away to wipe the tears from her cheeks.

"We have a lot of work to do. I suppose we should get to it," she managed in her best voice, though it still shook. "Everything is packed that can be. It's time to go. Let us assemble everyone, so we may make final preparations to move to the ruined city." She walked out of Kalamar's room purposefully, and Taylor followed close behind. As Rayla encountered her people in the caves, she sent them to spread the word to gather in the meadow.

Within the hour, Rayla stood in front of her people upon a small flat stone podium hewn from a boulder. It sat outside the Refuge's exit, under a great tree. The early morning sun shone on her, and as she raised her hand, everyone quieted. Using the Orb to spread her voice over the meadow, she began.

"Before I left, I set you packing so that we might begin our journey to our new home. Of all the locations that were found suitable, a ruined city is our best chance for re-settlement together. The city is no longer intact, but there is a wall of stone several men tall surrounding it to provide us protection. We will have to do a great deal of work to build a home there, but we have achieved against higher odds.

"We will need to travel for at least a month before reaching the city." At this, the crowd began to stir and talk amongst themselves, "Listen! Listen!" Rayla called out, and everyone quieted. "I know that it's a long journey for some of you. But we don't have a great deal of choice. Kalamar showed us how to come together and become stronger. I know many of the older and young generations will have trouble on this journey. But if we work together, we can achieve this.

"With the use of the wagons, horses, and supplies from the soldier's camp, for which we can thank their presence to our little-known residents, Kerisa and Daven, the moving process will be sped up ..." Rayla drew the crowd's attention to them sitting off to the side. Both of them were uncomfortable with everyone's eyes on them. "They were instrumental in us getting back as fast as we did, and they're a linchpin in us getting to the city. Together, the two can create gateways to other places, which is how we arrived here so quickly. They will do the same to make our way to the ruins."

"Our first stop will be at the hunting camp, and from there, Tae will take over navigating the portals. As many of you know, he's a shard carrier and has a special gift for finding the unseen. The path we traveled on before, the valley where the city lies, won't suffice for the wagons. He has agreed to use his gift to find clearings large enough to rest in as we travel." Tae wore an eager smile while Zem flourished his hands at Tae's side in a comical gesture.

"Our resident crystal holder, Budena," Rayla pointed them out, "will be on hand to move through the gateway first should we need to clear a larger spot in the forest. You may have seen Budena's ability to reduce plants to ash. Using the Power, as you might know, can be taxing. So we may need to wait for them to recover, should the need arise for them to use the shards. This might extend our time moving, but it can't be helped.

"Our packing of supplies is complete. Take the next two days to rest and pack what personal belongings you can carry. We will begin making our way to the ruined city in three days. We have only a few weeks before Tarak realizes that Wynfor and his men are all dead, and he begins to pursue finding us. Tarak will have a good idea of where to start looking from the location of the camp. I'll begin assigning tasks to you through your community group leaders for your work position. Careed will take care of militia deployments. If you're armed, see him. I need the group leaders to meet me up here as soon as possible."

The crowd stayed for a moment as they talked to each other. Some were excited. Others were more reserved in their judgment. No matter their feelings, within a short time they began moving and organizing themselves into groups. Kalamar had set up groups of representation for each of the communities, as well as setting up priority response teams should there be an emergency or an attack. Should something happen, the priority groups took the presidency over the community groups. This allowed healers, soldiers, and support staff to go about their business, while the bulk of the community could be assigned functionary tasks like cooking and watching the young.

Rayla stepped down to converse with Taylor, and Careed had walked off and stood to the side of the big tree. Those with soldiering skills had already started to group there. *Now begins the organizing*, Rayla thought.

Taylor reached out and grasped her hand and squeezed it for reassurance. Rayla's eyes were still swollen from the crying she had done. She took a deep breath, let it out, and composed herself. "Alright, I can do this," she said under her breath before she squeezed and released Taylor's hand. She turned to the podium where the representatives had gathered. She directed the groups in their tasks and the great deal of work needing to be completed. When she was finished, she returned to Taylor, her mind buzzing with lists.

"You have one more representative to assign a task," Taylor insisted, breaking her concentration. Rayla looked at him with curiosity, unsure of who he meant. "Me, I'm the only person here that doesn't have an assigned task. I can track, use a sword thanks to you, and heal ..." Taylor trailed off. He was smiling, but he felt out of place and a slightly useless. "I understand you have concerns. I know you feel a great deal depends on me. However, I need to do something. I can't sit back and wait for this ultimate purpose you see me fulfilling."

Rayla smiled in understanding, "You have one of the most difficult jobs I can think of. I'm not sure you noticed, but everyone stands a little taller when you walk by. By saving so many and defeating Wynfor's men, you have become a symbol of hope. Tarak has been a force that has suppressed these people since birth. I was hoping you could continue being that hope of Tarak's tyranny ending. All you need to do is be present with them, as hard as that may be for you."

She paused, "It's inspiring that you have been through so much and are still willing to help. There is a secondary job that requires your attention. It would be best if you continued to interact with Kerisa. Would you please stick with her and Daven for the first part of the journey? Kerisa wouldn't hear of you being anywhere else but with her. Which I'll deal with when we are a few days away from the city. Careed, you and I will lead a small team ahead of the column into the ruins.

"We haven't yet spoken of how you managed to open the doors, but we will. There will be a great deal of work there to create a new home. I only hope that the wizardess there can aid us, as she hinted. We first need to find another entrance into the city that the carts will fit through." She paused, "I think I can also keep you quite busy tracking, healing, and scouting in addition to keeping everyone's spirits up if you wish it."

"Opening the doors was sheer dumb luck. The door not having locks reminded me of how security doors are on

Earth. The panel being there made sense." Taylor shrugged. "I think I have as many questions as you, though. The obelisks, the murals, the wizardess herself, and how she exists. I'll do my best to help with anything I can when we get there."

Rayla looked at Taylor with a look of confusion. "You will have to tell me more about your obelisks—but later. For now, you could look in on those that need some healing in our community."

Taylor smiled and walked off toward the healing tent that still stood in the meadow. With the triage in the Refuge full, they had retaken the triage tent in the meadow and used it for the wounded prisoners from the base camp. For most in the Refuge, the following two days were filled with sleep and light packing of personal items. Taylor, however, passed both days healing the wounded. Each night, he returned to his quarters exhausted, only to find Rayla waiting there. After a quick meal, Rayla would usher Taylor into bed, then crawled in with her arms wrapped around him. Taylor fell asleep to the lulling floral smell of her soap.

At the end of the second day, with the Refuge emptied of supplies and its people packed, they stood ready to depart. Everyone turned in early to get one last night of restful sleep before the trek began. The following morning, a knock at the door awoke Taylor. He looked around the room and saw that Rayla was already up and at the table. A young boy of about ten opened the door and entered with a tray of fresh fruit and a skin of water. He smiled at them both as she put the plate on the table, and he left.

"Good morning," Rayla smiled at him as she took a piece of fruit.

Taylor stretched and yawned, "It seems early. I don't feel like I have slept very long."

"It's just before dawn. Kerisa and Daven will need a head start this morning on the roadway." Rayla tossed some fruit to Taylor. "Kerisa has already been here to make sure you would be accompanying her."

Taylor took a bite of the green fruit, and its tropical sweetness filled his mouth. He savored the flavor a moment before taking another bite. Taylor swung his legs off the edge of the bed and dropped his feet on the cold floor, sitting up. He finished the fruit ravenously before making his way over to retrieve a second piece from the table. Its juice gushed out, dripping on the dirty clothes he had slept in for many days. "Do I have time to freshen up and change?" Taylor inquired. "It would be great to start our journey clean."

"Yes, of course, you do. I have to go and start everyone moving," Rayla replied. She ran her fingers through her wet hair. "I'll catch up with you, and the twins once everyone is ready." Rayla stood, kissed him on the cheek, and left with her travel pack in hand.

Taylor hurried to make his way to the bathing area to find that it was devoid of people. This left him to fill his own basin to bathe. After this, Taylor quickly cleaned and changed his clothes. Back in his room, he grabbed his water skin off the table and the travel pack he had made up the night before.

He took one last look around. His life had changed entirely while occupying this room. He hoped that the city would bring better memories of change than his stay here had. The only thing he would genuinely miss here would be falling asleep with Rayla. He left, and he followed the caves out to the meadow at a quick pace. The sun rose as he exited the Refuge, casting its dim light. Off to the left stood Daven and Kerisa, waiting for him to join them.

The twins stood at the path that led to the hunting camp Taylor and Rayla's scouting team had begun their search from. The trail had a gentle slope up from here, and it would be easy for the wagons to move through the archway. He walked across the meadow in excitement of what the city might bring and joined them. Daven nodded to Taylor, and Kerisa sighed in relief and smiled up at him. "Good morning. Are you two ready?" Taylor asked.

"We are," Daven replied as he took Kerisa's hand and turned her to the path. Kerisa let her gaze linger on Taylor for a moment, then turned. Their rings began to glow, and the archway appeared. That while it's an awesome feat, it no longer held the awe it did a few short days ago. The journey to their new home was on its way, and after all that had happened, Taylor looked forward to exploring the ruined city.

Chapter Forty-Three

The first weeks of the caravan's journey to the ruined city went as everyone expected. The days were long and hard but uneventful. It was surprising how much energy it took moving the caravan each day. Even with all the effort everyone put in, they only actually moved for a couple of hours between sunrise and sunset. Getting everything prepared in the morning while the Shard Carrier Budena prepared an open space for them, and setting up at night took a lot of time. Most people did not bother to set up tents. There were not enough anyway. They simply slept in the grass by the wagons.

Kerisa and Daven worked diligently to create the roadway for the caravan to travel through. Taylor started his morning by finding the twins at first light at the lead wagon. Later they were joined by Rayla, something Kerisa was unhappy with, but Daven insisted was more than fair. Rayla and Taylor talked while chaperoning the twins to keep boredom at bay.

The twins were able to hold the gateway twice a day. Once the caravan moved through, just short of two hours,

Taylor, Rayla, and the twins stepped through, and the archway disappeared. Taylor and Rayla's past became a broad topic as they got to know each other further. They were interested in getting to know what the other's life had been like growing up. This was interspersed with discussing what to do when they first reached the city. They had plans to leave the caravan with a small group a few days before reaching the city, to explore.

They ended each day falling asleep beside each other, something Rayla and Taylor began to look forward to each evening. Midway through the third week, Rayla approached Taylor in the late morning as he watched Kerisa and Daven. She wore a grim look and was preoccupied.

"Is everything alright, Rayla?" Taylor asked

Rayla looked up from her thoughts and frowned, "Not really. I have talked to several women this morning that have experienced sickness in these last two days."

Taylor stood a little taller, "Perhaps there is something I could do, maybe some healing."

Rayla held up her hand to stall him, "It isn't that kind of sickness. A few of the women have missed their blood time. It was something that I had expected. I haven't quite had the time and presence of mind to prepare for it, though."

It was Taylor's turn to frown, "I felt the seed in many of them, but with all that had just recently happened, I thought it best they come to terms with being with child on their own. Was I wrong?"

Rayla was surprised by Taylor's statement and took a moment to consider his imposition. "You were under a lot of pressure. It would have been best to have consulted with me. Many of the women that were raped had already confessed to being scared of the fact. Being an Orb Bearer often has unanticipated burdens. Next time you have important information, share it with me."

He agreed to her request, and they carried on with their day. Though, Rayla was more preoccupied than usual. In the following days, the community seemed to weave back together. The women with child would need support in the coming months. Once there were newborns in their care, it would be especially so. For the first couple of years of life, children need a great deal of attention. In the current situation their community was in, to accommodate their needs would be difficult, perhaps even impossible.

Careed looked even more protective of Niea than before as he doted over her. Taylor nodded to Tae and Zem as they walked with their partners. Taylor had healed Maud and Ferina and told Rayla both were with child. The men had become more protective of their partners in the last few days. Even after all that had happened to these people, they still saw the blessings of life to come. All those years of tyranny had not taken away how precious new life was to them.

Rayla stared off into the distance, "If the new mothers wish to abort, they can ask their Babushka. They know the herb."

"The what now?"

"The Babushka are women who deliver babies." She said, looking back at him. "They care for the mother and child from pregnancy until a few months after the baby is born."

Rayla's voice was flat; she was having a hard time with this new development. She glanced up to the sky, "The rains will be here soon," she pointed up, changing the subject.

Taylor followed her glance up to the unusually thick

cloud cover. "In the last few days, the temperature has been colder in the morning and evening. I had thought that it was the altitude we were at. I hadn't considered a seasonal change. Rain will slow the trek to the city and be a damper on morale. What kind of rain are we talking about? A small storm every couple of days? Rain every day?"

"It will start with a storm every other day, but it won't be long before it's every day. By then, there will be enough rain each day to fill your travel cup thrice," Rayla replied distractedly as she calculated. "It's a bit early, but all the signs have started. Not great timing for us. I'd say we have just short of a week's travel at our current pace. If the rains start before we get there, that week will be more like two."

"I hope it will hold off for a few days once the column of people makes it to the valley. A large camp can be struck once we are there," Taylor responded. "Though, we will be short of tents for this many people."

Rayla grimaced, "That is something we will have to sort out when we are there. My people are great at wilderness survival. We may need to build temporary shelters inside the city using timber from the surrounding forest there."

Rayla looked to Daven and Kerisa. Taylor, Rayla, and a small team of people were due to head out in two days to start exploring the city. Daven and Kerisa were to stay behind and continue with the roadway. *I'll have to manage to convince Kerisa to keep going without Taylor. Not a small feat.*

Rayla woke early in the morning. She and Taylor were to leave for the city. The warmth of Taylor's hands still lingered on the skin of her arms from his embrace during the night. Each morning she woke in his arms, her heart swelled with joy. She could hardly believe that her visions of the man she would love had come to pass after all these years. As she slipped out of their tent, the first drops of rain began. They were large and cold as they landed on her hands and face as she walked. It was a perfect setting for how she felt about her task this morning. Kerisa was always a challenge, and this morning would be a test on an epic scale for Rayla's patience and negotiation skills.

She worked her way to the front of the column and found Daven and Kerisa's tent where it was always pitched. It was not separate from the camp, but it was not part of it either. Kerisa sat in front of it on a little stool as she ate her breakfast. At Rayla's approach, the sprinkle turned into a full rain. She could see that it did not touch Kerisa, though. It instead disappeared about a foot above her head into that unknown space only she and Daven knew about.

Rayla sat down on the stool beside her. As she did, Kerisa turned to Rayla and spoke firmly, "He may not leave."

Rayla looked at her, "How could you know? We haven't spoken a word to anyone."

"I have been reading thoughts for longer than you have been alive, Rayla. Did you actually think I wouldn't know," Kerisa said in her catty child's voice.

"It doesn't matter whether you want him to go or not. He's leaving with me today. Taylor isn't yours to command." Rayla spoke a little sharper than she had intended.

Kerisa stood, a hot expression on her face, "Taylor is not yours to command either! Your time with him will be short. You're not the only one he's to be with," Kerisa's voice was sharp and angry in return. The air shuddered around her, but Rayla knew Kerisa could not attack her with the Orb. Though she *had* found other ways to punish her before.

"You're a child. You could never be with Taylor in any capacity. I'm not up for your childish little games this morning!" Rayla shot back. This was going worse than she could have ever imagined.

"You're not the only one with visions, Rayla. In time you will see who Taylor ends up with after ..." Kerisa stopped short of her next intended statement, flustered. She said, "Let's see how far everyone gets without my help," before ducking back into her tent.

"That went well," Taylor said from behind her.

"It's one of the more productive conversations we have had. We should get ready to leave; grab your gear and meet me at the pathway as quickly as possible." Rayla looked back at the tent. Did Kerisa know? Could she know? She might not know the whole truth of the last battle and Rayla's part in it if she did.

"It didn't seem like she was willing to keep cooperating, creating the gateway, if I left. Do you think that is wise?" Taylor asked

"I have known Kerisa for a long time. She will keep up with the gateway and perhaps with a little less complaining. Kerisa not only has a crush on you, but she also wants to impress you," Rayla grimaced.

"And why do you think that?" Taylor looked at her inquisitively.

"Little girls aren't that much different than women when it comes to love. Both hate looking bad in front of the one they love. She will want to show you she's helpful because she thinks that's what you want from her," Rayla answered.

Taylor half grinned but did not say anything back. He left Rayla to deal with Kerisa and went back to their tent to gather his things. With Kalamar's sword strapped at his side and his travel pack in hand, Taylor looked around the tent and spotted Rayla's pack at the end of their bed, ready to go. With the rain's arrival, Taylor took the extra time to find a small tent amongst the supplies.

As he reached the front of the column, he saw to his surprise that Daven and Kerisa had already begun to work, creating the gateway. Rayla stood a short distance back, with Careed to her right. Neither of them spoke as he joined them, though Careed nodded to Taylor. All of them stood for a moment and watched the twins work at the crest of the pass. The rest of the journey would be all down from here into the basin where the city lay. Taylor noticed the gateway appeared quicker than usual. Rayla met him with a knowing smile on her face.

The arch solidified all at once, the city visible through the opening. "Look, we are almost there. That is the clearing in the valley I have been talking about," Tae shouted. Everyone at the front of the column stopped what they were doing and moved forward to look.

Kerisa and Daven turned as Taylor, Rayla, and Careed approached. Daven looked to Rayla with a confident smile across his face. He let go of Kerisa's hand and faced Rayla, the Orb half aglow in his ring. When Daven was only a few feet away, Rayla's eyes widened, and she looked into the woods to their left. Rayla started to run toward Daven, knowing an arrow raced toward his heart. Everything slowed down as she desperately tried to reach him while searching for the arrow in flight. Before she could achieve either, the arrow found its mark. It thudded into Daven's chest and pierced deeply into his heart. His body shuddered with the impact, and he fell to his knees. The smile was still on his face as he fell forward. Rayla skidded to a stop at his side, where he lay face down in the dirt.

Rayla caught the image of Kerisa, only steps away out of the corner of her eye. The Vidre in Kerisa's ring shone bright red and she let out a shriek, amplified by magic, that was so deafening that everyone had to cover their ears. It continued until Kerisa paused to take a breath. Her face was filled with fury. She fell to her knees on the ground beside her brother and rolled him over into her lap.

As she touched Daven, his Orb flared to life, turning red as well. Kerisa held him before letting out a thundering scream, "Nooo!" Another wave of magic emanated outward from her in every direction; the air shuddered, and the ground shook beneath Rayla's feet. She felt the full force of the wave of power hit her, pick her up and carry her backward. The impact broke several of her ribs and one of the bones in her forearms. Taylor and Careed were next to be caught in its wake as it passed them. It tossed them like dolls ten feet back from where they stood; Rayla landed beside them. The power from the Orb about Rayla's neck flowed through her and began to heal the breaks in her bones. The pain of her injuries was sharp as she lay there.

Everyone's ears rang as they sat up. Careed pointed to three men that ran through the woods. Though the ringing muffled his voice in Rayla's ears, she still heard him say, "Assassins, get them before they escape."

As Rayla looked back over at Kerisa, she slid Daven's ring off his finger into the palm of her hand and stood. The look of fury on Kerisa's face had been replaced by heartbreak. The Vidre in the rings began to glow the familiar purple hue. Rayla swung her head back toward the assassins and saw the three of them incinerated mid-stride. Their ashes floated in the air like flakes of snow before being caught in the rain and washed away.

As the ringing in their ears subsided, Rayla, Taylor, and Careed stood, all their eyes on Kerisa. She shook with fury as she looked over Daven's still body. Taylor took a step toward them, and when Kerisa did not stop him, he continued to walk toward them. When he reached them, Kerisa looked up at him, her face suddenly calm and sad, and a tear rolled down her cheek. "There is not anything you can do for him. I wondered all those years, why I never saw him with us in my visions of the future."

Taylor had overheard Rayla and her conversation earlier that day but had not endeavored to ask about Kerisa's visions. He looked down at Daven and felt for life in the boy with the Orb's help. Kerisa was indeed right. There was no spark left in him to build upon. "I'm sorry, Kerisa," was all Taylor could think to say.

Rayla ventured to take a step forward and was met by Kerisa's head snapping toward her. "Stay back!" Rayla froze in her place before she took a step back. Kerisa's face and voice had turned angry again. The Vidre in the rings she held began to glow, and Taylor prepared for the worst. However, instead of lashing out, the flows of power wove toward Daven's body. He rose from the ground and hung in mid-air beside her. If it were not for the protruding arrow in his chest, it would have looked as if Daven lay asleep on an invisible bed.

Kerisa returned her gaze to Taylor, saddened, "Everything will be different when I return." Kerisa walked off down the path, and Daven floated along beside her. There was a sudden flash of light, and they were both gone.

Rayla, Taylor, and Careed had stood there for a moment before anyone said anything, shocked at the happenings of the last few moments.

"Did you see the glint of something as the woman turned to ash?" Taylor inquired but did not wait for the answer. The others followed him to the spot where the assassins had died, and he bent, scooping up a small shard of Vidre set into a tear-shaped pendant. He handed the necklace to Tae, "Can your gift tell us what this pendant is for?"

Tae held it up, "It doesn't always work that way, but it's unknown what it does to me. I suppose." Tae closed his eyes, and both his earpiece and the pendant flared. "I see her before Tarak, telling him where Rayla is many weeks ago, and then her searching for Rayla in the woods." Tae opened his eyes in surprise. "I think this shard can find people. That is how they found us. They tracked Rayla."

Rayla's face fell, "So much pain has come from what I did that day. Going into the city was reckless, taking the book more so. I should have waited."

"You can't have known, Rayla," Careed interjected. "We wouldn't have had Taylor here to help us."

"I agree," Taylor put in, "How could you have known?

Rayla did not say more on the subject. "We need to figure out our next steps. Let us convene and discuss what to do." Rayla had recognized the assassins. They were captives from the base camp. The woman's quick thinking had led her to hide amongst the prisoners. She had taken an opportune moment when they had arrived close enough to the city to escape with the location. She had not accounted for Kerisa's power; that had been a mistake.

With Kerisa and Daven gone, it would take a significant amount of work for Budena to clear a path for the wagon. It also left them to walk the rest of the way into the valley, in the rain. Luck as it was, they were only a two to three days' walk from there. Still, now it would take several days to move all of the supplies down to the clearing and set up a camp. Nevertheless, Taylor, Rayla and Careed would lead a small team into the ruins to look for a desirable location before occupying it.

Rayla gathered together the leaders of the community and emergency team leaders. She had spoken with Maud, asking her to take the lead of the caravan. Maud had been left to grieve for her friends' deaths during the search for a better location. But with so many of the militia dead, few were left to lead. Maud was seasoned as a leader and agreed she could step up to the task. Rayla laid out a plan to move their people to the valley and set up a base camp. The horses would be unhitched and loaded with the wounded, elderly, and children, and the supplies needed for their care. The rest of the column's occupants would accompany them after they packed the essentials to establish a camp and triage. Once the tents were erected, and the camp was established, the leaders of the communities would take parties of people back up to the wagons. There were axes and saws in the army supply wagons they could use to create a path for the wagons to bring the remainder of the supplies.

The women with child, the elderly, and the children were tired from the long journey. And, as such, they needed a great deal of care. Each had carried their own burdens in the days of travel getting here. When they had started their journey back at the Refuge, they had initially paired the older children with the elderly, which freed up able-bodied members of the community to help as the column moved. It had worked at the start. But as the weeks wore on, the elders of the community needed as much help as the children did. Thankfully, those in need of rest and recuperation would get it in a few days.

After Rayla and Taylor settled the caravan members down, she worked through the new plan and afterward found the day was gone. Taylor, Rayla, and Careed all agreed to wake early the next day to move forward, going to the city. They all turned in, anxious to discover what lay there.

Chapter Forty-Four

Staring into the sky at the bright light that moved in a straight line, Tarak thought back to his arrival here.

As the Starport had come into sight above the planet it orbited, Tarak felt a sense of happiness. The shuttle that he had stolen was more extensive than most small ships, and it was in pristine shape. The law ship that it had come from would pursue him soon enough. But if he found what he was looking for here, it would not matter. Several Vidreian were logged as living on this Starport in the computer back at the post he and his men had raided a few months ago. A miraculous find! He had almost given up looking for this place. Shortly after finding the port, they were captured. "How was I to know that there were still pockets of Navaden rule after so long?"

The years since he had left Kardain and Sailock had been cruel to him. The disenchanted man from the Orb there had lost all touch with the universe outside of their world. The universe had become a terrible place, much worse than Tarak's home. He reached toward the panel and entered the sequence to dock with the station. The automated systems would take over once he was close enough and send a greeting across all channels. The station started to come to life almost instantly. Tarak smiled, "Somebody is home. The Vidreians here have survived all this time."

He could see a docking bay light up from the distance and waited for the systems there to take over. That was when an alarm began to blare.

"Weapons lock detected! Weapons lock detected!" The ship computer sounded.

"Chingar!" Tarak had expected a warmer welcome. The rail gun began firing, and he banked to the left, but not quick enough. "Why? I'm like you!" he shouted. The ship spun out of control toward the planet, and he did his best to pull the nose up to not burn up in the atmosphere.

"I'm going too fast," were his last words before he passed out.

The memory was sharp in his mind this morning; he had spent hours here at this small pond recuperating. With all the things he could do, this method of traveling drained him to the extreme. At least he could manipulate the water, creating a portal to the side of the lake on dry land. A trick he had learned early on. It would be dark soon, but he would shift once more. He had only been traveling toward the city for a short time.

He looked up to the sky, "I wish the magic could reach the Starport. What has happened up there since I crashed?" His mind shifted to the colony that lay only days away. Maybe there was a way there to get up to the Starport. According to the data found all those years ago, the tech here had been said to be superb.

His mind floated back to when he had awoken the first time on Daemor, and he smiled. These people had been so easy to fool. They had willingly told one of the best pirates in the galaxy all about the precious Orbs here. Once he had one in hand, he had used its power to taint everyone he came into contact with. They were using philosophy to fight against someone that had the equivalent of a rail gun. They never had a chance.

He smiled. He was not done tormenting these people yet. In the end, he would kill them all. A fleeting thought of Godry made his heart clench. He pushed it aside. Using the Orb to kill was sickly sweet, so sickly sweet.

Chapter Forty-Five

Rayla, Taylor, and the party gathered and began walking toward the city in the morning. Rayla was quiet as she thought about what might lie ahead. There would be a great deal of work to do and much planning behind it. Taylor and Rayla walked beside each other in silence for the first couple of hours before Taylor broke the silence. "The way they disappeared—" Taylor paused and looked at Rayla, "it seemed like the same way you brought me here."

Rayla nodded, "Those two spent years on their own doing who knows what in the woods. It seems during that time, they discovered how to travel, and without the use of water, no less. It wouldn't surprise me if they knew how to go to other worlds." Rayla looked at Taylor thoughtfully, "Where do you think she took him?"

"I have been thinking about the same thing. You don't suppose they ever went to Earth?" Taylor looked concerned.

"I doubt it. Daven would never have been able to keep a world like yours to himself. He was secretive, but he was always interested in impressing me with his knowledge about the Orbs."

Taylor and Rayla fell silent again as the rain began for the first time that day. It had been overcast since the rain had started the previous day and rained off and on that evening. This day wore on as they walked, and with the dark, clouded skies rolling in, the light had also begun to wane earlier. While the sun went down, they set camp, and looking forward to their dry tent, they turned in. The following morning the weather was much the same as when they turned in, cold and dreary. By mid-afternoon, though, the sun began to peek out through the clouds and warmed them and their spirits. As evening approached on the second day, they found themselves in the clearing outside of the city. Exhausted, they set camp and gathered around the fire. Each talked with excitement about the ruin's potential and Milthra before they turned in for the evening.

As Taylor and Rayla lay down in their tent at each other's side, Rayla looked at him, smiled, and touched his face. She leaned in and kissed him; "That was nice," Rayla whispered, lying back. "If I weren't so tired, I'd kiss you more." Her eyes slid closed, and she fell asleep.

Taylor awoke the following morning to Rayla staring back at him. Her deep dark eyes seemed to look into the depths of his heart. "You have turned out to be everything I had dreamed you might be."

"Is that so?" Taylor asked.

"I'm glad that I made it into your dreams," Rayla said as she leaned in, kissing him. Taylor became aroused and in turn; he felt the energy of her arousal at the back of his mind. Her lips were soft and warm against his. She slid closer to him and pressed her body against his. Passion flowed through Taylor as he kissed her back, enjoying the feel of her body against him.

Rayla and Taylor slowly undressed each other while they kissed. He could feel her heart racing as she lay against him. He could feel her joy at being there with him, when she kissed him, when she touched him. They began making love, and as they did, all at once, the Famsha opened up, and they both became a swirl of thoughts and emotions, allowing their lovemaking to be more pleasurable. They stayed entwined with each other for well over an hour. Their minds were separated when they were finished, and they lay back again smiling.

Taylor looked over at Rayla and realized his love had grown so much for her that he could not remember being happier. They both dressed and gave each other a small kiss before leaving their tent, only to discover that they were the first ones up and awake.

They ate and afterward decided they would have a quick look inside the city to plan how they would house all the people to come. They walked to the wall where Tae and Zem had found the entrance, peeled back the vines, and found the exterior door closed.

"That's odd, don't you think? It was rusted open." Taylor said as he looked at Rayla. "Do you see another one of those panels I got my hand stuck in?" He began moving the vines around and found what he was looking for—an oval panel much like the ones he had encountered in the hallway beside the doors. Though, this one seemed active; the pad's clean surface was back-lit to bright silver.

Taylor placed his hand on the panel, and the familiar magical liquid flowed out and around his hand. There was an audible click of locks in the door, and it swung open. The light illuminated the stone walls and floor inside the corridor, which was so clean and polished it gleamed. "Wow," he said.

"It seems the wizardess has managed to extend her power to here," Rayla said as she stepped through the doorway. "I find my hopes rising if she can do this so far from her Dome."

"Agreed, she may not have been candid with us," Taylor replied as he stepped through. "Shall we carry on and see what she has managed inside?"

Taylor placed his hand on the panel at the end of the corridor, and the door swung open. "Welcome back, Taylor and Rayla," the disembodied voice of Milthra said. "I trust you can find your way."

As they stepped into the grass, their eyes adjusted to the light. "It doesn't look as though Milthra has managed much else," Rayla said, disappointed.

"I wouldn't be so sure," Taylor said as he looked at the ruins. He did not see any apparent changes either, but the city had been enormous. "Let us go to meet with the wizardess and see what she has been up to."

As they walked toward the city, all seemed to remain as it had been. Fallen stone lay everywhere, vegetation sprang up through roadways, and there seemed to be no buildings untouched by time. That was, until they turned a corner in the road. "Look up ahead closer to the Dome," Taylor pointed. "I don't remember the buildings being so tall. And if I see correctly, the streets seem a little clearer ahead."

Rayla nodded in confirmation, then cocked her head to the side. "Do you hear that odd noise?" Rayla asked, peering up into the sky. "Look there," she pointed. "What a strange bird."

Taylor looked up as he heard the sound move away behind a large pile of rubble only a few feet ahead. "Come on, let's go and get a closer look," he said as he began to run. Rayla followed close behind. When they reached the immense pile of fallen stone, they could not find any birds. "I don't see anything. How about you?"

"No!" Rayla looked up and down along the road. "How could that be? No bird I know could fly that fast. Could it have been the wizardess somehow?"

"Maybe, I don't know much of magic, aside from the imaginings on Earth," he replied. "Let's keep on going. I doubt that will be the only oddity today."

As they walked toward the Dome, the streets began to look more maintained. A short distance from the Dome, they turned a corner where they stopped short. There before them stood a circular fountain spewing clear, clean water. Behind the fountain itself were several brand-new buildings making up a small downtown. Behind them lay a small city.

"How?" was all Rayla could say; her mouth hung open.

"This wizardess seems to have some rather amazing abilities," Taylor said. "We have only been away for a few weeks, and look at what she has done. Perhaps our troubles with Tarak are over."

"I could weep at the thought," she replied. "How is it that the inhabitant in an Orb could do so much? I could never have done this. Even you, with your accelerated gift with the Orb, you couldn't have managed."

"I don't know that I can answer you," he said, stunned. "Milthra seems more able than she let on. Shall we continue on to the Dome?" Taylor asked.

Both fell silent as they made their way. Taylor had not planned to walk in this far without the others, but nevertheless, here they were. The sun had reached a quarter of the way up the sky by the time they reached the Dome.

"She has cleaned here too," Rayla said, breaking the silence. "The steps look like they have been polished."

"I'm still astonished by her power," Taylor said distractedly. "Look, another bird," he said as they watched it fly into a hole in the Dome's glass top.

"Odd, don't you think?" Rayla said as they moved to walk up the steps. "Why would she allow birds up there?"

"I'm uncertain," he replied. "Though things are getting stranger by the minute." Taylor reached out to push the door open to enter. But before his hand touched it, the door swung open on its own.

"Welcome back, Taylor and Rayla," Milthra's voice echoed through the first floor. "I'm waiting upstairs for you. I have much to report."

They looked at each other, shrugged, and then walked through the doors. Nothing inside had changed, and the light was still dim as before. However, the walkway that led to the staircase had tiny balls of light framing it this time. They were a warm, soft white and hovered a few inches off the ground every foot or so.

"Do you think she wants us to go upstairs," Taylor chimed sarcastically. Rayla frowned at him; she was getting used to his bad humor. Though, she was not always up for it. "Right," he sighed and led the way forward.

At the top of the stairs, Milthra was waiting for them, perched on the windowsill. She was smiling with delight, "I'm glad that you were able to return. But you have come alone. Didn't you bring any of your people? None but you entered the city."

"How do you know that we came alone?" Rayla asked Milthra.

She smiled, "A wizardess has her ways. Magic has many faces and uses. What kind of protector would I be if I didn't know who was in my city? Now tell me, why have you come alone?"

"We have not," Rayla started, "but we had the opportunity to come ahead and see how we would set up lodging for my people, of which we have brought many. I was amazed to see that you have somehow managed to restore a small portion of the city. Your abilities seem to be a bit more than you let on."

This time Milthra's smile was less all-knowing. "I said my magic couldn't reach outside this Dome, not that I had no way to affect the outside. I have a few little helpers that can still do a little magic."

"The flying objects we saw. The ones Rayla mistook for birds?" Taylor exclaimed. "Only magic could explain that, but how could a bird do such a thing?"

"Magic isn't bound by what you believe it could be, Taylor," Milthra chastised. "Magic has many forms in the universe. Would you have believed that the Orbs you carry are a source of magic with sentient beings in them a few weeks ago?" She paused to wait for Taylor to respond.

"Well, no, but—"

"There you have it! Besides, I wouldn't call them birds per se. They are, however, my little helpers, but call them what you like," Milthra retorted.

Taylor felt flustered. How could he possibly argue about a subject he barely knew about. *I know she's hiding something. I can feel it.*

Rayla interrupted, "The restored part of the city. Is it ready for us to occupy?"

"Yes! I mean mostly," Milthra began. "The final construction should be finished this evening. This brings me to a small condition. You mustn't be out in the night after dark. That is when I'll have my little helpers out. They aren't all that smart, and part of their duties when the city was alive was to help protect it from intruders. They can be quite dangerous. Luckily, I detected your Orbs and called back the one close to you."

Taylor felt the unease in Rayla flow through the Famsha. *Do we trust her?* Sounded silently in his mind.

I don't know, he sent back as loud as possible. *We should agree for now.*

"We will abide by your terms," Rayla replied. "The safety of my people is what is most important. If these magic birds are dangerous, we shall stay away from them while they work."

"Magnificent!" Milthra exclaimed. "If you'd like, take a look around the restored area before dark. Return here for the evening to rest for the night, and bring the rest of your party with you." Milthra's form faded away quickly as if she was dismissing them.

"I suppose she means well," Taylor said flatly.

Rayla elbowed him. *She can probably hear you!* Her voice sounded in his head.

"Likely, but we don't have anything to hide," he said, "why make the pretense?"

Chapter Forty-Six

As Taylor and Rayla left the Dome, the sun hung in the midday sky. This left enough time for them to return to their camp and bring the others to explore the city's renewed part. Both of them kept a steady pace, and as they walked, Rayla looked up at the sky several times. Taylor felt her concern that they were going to be attacked by birds at any moment.

"Relax, why would she attack us," Taylor said comfortingly. "If Milthra wanted us dead, she would have done it already. We know that she's not telling us everything, but Milthra could be a great ally. Imagine what else she might do if she could create a home for us and our people in weeks."

Rayla smiled, "You said our people."

"I did!" Taylor replied with his own smile.

Rayla took a deep breath, "I suppose you're right. It just seems like it's too easy. Why would she go to such an effort?"

"Perhaps it's a sense of duty to our ancestors, or loneliness, but does it really matter?" Taylor asked rhetorically.

THE RUINS OF DAEMOR

"She *is* willing to help! And that is something we need a great deal of right now."

Rayla smiled, "You're right. Can you imagine that she could once destroy whole armies? That is something we could use."

"I think 'once' is the key here. Milthra didn't allude to it being possible again," Taylor replied as they reached the metal door leading through the wall.

They walked in silence until they exited the door on the other side. The others were waiting there uneasily. Tae was the first to call to them, "You had us worried! Trust the two of you to wander off and give us a fright over your wellbeing."

"While your concerns weren't entirely misplaced, we have something to show you that will make them seem acceptable," Rayla called back to Tae as she and Taylor approached. "You will find it quite unbelievable."

"We don't have much time before we have to return to the Dome," Taylor said as he glanced up at the mid-afternoon sun. "Grab your gear, but leave the tents. We will be sleeping inside tonight. We leave as soon as we can."

"What is the hurry, Taylor?" Zem asked. "We have plenty of time to get to the Dome at this time of day."

"We will explain on the way," Rayla interjected. "It's unbelievable."

The story of the morning's events did not take long to inspire a little speed in the party. Rayla was not the only one who glanced up at the sky, wondering if they needed cover as they walked.

"It's just around the corner," Rayla said eagerly. "I cannot wait for you to see what Milthra has created."

"Nor I," Tae put in. "I could never imagine that there

were people in the Orbs. Let alone that they could wield such powerful magic. She rebuilt parts of a city!"

"It's amazing to think of it. I bet even you couldn't do such a thing, Taylor," Zem put in.

When they all rounded the corner, Tae and Zem stopped and looked at the wonder of it. "It's seamless," Taylor said. "Every stone is flawlessly set."

Spread out before them was the small downtown area. Sitting inside the immense ruins, it was in deep contrast with its ornately constructed stone buildings. The glass windows gleamed. They were so clean; the metal accents were polished, and the streets were cobbled, as were the sidewalks. There were even lamp posts with tiny flames in them at every corner they could see.

At the entrance sat the large round fountain in the center of the road—the elegantly sculpted spout spewing clear, clean water. The rooms behind the windows were dark, and from what Taylor could see, there were no power lines or poles.

"It's unbelievable," Careed said. "This will house everyone coming and then some."

"Yes, it will!" Rayla marveled. "Shall we take a look? The sun is getting low. The walk to the Dome is only a short distance, but let us make sure our tour is finished at a thumb space to the horizon."

Taylor held his hand up and checked how many fingers were between the sun and the horizon. It was almost three. Remarkably, it was pretty accurate from what he had been able to tell from his pocket watch, a treasured timepiece he had inherited from his grandfather after his death. "I wish we had more time," Taylor huffed.

"There will be tomorrow," Careed remarked, "and the next day, and so on. Let us have a look and get to the Dome.

I've always been on the side of caution when it came to the advice of the Orbs."

They walked the main street and took in everything in awe. After the first three blocks, Rayla pointed out that there were residential blocks on either side of the road. They took a side road and walked through the residential area for several blocks. So overwhelmed with what they saw, no one thought to look inside any buildings or houses. Rayla held up her thumb to the horizon. "That went fast," she said to herself. Then she spoke louder to the others, "It's time!"

The others turned back and began walking out toward the Dome without a word. An hour later, everyone stepped through the doors. They filed upstairs to greet Milthra, only to find she was not there. After calling out to her several times, she appeared before them.

"Milthra, why can I see through you?" Taylor asked urgently. "You were fine earlier.

"Was I? Illusions are easily made here in this room. I had to decide when you returned all those weeks ago," she started. "It has been so long, and my magic had lessened to almost nothing. I served your ancestors faithfully and kept the Dome intact all those thousands of years. When you came here, I had enough magic left to stay awake but be bound here for eternity, or to use what remained to rebuild part of the city."

"Milthra, why not tell us so that we could choose?" Rayla asked. "Perhaps we could have come to a better solution. How much longer will your magic last?"

"It's all but depleted," Milthra replied. "After my birds finish the city tonight, I'll be exhausted of my magic."

"But there has to be something you can do," Tae broke in.

Milthra looked to Rayla's chest, then Taylor's. "Taylor could place me in the hand of one that does not wake—" Milthra's image wavered, then vanished from sight.

"Huh?" Taylor exclaimed, "Anyone have any guesses at what she meant?"

"Not a clue," Rayla said as the others shook their heads.

"What do we do now?" Zem asked.

Taylor looked out into the darkness through the glass of the Dome. Off in the distance, he could see glowing lights dance about the reclaimed city. The glass clouded over so they could no longer see out, and the familiar silver liquid filled in the landing of the stairwell opening. Taylor watched Zem, standing close by the stairwell, investigating the surface. First, he stepped lightly, then stomped on it.

"Albax!" Tae ran to the stairwell in a panic. "How are we going to get out!"

"Relax Tae," Rayla put her hand on his shoulder. "She won't keep us in here past dawn. It's just to make sure we stay put, she doesn't want us to get hurt."

"So what do we do?" Tae said in an agitated voice.

"We sleep?" Taylor said with a shrug. He laid out his bedroll, and the others followed suit.

Rayla butted her roll up to Taylor's and lay beside him. "I guess I was wrong, in a way. She was hiding something. Only not like I expected. She sacrificed herself for us." Her words were solemn, and she had a small tear in her eye.

"I was wrong, too," Taylor said quietly, wiping her tear. He leaned in, kissed her, and they curled up together and fell asleep.

When Taylor awoke, Tae stood looking out at the now-clear glass of the Dome. "The city looks the same except for the weird tower with no covering," Tae said as Taylor joined him.

Taylor looked at the tower in question. Its wire frame was indeed a bit odd when compared to the rest. He smiled a little. "I'd say that it's a unique sculpture for sure." *I knew you were hiding something, Milthra.*

An odd mechanical *click* from the pedestal behind them drew Taylor's attention. The Orb inside turned from its blue color to a dull gray, and the protective glass over the Vidre rolled back, exposing it to the open air.

Rayla sat up at the click of the glass of the pedestal. "What do you think that means?"

"That she has completed her task would be my guess," Careed put it. "She must be surrendering herself to you, Taylor. So you might do as she instructed. If you ever figure out what she meant."

Taylor walked over to the stairwell to see the magical barrier was no longer there. "How many days do we have until the rest of our people arrive?"

"A couple," he heard Careed say from behind him.

Rayla stepped up beside him and gave him a kind smile. "We have a larger door to look for. Otherwise, we will be loading the supplies in by hand." When Taylor looked back at the party members, they had packed their gear and stood ready to go.

Rayla grabbed Taylor's hand, and when he looked at her, she motioned toward Milthra's Orb. "That is an awfully dangerous thing to leave lying around. What if someone gets a hold of it?"

"Tae and Zem, make sure everyone knows the Dome is off-limits," Taylor commanded.

"Done," they said in unison, then smiled at each other.

As they walked out of the Dome's main door, the morning sun shone on the horizon of the clear blue sky. Rayla could see the revived city, an odd contrast to the piles of rubble and partially intact walls of the ruined city, stark to the eye. "We have some exploring to do. Why don't we split up and report back at the fountain later today?"

Everyone stopped short of the fountain. An odd light could be seen through the windows on the darker sides of the buildings. They all stood silent a moment before Taylor broke the silence, "I'd say that Milthra's workers have done the last of the building to make this part of the ruins inhabitable. Light, water, and with luck, sewers."

"Great gods, to poop and not bury it," Careed said. "It's the small conveniences you start to miss when you get older."

"I've heard of these pots you sit on and pull a lever to wash things away," Zem said.

"So strange these city folk," Tae gibed.

Rayla laughed, "Taylor's world is quite fond of them."

"Really?" Tae asked. "Are they everywhere?"

"So, we are about to explore a city made of magic and wonder, and you want to talk about where my people go to the bathroom?"

"You brought it up!" Zem stated.

Tae looked eagerly at him, so Taylor relented. "Some people have their own private one attached to their bedroom."

"You can't be serious!" Zem exclaimed.

"You will have to forgive them," Rayla exclaimed.

"Indoor plumbing is something that fell away some time ago."

Taylor laughed at them, "Can we go explore now? Why don't you see if they have toilets here?" Everyone but Rayla looked confused. "That is what they call the pots on my world."

"Huh," Tae said, "That is an odd name. "Thumb's width to the horizon?" Tae suggested, eager to spend as much time exploring the new city.

Rayla nodded her agreement, and Tae and Zem began to make their way off into the city. "Would you care to join us, Careed?" she asked.

"I'm going to go by myself," he replied. "I feel like a bit of extra time alone."

"See you in a few hours then," Taylor said as they took different streets.

As they walked up the street, Rayla looked excitedly into the windows of some of the shops. The first two blocks were full of different types of ready-made retail stores, with a second story for what she suspected would be the shop owners' residences. It was almost too much to conceive. "Taylor, there are places for craftspersons, bakers, weavers...." Rayla paused, "everything I could think of we would need for our people is here."

"It's hard to imagine that she managed all this," Taylor said as he stopped in front of what looked like a bakery. "You have yet to go into any of the buildings. Is there one you're specifically looking for?"

Rayla stood, staring with a blank face at him for a moment. "No, I hadn't considered going in. It has been all too much. I thought that we might explore something bigger once we had looked about. But why not these?"

Taylor reached out and pressed down the lever for the

door. Rayla was more anxious than she suspected, and her anticipation of the door being locked almost broke her. The door swung open to her relief, and she stepped in. Taylor followed behind her to the front of the glass-faced counter, built from solid wood and stained dark. The patron area inside was filled with the same wood accents, wainscoting, and decorative plaster. There were beautifully carved chairs set at the round wooden tables.

"I don't even know what to say," Rayla breathed.

"How about 'wow'," Taylor exclaimed as he looked around. "I can't wait to see the kitchen in the back."

"The kitchen ..." she said as she followed Taylor around the counter into the back. Rayla walked into him full on in mid-step when he stopped short. "There is everything in here, right down to the mixing bowls."

Rayla looked around; indeed, the kitchen was packed, with butcher block countertops, spoons, pastry utensils, a large wood fire stove, and everything you might need as a baker except for dry and wet goods. "Could they all be like this?" she said, shocked. "Could they be all equipped as such?"

"Should we look upstairs?" Taylor gestured down a small hallway at the back. "I'd guess that there is a residence up there."

Rayla felt giddy. Her biggest dreams would never have amounted to this. "Lead the way."

Upstairs they found a well-laid out, three-bedroom, simple home. It had all the amenities one could want. "It's like she left all the personality out. Even the linens have no personality," Rayla said to Taylor after they had looked around.

"It makes sense. Milthra has left the decorating to whoever will be living here," Taylor smiled. "How could she have decorated for someone she did not know? She left it blank for whoever lives here."

Rayla smiled, "Aren't you the smart one. Let us look in a couple more and then move on."

Rayla and Taylor spent their day looking excitedly through various buildings. All of them were finished to a state that would allow someone to begin either working or living there without so much as unpacking. After a while, it was almost like walking through a city that had been abandoned. Rayla had to remind herself that it was a city in waiting, and its residents would arrive in a little over a day. *I'll need to start talking with everyone to set up how we settle everyone and where.*

At the end of the day, they met with the others to find they had encountered the same thing. Careed had found a barracks, his primary hope when he had set out. "It's well supplied with every type of weapon one could want. There are also enough raw materials to make everyone in our militia full suits of armor. We will have to get the smiths to start straight away. Strangely though, there is no feathers for working or fletching for arrows."

"We found much of the same as you, Rayla," Zem began, "we were curious what amenities there might be. There are several pubs with equipment to brew but not a drop of mead anywhere, to our dismay. We found a store with many musical instruments and a school, like you said they had in the cities. Though there did not seem to be any books anywhere. And we spent the afternoon in a park—"

Tae elbowed Zem, "Not the whole afternoon," Tae interrupted. "We walked loads, and the school took a lot of time to look through."

"Uh-huh," Rayla chided, "You two need to work on getting your stories straight." She laughed. "Tomorrow, you will need to put on your grown up pants. We have plenty of people to contend with. We need to figure out who goes where, what skilled people we have to fill the shops, what tradespeople are left, and all the other jobs required to run this city."

Zem's shoulders drooped, "That sounds like a lot of work."

Tae patted him on the back, "We should start with Garny. He was always good with stills. The brandy he turned out was always darned tasty."

Zem stood a little straighter and gave a knowing nod at Tae, "You always know how to cheer me up!"

Chapter Forty-Seven

Rayla woke up early as the sun shone through the glass of the Dome. They had decided to wait until everyone had arrived before choosing a house. It only seemed fair. How could she expect order and patience from her people if she let those close to her start taking precedence? Everyone was equally important, whether she knew them well or not.

She arose to find Taylor standing at the pedestal, sipping cold tea. "Good morning," he said, slipping his arm around her and giving her a tender kiss. "I couldn't sleep; the caravan is close. I can hear their voices a little louder this morning. They might be here tonight if they push hard enough."

"That soon!" Rayla croaked, panic in her voice. "I'm not prepared enough for that. We have yet to sort out how to set up the encampment in the field outside the city. I have so much to do."

"You should trust your people more," he reassured her, pulling her tighter to him. "Kalamar prepared them well.

You have many people that you can count on. I'm sure Kalamar didn't do it all on his own."

Rayla smiled at Taylor. There had been hardly any time for them to be alone since they had entered the city. They'd had a brief cuddle in the evening before exhaustion took over and they fell asleep. Rayla could scarcely wait until this was all settled and they had their own quarters. Rayla's heart swelled to think she could have him all to herself. Rayla desired to spend time talking and getting to know more about him. And she wanted to make love to him. "You're right, and he did have a great deal of help." She looked back at Tae and Zem, "Those two will be my first recruits. They know everyone, and the trickery aside, they're trusted."

Taylor changed the subject and gestured to Milthra's Orb, "I wish I knew what she meant about one who does not wake?"

"That is a problem for another day," she replied. "We need to get these three up and get started if you think they will be here tonight."

They woke the others and had a cold breakfast of dried meat and hard bread, then ventured out to the front of the city. "Careed, your job will be to set up the design for the camp. These two will help you stake things out." Careed nodded his agreement. "We will need the camp to function for at least two weeks as our base camp. Tae and Zem, while you help him, I want you to discuss the best way to assign housing and who will take over the shops."

"More work," Zem said, slumped.

"Nothing we can't handle, my friend," Tae said as he patted Zem on the back.

Rayla turned to Taylor, "As for us, we need to hike around the city outskirts to see the wild game situation.

There are eighteen thousand mouths to feed coming our way. The food supplies we have will last another week at the most. With the help of Shard Carriers, we will have crops to harvest in a few weeks. Until then, we will need a lot of quarries to keep us going."

Rayla's take-charge nature was something Taylor admired in her. She'd had a significant role in running the Refuge, but this was more than taking over a smooth operation. Taylor realized how much he had become accustomed to life here and the Orb that hung around his neck as they stood there. The gifts it had bestowed in him were now a part of his life. He was still discovering new ones.

Like the one now that told him of the teeming life in the forest around them, though he could not distinguish between the large and the small. They were all separate, yet a part of one another. Feeling the life out there was like being connected to life itself. He felt Rayla move to the forefront of his mind. *It's beautiful, isn't it. It gets easier to sense them individually. But I must warn you that it's hard to hunt them once you feel their presence and individual personality. I suggest the old-fashioned way.*

Taylor thought a moment, of the voices in his head after the attack in the Refuge, then on how he had lessened them. Taylor had needed it to turn down, or it would drive him crazy. He had eventually pleaded, and like someone had heard him, it had abated. He had not thought of what had taken it away, but now as he thought of it, the only reason it could have decreased was the Orb. He took a breath and directed his thoughts to the Orb, asking it to help him.

The skin where his Orb touched began to tingle. The

feeling triggered a distant memory of the same thing happening that day he had pleaded. As the tingling continued, he felt his ability to sense the life in the forest come more under his control. Taylor experimented a little, and he found he could lessen and increase the sensing as he wished. While he practiced with his newfound control, a sense of happiness came from the Orb. He remembered Milthra saying that the Orbs had a consciousness within them, but he had not yet felt it. Why had Rayla not mentioned that this was possible?

"Are you coming or not?" Rayla's voice brought him out of his thoughts. "What's going on with you?"

"You never told me that you could feel the beings inside the Orbs," he said to her.

"I was as surprised as you when Milthra told us there were people inside them, but I don't know what you mean by feeling them?" Rayla looked at him with curiosity as she touched her Orb. "I had often considered them to have their own will, as have many others."

Taylor was left speechless, with yet another question about the Orbs and his ability to connect with them. Rayla stood, waiting for him to say something. "L ... lets go then."

Rayla eyed him, wondering what he was thinking—he was getting better at blocking her—before she led their way out into the woods. For the remainder of the afternoon, they found several well-used game trails starting around the lake and leading into the woods. At midday, they found themselves at the back of the city, up against the mountain wall. When Taylor's stomach growled, they decided to stop for a break to snack on hard bread and fruit. While they ate, Rayla commented, "This place will indeed be able to feed us for the first few weeks. And while the mountains circling the city provide a perfect defense, the terrain still lends to hunting."

At the base of the mountain, where it had been cut away, there was a small hill butting up against it. The forest there was thin and while Rayla spoke, the sun peeked through the trees, and small streams of light shone on the ground further ahead. "Huh, look at that," Taylor said. "Those look like stairs." He pointed a few paces ahead. "Want to check it out?"

Rayla looked ahead, "I don't see anything. But sure."

Taylor took the lead, and within a couple of minutes, they stood at a well-concealed set of stairs carved into the mountain. "Very clever. We were lucky to have been at the right angle. Otherwise, I would never have seen these."

"I don't think I would have seen them at all," Rayla said with dismay.

"If it makes you feel any better, I trained a long time to spot those types of things." He stuck his lip out in a pout.

Rayla slugged him in the shoulder, "Jackass," she laughed, "It couldn't have anything to do with the magical Orb around your neck?"

Taylor rubbed his shoulder, "Ooowww, that hurt."

"Don't be a baby," she laughed again. "Let us see where this goes."

Rayla felt the pressure of all her responsibilities lift. It had been several days since she and Taylor had been alone. "How far do you think they go up?" She watched Taylor ponder her rhetorical question. "Shall we race to see who can reach the top first?" She did not wait. She began running, first at a regular pace. She looked back, saw Taylor on her heels, and picked up speed until her surroundings blurred.

The experience of this speed was always surreal; the faster she went, the more focused the ground before her became. She could have counted the leaves on each step if she chose to. At the back of her mind, Taylor's emotions told her he was elated with the feeling. He was only a few steps behind her, but he could not bridge the gap between them. Maybe this was one area he could not best her with the Orb? Her senses snapped her attention ahead of her, where the stairs ended on a ledge above.

She slowed, as did Taylor, and they both came to a halt a few paces onto the ledge. It was apparent that the shelf had been carved out of the mountain and was almost an acre in size. Nothing but grass and moss grew here, and if not for the trees growing below, blocking the view, they would have been able to see the whole of the city and meadow.

Taylor smiled at Rayla, "That was awesome! I can hardly wait until we go back—" Taylor stopped mid-sentence when he saw something he hadn't expected. "On our way up, I had thought this might have been a lookout. But look!" He pointed to the face of the cliff.

"Is that a door?" Rayla gasped in disbelief. "Carved into the mountain?"

"I do believe it is!" Taylor replied as he walked toward it, "and it has a pad like in the entrance to the city." When he placed his hand on it, the pad came to life, and liquid goo shot out and receded. He expected the door to swing open, but instead it disintegrated from the top down. As it did, a rush of air swept through the entrance.

Rayla gasped, "That is exciting! This is turning out to be an unexpected adventure." She smiled at Taylor and shot through the door.

"Wait! We don't know what is in there." Taylor rushed in after her before the door re-materialized. Globes of light hung at the wall, dimly illuminating the chamber inside. Before them was a fully functional living space; Taylor could make out a small kitchen, a living space, and a sleeping area in the dim light. As they stood there, the globes brightened, showing the room in more definition.

"It's perfectly preserved," Rayla said. Walking up to a writing desk, she picked up one of the papers atop it. "It's still pristine," It crinkled as she waved it at him, then looked at the writing there, "This looks similar to my language, but I don't understand it clearly. I bet if I took some time with it, I could figure it out."

"Wouldn't that be something, if we could find out what this place might have been like," Taylor said, pointing to the full bookcase. He walked over and pulled a book off a shelf. "There isn't even any dust on them. Who do you think might have lived here?"

"There is a name here on the bottom," Rayla added. "'Tess Ravena,' hmm. That name seems familiar."

Taylor put the book back and sat down on the writing desk bench beside her. "She obviously didn't want to be disturbed, living all the way up here."

"Obviously," Rayla said sarcastically. She put the paper in her pocket and walked toward the sleeping area, "Even the sheets are pristine," she said as she pulled the blankets back. She looked at him, "Care to see how they feel?" she teased.

Taylor's eyes widened, "Oh yes, I do." He jumped up and was before her in an instant. He leaned in, embracing her. "This is indeed turning out to be an unexpected adventure."

She kissed him passionately, shoved him onto the bed, slinked over, and straddled him. "I was beginning to think that this moment might not ever come again." Their Orbs began to glow, and once again the Famsha opened, and they were entwined, making love.

As they slowly walked back down the stairs, the sun was low in the sky. Taylor hoped they would be prepared for the caravan's arrival tomorrow. It would be a long few days coming up, and privacy might be hard to steal. Though if they needed it, they now had a little getaway that was very hard to find. They followed the stairs down past where Taylor originally spotted them. An hour after leaving, the hidden stairs had stopped, leaving them on a small clearing halfway up the mountain. "Purposeful, I suspect," Taylor commented looking down at the city, "After all, what would be the point in having a secret place if anyone can stumble across it?" Only a sliver of the sun remained as they made their way into the meadow.

Taylor and Rayla found the field staked in several different areas outside the city where they had left Careed, Tae, and Zem. The three of them had been busy. They were, however, nowhere to be found. They had likely returned to the Dome with the sun at a thumb's width. Hand in hand, Taylor and Rayla walked back to the Dome and found their friends there eating a cold dinner.

"We thought we might have to come looking for you,"

Zem laughed. "I thought you two were looking for game? And you have returned with none." Tae snickered but did not add anything to the conversation.

Rayla's face heated two-fold, "We found plenty of game and trails that will lead to good hunting!" she spoke sharply. She felt the weight of responsibility back on her shoulders as her friend looked with hurt on his face. *I mustn't let myself get overwhelmed. I have many that can help me bear the responsibility.* "Besides, I have had the displeasure of tasting your cooking. I wouldn't waste my time with the hunt to have you spoil the prize."

Tae laughed boisterously and clapped Zem on the back, "She's right. You're the worst cook I have ever crossed paths with."

Even Careed smiled as he sat eating his meal. Rayla and Taylor sat, joining the others, and pulled hard bread and dried meat from their packs. They discussed the coming of the caravan the next day, and Careed filled them in on how he had decided the best way to set up the camp.

"We have some rather good news to finish off with," Careed said. "I got tired of these two and their nonstop blather. I sent them to go explore this afternoon. Tae has found a large door into the city through the wall, under all those vines."

Tae smiled, "I did indeed!" He looked like a child being praised.

Zem elbowed him in the side; with a mouth full of food, his speech was broken, "Ou orgot o tel m za bes par-tt" He swallowed his mouth full, "He couldn't find the pad thingy on either side of the door. We can't open it!" he laughed.

"I'm sure with a little more time tomorrow, I'll be able to!" Tae said, elbowing Zem in the chest, knocking him back off the pack he used as a seat. Arms failing, Zem's plate of dried food spilled on him. Everyone laughed at the spectacle.

"The sun has gone completely," Taylor put in, "we should get some rest soon. And I'm sure you will find us the way in, Tae. It might just take some time."

Everyone nodded their agreement, and the party prepared their bedrolls for the evening. Careed stood to tend to the glow of the globes at the wall. He moved to a small square panel on the outcropping where one of the globes hung. He had found it the evening before when he had tired of the glare keeping him from sleep. He swiped down the center of it, and the lights went out. The sliver of the moon cast enough illumination for him to make his way back to his bedroll.

Chapter Forty-Eight

Taylor had felt weary from the days that passed. Making love to Rayla had reminded him of the beauty that life could hold, the beauty *their* lives held. The moment his mind mixed with hers, the preciousness of life had filled them. He turned to her as she slept beside him. He did not think that he could imagine his life without her now. Not having her presence in the back of his mind seemed appalling to him.

She opened her eyes as he stared at her, "That's creepy!" she laughed at the uncomfortable look on his face and leaned in, kissing him. "You make my heart sing."

Taylor smiled at her, "You had me going there for a minute. I can't wait to see how it is that our lives together end up when we are finished with all of this." He took in the wholeness of the woman before him. *How could I be so lucky?*

Looking out the Dome's glass, Rayla breathed in a sigh, "We have a great deal ahead of us before that happens. Starting today!" She patted him on the stomach. "We should get up and prepare for them to get here."

Taylor could see Rayla's excitement. They had almost accomplished relocating her people, possibly avoiding detection altogether. After they had eaten and made their way to the exit, Tae and Zem broke away to further look for the way to open the gates. Taylor could feel Rayla's excitement to have her people settled in the back of his head, along with the mixed feelings of anxiety and dread for the days to come. Sorting her people out was going to be a big deal indeed.

Rayla had given Tae and Zem instructions to come with haste when they heard the caravan approaching. Taylor, Rayla, and Careed would spend their time finishing up the plans for setting up camp for her people. It would take several days to sort everyone into the New City. They busied themselves laying out marker posts and stakes they had grabbed from a supply store.

As midday approached, Rayla stopped Taylor. "I think I hear them," she cocked her head and then looked up to a stream of people emerging through the trees. "Now it begins."

Tae and Zem stepped up beside her. "We have had some luck," Tae said. "We found a stairwell beside the main gate into the city. There is a room above that was locked up, but there is a pad beside the door. I think it may contain the controls to the gates."

"That is great news! But we will need to see to that later. Are you two ready to begin assigning quarters to a few thousand people?" Taylor asked wryly.

Zem sighed, "Let us get them settled here first, then. That is going to be a feat all on its own."

Careed sighed, "That is an understatement. This is going to take days! As the people weave their way down to us, guide each person to their area of the camp."

Expectant mothers, the elderly, the young, and the sick or wounded were all settled into different areas. Each group would need a different level of care. Their able-bodied caretakers from the caravan were sent to a separate part of the camp. They would need a place of their own to rest, away from their charges. Careed had staked out a different command for the militia further out in the field. There were not enough of them to protect the camp, but it would provide the illusion of safety for everyone's minds.

At the end of the day, the tents were sprung for those in the greatest need, fires were being lit to keep warm, and tomorrow they would start building shelters. The rains had held off, but the cold and overcast skies spoke of what was to come. In only a week, maybe two, it would rain steadily. They would need to move quickly.

A week passed by quickly with the arrival of their people. One morning Taylor bumped into a familiar face. "How is it moving along, Tae?" Taylor asked. That there was an empty city inside the walls had lifted everyone's spirits.

"As Zem and I work with the community leaders, it seems there is ever more to consider in settling everyone. The infirmary is staffed, and the sick and hurt are well taken care of. Thank you for stopping in again last night to heal more of the wounded. That will give us more strong bodies in a day or two. And less of a burden on the healers."

Taylor had missed healing the wounded the two days they had been in the city alone. As such, he had stopped in each night since and spent the time helping three or four people. After this, he had met Rayla in the Dome, where they spent their evenings alone. Tae and Zem had taken tents for their partners and themselves, but were due to take a large home in preparation for their children to come.

"There are just so many people to contend with," Tae said. "And how we decide who gets to take possession of the shops has been a heated topic of discussion with community leaders." Tae sighed. "I thought this would be easier!"

Taylor put a hand on Tae's shoulder, "Your people have been through a great deal in the last months. It would have been unsettling to the calmest person. Give it time, and they will settle in." Taylor thought for a moment, "Have you considered using a lottery for the most desired businesses or even perhaps a co-op?"

Tae took some comfort from Taylor's reassurance but looked a little confused, "What is a co-op?"

"Ah, yes. It's when everyone shares the business space but does their own work. Like, say; artists, potters, painters, photographers, woodworkers... didn't your people use such things at the Refuge?"

Tae nodded, "We never had a want for space in the Refuge, but I understand, except for the photo ... thing. Thanks, Taylor!"

"And don't try to do this all on your own," Taylor put in. "You know these people; find some help."

Taylor moved to carry on, but Tae stopped him, "Wait! Zem and I have been thinking. You and Rayla should have your own place instead of staying in the Dome. We weren't sure, but we thought you might like an apartment in the city square."

Rayla had joined them just as Tae had proposed the apartment, "I think that is a wonderful idea! It would be very convenient."

Taylor nodded his agreement, "I suspect you have a place in mind, by the look on your face."

Zem piped up from a small distance away, "We do, actually. Follow me." Tae beamed and set off in the lead with Zem at his side, Taylor and Rayla in tow.

Taylor gave Rayla a small smile. *I can't wait for a proper bed to have a whole night's sleep,* he sent.

Who says you're going to get to sleep? she sent back and gave him a wry smile in return.

Tae and Zem led them past the fountain through the New City entrance, to face the pie-shaped building centered between the two roads leading into the city. "Strangely, we were so excited that we didn't even look about in the first few buildings. That arrow-shaped one has an apartment above it that is quite elaborate. In fact, the apartment takes up the whole floor."

Rayla stammered, "Tae, we couldn't possibly take an apartment of that size for just the two of us."

Zem raised his hand in a wave, "It's unique in that it only has one bedroom. The rest of the apartment has a sitting room, a room for entertaining, a library, a conference room, and a large dining room. With the abundance of housing, who better to use it than the people in charge of our new city and our people?"

"It couldn't hurt to at least look. Could it?" Taylor put in.

Rayla rolled her eyes, "I don't think I have a choice."

With Zem in the lead, this time, they walked to a door at the side of the building and led them upstairs. "It's amazing up here. I can't wait to come to visit!"

It was exquisite indeed, filled with fineries that Taylor thought would have rivaled penthouses in New York. To his surprise, it was set up with beauty and functionality for entertaining stately guests and conferencing with the business people of this new city. "You two have outdone yourselves. It's perfect for what we need." Rayla nodded her agreement. Tae and Zem excused them to explore the new home.

The sun was low, and Taylor was tired. The bedroom was enormous, with a sitting room and a spacious five-piece bathroom. He turned the shower on, and hot water gushed out and filled the room with steam. He noted the second set of taps and a shower head to the other side. "Care to join me?" he lifted his eyebrows.

"Only if you wash my back!" she said saucily.

After a long hot shower filled with lovemaking, they made their way to the bed. "I cannot wait to sleep in this."

Rayla rolled him over and slid on top of him, "I told you there would be no sleep for you tonight." She leaned in, kissing him as she took him inside of her.

Several days passed as the people in the temporary camp moved into the city. The elderly, the young, and their caretakers were the first to be assigned homes. To Tae and Zem's delight, the parties sent out to explore the city found several large apartment buildings created to care for the elderly. Others found houses that could house several children in each, much like a community home.

Taylor had taken to spending time healing more of the wounded from the battle. One evening he took the time to check on Marita, the woman that had cared for him when he had first arrived. She had taken the pommel of a sword to the side of her head during an especially violent rape. Taylor had healed her on the first night back at the base camp, but she still lay in what Taylor suspected was a coma.

He sat by her bed in the infirmary, holding her hand.

She was gaunt and skinny. Concerned, he called to the Orb, using its power and attempting to reach into her mind. He closed his eyes, preparing for the memories that could draw him in, those he might get lost in. To his disappointment, he found a nothingness within her. Whatever had made up Marita no longer existed inside her body. He retreated and laid her hand down.

A voice startled him from behind, "Poor dear, that one will never wake!" Taylor turned at the words to see a kindly old woman. She wore the clothes of an attendee, something akin to a nurse. She spoke again, "You should move on to someone that can be helped, young hero."

"What did you say?" It came out a little harsher than he meant.

The woman was not taken aback. Instead, she pursed her lips, "You will have to pardon me, I'm an old woman, and I do not have the time to always be pleasant. You should move on to someone you can help. She's not worth your effort any longer. We can get water down her throat, but nothing else. We do not have the means to feed her in her condition. She will likely be dead in only a few days."

Taylor grinned to himself; most of the people here saw him as the prophesied savior and did not have the will to speak to him that way. It was a little refreshing, "Sorry, you misunderstood me; I meant what did you say when you first spoke to me."

The woman thought, "Ah, yes, 'She will never wake.' She's in the death sleep. Her spirit has moved on, but her body does not know it yet."

"I do not believe it," he said to himself. "That's it! I have to go." He stood and ran out of the infirmary. He made his way back to the apartment, knowing Rayla would be there. It was several blocks, but he began to move in a blur as he accessed the Orb. When he reached the door at the side of their building, he opened it with such force that it almost came off the hinges. He took the stairs two at a time and was met by Rayla at the top of the stairs, her sword in hand, standing defensively. He stopped in front of her.

"Taylor, you scared the wits out of me. What is going on?" she asked, dropping her stance.

"I have it!" he explained. "I know what to do with Milthra. I know how to revive her!"

Chapter Forty-Nine

As Rayla had helped carry Marita on the stretcher, she was not convinced of Taylor's plan. She had known Marita since birth, and this seemed wrong, somehow. But Rayla's trust in Taylor pulled her to follow him in this. They laid Marita on the floor beside the pedestal in the Dome, and Taylor looked at Rayla for her permission to proceed. She took a deep breath, "The Orb isn't glowing golden like ours do when it's time to move to a new Bearer. But if you think this is what we should do?"

"It is," he stated. The Orb atop the pedestal flared to life as he touched it, and Rayla saw him shiver. It could be like that sometimes when a Bearer held another Orb. It was Taylor's Orb communicating; he was already aligned. "Ready?" he asked as he looked at her once more.

She agreed, and he bent down and placed Milthra's Orb into Marita's hand and cupped it closed. The Orb turned a blinding bright red, something Rayla had never seen or heard of. Her heart started to pound in her chest. After only a moment, Marita's eyes snapped open. She sat bolt upright and took a deep breath. Taylor had been knocked back in the process, and he lay sprawled. Careed, who had helped with the stretcher, unsheathed his sword. Tae and Zem stood, not saying anything, horrified at the scene.

Everyone held their breath a moment, watching. Taylor moved to kneel at who Rayla now thought to be Marita's side. The woman sat wide-eyed for a moment before she exhaled and relaxed. "Thank you, Taylor! I hadn't known if you had understood."

"Marita?" Zem asked.

The woman before Taylor looked at Zem. He had been a dear friend of Marita's. "No, Zem. Marita is gone. She has been for some time. This mind was blank. It's me, Milthra."

Everyone but Taylor stood shocked. In Rayla's doubts, she had not fully disclosed what they were doing. The others had thought this was the last chance for Marita. But here Milthra was. Or so it seemed. "How?" was all Rayla could muster.

"Indeed, how?" Zem shot at Rayla, then glared at Taylor.

Milthra opened her palm to look at the Orb, "How strange to look at it from this angle." The tinkling of the brass bracelets at her wrists caught her attention. Someone had thoughts that Marita might be comforted by them in the infirmary. "These will do," she said as she touched the Orb to them. The metal began to twist and bend, forming a setting shaped like the foot and talons of a bird around the Orb. The rest of the metal shaped itself into an elegant chain, and she brought the Orb up to her neck. The last of the metal left her wrist and created a clasp that clicked into place around her neck.

Milthra turned her attention back to everyone standing around her. "The Orbs that your people carry here are a rarity," Milthra began. "It's something we only have sparse records of in the times of our people—time that spanned more than you can comprehend. The Orbs like you carry were most often destroyed or disappeared, never to be seen again. They were a magical item of immense power, allowing those that couldn't wield magic the ability to do so, giving the wearer magic at a level parallel to that of the strongest of wizards and wizardesses. Something that was most undesirable. Though, no Orb ever wielded extended life as they have for your people."

"Our Orbs are different than the one you inhabit then," Rayla asked.

"The Orb that I'm in, all Orbs, are quite different from yours," Milthra said matter-of-factly. "The key difference is that Orbs don't lend their magic; their consciousness takes over the body of those that carry no magic. Sometimes with dire consequences, completely erasing the consciousness there."

Taylor stepped in, "That is why you wanted someone that was brain-dead. So you wouldn't damage anyone. That's very brilliant."

Milthra moved to stand and, with wobbly legs, managed well enough. "Thank you, Taylor. It can take some time for one of us to remember how to function in a body. She stumbled, and Careed caught her by the elbow, steadying her. Milthra smiled kindly at him. "Thank you, Careed!" She turned her attention back to the others. "There are other differences, but we need not speak of them now. I'd love to have a look at the city from the ground. I have been relegated to this room for a long time and would very much enjoy a different view."

Taylor led them out, with Rayla at his side. Careed offered an arm to steady Milthra, and she took it kindly. Tae and Zem followed behind, whispering to each other.

Milthra took a deep breath of air as she stepped into the night. There was a clear evening sky, the stars shone bright, and a cool breeze touched their cheeks.

Taylor wondered what it would be like to not feel sensations for so long and have them return so suddenly. It was odd to watch Milthra in Marita's body. Marita was kind and feminine in her own right. But she was the daughter of a peasant farmer and had moved with steady coordination and her feet planted on the ground. In contrast, with each step Milthra began to flow, and in only moments she walked gracefully like a dancer and with the demeanor of a well-educated person.

A tear fell from Milthra's cheek, and her chin quivered, "You have no idea what you have given me. It was against the law to inhabit a body as I am now when my people ruled. I'd never have been allowed this!" She looked up at the stars, "I have watched them over the centuries, but to see them like this once more ..."

"Are you sure you're alright?" Careed asked with concern.

Milthra tapped his hand, "Quite, but I fear I have overdone it. There is a place in the city I'd like to go to." She smiled to herself, "I took the liberty of recreating my apartment when I was young and fresh in my work as a dignitary. I thought that someone would enjoy it as much as I did."

"Gladly," Rayla said. "Tae and Zem are quite familiar with the city. Could you direct them to the area?"

"It's on the corner of Fifth and Twiddle Dee Dee," Milthra giggled, "such a funny name."

Zem laughed aloud, "Very silly! I know where it is, and I had a good giggle myself."

The walk was not a long distance, but Careed had carried her in the end. When they reached the building that she directed them to, they took the stairs in the apartment building up to the sixth floor, to apartment number eight. Rayla swung the door open, and Careed placed her on the bed, and she fell fast asleep.

Milthra slept the night and almost through the next. The five of them had set a schedule to check on her. Each of them was eager to ask the many questions they had for her.

The five gathered in Taylor and Rayla's apartment conference room with the community leaders that afternoon. Rayla stood and addressed them. "I'm glad to see everyone has made it. Taylor and I have talked with a few of you over the last two days. We have heard many concerns over the move into the city and the current food supplies."

One of the men stood and, with anger, spoke, "Many of my people have asked when they would be allowed into the city, only to be put off by Tae and Zem. I want to know what is taking so long?"

A heated look erupted on both Tae and Zem's faces. Rayla forestalled them, seeing they were about to have words with Brek. "I know that Tae and Zem are working hard to safely get everyone into the city. It's an arduous task, though. There are so many people to work through and assign housing to. And as they do so, they need to distribute personnel to that area to make sure everyone there is taken care of properly."

"I don't want to know about the clerical work these two are doing," Marg, another community leader, said. "I'm with Brek. When are our people going to see the inside of the city?"

Taylor stood, and everyone settled a little. Some people here were still distrustful of him. "We are all weary, but bickering will get you nowhere. If I could suggest that you go back to your people? Ask who is willing to be on work crews. We need help keeping the city's residences cared for and others to help those who are settling. Tae, what are the jobs that need to be done the most?

"Ahhhh, hmmm," caught off guard, Tae was unsure where to start.

"We need more staff for the infirmary!" Zem cut in, still red in the face with anger. "And we need to staff some of the restaurants to prepare food. It's proving hard to get meals to the young and the elderly from outside the wall. While we are at it, we should bring the food supplies inside. That way, everyone could eat here; maybe that will soothe these turds." He paused, looking at Taylor; he had liked that one when he had heard Taylor use it. "Once that is done, the shops can start to be staffed."

The community leaders shifted in their seats, "And would these individuals get housing inside the city?" Glaith, a third community leader, asked inquisitively.

"Of course they would," Tae interjected. "We also need to begin forming hunting and foraging parties. Some of you could also look for volunteers to begin breaking the land outside in the field for crops. I'm surprised the rainy season has held off this long. We need to get our winter crops started. If the seeds aren't sprouted before the rains, the seeds will be ruined. Even with the help of the Shard Carriers, it won't be easy. All these people would also get housing once they volunteer."

"Tomorrow, all of you can report here," Zem continued. "Brek, you can arrange the food getting in here! And look for some cooks. Glaith, could you work out finding hunting and foraging parties? And Marg, you were one of the gardeners, how about you sort out the crops? We start a thumb's width after sunrise."

Relief spread on the faces around the table. Aside from

Brek; he was not easily pleased with anything. Zem had done well, giving the leaders that were unhappy about the progress something constructive to do. Taylor was starting to feel hopeful. "It might even be best for the farmers to construct homes outside the walls. If they so choose." This brought nodding amongst a few around the table. Many of them began to actively speak about solving the more minor problems they all faced in the camp.

Taylor looked to Rayla. The day was getting late, and they still had to work out the details of accomplishing the opening of the restaurants and the shops. *Perhaps we should let Tae and Zem deal with this?* He sent. Rayla gave him a nod. She whispered in Zem's ear, and Zem agreed, both slipping quietly out of the room.

Chapter Fifty

The community leaders would likely talk for some time, then be off to ask for volunteers. Tae and Zem would then return to admitting their people to the city. Curious about Milthra's well-being, Rayla and Taylor stopped to check on her. She was awake and sitting at the kitchen island, eating foraged berries and a freshly cooked wild hen.

She spoke with her hand over her full mouth, "Oh... hi..." then swallowed and stood. "Careed stopped in with some food. He just left. Such a sweet man! He took the time to get all of this for me. I had no idea you had such things with you."

Rayla smiled at Taylor, "Oh, you know, Careed is resourceful." *I don't think I have ever heard of Careed making someone's dinner. Let alone hunt for them.*

Taylor took in the sending. *Perhaps he just needed the proper motivation,* he sent back.

"Please, don't stop on our account," Taylor continued. "I have some questions for you when you're done." Rayla gave him a curious look.

"Oh, thank you," Milthra said as she sat. "This body hasn't eaten in some time. And I must admit I'm enjoying the sensations it brings. It has been so very long since I have tasted or felt hungry. Or had to pee... I think that is what this sensation is. Excuse me." Milthra shot up and ran for the bathroom.

She returned with a smile, "I haven't had a peegasm in some time, either."

Rayla caught Taylor's curious look and smirked, "I'll tell you later. You had questions you were going to ask Milthra?"

Taylor directed his gaze at Milthra, who said "Oh, please go ahead." She took a small bite as she waited.

"I have plenty of questions," Taylor said, pondering. "Perhaps I'll start with something simple. How old is this city?"

"One hundred twenty-nine thousand eight hundred fifty-three rotations of the sun around this planet have passed since this city was constructed," she stated in a flat tone.

Taylor's jaw dropped, "That's unbelievable, more so that the Dome stayed intact."

Milthra looked to him, "Oh, that's nothing. Some of the other—" she stopped.

"What were you going to say just then?" Rayla asked. "Are there other cities like this on my world?"

Rayla felt Taylor's suspicion; there was more. "I suspect other worlds? After all, even with Rayla's small amount of knowledge of the Orbs, she was able to come to Earth. The murals on the walls of the Dome depict other worlds, do they not?"

Milthra nodded, "This is but one world that was known to our people. The construction of this city was one of the more recent. Though I don't have much information about the conditions of any other worlds after I evacuated the city. Due to the sickness, the Navaden regime had lost many outposts and colonies. All communication with other worlds stopped shortly after the city was empty. I can only assume the sickness annihilated the regime."

Rayla stood shocked, "Then it's true! The Song of Reminder was true."

"I had asked the survivors to set a warning to the other generations," Milthra stood soberly. "And it has worked. Though I had expected you long ago. I was unable to keep our great city from crumbling through all that time."

Taylor took the opportunity to ask another question. "But you managed to create a home for Rayla's people out of nothing. How?"

Milthra was quick to answer, "Why with magic, of course." She laughed but did not offer any more information.

"Magic is only something science hasn't come to understand," Taylor put to her.

Milthra did not retort; she took a bite of her food and held Taylor's eyes levelly. "Do you have more questions?"

Taylor looked back at her in dismay but did not push. "You said you could have destroyed entire armies in your glory. Is that a power you can still wield? As you are, I mean."

Rayla cut in, "You mean hold off an army!" Rayla gave Taylor a look of dismay. "If I don't have to kill my people in Tarak's army, it would be preferable."

"That's an interesting question," Milthra drummed her fingers on the counter. "I'm still a creature of magic and the keeper of the city. Perhaps we should find out." Without

THE RUINS OF DAEMOR

another word, Milthra walked off toward the stairs and down to the door.

Taylor and Rayla followed, very surprised at Milthra's abrupt decision. She led them past the New City, through the ruins, and to the barrier wall. She took the stairs Tae and Zem had found without pause, which led to the gate control room. There they found Tae and Zem up to their usual antics. There were tools everywhere, broken and bent, lying on the ground at the base of the door. "I wouldn't if I were you," Tae said to Zem as they approached. Not listening, Zem hoisted a giant hammer over his shoulder and, with all his might, slammed it into the steel door. The hammer gave a loud crack but did not leave the slightest mark as it bounced backward. Zem let out a grunt of pain from the vibration, and the hammer slipped from his grip and straight for Milthra.

Milthra lifted one hand with fantastic speed, and the hammer halted a foot before her before dropping to the ground. Tae looked wide-eyed and as she approached; Zem hurriedly stepped aside. Milthra came to a halt a few inches from the door, at which point her Orb flashed orange. The door slid aside, and she stepped in, while the others followed.

They could see the vines covering the wall from inside the room through the large, thick-paned windows. Under the windows and along the perimeter, a counter wrapped itself around the curve of the otherwise empty room. Milthra stepped up to the counter, and as she did, the vines in the window withered away and disintegrated in the wind, giving them a view of the field outside.

She placed her hand on a panel in the sloped counter below the window and closed her eyes. Her Orb glowed orange, igniting vein-like lines that flowed outward from the center of the panel, creating an intricate pattern. Milthra frowned, "The wall's magical defenses are quite damaged. I can repair them with my birds, but it will take time."

Careed stepped into the room, looking at Tae and Zem, "I see you two finally—" He stopped short as his gaze caught Milthra's presence, and he stood a little taller, "I hadn't realized you were about, Milthra. It's good to see you're up." He smiled at her, then looked at the counter. "Well, that's something!" Milthra looked back over her shoulder and gave Careed a flirtatious smile but did not say anything.

Taylor, taken back by the display of magic Milthra was performing, was finally able to say something. "You said that you used all your magical power to create the New City."

"And I did," Milthra said plainly to him over her shoulder again. "The wall, however, has its own reserve." Her expression changed to confusion. "That's odd. I didn't expect that." She lifted her hand from the panel, and the veins of light faded.

"You didn't expect what?" Rayla asked.

"Oh, it's likely nothing," she replied, "An old lingering magic." But Milthra's face betrayed her. She was not telling them something. "It seems I have a great deal of work to do. I will need to use my birds for the next few evenings to remove the vegetation from the walls. There are focal points built into the wall for deploying its magic. They will not be effective, covered as they are. Please let your people know to stay indoors." She turned to Careed, "Would you walk me to my apartment? I'm suddenly feeling tired." Careed took her arm and led Milthra away without so much as a word.

The door closed behind them as they stepped past the threshold.

Zem held his hands under his armpits, trying to soothe his pain. He looked over at Tae, "Let's go back to our quarters. I'd like to see if that magic cold box for our food will make my hands feel better."

Rayla looked at Taylor, "What do you suppose that was really about with Milthra? The 'old magic' bit?"

Taylor shook his head, "I'm not sure. I sense we can trust Milthra, but she's definitely keeping secrets. For our benefit or hers, I'm not sure."

"I hope it's for both our benefits," Rayla retorted. "She did, after all, sacrifice herself to build this city."

Taylor nodded his agreement, "My hope is that it won't end up causing us trouble."

That evening as they lay down in bed, Rayla held up her Orb. "Something has been weighing heavily on me since Milthra took over Marita's body. My people have been using these Orbs through the generations, unknowing of the entities inside. They have been like slaves to us, something that is against all that my people came to stand for. Considering that Milthra was able to take over Marita's body ... I'm curious if the beings in our Orbs could be set free in the same way she was."

Taylor took in what she had to say. "That's an interesting thought. That might mean a considerable change for your people. Why don't we ask her thoughts on it when a proper time arises?"

The days to follow were filled with a bustling of Rayla's people moving into the city. The first shop to open was a restaurant with a limited menu of wild meats, foraged roots, and berries. Many of the cooks from the Refuge happily took the opportunity to take on a restaurant. They agreed that they would continue cooking as they had in the Refuge food commons and work together to feed those that came to them. The shops opened a couple of hours each day at first, and then to full days after everyone found their bearings.

The hunting parties began hunting the next day and at the same time, the gardeners divided their time between breaking the ground, planting crops, gathering, and foraging in the woods. Once the seeds were planted in the fields, the Shard Carriers moved about in the gardens, speeding their development. The community would have plenty of food for the rainy seasons.

Within two weeks, most of the camp outside the walls was emptied, and life again felt a semblance of normal. The community leaders met each day, working to recreate how the Refuge had run, which had served them well. Taylor and Rayla looked forward to when the camp was emptied and disassembled.

Milthra told them that her magic was limited now, needing to use so much of it to occupy her new body. The work of clearing the wall would be slow, but it would get done. True to her word, they woke to a different section of vines and trees in the walkways cleared away each morning.

Chapter Fifty-One

Tarak had spent hours at the lake recuperating. After days of traveling, he was growing weary; he could have slipped back to Glydane if he wanted, a luxury of having been there before. But to move forward, he would have to keep sensing water at the outer reaches of his abilities. The sun was setting, leaving him only enough time to shift once more. He had been traveling toward the city for days, and he would be there in a short time.

Would he be lucky enough to find a colony intact? So many of the Starports he had found were burned-out shells, decaying in their orbits. The settlements were ruined and crumbling, unlivable, and none pointed in a direction that would have led him to other Vidreian civilizations. Tarak kicked up the dirt at his feet, "How much worse could my luck be?"

He sighed; he had changed in the time he had been here. He had always wanted the Navaden dead. They were the Vidreian's death enemies. But with the Orb in his possession, he could rule them, bend them to his will. What would he do here if he didn't have them? There was no guarantee that he would find a way to the Starport from the colony.

"Godry!" He paused, forgetting where he was for a moment. Forgetting what he had done. "I'll figure it out myself! I'm at least capable of that." He filled himself with the Power, the feel of it washing over him, and the desire to kill beckoned to him. But there was no one here.

"Time to move on." Tarak stood and used the Orb's power to create a portal in front of him. "How tedious!" Stepping through, he found himself in a marsh; water rushed into his boots, aggravating his temper. The smell of cooking brought his attention to a dim light off in the distance. "Let us see what is cooking." He smiled. He was not done tormenting these people yet. In the end, he would kill them all.

As he sat in the chair by the fire, he ate a bowl of hearty stew . The owner of the little shack lay on the floor, staring upward. The hole in his chest smoldered still. Tarak spilled some stew and looked over at him. "How dare you not have baked bread for your king."

Chapter Fifty-Two

One morning, Taylor moved through the city while Rayla slept. These last weeks had pushed her hard, especially with the resettling of her people. He had kissed her softly and left her to rest. Taylor had also gone beyond his limit and thought a little time to himself was in order. As he walked, his life back home seemed like a lifetime ago.

Taylor stopped suddenly and found himself standing at the Dome. He had not had a destination in mind but had subconsciously taken a path he had often traveled. Taylor carried on through the main doors and to the center of the main floor. Pausing there, he studied the murals behind the obelisks. They were each painted in such a detailed quality they would have rivaled a high-definition picture back on Earth. Each painting was of different sorts—jungles, palaces of ice, and forest scenes.

"They're splendid, aren't they!" Milthra's voice startled him.

He turned to her, his Orb glowing brightly, "It's not

nice to sneak up on people. I could have done something brash."

The body Milthra had taken as her own had regained its robustness and was now full of life. She stood beside him in a long flowing dress, much like what she wore when they first encountered her. She smiled, "I have my own protection, thanks." She nodded toward the murals, "I had forgotten how vivid they were. It has been so long since I looked upon them."

Taylor turned to her, "What are they, Milthra? Gateways? I would have thought of them as works of art if it weren't for the obelisks." He pointed to the one they stood in front of. "They're a symbol on Earth as well."

"You're very perceptive," she said. "They lead to places that no longer exist, I fear, as they were in these depictions, anyway. Scenes, frozen in time from their last use."

"When this place had power, you mean," Taylor dug for information.

"Perhaps," she said, leaving his side and walking up the stairs to the upper level.

"And how is it that you actually activated the magic at the walls?" he asked.

She stopped and turned to him, "From the very same place that you get yours, of course. But this place didn't only run on magic. Are you coming?"

Taylor followed her up the stairs and to the window that viewed the New City. "Why are you so vague?" He asked, "You have, after all, created a city with electricity for Rayla's people. Although, all but Rayla believe it's magic."

"You assume that it isn't something that I pulled from your mind," she said, not answering his question. "You still don't see the obvious for all your brains."

"What does that mean?" he asked.

"Rayla's people, in all their recent remembering, only know of rudimentary machines," Milthra started. "What I have created here is beyond their capacity to grasp. I made everything here look archaic so that they could grasp the city's workings. The illusion that magic runs the city enables them to accept it. This ruined city once held wonders that you couldn't even comprehend, mechanical and magical."

Taylor thought a moment; she was right. Rayla's people were living in caves until weeks ago. He had not been to one of their cities, but Rayla had described them. At their peak, they were a wonder of architecture. But they had never created electricity and had only basic machines driven by steam, and those were few and far between. "What are you, Milthra?"

"Does it really matter?" she said flatly.

Taylor looked out to the city and the ruins surrounding it, "No, I suppose not. But I hope someday you will tell me."

"Maybe," she replied. "She's coming for you," Milthra motioned to Rayla's footfall on the stairs.

It was something he already knew. Taylor had felt Rayla wake and begin to search for him as he left the city. Though, he had hoped to extract some answers from Milthra before she caught up with him. "Can I trust you?"

"Do you have a choice?" she replied.

Rayla reached the top of the stairs with a surprised look, "Hello, Milthra, I hadn't expected you as well."

Milthra smiled, "How lovely to see you, Rayla. Taylor and I had the same destination in mind this morning, it seems. With Careed off early looking to train the militia on the wall, I found myself reminiscing about this view. It did always calm me."

Taylor moved to intercept Rayla. His conversation had left him seeing the larger picture of who Milthra was, even though she had skirted many of his questions. "We shall leave you to it then." Taylor walked past Rayla to the stairs, not hiding his irritation with Milthra.

Rayla moved to follow him down the stairs, but stopped. "Wait, Taylor." She stroked the Orb at her neck and then spoke, "Milthra, could you tell me something of our Orbs? Since meeting you, I feel like a captor to the person inside my Orb. Could we do with them, as we have for you? Give them bodies?"

Milthra looked kindly at Rayla, "You are a true rebel if I ever met one," she said under her breath. "Unfortunately, they're safer as they are and as you use them. Remember when I said that your Orbs were damaged. From what you have told me of the Orb's arrival here, I suspect that the consciousness inside your orbs were altered when they fell from the sky. The Incoa inside are that of no more than small children. Giving them a body would allow them to use immense magical powers in the world—a responsibility they couldn't carry. Fear not, though; the presence inside your Orb is happy where it is."

Rayla nodded and joined Taylor, leaving Milthra to her view. They made their way down the stairs to the bottom. "What happened up there?" Rayla asked.

"I ended up with more questions than answers is what happened," Taylor grumbled.

Rayla reached out, grabbed his hand, and squeezed it, "Maybe we could take the day off tomorrow and spend it in our little hideout."

Taylor felt himself soften, seeing her obvious concern for him. He smiled, "I'd like that. We could slip off to the little hideaway. It has an interesting oddity here, with its own little mysteries, and no one can find us there. To sit and be quiet would be something of its own."

They made their way back to their new home in the waning afternoon to find the apartment empty. They ate a dinner of dried meats and hard bread and then moved to lie on the couch. "Taylor," Rayla said as she lay propped with her back against his chest, "I'm not sure that I can, in good conscience, keep wearing this Orb."

"I know that it bothers you," he empathized. "But Milthra told us it was for the best that they stay as they are. Not to mention they have guided your people for thousands of years and helped create a golden age."

"Until a maddened man destroyed it all," she replied, holding the Orb up and staring at it. "What she has shown us has made being a Bearer a burden in a way I didn't think possible. It may be time for me to pass on my Orb to its next Bearer. Perhaps we could try a little experiment." She enveloped the Orb in the palm of her hand. As if by command, the chain fell free of her neck. "What if we didn't wear them tonight?" Taylor nodded, removing his as Rayla turned about and kissed him lovingly. At first, he knew out of happiness that he was so willing to support her, but passion ignited as they pressed against each other. She leaned in and kissed him, and he caressed her cheek. How good it felt to touch her! They slid into bed and began making love, and as they did so, their minds mixed together as they had so many times, despite not wearing the Orbs.

Taylor fell into a deep sleep, and dreamed he had awoken in the night with his arms wrapped around Rayla. A woman had sat across from him in one of the plush chairs, dressed in combat gear of a sort; it looked modern, almost as if it could be of Earth. Her fair hair was pulled back in a braid, allowing a clear view of her face's striking beauty and bright blue eyes.

The woman leaned in. "When the time comes, I will be there for the two of you. It won't be long before Prophecy fulfills itself. You're both as heroic as I remember, Taylor. I'll see you soon."

There was a bright flash as the dream ended. When Taylor woke up the following day, the dream was still vivid, and the woman's face was imprinted in his memory. He rolled over and saw Rayla sitting across from him in the same chair the woman had. Still in her clothing from the previous day, she held out a small brown paper package of tea in her hand.

"Taylor, did you use this for the tea we had after eating last night?" she inquired, holding it out.

"Yes, of course. I followed the instructions you put on it as well. It said, 'for us, darling.' Why, what's wrong?" Taylor asked, confused and still groggy.

"This is Mortis leaf. If not properly prepared, it's deathly poisonous. If you don't boil it long enough or let it cool too long, it kills you within minutes. But if you do it just right, it's a powerful sleeping aid that revitalizes the body while you sleep." Rayla looked at him curiously. "You said there was a note?"

Taylor stood and reached into his pocket, "I kept it cuz I thought it was a little sweet of you." He had a small embarrassed smile as he handed it to her.

Rayla took the note looking at it, confusion filled her face. "This looks like my writing, and the directions are correct on how to prepare it. But I didn't write this, Taylor. Who would go to such great lengths to make us sleep the night away? And why make it look like I wrote it?"

"I have no idea," Taylor began but was interrupted by a loud pounding at the door. "Who do you suppose that is?" Taylor groaned.

Rayla shrugged her shoulders. "I have no idea."

Taylor answered the door to find an out-of-breath Milthra, leaning against the door jam. "Sorry to bother you," she huffed.

"What, in the name of Albax, is it?" Rayla asked. "Are we under attack or something?"

"A man has appeared outside the wall. He's wearing a Vidre of unknown origin. If I had to guess, I would say that it's the man you call Tarak."

A look of panic filled Rayla's face, while Taylor's heart began to pound hard. "How could he have found us so soon," Rayla murmured. "How can this be?"

They stood in front of Milthra, taken back. Taylor grasped Rayla's hand, both to give support and in need of some of his own. "Milthra, how many of his men are with him?" he asked. His body filled with adrenaline; he didn't wait for the answer as he pulled Rayla through the door past Milthra. "We need to go to the outer wall!"

Milthra coughed, "It appears to be only him. I didn't detect any other soldiers."

Rayla stopped short in bewilderment, "He's here alone! That means we still have time." Rayla no longer needed to be coaxed and ran back through the door toward the kitchen, where a giant crock of water sat on the counter. She slid it off with a swipe of her hand, knocking to the floor braking open. Water splashed everywhere, leaving a large pool on the floor.

She looked down at the Orb she held in her hand, "A

burden indeed. This won't take a great deal of energy if we do it together." Rayla held the Orb tightly in one hand and reached out with the other to Taylor. Without hesitation, he clasped her hand, holding tight to his own Orb. There was a familiar feeling of being pulled somewhere. Taylor's eyes went out of focus for a second, and his body tingled everywhere. The sensations disoriented him enough so that he had to close his eyes. The feeling of being pulled lasted only a few seconds before it subsided. Upon opening his eyes, the field outside the city came into focus.

He and Rayla stood on the top of the defensive wall, in the walkway. Rayla had ported them to where Milthra had removed a tree; its roots had grown into the walkway. The large hole left behind had provided a space for the night's rain to form a pool. Knee-deep in the water, they could see through a broken portion of the defensive tooth-shaped parapets. The two of them stepped up out of the hole toward the crumbled part of the defensive wall. There, below in the field, stood a tower of a man dressed in a full suit of black armor.

Chapter Fifty-Three

Tarak looked as Rayla had described him. His voice boomed through the air, breaking the silence and, not expecting the level of volume he spoke at, it startled Taylor.

"Ahhh, there you are, Rayla, and it looks as though you have found a new friend. The magic tells me that he also has an Orb. Where is that troublesome nuisance of a man Kalamar?"

Rayla had not yet released Taylor's hand. She tightened her grip with exceptional strength. Taylor could feel her mixed emotions of anger toward Tarak and sorrow at Kalamar's death now that she wielded her Orb again. He also sensed her struggle to hold back her desire to engage Tarak in battle. Anger was a dangerous enemy on the battlefield. He had seen it cost lives more than once in her memories.

Tarak spread his arms, "I have searched for this place for hundreds of years. When I entered your orbit with my damaged ship, I didn't have time to scan for it as I had hoped to. You see, I found mention of your world in an abandoned base like the one you stand upon, back on my home planet, though its construction was much less mystical in origin.

"Imagine my surprise when I arrived to Navaden descendants instead of Vidreians. Navaden, who had built a paradise achieved by wielding Vidre they shouldn't have even been able to touch. I have been somewhat stuck here all this time. A time I have so enjoyed, though; I find it rather lovely. I like how malleable your people are, Rayla. It was relieving to have such a wonderful welcome, and they were so eager to have me lead them.

"But now that I have found you, Rayla, and your new friend, I can finally put an end to this Navaden civilization.

"To think, if your lovely Milthra hadn't sent that message a couple of days ago, looking for any surviving Vidreian people, my guards would never have notified me that my ship picked it up."

Tarak lifted his right arm and waved, "Thank you, Milthra!" he said in delight. "I do, unfortunately, have to go, now that I see with my own eyes that you're here. I had hoped that you would be! And your friend there beside you will be a bonus. I need to go gather my army now. But I'll see you soon." Tarak turned, and as he stepped into a large pool of rainwater, he dropped into it and was gone.

Rayla and Taylor stood motionless, gripping each other's hands tightly. One word resided in Rayla's mind. "Milthra!"

Chapter Fifty-Four

"Why, Milthra? Why?" Rayla screamed at Milthra as they stood in the living room of her apartment. Rayla's fists were clenched at her side, and her face was full of fury. They had been in there for ten minutes, and Rayla had screamed at Milthra the entire time to no avail. Milthra had stared out the window, stubbornly refusing to answer.

Back at the wall after Tarak left, Rayla had pulled Taylor back to the puddle and stepped in. They shifted to the nearest pool of water to Milthra's building. Rayla's Orb swung from its chain in her hand and she had dropped it into Taylor's hand the moment they were through. With the Orb's power at hand, she was unsure she would not destroy Milthra.

Rayla was beyond words at this point. Taylor had known there was more to Milthra. That she could still signal other worlds was something of a surprise. *What had Milthra been thinking?* Taylor thought to himself, *And why does she not answer?* The door burst open, startling Taylor, and on impulse, he tensed himself ready to strike.

Careed moved through the door with purpose, "RAYLA!" he shouted, putting himself between them. "Perhaps you should allow Milthra to explain herself," he barked. Then turned to Milthra, who stood tall and dignified, dismay on her face. "Milthra, my dear, I'm sure that you had good reason to send the ... single ..."

A small smile spread across Milthra's face, "A signal, my darling."

"Please explain yourself, Milthra," Taylor implored, "You have put us in jeopardy." Taylor glanced at Careed.

Milthra sighed, "I can't answer your question. It's against a direct order."

A vein in Rayla's head began to pulsate, "What direct order? You run this place!"

"But there were others higher in status than I, once," Milthra explained. "I'm obliged to obey any orders given by them. Someone sent a letter containing orders with a signet attached. The signet they used was that of the Resistance's original leader."

That gave both Taylor and Rayla pause. "How is that even possible, Milthra?" Taylor inquired.

"I'm unsure. I detected unidentified magic in the city that first day in the wardroom above the wall. I dismissed it because I thought it couldn't possibly mean anything. I was out for a walk with Careed yesterday, and when I returned, I found a parchment with the orders," Milthra responded. She caressed Careed's arm and smiled at him, and he relaxed. She went to a small writing desk in the living room and, from a drawer, produced the parchment. "This is the letter."

Taylor took the letter and looked through it quickly. There at the bottom was a signet, and beside it was the signature of Tess Ravena. "How can that be?" he handed the letter to Rayla.

Rayla's anger turned to wonder as she saw the name at the bottom. "Milthra, this isn't possible. This woman has to have been dead since the fall of the city. Who was this woman?"

With suspicion, Milthra eyed Taylor and Rayla, "How is it that you know Tess's name?"

"We found part of a building intact in the city," she lied. "We found a document with her name on it."

Milthra's suspicious look stayed on her face. "Not everyone was happy with how the Navaden ruled; some such as myself worked with a resistance. One such person who wanted to protect magical worlds and their inhabitants, Tess Ravena, was a high-ranking Navaden official and the creator of the Resistance. She kept it going while in seclusion for almost fifty years. Tess disappeared mysteriously but left orders to await her return. No one alive today would know her private signet aside from surviving Vidreian resistance operatives such as myself. I was, however, bound to obey once I saw the signet."

"Wait!" Taylor stopped the conversation, "You were in the resistance?"

Milthra stood tall, "In the last thousand years of the war, many of the Incoa were. We volunteered to help win the war effort only to realize that we were enslaved afterward. Some followed blindly for the cause, but after a few centuries, most could not."

Rayla sighed, "It seems that the battle still rages after centuries. Tell me, though, how is it that someone used a signet that is thousands of years lost, Milthra?" Rayla asked.

"I can only assume that it was her," Milthra responded. "Her disappearance was not the only strange occurrence when it came to Tess. She often appeared in the oddest places, and questioning one of her stature without merit was high treason."

"That's what we needed, another person in the mix, making things more complicated than they already are." Taylor said, with sarcasm, "Did she leave any other orders that you might want to let us in on Milthra?"

"NO," Milthra denied, "The last time I detected the foreign presence in the city was someone in your apartment. The presence was there for a few minutes; you weren't there the first time, and the second was while you slept last night."

"Good God," Taylor said aloud, "She talked to me while I was waking up. She knew me. She had a strange familiarity that I couldn't place. Milthra, why didn't you tell us?"

"As you read in the letter, she says to not report any anomalous magical presences in the city unless asked."

Careed took the letter from Rayla, "How can you read this? It's in a language I've never seen.

Rayla grimaced at Taylor, "We didn't find a building in the city. We found a little hideaway in the woods. It's a completely preserved apartment cut into the mountain. Taylor has been looking through the books there."

It dawned on Taylor then that, indeed, the letter was in the language from the books. "The Orb! I had not even realized the books were in a different language."

Rayla had calmed down somewhat. Knowing that Milthra had not betrayed them purposefully made her feel more at ease. What could Rayla do about a stranger that wandered about with access to everything because of a long-lost signet? Nothing! Milthra did not seem to be able to help them, and she was the warden of the city. After all, the mystery woman could slip into their apartment undetected by herself, Taylor, or anyone else.

Rayla dropped herself into a chair, a tear rolling down her cheek; the stress of the day was getting to her. "Taylor, we should have a look at the hideaway and see if anything is amiss there." The threat of Tarak was paramount, now that he knew where they were. The months of preparation time they thought they had would only be a matter of weeks if they were lucky. "Milthra, you had mentioned the wall had defenses. Of what kind?" Rayla asked as she wiped her cheek.

"The city was equipped with a magical shield that wrapped around it. It was impenetrable as long as there was enough available magic to maintain it ..." Milthra paused and looked as if she were calculating. Taylor could barely hear her mumbling. *I could train her people in the necessary skills to help repair it, but I'm not sure there are enough magic reserves in the wall to make it work* ... Milthra eyed Taylor, a knowing look on her face. He realized then that she had not been speaking at all. He had been hearing her thoughts. "It would take six to eight months with the help of your people to find out."

"That will not do," Taylor interrupted, "Are there any offensive weapons in the lookout posts?"

I won't spoil their simple life here with machines and weapons! Milthra's voice echoed in his mind. Milthra turned to Rayla to address her, "There were once offensive magics here, but again there isn't enough magic to use them. If they even work. There may be a way to make the opponent sleep, though. Giving you enough time to disarm any that approach the wall."

Rayla stepped up to Milthra, "Tell me more. Would it do any kind of damage to them? I would like to know everything before I consider it. I don't want to harm any of them if I don't have to."

"The Sleep is just that. It won't kill your attackers, only disable them, and would work immediately on Tarak and his soldiers. They would remain unconscious for a minimum of twenty-four hours. This would give you enough time to subdue them, would it not?"

Rayla stood there, beaming, "That is the best news you could have given me. I never imagined that I could save so many of them. Tarak's men would fight to the death for him if the situation required it. I have hope that once he's gone, Tarak's followers will come back from his madness."

"However," Milthra cautioned. "While I have managed to remove the vegetation from the outer wall, I have yet to clean and examine the focal points—a tedious task, even with my birds. I'd say three or four weeks to have them all in proper order. Then we can test the wall's magic to see if it works."

Rayla's smile fell a little. "Where do we begin with the focal points?"

Milthra began cleaning the focal points that very night with her birds. Working diligently to complete the task, she slept during the day. Not long after, Careed was no longer seen during the day either. Rayla, Taylor, Tae, and Zem busied themselves with settling their people into the new city.

Each night, a guard was posted at the entrance to Rayla and Taylor's apartment; a precaution, should the mystery woman reappear. Everyone in the city had been alerted to her presence, but none had yet reported seeing her. As the days passed, each evening they returned home, and the two of them talked, ate, made love, and fell asleep from exhaustion. Rayla had all but stopped wearing her Orb, unable to reconcile her feelings. It felt strange to Taylor to wear his while Rayla had given up hers, so he made it part of his routine in the evening to remove his. Though, he kept it close by and put the Orb on as he went about his day outside the house.

One evening, Taylor and Rayla walked home in the darkness of the streets. The sun wouldn't be up for hours yet. The city lay dark in front of them except for a few street lamps. The little moon hung in the sky above in its fullness, casting its light down on them, illuminating the streets well enough to compensate for the dimness of the streetlights.

As they walked in the darkest part of the street between the lights, where a tall tree blocked the moon's light, Rayla halted and stared off out toward the defensive wall. Taylor followed Rayla's gaze out past the defensive barrier to the forest.

"It can't be!" she said. In the stark night outside the defensive wall, Taylor recognized the telling red glow of massive fires off in the direction of where the Refuge lay. Tarak was almost here, and they were nowhere near ready.

Careed stopped short of them, breathless, "Taylor, Rayla, I have been looking for you all over the place," his voice sounded agitated. "You need to come with me to the Dome. You need to see the fires from there."

Chapter Fifty-Five

When Taylor and Rayla arrived at the Dome with Careed, Tae, Zem, and Milthra were waiting for them. Together, the group stood at the Dome's windows and stared out at the mass of fires that burned in Tarak's camp. "I sent one of my birds to stay out in the woods after Tarak's surprise visit so that we might have warning of his return. There are enough fires to account for a hundred thousand men," Milthra said. "The camp is only a few days away, meaning he could strike soon."

"What is the readiness of the wall?" Rayla inquired.

Milthra turned to Rayla and Taylor, "The repairs are almost complete and will likely be ready when Tarak's army arrives. But I can't promise it.

Everyone went silent; Taylor could feel Rayla's panic rising. *There isn't enough time!* she sent in thought to him. Looking at the others, he opened up his mind, and he heard similar thoughts from Tae, Zem, and Careed. Milthra was shielding hers, and she gave him a knowing smile. As other voices from the city started to rush in, he slammed the door closed. He sighed and spoke, "We all knew this was coming, and we each have our duties. We follow the rules Kalamar set in the Refuge.

"Tae and Zem, take word to the community leaders to lock down the city. Careed, you planned for battle if the wall isn't ready, I assume?" Careed nodded. "Then we all know what to do." Rayla had slipped her hand into his as he spoke. He felt a fear in her that she tried to mask but was unsuccessful. Something had changed when she saw the fires; she was fearful now, something that had not been so before. "The next few days will be long and arduous. There is still a great deal left to do."

Rayla rose early the following day and left Taylor asleep in the apartment. After lying in bed for a long while thinking of their situation, she needed answers. Rayla moved through the city with speed toward her destination. When she reached Milthra's door, it opened before she had a chance to knock.

"Good morning Rayla," Milthra nodded. Careed kissed her on the cheek and nodded to Rayla. Then, he walked out into the hall towards the exit without a word.

"Come in, won't you." Milthra walked further into the apartment, leaving the door open.

"You were expecting me?" Rayla said, closing the door behind her. "How did you know?"

Milthra sat in one of the firm cloth-covered chairs in the living room, "I have been alive long enough to know that one of you would be here ... I suspected it would be you. You have a single-minded goal in hand, and in my experience, a woman with a goal is hard to stop." Milthra smiled at her. "How can I help you?"

Rayla sighed, "I have gone this alone for so long that I admit it's novel to have the company of someone who has borne the responsibility for others. I was hoping that you might be able to give us more of an advantage with the coming battle."

Milthra grimaced, "I'm afraid that I'm putting all the efforts in that I can, and I'm not very good at wielding a sword." She yawned.

"YOU ARE A DAMMED WIZARDESS..." Rayla broke off, not having meant to raise her voice so. Milthra seemed unfazed, so she carried on. "I have seen Taylor win this battle, taking Tarak down with his sword. But the Prophecy never showed me the odds he would have to traverse getting to Tarak. One hundred thousand men against our few thousand with pitiful weapons and armor. Our rusted swords and leather armor won't bode well against them. We are doomed if you don't get the wall's magic ready in time."

"I'm a wizardess, but everyone has limits to their power," Milthra said. "The work I'm doing to prepare the wall is taxing me beyond what you can imagine. Your Orbs have some of the most amazing properties I have ever seen. They can lend their magic in an uncharacteristic way. But I AM the magic in my case, and I use it in ways you can't possibly understand."

It was then that Rayla saw the haggardness in Milthra, and guilt began to set in. Milthra had been resurrected only days ago and had not stopped helping them since. "I know that I can't understand your plight. I'm not even sure what I thought you could do." Rayla was silent a moment, "If only there were a cache of weapons still here somewhere."

"The weapons here turned to dust long ago, Rayla. Alas, it isn't something that I had the time to construct. Return to me tomorrow night. I'll see if I can work something out by then."

Rayla smiled, "Thank you, Milthra. I hadn't trusted you at first. But you have turned out to be a great asset. I'll leave you to your sleep." As Rayla reached the door, she stopped, "Be sure to take care with Careed. And Niea." She left without waiting for a response, and when she reached the street, she turned to her second destination. Tess Ravena, that name had been ringing in her ears since Milthra had said it. There had to be a clue in the hideaway they had found.

When Taylor awoke and Rayla was not there, he assumed that the sound of someone making tea in the kitchen was her. He was a little embarrassed when he stood naked in front of Milthra as she sat, sipping her tea at the little kitchen table. "What the ..." he stammered.

"Good morning Taylor," she eyed him up and down and smiled. "No wonder Rayla has such a satisfied smile on her face in the mornings. Would you like to put some trousers on?"

Taylor felt the heat in his face, "I would," he said embarrassed and stepped back out of the room. *This is unexpected.* He found his clothing in a heap on the floor at the end of his bed, slipped them on and returned to the kitchen.

"Feel a little more secure now?" Milthra inquired with a knowing smile. "I find myself in a dilemma, Taylor. In my time in the Resistance, I had always wanted those with magic to have peace. There were only a few among my people that felt the same. They saw the Vedreians as a nuisance and disposable in their plight to find Vidre to mine. This city was to be a haven for The Resistance after the virus. A world where they could live and be free of repercussion once the war was won. But the virus made its way here despite our efforts and the quarantine."

"I—" Taylor started.

Milthra lifted a finger to silence him, "I was supposed to protect citizens of this city and was, in the end, forced to send the uninfected out into the untamed wilderness. Never had I guessed that they would build such a utopia left to their own devices. So here is my dilemma; if I do nothing to help, they will all die here. Leaving a crazed Vidreian to do whatever torment he desires to the people he rules. If I help them by giving them weapons even as rudimentary as your world, it goes against my mandates and would likely take them on a path of destruction eventually." She sat back and took a sip of her tea.

Taylor had not yet joined her at the table. He had chosen to stand in what he thought to be an authoritative stance while listening. He realized now that it was a ridiculous thought. This woman was more powerful than he could imagine. He sat and poured himself a cup of tea, "Then give them something in the middle." Milthra tilted her head in curiosity. "I have seen the weapons here. They're poorly designed at best. Have you had a look at the sword craftsmanship? If you can still use your 'magic' to create weapons. Give them well-crafted crossbows and swords that hold an edge. Give them ballistae that throw burning balls of pitch."

Milthra eyed him, "Isn't that only another step toward guns?"

"Not if you allow the Bearers to return to power," he replied.

"And what of those like Rayla that see that there are entities in the Orbs? And don't wish them to be enslaved?" she asked.

"As far as I can tell, these Orbs can't function without a host. Correct?" he suggested. Milthra nodded her agreement, and he continued, "I believe that the entities are a small piece in a larger picture. With her daughter's death and everything else that has happened, I don't think Rayla has the heart to wear hers any longer. She wishes to live a life of simplicity, where she can live without everyone relying on her. The Orbs are dear to the people here. The next Bearer will appear as they always do."

That brought Milthra pause, "Perhaps you're correct. She has had a change in her since her first arrival here." Milthra sighed and put her tea down. "Your desire to have weapons shows your people haven't lost their blood lust in all these years. Perhaps it truly can be of use to save this world. I'll find you tomorrow morning and give you my decision." Milthra left then, leaving Taylor to feel out where Rayla had gone. He could sense her off in the woods toward the hideaway. She was ever curious about mysteries laid at her feet. He could not blame her. He, too, had thought to go up there and have a second look. Though, he would have included her in the excursion.

Chapter Fifty-Six

"Where are you?" Rayla said as she stood in the living area of the hideaway. The bed had been made, and the place had been tidied. Not a move for someone trying to keep it a secret that they were about. She could feel Taylor approaching the doorway and his upset that he had not been invited. "Hello, lover," she said as he entered. "It took you long enough." She felt his feeling cool somewhat at the game she implied.

"I wasn't sure I was invited," he replied and slipped his arm around her waist from behind and embraced her.

It sent tingles through her body and in her womb. This man she loved to her core. "You're always invited!" She placed her hand over his at her waist and took a moment. She sighed, "She has been here."

Taylor pulled away and looked about, "She even cleaned," he said, astonished. "Not very secretive of her."

"My thoughts exactly. I looked around, and I found this." She showed him a glass jar filled with leaves. "It's Mortis leaf. I found it on the kitchen table. And she even made the bed. Help me look around."

Taylor looked over to the small bedroom. "You remember the bed wasn't made? Maybe we should check it? Maybe if we replayed the scene when we were in it last, we would find something."

Rayla rolled her eyes, "Just look!"

"Hmph!" Taylor began searching for anything that would give them a clue about this woman's presence here. After looking in the living area, he found himself standing at the writing desk in front of the bookshelves. He looked down at the desk and smiled. "Aren't you a bit of a smartass!"

"What was that?" Rayla asked.

Taylor picked up a piece of paper, waved it at Rayla, and then read it aloud. "'Welcome back, Taylor and Rayla! See you soon.'"

"Huh." Rayla looked around suspiciously.

"Are you expecting her to jump out and announce herself?" Taylor asked snidely, immediately regretting it. "Sorry, she seems so cheeky."

Rayla sighed, "She does! I doubt we will find any clues other than what she wants us to. And that is likely no more than we have found."

"You're probably right," Taylor said as he looked at the note again. "But why the games?"

Rayla shrugged, "We have better things to be doing. Let us go back to the city and see how the preparations are going."

They spent the rest of their day calming the people they saw on the streets. The fires of Tarak's camp had spread fast, and people were scared. After briefly talking with Tae and Zem, they made their way to a new apartment the two had set up for them. Taylor thought it was likely for nothing. The woman seemed to know more than they did about the city's happenings.

In the morning, just after they finished breakfast, there was a knock at the door. Rayla opened it to find a grumpy looking Careed and a much haggard Milthra. "This is unexpected. I had thought I'd have to come to find you." *Is that a freckling of gray I see in her hair? That wasn't there yesterday.*

Milthra smiled delightfully, "If you and Taylor would come with me?"

"Oh, of course, I was just surprised at your presence," Rayla fumbled, opening the door wider. "Taylor, Milthra wants us to come with her," she called back, then leaned in and whispered, "Was this about the thing I asked?"

"In a way, yes," Milthra replied as she turned and began walking down the hall. "I had a chat with Taylor yesterday morning after you left. He had some good advice."

"Did he?" Rayla turned to him, eyebrows raised, as he stepped up beside her. "I'd have loved to hear about that." Rayla elbowed him in the side.

Taylor took it in good stride. "Where is it we are going?"

"To the industrial section," Careed said harshly over his shoulder.

Taylor was a bit taken back. *Is it just me, or is Careed angry with us?* Rayla heard him send.

"Calm down, my dear," Milthra said to Careed placing her hand on his shoulder. "I'll be alright."

HE'S ANGRY WITH YOU BUT JUSTLY SO! Milthra's voice echoed loudly in Taylor's heads. Rayla screeched in pain and put her palm to her forehead. Taylor had to lean against the wall while he retched. *Sorry for that!* Came into his mind much quieter. *It's a new experience to be able to communicate in such a way, and I had a rather long night. And no, Rayla, I'm not controlling him in any way. He's free to do as he wishes.* Milthra said no more on the trip down. Careed said nothing; he had a satisfied look on his face as they left, though.

When they exited the building, Taylor saw four horses tethered to the left. "It's a bit of a walk then?" He did not bother waiting for an answer from Milthra and mounted up. "Lead the way."

The four of them spoke little as they rode through the streets. A thumb's width of the sun's passage later, they were in a small block of warehouses. "I don't think I have been here," Taylor said. "I'm curious why you built so many things that we wouldn't need for decades."

"I only had one shot at getting it done," Milthra replied. "I didn't want your people to want for anything." She stopped at a little windowless warehouse and dismounted. "Follow me."

After walking through the warehouse's front doors, the contents left Rayla stunned for a moment. "I can't believe it!"

From the look on Taylor's face, neither could he. "Crossbows, long and short swords, recurve bows, there is every kind of mid-level weapon I could think of. Is that an entirely separate section for armor? You made an armory..." Taylor turned to Milthra. "When?"

Rayla did not need an answer. She walked over to Milthra and touched her gray-freckled hair. "You did this last night while we slept. That is why you have aged, isn't it? That is what you meant, that your Orb is different."

Milthra smiled kindly, "It's the effect such a symbiosis has on the Navaden body. I failed your people once. I won't do it again."

Rayla's stomach turned, looking past Milthra's shoulder at the rows upon rows of weapons. Weapons that she would potentially use against her people. She had seen many different forks in the Prophecy that pertained to Taylor. Those with weapons of these types never ended well for her, her people, or Taylor. But if they had reached a point where weapons like this appeared, they would soon run out of forks that led away from the darkest forks of Prophecy. None of the Prophecy she had seen led to an all-out victory; there was always going to be a sacrifice to be made.

Understanding Prophecy was always complex; one never really knew when it would begin to transpire. That was, until you were in the midst of one. You needed to act fast and decipher what the Prophecy revealed if that happened. Moving quickly enough could redirect you into another, more desirable, fork.

Rayla had yet to adjust her timing during one of the crucial moments of Prophecy to stop them from heading to this moment. Each time she'd kept silent when she missed the moment or chose the wrong approach. It made no difference. She had lost the opportunities to change the path, and nothing was to be done about it. She had missed the last critical fork that kept Tarak from finding them. Rayla had thought using the twins and their abilities would throw him off long enough for them to get to safety, only to have the mystery woman broadcast their location.

Rayla had seen the moment that Kalamar had died in her arms some twenty years past. She had also seen the smoke billowing out of the Refuge many years before her vision of Kalamar. But she had not known when or how it would happen. Had she encouraged the search party to move a little quicker or selected smaller areas to search, she might have prevented Kalamar's death, but would she have missed the opportunity to find the ruined city?

Seeing Tarak standing alone in front of the gates and the fires a few nights ago were only her most recent prophetic visions. That left only one more fork in the Prophecy that would enable her to change the course they were on—one where the whole of Tarak's army fell to the ground and slept for days. The second outcome was that most of his army stood unaffected, and they would lose everything. She realized by the look on Taylor's face that there would be no dissuading him from using the weapons. Things were not going well, and she needed to figure out how to change that. Her hormones were raging; to top it off, she had not considered how her body would react without the Orb. It had been so long since she dealt with the rise and fall of her hormones and mood each month.

Taylor walked over to the rack of crossbows closest to him, then pulled one free and moved it from side to side, admiring its craftsmanship. The wooden stock and limbs were smooth and polished, and the metal of the rail, limb and crannequin gleamed in the light. On the shelf below was a quiver full of bolts. "This is a nice piece of work! Is there a target range close?" Taylor inquired as he slung the quiver over his shoulder and grabbed the crank beside it.

"The range is in a separate room at the back of the warehouse. I can guide you through shooting one if you like."

Taylor looked down at the crossbow and placed the butt of it to his shoulder. He looked through the crosshairs down the row of weapons to the wall at the end. "I've shot one before, thanks. I'm good."

Taylor lowered the crossbow down to his side and looked at Rayla. Where he had expected to see relief, or perhaps curiosity, he saw concern and what might have been fear. "We will only use them as a last resort," he said to her, which he hoped would ease her worries. Rayla feigned a smile that Taylor saw through immediately. He had realized that Rayla would not be entirely comfortable with weapons that would kill her people in swaths. He had hoped she would see that they were necessary.

Rayla dropped her smile and walked over to the rack of crossbows. She grabbed one and took the quiver and crank from below it. "Lead the way."

Tae, Zem, and Careed followed suit. Tae and Zem were less graceful with the crossbows, almost dropping them as they took them off the racks. Careed took his in hand like he had used one his whole life. Milthra led them to the range when they were ready, silent throughout the entire ordeal.

Taylor stepped up to one of the fifty stations there, cranked the string back, and loaded the bolt. Taylor recalled summertime at his grandparents' in Wyoming on their ranch as he did. His father was a school teacher, which allowed him to spend the summer months at the ranch with Taylor. There were always more chores for the two of them as they helped Taylor's grandfather.

"When he was ten, my father taught me to shoot gophers with a twenty-two caliber rifle during the summer," Taylor smiled.

"Fewer holes in the ground mean fewer cows and horses with broken legs," his dad had said stoically.

After his lesson, his grandfather had brought out his prized crossbow. "When you get older, I will teach you to use this." His grandfather set off a few shots, hitting the target with remarkable accuracy.

Every summer after that, he spent the day shooting gophers and targets he made with cans or bottles. One day in his teens, he came home and found a brand-new crossbow on the kitchen table. It had taken a bit of time to get accustomed to shooting it. After he had it, though, he had been a decent shot.

Taylor's grandparents had the largest ranch in the county, which left him to wander the land. His father took him out into the vast ranch for campouts and adventures during the summer months. Taylor and his father had found tepee rings and an old grave on one of their camping adventures. The rings and grave had led his imagination to what Native American life would have been like. That imagination turned to curiosity, which eventually became a desire to study archaeology. He would never have thought his ability to shoot and being an archaeologist would be a combination of skills helping him on an alien world.

"Are you alright, Taylor," Milthra asked?

Taylor realized he had been standing there for several moments, motionless. He looked at Milthra and nodded his head, "Yes." Taylor raised the crossbow to his shoulder and fired at the target down the lane without hesitation. The bolt shot out of the barrel's end and veered off to the side of the lane.

"Hmmm, you're going to need a little practice, I see!" Milthra said.

He stared at the three-dimensional target dummy at the end of the firing range. It felt odd that at some point killing had become part of his nature. It was a part of his life now. "Who's next?" he asked woodenly.

Milthra guided everyone else through how to load and

fire the crossbows. After a few shots at the targets, most of them were more comfortable handling the weapons. Rayla and Careed were even decent shots. When they had completed, Rayla asked Milthra to contact the squad and community leaders and have them come to the armory. Milthra could brief them and choreograph the militia getting new weapons and training where they needed it. The exception being that crossbows would be a mainstay for those assigned to the wall.

The squad leaders would coordinate ten militia members to come in groups until the whole of the militia had been to the armory. The squad and community leaders would then organize the militia to train civilians who wished to fight or defend the vulnerable. The first civilians to be taught would be those that could be spared from work duties.

The quickest armament that would take place would be the infantry. Swordsmanship was something they knew. Well-crafted swords that held an edge would make them deadly. The retired warriors that no longer had the stamina to fight for hours could all be armed with the new crossbows and returned to the militia.

The small militia of just over two hundred warriors they had would become two or three thousand strong. Taylor knew these people to be gentle and kind, but Tarak's tyranny had changed some of them. Others had taken on the mantle of the fighter they saw in him. If the magic in the wall did not hinder the army, at least half of the militia would be on the wall's walkway with crossbows. Archers would be interspersed between them. There were at least four hundred well-trained among the people. With archers and crossbow squads firing at a fast pace, they would take out a good deal of Tarak's men.

Tarak would quickly learn how deadly the crossbows were, though, and would move his troops back. Taylor would need to start planning on how to use guerrilla warfare. He would need those spirited fighters at that point to get to Tarak. This battle was a coin toss as to whether they would win or lose. If they took too long to defeat him, Rayla's people did not have the supplies to outlast a siege.

With the training in Milthra's control and Careed at her side, the other four left together for the city center to prepare for Tarak's army. As they walked, they talked of the plans needed to ready themselves, though Rayla seemed preoccupied and resigned to the whole idea. Rayla had put on a good show, but Taylor felt she was resistant to the concept of the weapons Milthra had provided them. She had begun guarding her thoughts when they entered the armory, and he had no clue why. He would speak with her when they were alone.

"Rayla!" a familiar voice called. She turned to see Niea approaching her, and the girl was sobbing. "Niea, whatever is the matter?"

The young girl could barely contain herself, and when she reached them, she exclaimed, "I'm with child." She collapsed into Rayla's arms.

Taylor felt Rayla's heart wrench; he had warned her that this was true, but Niea was not even thirteen. Rayla hugged the girl. "Let us go somewhere private. Taylor, do you mind if we use the apartment to talk?"

"Not at all," he said with a saddened face.

"Excuse us then," she said and walked off with Niea leaning into her.

Taylor watched them walk off toward their current apartment. The sun was high in the sky, and he had not eaten since the morning. He walked to the downtown area and found a restaurant. Not surprisingly, it was busy. The food commons at the Refuge was a place where everyone could gather and talk. With that space missing, the people here had turned to the smaller restaurants. For the remainder of the day, he found himself wandering through the little shops. There was a distinct unease in the people, but they were carrying on with their lives. These people would not be prisoners to the situation they found themselves in. When Taylor arrived at his and Rayla's accommodation, the guard at the front door delivered a message to him from Rayla. It read:

Taylor,
I will be back late tonight. I promised Niea I'd stay the day with her.
I will talk with you in the morning.
Love
Rayla

As the next couple of days passed, Taylor was sure Rayla was avoiding him. And when he was in her company, her mind was elsewhere. He did his best to give her the space she needed. Niea's pregnancy had been a reminder of so many other women that would bring new life here. He knew the thought weighed on her. She had changed after the business with the armory; the pregnancies seemed to have pushed her too far.

On the third morning, Taylor awoke to the bed empty next to him. A note lay there saying she would find him for lunch. He made his way down the stairs and found Milthra in their living room, waiting for him. She had a concerned look on her face.

"I believe I have restored the wall's ability to create

magic once more," she said. "We will have to run a small test using the focal points to make sure. I have asked everyone to leave the area and stand back from the walls should something go wrong. If you'd come with me."

"That is amazing news, Milthra," Taylor almost hugged her but reconsidered when she gave him a cold look. She looked more haggard than ever. "Shall we," he said as he motioned to the door. Taylor stopped at the door and strapped on his sword. He had begun wearing it since they had seen the fires of Tarak's men. Milthra had assumed he would want to come and had horses ready for them.

As they stood in the room above the wall, Milthra leaned over the console and placed her hand down on the pad. It came to life, and she said, "I will only set the focal points to dispense the magic five yards for the test." Without another word, the light from the panel brightened, and a hum began. Out of the corner of his eye, he saw several birds fall from their perch on the wall. "It's done. The wall's magic is working. We have a viable defense!" Milthra looked up and to the woods in the distance. "And it appears we have finished in time to save Rayla's people, but not by much. Tarak's army is marching into the field outside the wall."

Taylor looked toward the edge of the field, where it met the woods. There stood Tarak, his army fanning out to the sides of him. Taylor stood frozen for a moment there in the control room. He had known this was coming, but it still hit him hard, seeing Tarak and his massive army. "Taylor!" Milthra's voice jarred him out of his shock. He realized that Milthra had been speaking to him, but he had not heard her. "Rayla and the others need to be alerted. It would be best if you gathered the others. I'll remain here."

Taylor was out the door before she finished and ran

bolting down the stairs. "I'll return shortly with everyone." At the bottom of the stairs, Zem and Tae reined their horses to a halt beside his mount. "He's here!" he declared, mounting his horse. "You two find Careed, and I will look for Rayla." They all sped off in silence.

Chapter Fifty-Seven

"I can't believe how many there are," Tae said blankly. He and Zem stared into the field below, concerned looks on their faces.

Rayla shifted uncomfortably, "You're certain the wall's magic is ready? It will function when we need it?"

"I tested it, and it's working perfectly," Milthra replied. "It will put them to sleep when we turn it on. The army will have to be closer to the wall, though. Its magic will work as far as two hundred strides."

Taylor felt a moment of panic flash through Rayla. "I saw the birds on the wall fall," he put in, trying to comfort her. "They're still on the walkway, as you can see."

Rayla nodded in acknowledgment and feigned a smile, "We need to start preparing our militia and have our civilians ready."

"Indeed," Careed looked toward Milthra, "Stay safe, my dear. I'll come to check on you later." He kissed her on the cheek and left, knowing his part in all of this.

The others stood and watched the scene below, where Tarak's men set up camp in the field. The squad leaders joined them, and with dusk set in, Taylor, Rayla, and the rest of the command believed that Tarak would wait to attack until tomorrow. Taylor rested his hand on the pommel of his sword, its magic mingled with his. Memories of battle from previous owners flowed into him. "Have watches placed on the walls and rotate the shift for sleeping," Taylor instructed the squad leaders.

Then Taylor turned his attention to Zem and Tae. "Let the community leaders know that it's time for them to gather your people. Then join with your squad back here."

Rayla looked at Taylor and met him in the eye for the first time in days. "We should get some rest. It will be a long day or two coming up. Even if our plan with the weapon goes well." She turned to Tae and Zem, who would take the first watch, "Send word for us if we are needed." Rayla took Taylor's hand and led him back to their original apartment and straight to the bedroom. She crawled into bed, fully clothed, and patted the bed beside her. "Sleep, Taylor. You will need it."

Rayla watched as Taylor crawled into bed and quickly fell asleep. Her eyes, heavy with sleep too, closed, and she drifted off, wondering if she had done enough to protect him.

During the night, she dreamed the mystery woman stood at the end of their bed and watched them with a worried look on her face. Rayla, too, saw familiarity in the woman but could not place her. The dream suddenly changed, and she watched in horror at Taylor being collared and chained, and led around like a dog while people laughed and jeered at him. All the while, she could feel he pined for her loss.

She awoke with a start and sat straight up in unison with Taylor as the apartment shook. A second explosion sounded off in the distance and rocked the apartment. They both jumped out of bed and ran for the front window.

Out in the darkness, toward the entrance gate, a sphere of bright light impacted the city wall. They almost lost their footing as the apartment shook again. Tarak had started his attack, and surprisingly, he had begun the assault on his own. They looked on in horror at the horse-sized chunks of rock that flew in every direction with each impact, leaving smoldering craters of red-hot rock glowing in the night. Rayla turned to him, "Albax," she cursed, "How are we going to hold against that?"

Taylor took a deep breath, a look of concern on his face, "Considering neither of us could do so, let us hope that he can't maintain that level of magic for long." Taylor turned back to the living space, a measure of confidence returning to him. "I had Milthra make us armor a couple of days ago. She was happy to comply, saying it was a simple task and wouldn't cost her much. Now is a good time to put it on."

Rayla followed him to a chest she had not noticed. She had been preoccupied, and Taylor lifted the lid. Inside, she saw a leather jerkin similar to what she had worn when he found her on Earth. "I have to admit; I don't know much about armor. Careed designed them." She reached in and found the leather soft and malleable. At the bottom of the chest, she saw chainmail, something that was hard to come by. Careed had appropriated the piece she had left behind on Earth. "I did recommend that she make the arm and shin pieces out of metal instead of hardened leather." In the chest beside hers were larger versions of armor for him.

"Well, let us get to it then," Rayla concurred and reached into the chest, taking out the linen pants and shirt Milthra had kindly made. They quickly undressed, donned the armor and grabbed their swords. Lastly, they grabbed their Orbs from the night tables beside their bed and put them on. This would be the last time.

There were fresh mounts on the street, and they rode hard toward the control room at the wall. They were hastened by the explosions and the crash of breaking rock hitting the ground. The large doors had turned out to be made of solid steel an arm's length thick, but would they hold up to such an attack, Rayla wondered. It took them a full thumb's width of the moon's movement to reach the wall. The volley lasted the entirety of that time, to her chagrin. Rayla and Taylor knew all too well the energy needed to do as Tarak was doing. That he had done so for so long was impossible.

At the wall, bodies of the crossbow and archer squads lay on the ground everywhere. Dispersed among them, pieces of rock of all sizes littered the ground. Taylor looked up the wall to the control center, "God damn it," he cursed, "Tarak hit part of the wall beside the control center. I can see right into the control room from here."

Rayla pointed to the other side of the control room, "The upper corner is gone on the other side. This is not good! I hope no one was in there." They took the stairs as fast as possible, but those few seconds it took seemed like hours to her.

When they reached the top, Rayla flung open the door to a half-exposed ceiling. There was dust in the air, and windows were shattered. The sun rose over the trees as a large, black carrion bird landed on the sill. It let out a cry that pierced their ears before it flew away. Rayla saw Milthra standing off to the side, somewhat dazed and covered in dust. Rayla ran to the window in concern. There in the field stood a hundred thousand soldiers; their chest plates gleamed in the morning sun in formation. Tarak was at the head, in full armor, sword drawn. "Deploy the wall's magic, Milthra!" she screamed.

Rayla's words brought Milthra around, "I'm sorry!" she shook her head. "I hadn't considered Tarak using this tactic. The wall was created in conjunction with the shielding to protect it. The wall's incapacitating magic was never meant to stand alone in a direct battle of this sort. The focal points will have taken too much damage. Tarak is much more powerful than we had considered." Milthra stumbled to the control center and placed her hand on it. The console pulsed erratically. "The magic of the whole system is fluctuating, Rayla; I'm not sure I can even deploy it. And if I can, I would *not* advise it."

"FIRE THE DAMMED WEAPON!" Rayla shouted at Milthra.

Milthra sighed, "Setting the focal points to a maximum range. Deploying now."

Taylor stepped up to the window beside her as the weapon went off, hope in his eyes. A hum began, and with it, a loud buzzing alarm, lines in the console flickered, and the hum ceased with it. The globes on the wall went out, and the whole place darkened with only the rising sun's light coming in.

Milthra straightened, "The weapon has been deployed, but I fear that only to the left of us. Roughly a third of Tarak's army is on the ground, unconscious." Careed rushed through the door to his beloved as she swayed. He caught her arm, steadying her.

Rayla watched those of Tarak's army that stood close enough to the fallen glance around, frightened. A ripple of unease passed through the rest of his soldiers. The Prophecy was fulfilling itself, she knew. The sun was peeking up over the woods and illuminating the army, the black bird's cry, and now the odd arc of men lying on the ground. They all pertained to the Prophecy's darkest fork, where Taylor lost and lived out his days as a prisoner. The one where Rayla's torture led to him giving up his Orb.

Tarak created another ball of light, more immense than any they had seen him generate before. However, this time he flung it at the large central doors below them leading into the colony. The impact shook the wall, and more glass fell from the windows behind them. "That blast has buckled the doors, but his magic must be weakening. It didn't disintegrate the door on impact," Milthra said.

"I don't understand how he can do that?" Rayla asked, turning to Milthra.

"Tarak revealed during his last visit that he was a native Vidreian. He said there were only trace amounts of Vidre on the planet, which should have lessened his magical ability. I have made a mistake! I misjudged how much power the Orb would give him. With the use of the Orb, he's unimaginably powerful."

Out of the corner of her eye, Rayla caught sight of Tarak turning and sending a ball of light straight at the command post. Rayla shielded everyone as best she could as it sped toward them, but the impact still knocked her back, and her shield failed.

It took a moment for the dust to settle, and when it did, Milthra began to howl. "No, no, nooo," Milthra cried over Careed's broken body. Rayla had not reacted quickly enough, and a large piece of debris had hit Careed. Milthra let out a wail for her lost love. Then the Orb at her chest turned a bright red, and she stood walking to the window, hatred on her face. A sound came from behind them, like a giant movement of air. Milthra stopped at the window, glaring at Tarak and his army.

Whoosh, whoosh, whoosh, came a sound as Milthra's birds flew overhead at Tarak's army. Twenty in all, Rayla counted as each burst into flames before they crashed into different parts of the standing army. The fire erupted outward from the impact, consuming the men around them. Hundreds of men flailed about on fire.

"It's not enough! They all have to pay!" Milthra hissed. She threw out her hands, and a wave of heat erupted at the front lines of Tarak's army, incinerating the men there into dust. Milthra's Orb grew brighter and brighter, and more troops died, thousands this time.

Rayla watched, horrified, as the Orb drew life from Milthra to power her fury. As each second passed, she aged more and more. Within moments, Milthra looked like a woman in her nineties. Her hair was gray and wispy. She was hunched over, using the windowsill to stay standing. With the last of her strength waning, she looked at Rayla and Taylor, then she slumped to the floor.

Rayla rushed to her, "Milthra! How could you be so careless?"

A tear rolled down Milthra's cheek, and in a creaky old voice, she spoke, "Darned emotions! It has been so long since I could love." She turned her head toward Careed, then back to Rayla. "KILL them. ALL of them." Her eyes slid closed, and her body went limp.

The room was silent for a moment before Rayla turned to Taylor, her eyes glistening, "I won't let him take any more innocent lives!" She took a deep breath hoping her Orb would counter Milthra's magic, and reached down with a shaking hand, wrapping it around her Orb. The clasp on the chain unlatched, and she stood. "I'll meet you on the battlefield. Be swift in getting the crossbow and archers squads firing while Tarak's men are in chaos. If his men get through the wall, he will reign over my world for an eternity." Rayla ran for the door.

Kalamar's words rang in Rayla's ears as she descended. *Some are not so bound by Prophecy!* Words she had always thought were about their coming savior. *I'll not let him have you, Taylor!*

Chapter Fifty-Eight

Taylor followed Rayla out the door, "Where are you going?"

"I'll meet you on the battlefield," she called over her shoulder. "I have an idea that may win us this battle."

He watched Rayla's shape blur as she moved down the stairs, feeling concerned for her as she went. Until now, he had not considered that the people he loved most might die. His heart was heavy with the deaths of Milthra and Careed; he had counted them as friends. He felt anger rise inside at the idea of Rayla dying and the deaths he had just witnessed. Outside he could see the skies above were beginning to gray and the storm clouds rolling in from the west. The lines of crossbow squads that peeked over the edge of the wall had also witnessed the devastating blow Milthra had dealt. "Crossbow squads, archers!" he shouted, "Shoot them down! Their defenses are scattered. Everyone on your feet! Pass the word on. Start shooting!"

The squad leader standing closest to Taylor straightened to attention and bellowed, "STAND READY! STAND READY!"

The call echoed down the lines, and the militia answered, nocking bolts and arrows alike. Taylor felt the tension from the men and women here. He nodded to the squad leader closest to him, and the woman called out, "WEAPONS FREE!"

The twanging of bowstrings and clicking of crossbows commenced, and Tarak's men began falling everywhere as volley after volley rained down upon them. Thousands died in only minutes. All the while, Tarak sat with a smile on his face at the back of the battlefield, encircled by some of the largest men Taylor had ever seen.

"It's something to see. Don't you think!" Tae's voice said from above Taylor.

Looking up to the top of the command center, Taylor saw Tae and Zem standing on what remained of its roof. "Only you two would be bold enough to stand up there."

Tae loosed an arrow into the chaos below, "It's a great vantage point. I can see so much more up here."

Zem cranked his crossbow, "What better place to see them all die?"

Taylor nodded. He could not deny that. "It's time to head into the battlefield. We need to take advantage of the disorganization. Tarak is down to a few thousand men, and they're scattering."

Zem fired off the bolt he had prepared and jumped down. Tae was at his side a second later. "Let us go," Taylor nodded and moved to the stairs taking them two at a time; they followed.

Taylor looked to the military tents pitched in the field below them. Men and women were moving in formation toward the wall. "I sent word to the militia to ready their position for this morning," Taylor called back to them. "Careed advised that they set camp here last night." At the mention of Careed, a pang of pain hit his heart. "That precaution will save us time in deploying the militia through the exit doors.

Taylor looked down and saw the militia personnel standing at the assigned positions. Taylor was surprised again by the speed at which Rayla's people had adapted. They had integrated the new weapons, shields, and armor into their knowledge of warfare seamlessly.

Tae and Zem moved to lead the squads they had been assigned at the bottom of the stairs. "Stand ready! When the doors you're assigned to open, file through, and make your formations."

There had been several more exit doors like the one they had first entered the city through, likely for the same purpose they were using them for now. Taylor heard the ring of swords being drawn and crossbows being cranked. He looked to the outskirts of the city, where he could see Rayla. Part of him hoped she would miss the entire battle. The other part of him recognized how much of an asset Rayla was on the battlefield. She was a well-trained warrior, and her presence would also empower her people; they would fight fiercely for her. Taylor ran the forms of the sword she had imparted to him through his head. He placed his hand on the pommel of his sword allowing the tingle of its magic to fill him.

He pushed aside his concern for Rayla as best he could and closed his eyes, then continued to run the forms of wielding a sword through his mind—the very same ones Rayla had practiced when Kalamar had taught her. Taylor worked to keep calm. This fight with Tarak would decide so much. Feeling the pressure of what he needed to do, he tightened his grip on the pommel of his sword as it rested on its scabbard. The idea of his friends dying filled him again, and his anger bubbled to the surface. The magic of his Orb filled him and swirled together with the sword's magic.

He looked up at the storm-cloud-filled sky and took a big breath. Rain would make today's battle more challenging. Taylor moved toward the assigned door for his squad, his team following into formation behind him. The door Taylor's team was to go through would be delayed a few minutes. The militia would engage Tarak and his army and draw their full attention. It was a distraction away from Taylor and his team as they moved through the door onto the battlefield.

Several moments after they reached their position, Taylor saw the flag raised for his team to move through the corridor. There was another explosion at the large doors, and the ground shook, but they held. Tarak had recovered already. No wonder he was still smug while his men died. The wall and ground shook with another hit. Taylor had positioned himself in the middle of the formation of his team. They would surround him as they exited to protect him from danger and do so until he reached Tarak. He glanced back over his shoulder and wondered if Rayla would make it back before he moved onto the battlefield.

He was still in thought as he heard the click of the locking mechanism releasing the door. It swung outward, exposing the long corridor through the wall. His team moved through the door, two abreast. The sounds of steel upon steel of the battle outside were muffled in here. The wall shook again. This time Taylor heard the cracking of the large doors buckling. *I need to get out there!*

The outer door swung open, and his men filed out, allowing Taylor to see how the battle unfolded. *It's going well for our side!* Some of Tarak's men had reorganized and formed a protective wall before him. Taylor saw that the militia had moved into position protecting his squad. The militia was thus far repelling any attacks and inflicting a fair amount of damage on Tarak's disorganized army. There were casualties to the militia, most from arrows, but it stood strong. Taylor saw some of Tarak's men retreat into the woods. *That's a good sign!*

Taylor was confronted by a blinding light and an explosion to his right, only a few steps from the door. Bodies, dirt, and debris flew everywhere, knocking Taylor to the ground. Tarak had redirected his assault toward the militia in front of him, but would soon need a few minutes after his volley of attacks on the door.

"Everyone, scatter, and begin your frontal attack!" Taylor screamed and picked himself up. The militia broke into smaller formations and ran toward Tarak. With shield lines in front and crossbow squads behind firing through openings between the shields, they took ground quickly with the constant barrage of bolts firing into Tarak's army. All Taylor needed to do was get to Tarak, and he could confront him. His men moved swiftly, and once they reached the designated distance to the front line of the main body of Tarak's men, the teams merged back into formation, latched their crossbows at their sides, and drew their swords. As one, they formed a wedge that headed straight toward Tarak.

The number of men standing in front and around Tarak had dwindled significantly. Taylor could see that large groups of soldiers fled the battlefield off into the woods. If he had to guess, their numbers were almost even now. Tarak's remaining men were having trouble matching the militia's lighter armor and more exceptional weapons.

Taylor was becoming hopeful that all of Tarak's men might abandon him. With the speed at which they approached him, the long-prophesied battle between Tarak and him would begin shortly. At the moment Taylor had that thought, another flash and subsequent explosion occurred. Taylor's Orb came to life instantly at the flash. An opaque dome of light rushed outward, with Taylor at the epicenter.

The dome expanded outward to meet the explosion. The force of the blast was deflected, rolling over and around them as it hugged the protective field. It happened quickly enough to protect a large portion of the militia from the blast. Taylor watched as the unprotected militia in front were vaporized. Those at the outer edge of the explosion were thrown back like rag dolls. The men in Tarak's army stood back, halting their assault as the smoke and dust settled.

The militia was in awe, shocked for a moment at both the protective field and the explosion. The dome vanished with the threat ended, and the militia turned to Taylor. A cheer arose from them with a renewed vigor. The loss of so many men in the militia had not broken them. It had angered them. The magic Taylor wielded inspired them, and they rushed in and pushed harder toward their goal. Some of the fallen militia had escaped the full force of the explosion outside of the field; they staggered to their feet and rejoined the battle. The militia formed the wedge around Taylor once more and carried on forward.

Taylor felt a drop of wetness fall upon his cheek just

before an arc of lightning flashed from the sky and struck the trees behind Tarak's army. Thunder boomed in their ears, and rain began to pour from above. It came down hard and made the ground slick, soaking everyone. The militia moved onward despite it and closed the gap.

Finally, Taylor caught a glimpse of Tarak. He stood, his sword in hand, surrounded by his ring of hardened massive soldiers. Taylor was not sure, but he thought Tarak looked concerned. The ground beneath Tarak's feet held small puddles from the rains, but not enough yet for him to use as an escape. Tarak's Orb began to glow at his chest, which Taylor thought might be in preparation for a retreat—a retreat that was only moments away as the heavy rain fell. Taylor could not allow that.

Rayla had run with all her might to the fountain where she knew she would find standing water. She had been right. Her Orb had protected her from Milthra taking her over. She could even communicate to a degree with her as she held Milthra's Orb in her hand. Rayla looked at her reflection in the water. *Help me, Milthra! If Kerisa can disappear as she did, you can at least help me to get to Tarak so we might kill him?* She had finally taken in the full understanding of Kalamar's words. He had not meant Taylor; he had meant her. She could change the Prophecy!

Rayla began accessing her Orb's magic and was about to open a doorway when the rain started to pour down upon her. *WAIT!* Milthra's voice sounded in her head. *Allow me.* Rayla felt Milthra's power flow through her hand, entangle with her Orb's magic. The chain of

Milthra's Orb wrapped itself around Rayla's wrist and secured itself.

To Rayla's side, the rain began to swirl, and as it did, a doorway opened. Through it, she could see Tarak standing before her. She gripped the pommel of her sword in both hands and jumped through.

Chapter Fifty-Nine

Taylor pushed forward through the militia in an attempt to get to Tarak. When he reached the front of the formation of his men, Taylor broke free, which brought him only a few feet away from the circle of Tarak's soldiers. Tarak turned, and a knowing smile spread across his face. He had felt Taylor's approach through his Orb.

With his free hand, Tarak tossed up what at first appeared to be several small stones. As the stones launched into the air, Tarak turned his hand so his palm faced Taylor. The stones all paused in mid-air. The completely round shapes, each the size of a small marble, gleamed like steel. The balls coalesced themselves into a circular pattern and hung motionless again.

What is he— The realization came too slowly of what Tarak was doing. Tarak glared at him, and the metal balls shot in his direction, spreading out like a shotgun blast. *Bullets!* A shield again sprung to life but not in time. One of the bullets sunk deep into Taylor's side; pain ripped through him, his knees buckled, and he dropped to the ground. The Orb dulled his pain, and he was able to take his hand from his side, exposing the wound, and blood poured out. *Ughh, I need to get that out.* In shock, though, he looked up at the wounded around him. The other bullets had ricocheted off his protective field, hitting the militia and Tarak's men alike. Several men and women had gone down, their injuries fatal. His eye fell on Tarak and the large leather pouch on Tarak's belt. *No! He has more!*

Taylor reached down to the wound, sinking his fingers inside. As he dug around in his flesh, twinges of pain made him nauseous before the Orb again soothed him. Finally, he could get his fingers on the misshapen bullet, and he pulled it free and tossed it away. He felt the Orb pulse as it worked to heal the wound. His eyes found Tarak again, and the man held another volley of steely balls in the air. He shot them off to Taylor's right, where they shredded through the militia.

Taylor mustered all his strength and stood. His legs wobbled, but he managed to stay upright. He could see his sword where it lay out of reach ahead, toward Tarak. A broad smile still lay across Tarak's face as he stood there. Many of his bodyguards that stood close to Taylor lay dead, leaving the way clear for him. Taylor walked forward with the last of his strength and retrieved his sword.

Severely wounded, even though the Orb had stanched the blood flow, he knew he was in no condition to fight yet. *But I must... the tissue is knitting back together. It will be healed soon.* Taylor moved forward, closing the ten-foot gap between them, but it was then that the most peculiar thing happened. The rain started to bend together behind Tarak and became a seven-foot mirrored circle. At first, Taylor thought that it was Tarak, retreating to fight another day.

To his horror, though, he saw Rayla soar out from the liquid mirror, sword over her head.

Rayla was full of fury. Tarak had to die! As his image cleared through the watery doorway, she leaped through, bringing her sword up over her head to strike him down. She thought she had surprised Tarak, but he turned toward her mid-strike to protect himself. Her sword still hit clean; its edge sunk down through the metal of his armor into his shoulder.

However, Tarak's momentum and enormous strength were more than she could have imagined. The pommel of her sword ripped from her hands as he turned toward her, throwing her off balance. As that happened, Tarak brought his sword up from the ground in a slicing move. The blade struck a solid hit across her chest, cutting her open, and squarely caught the Orb at her chest. It exploded into a thousand smaller pieces, and Rayla fell back.

She hit the ground hard, and Tarak stepped up to her, her sword still protruding out of his shoulder. She watched as he raised his sword. *Gods no, it cannot end like this. Not with Taylor's child inside me!* Tarak drove his sword down toward Rayla's belly. *Milthra! Protect her!* Milthra's Orb pulsed and shifted Tarak's sword up toward her chest. It pierced into her lung, and she felt her body twitch. Fear flooded her—like all her visions, she had only glimpsed this moment, and before had not understood that she was pregnant. Her heart ached at the thought of not seeing her daughter born, of not raising her.

Dear Gods, let me have changed prophecy to save Taylor and our child! Out of the corner of her eye, she saw Taylor rushing forward; she trembled as a tear leaked out of her eye. The horrified look on Taylor's face pierced her deeply as she fell unconscious.

Tarak's remaining soldiers swarmed in to protect him. Taylor's body filled with rage, and he ran toward Rayla, and into the swarm. He shredded the men before him into pieces with his magic. The field around him turned into a mass of blood, flesh, and bone. The soldiers closest to Taylor tried to run, but he would not have it. They fell into heaps of flesh as the others had.

Tarak pulled his sword free from Rayla's chest as she lay there limp, then grabbed the sword's pommel in his shoulder. The blade came free with one pull of Tarak's brute strength, and he raised it over her like an ax.

The Orb's magic pulsed through Taylor as he pulled more to him, and it filled him as it had never before. Even with the wound in his side, Taylor felt an astonishing amount of strength. He made the final distance between them with a leap, soaring through the air. Sword raised above his head, he landed on his knees, sliding through the mud, knocking Rayla to the side while deflecting the sword. Using the last of the momentum to stand and flow into a protective form, he was ready to dance with his blade.

As Taylor moved from form to form, the melee continued for several minutes before Kalamar's words ran through his mind. "I do not have the stamina at my age to maintain the swordplay needed to defeat Tarak." Rayla did not have time for a prolonged fight. Concerned with her well-being, he took a chance and looked at her. She was still breathing, but the blood from her wound was turning the ground a deep red, even with the rain diluting it.

Had Taylor not felt an urgency from the Orb alerting him to the coming blow, Tarak might have ended him. Barely managing to deflect Tarak's blade, something out of the corner of his eye caught his attention. Something he should have been prepared for. An arrow sunk into his thigh. Two more quickly followed, one in the shoulder and the other in the side. He had allowed himself to be distracted by Rayla, and now as he faltered to one knee, he knew he had lost.

There was nothing that he could do quickly enough to change what came. Tarak inverted his sword and struck Taylor in the head with its pommel. Taylor's vision blurred as he fell to the ground on his side. He summoned the last of his strength as he worked to heal the concussion. He rolled over onto his back as the dull pain of the protruding arrows reminded him there was little hope of recovering enough to save Rayla. *If I give up, she will die! I cannot let that happen.* Tarak stepped down heavily on Taylor's chest and pinned him to the ground. He wore a confident smile, believing he was the winner of the battle between them.

Taylor reached to the side of his sword belt, and with deft speed, he pulled a knife free and jammed it into Tarak's inner thigh. The blade sunk deep into the artery there, a wound that would have bled out an average person. He knew better though; Tarak's Orb would repair the damage once the knife was removed.

The large man stumbled back in pain, and he pulled the knife free from his leg as blood spurted out of the wound. The knife dropped to the ground while he still wore that unnerving smile. The smile faded as Taylor vanished from sight, and was replaced by shock. Taylor had not intended that he disappear. The Orb saw his need and had done as it had that first time, acting on his emotions. He rolled to the side and up onto one knee, his Orb lending him strength. Tarak rushed to the spot he last saw Taylor and began chopping the ground in fury. Taylor had managed to stand and move a few feet away.

Taylor rolled three steel balls in his hand, three of many from Tarak's pouch. He levitated them above his palm as Tarak stood screaming in rage. With a smile on his face, he sent them whistling toward Tarak and ripping through his throat and neck. Four more followed, severing Tarak's head completely.

Taylor let the pouch he had yanked from Tarak's waist drop from his hand. Taylor grinned at Tarak as his head fell away to the side and the rest of his lifeless body crumpled to the ground. Taylor let a breath out and frantically searched for Rayla, finding her limp body in only seconds, a few feet away.

Panic ran through him. In her strange tactical armor, the mystery woman leaned over Rayla, sword in hand. "Do not hurt her!" he shouted. *What did this woman want?* Stepping over Rayla, she walked over to Tarak's body, a slight smile forming as she leaned down to pick up something. Taylor saw her drop the item into the pouch at her hip as she broached the distance between them.

Chapter Sixty

The woman looked Taylor over as she knelt beside him, then grimaced, "You will be alright, Taylor, but we need to get Rayla to safety. This is going to hurt," she wrapped her hand around the shaft of the arrow there and pulled it free.

Taylor screamed in pain, "Stop! Stop!" he screamed. The arrow had struck him mid-chest, just missing his vital organs. But she did not abate. She pulled each of the arrows from his flesh. As the last one came free, he thought he might pass out.

"I'm here to help, Taylor," she said and helped him to his feet. His vision still blurred as he stood. The effects of the concussion and the loss of blood were not entirely healed. But he managed to stay standing with the woman's help.

"I'm at your mercy," he groaned. "I have no choice but to trust you in our current predicament." He knew he would need to sleep to use magic of any consequence; healing his wounds was out of the question.

"That you will," she retorted.

He relied heavily on the woman as they walked toward Rayla. She was stronger than she looked, but Taylor was too focused on Rayla to care why. At Rayla's side, he dropped to his knees. The pain of his wounds and concussion started to subside as his Orb worked hard to suppress it.

The woman knelt across from Taylor and lifted Rayla's head into her lap. She stared down at her with a look of loss. Rayla was pale, her breathing was ragged, and air bubbles formed at the wound in her chest. Tarak's blade had pierced her lung, and as Rayla attempted to take another breath, she stopped short.

Rayla opened her eyes and looked at the woman, "There you are, all grown up. I thought it might be you who would come. Save her!" Rayla choked out before her eyes slid closed and went she limp in the woman's arms.

Tears sprang out of his eyes, and his heart sank. *I think she is dead. It can't be! How can she be dead?* Shock set in; he felt like he couldn't move. He tried to scream, but nothing came out but a low cry of pain. .

The woman shed a small tear, and she looked up at Taylor. "I need Milthra's Orb to help Rayla. With her Orb shattered, her body is on its own; She'll need yours."

Taylor felt his whole body shaking; he was having trouble forming thoughts. "She's dead." was all he could choke out.

"I know, Taylor. That is why I am here. I need your Orb," She replied holding out her hand.

A confusion of thoughts moved through his mind, and then the oddity of the woman taking something from Tarak's body floated in. "Did you take Tarak's Orb? Could you not use his?" Taylor asked. He knew it was a strange thought, but he could not process Rayla lying there. His mind was deflecting the truth of what was right before him.

The woman placed her hand on Rayla's abdomen and looked at him sternly, "His Orb can't do what yours can. We may yet save her, but you must do as I say!" The woman frowned as she reached down to Rayla's hand, where Milthra's Orb glowed brightly. As she took hold of it the chain let go and uncurled from Rayla's wrist.

Taylor nodded but did not say anything. He felt his mind slowing; his thoughts were like mud. "I think I'm going into shock."

"Taylor, stay with me!" she said sternly. "We need to hurry!

Taylor's hand shook as he reached up and grasped the Orb around his neck. He did as she asked; the ache in his heart was more than he could bear. His mind was now completely numb. As if the Orb knew his intentions, the clasp let go, and the chain fell free from his neck. The Orb began to glow a golden color as he lowered it to Rayla's chest, and the chain extended itself around her neck. He placed his hand there on her chest, finding her skin already cold, to his surprise. Tears dropped onto her face as they flowed from his cheek. The clasp clicked into place. *Breathe, Rayla! Breathe!* "Why won't she breathe?" He said as he looked up at the woman.

"Taylor." The woman held Rayla in her arms. "She's gone; it's too late for her; magic cannot bring back the dead," she was saying. Taylor looked at the woman before him. The rain no longer touched them; instead, it poured down an invisible shield in an arc. He could see the tears that flowed down her face. Something on her hand caught his eye, a ring that bore a perfect, half-shaped, glowing, purple-hued Orb. Taylor looked up at the woman's face, the matching ring hung around her neck.

"Kerisa?" Taylor asked.

She smiled slightly and nodded, "Yes, Taylor. I will tell you everything. But we need to get Rayla's body to safety. We can repair the damage where I'm taking you. I have everything in place there." Kerisa reached out and placed her hand on Taylor. As she did, he felt a cold tingle, and everything went white for an instant. When his vision cleared, the three were on the floor of a room, dimly lit by globes of light that hung at the wall. An illuminated console, much like the one in the control center, stood against the far wall. In the middle of the room, cut from solid rock, was what Taylor could only describe as a stone platform, the size of a small bed. There was a second, smaller room adjacent to the console, with an entranceway with a large window beside it.

Kerisa stood and pointed to the stone bed in the center of the room, "Put her there. Quickly. I have to activate the magic." She moved toward a pedestal to the side of the console—the same kind which had once held Milthra. Kerisa placed Milthra's Orb inside and slid the glass dome shut. The pedestal and console came to life.

Taylor took Rayla into his arms and took her to the bed. It had been carved out on the top to create an oval concave large enough for an adult to lie in. As he placed her inside the recess, the familiar silver liquid oozed out, lining it so the liquid hugged Rayla's body where it touched the stone's surface. Taylor leaned over to the side and retched. Kerisa ran over to him as he straightened, pulled free the Orb she had taken from Tarak's body and handed it to him. "This is yours now!" Kerisa rushed to the center of the console and placed her hand on it. The lines embedded there came to life. However, these flowed all the way across the floor to the altar. Astonishingly, above the bed, attached to the ceiling was a crystalline cluster twice the size of the platform. He could see that the veins of light from the console flowed up the wall, across the ceiling, and attached to the crystal.

Milthra stepped up beside Taylor in her original image, "Hello, friend. I'm sorry for what has happened to Rayla. There has been so much death."

He turned to her, "Milthra?" He blinked, trying to clear his eyes. "I can hardly believe it is you. I thought we had lost you. Rayla is dead ... I can't ... can you help her?" he finally asked with a blank look.

Milthra, frowned, "I know Taylor. I will do what I can," she replied. The altar came to life. A large projected control screen appeared to the side, and rays of white light emitted from the crystal's points. As the light fell on Rayla's body, a holographic representation of her muscular and skeletal system appeared over its surface. "So you did have advanced technology," Taylor started.

"And no one will ever know but you!" Kerisa moved her hand around on the screen, and the image on Rayla's body changed from her rib cage and muscles to her lungs and heart. The model revealed what Taylor had feared; Rayla's heart and lungs lay still. However, it was counter intuitive that the Orb around her neck was glowing a fierce golden color.

"I don't understand, if she's dead. Why is the Orb glowing," Taylor asked woodenly.

Kerisa turned to Taylor, "Because it still detects life."

"What do you mean? That doesn't make sense." Taylor replied. "Tell me what is happening," he implored.

Milthra appeared on the other side of the bed. "I'm relieved to inform you that Tarak's armies are either fleeing or subdued, General Ravena."

Kerisa pursed her lips and turned to Milthra, "I told

you to stop calling me that." Her voice was angered and annoyed.

"My apologies; it's so hard for me. You created the Resistance. You commanded our armies for so many years," Milthra said. She caught the antagonized look on Taylor's face as she spoke. "I'm sorry, Taylor, but she ordered me to keep it a secret. I couldn't refuse her. She outranks me."

Kerisa moved over to Taylor, put her hands up to his face, and moved his gaze back in her direction. "I saw Tarak's death and us here in this room over two thousand years ago, when I was a girl living in the Refuge. You need to trust me; I'm on your side."

"Allow me to take over Rayla's care," Milthra said and turned her attention toward Rayla. Two liquid metal arms flowed out of the crystal overhead, and the crystal points began to glow blue. When they had fully formed, they were only inches above Rayla's chest.

"Taylor, Rayla's consciousness is gone, her body is dead, but your and her child is very much alive." Kerisa paused to see if he understood.

Taylor's mind felt thick and wooden. It was hard to comprehend what Kerisa was saying. As her words sunk in, he noticed the crystal ends were glowing.

"Taylor? Taylor!" Kerisa's voice brought him back from his thoughts.

"She's pregnant?" he said aloud.

"Yes, she's pregnant, and your unborn child will die soon." Kerisa looked him in the eyes, "Do you understand?" The crystal ends discharged arcs of electricity into the liquid metal arms, which in turn arced into Rayla's chest, and her body jumped. Taylor jumped as well. Tears sprang from his eyes as he looked at Kerisa. He could not bring himself to look at Rayla as charges arced into her chest again and again. After several jolts, the holographic image of Rayla's heart began beating.

"You've done it! You have brought Rayla back!" Taylor was finally able to look at Rayla, searching her face for signs of life.

"No, Taylor. Her body lives, but Rayla is in the death-sleep," Kerisa responded. "That is why I quickly took Milthra's Orb from her when she died."

He watched beams of light emitting from the crystal, knitting Rayla's wounds back together, healing them seamlessly. Rayla's body now breathed with ease, though he knew she was no longer there. His heart ached in his chest so much that he thought he might collapse. "Is the baby okay?"

"Yes, Taylor." Kerisa smiled. "It's healthy, and I believe the Orb will begin to protect them both now. No woman has ever worn an Orb while with child. I suspect that it didn't understand what it should do."

"I'm going to be a father ..." Shock seemed to fill his face, and then he went quiet.

The light from the crystal slowly diminished and finally stopped. "It's finished!" he heard Milthra say. She turned to Kerisa, "He will need help in all this; losing Rayla yet gaining a child. It's a great amount to deal with."

Kerisa nodded, "He will. I saw that so many years ago." She moved to the table and looked down at Rayla, "We can move her to a more accessible place in a few days," she said. "Until then, we can keep her in the room over there." She pointed to a small hospital-looking room where a bed sat waiting.

Taylor still felt like he was watching himself from outside of his body, "You have a great deal of explaining to do, Kerisa. But first, where are we?" Taylor asked.

With a saddened face, Kerisa put a blanket over Rayla and tucked her in. But as she stood there, curiosity appeared on her face, and she reached out to touch the Orb that lay on Rayla's chest. A blue arc of light shot out toward Kerisa's hand. She retracted in pain, "AAhhhh!" she howled, shaking her hand. "I thought so; that's going to be interesting." Kerisa turned to Taylor, still shaking off the pain in her hand, "We are in a secret room below the command center in the wall. I had it installed when the wall was built.

"I have been very busy while I have been away. It's a long story, which I will tell you. We have other business to attend to first, though. You have a people to lead." Kerisa pointed to Rayla's chest. "And we have to figure out how to get off this Orb. Otherwise, your child will never grow to be birthed."

Taylor's heart sank. "I hadn't thought of that, that my child wouldn't grow." He slumped a little. "Will this day deliver me something other but death and disorder?" He took Rayla's hand and held it, "How could this happen, Rayla?" Fresh tears filled his eyes. "How do I go on?" he whispered.

"With our help and the help of the Orb you carry," Milthra stepped up to the other side of the bed. "We will be here for you; all your friends will be. We will help you through this while we put this world back together."

Taylor looked from Rayla to the Orb in his hand and back again, "I can't lead these people! Rayla is in a coma, and my child is frozen in time."

"You always were a bit of a reluctant leader. Why don't we start with going to the surface." Kerisa looked back at Rayla again and frowned at the woman lying there. "We will move her into the room tomorrow once I can be sure her body will keep going."

"Not now, Kerisa. I can hardly believe that for the second time in my life, I have lost the love of my life. Leave me be with my grief. I want to sit with Rayla and my child." Taylor took a deep breath, "You two can manage without me."

Kerisa knelt before him, "She did this so that you could live, so your child can live. She did this for you! She loved and protected her people for a hundred and fifty years, Taylor. Don't let her sacrifice go to waste. We will find a way to release the Orb so your child can grow. Stay here a while; I will prepare a room for her to be moved to. This is hardly a suitable place for either of you to stay." She nodded to Milthra before there was a flash, and she was gone.

Epilogue

DAEMOR

NAEIM, THE NEW CITY

Twelve weeks later:

Taylor stared out of the window of the Dome's top floor in thought. Word had spread quickly about Tarak's defeat and of the new city inside the ruins.

It had taken Kerisa and Milthra days to convince Taylor to let them move Rayla to her new room. Weeks more had passed before someone could convince him to leave her side. His heart had ached every moment of the waking hours. It hadn't been until the old nurse that had watched over Marita had confronted him one day, that he had been shaken out of his despair to a degree.

He recalled her standing there at Rayla's bedside. "Are you going to just sit there like a lump for the rest of your life? You need a bath; you stink! You can't help your child by being in despair the rest of your life."

"I—" He stumbled. So few here talked to him like that here. "What do you suggest? I'm of no use to anyone here."

"How about you put on that fancy sphere you hide in your pocket on and take a shower? Rayla would never have sat around like you do. She was a woman of action." The nurse chastised.

"How would you know what she would have done?" Taylor stood, agitated at this woman.

"She helped raise me! You are but a blink in her life. She was a mother, a teacher, and a friend to countless people here. She saved every one of us."

He had been taken aback, but the old nurse was right. Word had spread quickly about Tarak's defeat and of the new city inside the ruins. More and more people arrived each day, seeking refuge from Tarak's soldiers, who had, in his absence, turned bandits. This world would not find peace easily. It had too long been ruled by tyranny and despair.

There was hope here in this city though; its walls were secure, and the militia had become the residing police force. Taylor, after some reluctance, had donned the Orb Tarak had once worn. It was a symbol for the people here, and it helped the people identify his authority. However, this Orb had an entirely different feel to it. Stranger than the Orb that was with Rayla now. It was more ... malleable, and less willful.

A loud knock disturbed the silence and startled Taylor. He turned to see Kerisa on the other side of the glass wall. She stood in the room they had built for Rayla to reside in.

It was a room made of the same special glass the Dome's windows were. It could be transparent or opaque at a touch. Taylor had insisted that Rayla be up here, where he spent most of his time. They had partitioned off the new space closest to the glass facing the new city, so he could both see and visit her with ease. Milthra had somehow created a pathway for the crystalline cluster's magic to be used here, allowing them to keep a close eye on Rayla.

Kerisa waved him into the room again. He walked over to her and pushed through the glass doors. Kerisa began speaking as soon as he opened the doors. "It's as I suspected, the Orb is getting smaller, and at this rate, it will be half the size in twenty-three weeks." It had not been noticeable at first, but two things had happened in the last few weeks. The Orb had gotten noticeably smaller, and Rayla was showing. The baby inside her grew. The fetus should not have developed with an Orb present, yet it did. Taylor started to believe more each day that there was an unseen force at play in the universe. It was only pure luck that Rayla and Taylor had conceived a child. The window of the chance had been concise.

Milthra appeared and looked at him excitedly, "I have news." She used the display, a duplicate of the one at the platform, and moved it to Rayla's abdomen. There, Taylor could see the child in Rayla's womb. The thump-thump of its heart beating reverberated through the magic. "The missing Vidre isn't missing at all. It is in your child!"

"Taylor. Your child will be a fully developed Vidreian. It will be a child of magic."

"I hadn't imagined that another prophecy would begin fulfilling so quickly!" Kerisa said in exasperation.

"What are you talking about? Prophecy has been fulfilled," Taylor said.

"The one here has. But this isn't the only world with Prophecy. Prophecy isn't done with you yet, Taylor."

The End